Praise for

"Brenda Novak spins a taut, spine-tingling story
with imagery so vivid it leaves you breathless."
—*New York Times* bestselling author Christine Feehan
on *Every Waking Moment*

"Once again author Brenda Novak delivers
a stunningly magical performance."
—*WordWeaving* on *A Family of Her Own*

"A one-sitting read! Kudos to Brenda Novak
for an insightful and emotional story that
tore at my heartstrings!"
—*The Best Reviews* on *A Baby of Her Own*

"Novak's story is richly dramatic, with a stark setting
that distinguishes it nicely from the lusher worlds
of older romances."
—*Publishers Weekly* on *Taking the Heat*

"Brenda Novak always writes a wonderful story,
whether it's her Superromances or her single-title
books. I know when I pick up something she's written,
I'll be totally satisfied."
—Allyn Pogue, *Old Book Barn Gazette*

"This story should appeal to readers
who like their romances with a sophisticated touch."
—*Library Journal* on *Snow Baby*

A Home of Her Own "kept me on the
edge of my seat, Kleenex in hand, totally
enthralled to the last page. This is a
forget-about-dinner-just order-a-pizza kind of read."
—*Romantic Times*

Dear Reader,

When I set out to write this story, I was contemplating the measure of a man. Do we value people for how they look, what they can do—or who they really are? In the beginning, the hero of this book measured his self-worth by what he could accomplish. There didn't seem to be anything wrong with that. He had it all and could do almost anything. Then he lost certain physical abilities. He had to dig deep to find his purpose in life, and I think he turned out to be a better man for it.

I enjoyed getting to know these characters, especially Gabe because I came to admire him so much. At this point, you're probably chuckling. You're thinking I created him and could make him as heroic as I wanted. But that's only partially true. Sure, I'm the one who's written his story, but he strongly objected whenever I took a wrong turn. Seems there's no forcing Gabriel Holbrook.

By the time you finish *Stranger in Town*, I hope you think Hannah is as lucky as I do.

I love to hear from readers. Please drop by my Web site at www.brendanovak.com, enter my quarterly draw to win a $500 shopping spree at the store of your choice, see how I'm doing with my goal to raise as much money as possible for juvenile diabetes and send me an e-mail to let me know you took the time to visit all the characters in Dundee.

Here's to overcoming whatever fate throws our way!

Brenda Novak

brenda novak

Stranger in Town

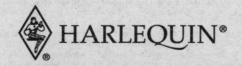

HARLEQUIN®

TORONTO • NEW YORK • LONDON
AMSTERDAM • PARIS • SYDNEY • HAMBURG
STOCKHOLM • ATHENS • TOKYO • MILAN • MADRID
PRAGUE • WARSAW • BUDAPEST • AUCKLAND

If you purchased this book without a cover you should be aware
that this book is stolen property. It was reported as "unsold and
destroyed" to the publisher, and neither the author nor the
publisher has received any payment for this "stripped book."

ISBN 0-373-71278-2

STRANGER IN TOWN

Copyright © 2005 by Brenda Novak.

All rights reserved. Except for use in any review, the reproduction or
utilization of this work in whole or in part in any form by any electronic,
mechanical or other means, now known or hereafter invented, including
xerography, photocopying and recording, or in any information storage
or retrieval system, is forbidden without the written permission of the
publisher, Harlequin Enterprises Limited, 225 Duncan Mill Road,
Don Mills, Ontario, Canada M3B 3K9.

All characters in this book have no existence outside the imagination of
the author and have no relation whatsoever to anyone bearing the same
name or names. They are not even distantly inspired by any individual
known or unknown to the author, and all incidents are pure invention.

This edition published by arrangement with Harlequin Books S.A.

® and TM are trademarks of the publisher. Trademarks indicated with
® are registered in the United States Patent and Trademark Office, the
Canadian Trade Marks Office and in other countries.

www.eHarlequin.com

Printed in U.S.A.

To my sister Pam, who wouldn't hesitate to take on the whole world for the people she loves. Pam, I admire your forgiving, courageous heart, your unfailing loyalty, your generosity, your incredible artistic talent and your lovely face. Thanks for remaining in my corner, always. I love you.

Books by Brenda Novak

HARLEQUIN SUPERROMANCE

899—EXPECTATIONS
939—SNOW BABY
955—BABY BUSINESS
987—DEAR MAGGIE
1021—WE SAW MOMMY KISSING SANTA CLAUS
1058—SHOOTING THE MOON
1083—A BABY OF HER OWN*
1130—A HUSBAND OF HER OWN*
1158—SANCTUARY
1195—A FAMILY OF HER OWN*
1242—A HOME OF HER OWN*

*Dundee, Idaho stories

HARLEQUIN SINGLE TITLE

TAKING THE HEAT
COLD FEET

HQN BOOKS

EVERY WAKING MOMENT—coming in July 2005

Don't miss any of our special offers. Write to us at the following address for information on our newest releases.

Harlequin Reader Service
U.S.: 3010 Walden Ave., P.O. Box 1325, Buffalo, NY 14269
Canadian: P.O. Box 609, Fort Erie, Ont. L2A 5X3

PROLOGUE

THE ROAD WAS COVERED with black ice. Leaning forward, Hannah Price focused intently on the strip of narrow highway beyond her beating windshield wipers. But the dark countryside and the whirling snow made it difficult to see. Gripping the steering wheel until the stark white of her knuckles glowed in the light of her instrument panel, she took a deep breath in an effort to calm down.

They can't be far. I'll find them.

The thought of her two sons being whisked away without her permission had pumped her body so full of adrenaline she barely blinked when her tires slid around the next curve. The back end of her minivan swung onto the shoulder and almost hit the guard rail separating the road from a steep drop. But she quickly gained control and, fixing a picture of Brent and Kenny in her mind, increased her speed. According to her neighbor, Mr. McDermott, her ex-husband had less than a five-minute jump on her. She could make that up if she hurried.

Sleigh bells ring, are you listenin'… Christmas music played on the radio, but she wasn't paying much attention. She was too focused. She'd find Russ. She *had* to. According to Mr. McDermott, Russ had loaded his Jeep with beer and had obviously been drinking already. Her neighbor had also mentioned that Russ had two carloads of his survivalist buddies following him. No doubt they'd have a grand time at the cabin, getting drunk and shooting at anything that moved. It wasn't safe for the boys.

Brent and Kenny were to remain with her for the holidays; it was all laid out in the custody papers.

...A beautiful sight...We're happy tonight...

The most perilous part of the journey between Dundee, her small hometown, and Boise was coming up fast. She managed to navigate the first of the hairpin turns without sliding all over the road, but then came up behind a pickup that was barely moving.

With a curse, she slowed to a crawl. At this rate, Russ would cross into Oregon before she could reach Boise. If that happened, her boys would be lost to her until her ex decided he didn't want the responsibility of caring for them anymore and deigned to bring them home. Provided they survived until then.

She needed to get them back now, where she knew they'd be safe. Before there was another incident like last year, when one of Russ's redneck friends had held a knife to Kenny's throat.

...He sings a love song, as we go along, walking in a winter wonderland.

The lyrics mocked her anxiety as she glanced hesitantly at the double yellow lines in the middle of the dark, shiny road. Veering into the other lane, she hoped for a chance to get around the truck. But it wasn't possible. The turns were too tight.

The disc jockey came on to say the next song was believed to be Welsh in origin and came from a tune called "Nos Galan" dating back to the sixteenth century.

Deck the halls with boughs of holly...

Panic prickled Hannah's scalp as she remained trapped behind the slow-moving truck. She felt the seconds tick by, imagined Russ taking the boys farther and farther away from her with every passing minute.

...'Tis the season to be jolly...

Russ insisted the knife incident had been a joke. But Hannah didn't find it funny, and Kenny hadn't laughed about it, either. The only joke, to Hannah, was that she'd ever been stupid enough to marry Russ in the first place. If her mother hadn't died when she was just out of high school, leaving her all alone... If she hadn't felt so cast adrift and desperate for an anchor... If she hadn't succumbed to Russ's unrelenting pursuit and gotten pregnant... *Then* things could have been different.

But there was no use wallowing in regret. She'd made a colossal mistake, but she'd been young and naïve. And once she'd become pregnant, she'd felt she had no choice.

...Follow me in merry measure...

Brent and Kenny. Her sons were all that mattered now. She couldn't let Russ get too far ahead. She didn't know where the cabin was located.

Hannah floated to the left again, her eyes boring holes in the thickly falling snow as she tried to see around the next bend.

It was no use. She couldn't pass.

...Heedless of the wind and weather...

Easing back into her own lane, she laid her hand on her horn, hoping the truck would pull over or at least speed up.

Brake lights flashed as the driver slowed even more—she'd only succeeded in rattling him.

They wouldn't be out of the mountains for another twenty miles.... Hannah wanted to bang her head on the steering wheel in frustration. She had to pass. It'd only take her a moment. A quick dash around, then she'd be on her way.

...Fa la la la la, la la la la.

Once again, she checked for oncoming traffic. A car rumbled past, then nothing. There was another curve not far ahead, but she felt fairly confident she could get around the truck if she didn't hesitate.

Another carol, Hannah's favorite, came on as she pushed the pedal to the floor. The engine shifted and the van lurched forward.

Silent night, holy night...

Moving into the other lane, she came even with the truck, but a pair of oncoming headlights suddenly appeared, seemingly out of nowhere.

...All is calm, all is bright...

Hannah slammed on her brakes and tried to swerve to safety, but her tires couldn't grip the ice-covered road. The van swayed sharply and began to fishtail; headlights rushed toward her, blinding in their brightness.

...Sleep in heavenly peace...

She screamed as a sudden, gut-wrenching jolt threw her chest into the steering wheel. The unforgiving crunch of metal on metal clanged in her ears. Then she tasted blood, and everything began to spin around and around as her van shot over the edge and tumbled toward the bottom of the ravine.

...Sleep in heavenly peace.

CHAPTER ONE

August, nearly three years later

GABRIEL HOLBROOK FROWNED as he saw Mike Hill get out of his SUV and walk through the dappled sunshine toward the cabin. He'd known Mike would be paying him a visit. He'd been expecting it for more than a week, ever since he'd heard the Hill family's sad news and attended the funeral. But he still wasn't prepared. What was he going to say?

Mike's knock sounded—as solid, decisive and determined as Mike himself.

Lazarus, Gabe's Alaskan malamute, dashed expectantly to the door.

With a sigh, Gabe let the blind fall back into place at the front window and wheeled himself across the living room. It wasn't as if he could pretend he wasn't home. Mike knew, since the accident three years ago, Gabe hardly went anywhere.

At least Mike hadn't brought his wife. Gabe wasn't ready to deal with Lucky….

As always, the heavy pile of the carpet made it difficult to maneuver. Turning too soon, he accidentally clipped the corner of the kitchen table. Because he'd made that table out of metal and hadn't yet finished off the edges, it cut his shoulder. Irritated that his preoccupation had caused him to be careless, he cursed, and Lazarus whined as he opened the door.

Mike's somber expression turned to concern as soon as he saw Gabe's arm. "You're bleeding."

"It's just a scratch." He moved back and whistled for Lazarus to do the same. "You wanna come in?"

Tall and lean, with close-clipped brown hair and hazel eyes, Mike doffed his cowboy hat and stepped inside. "How'd you cut yourself?"

Gabe glanced at his biceps. He'd been lifting weights when he heard Mike's car pull into the drive. Had he been wearing anything more significant than a muscle shirt, he probably wouldn't have been hurt. "It's the damn carpet," he said with a shrug.

"So why don't you tear it out and put in a hardwood floor? Make life a little easier?"

Because Gabe permitted only the most necessary concessions to his handicap. Special allowances made him feel weak, feeble…useless. Besides, he wasn't planning to be in a wheelchair much longer. He was going to walk again.

He didn't say so, though. He knew Mike would only give him a patronizing smile. No one believed him.

Absently petting his dog, a gift from a guy he used to play football with, given to him as a puppy just after the accident, Gabe curved his lips into the good ol' boy smile he used to deflect certain questions. "You kiddin'? It's real wool. Cost me a fortune."

His hayseed charm didn't work as well on Mike as it did on other people. The way Mike's eyebrows lifted indicated he knew Gabe had sidestepped the real issue. "You can afford it."

Gabe wasn't particularly eager to bring Mike to the reason for his visit. But neither did he want his friend to start harassing him like he had for the past year. *When are you going to quit holing up in that cabin of yours and get back to the business of living?*

Gabe couldn't exactly call what he was doing living. It certainly wasn't life as he'd always known it. He avoided people, even his family, and attended few events. But he was meditating, training, growing his own food and working. Mike just didn't understand. Mike hadn't lost his ability to walk, and with it his life's dream, right before the play-offs. He hadn't been forced to sit back and watch his team lose the Super Bowl because their starting quarterback had nearly severed his spinal cord. The site of the injury was Gabe's lower back, which meant he could do more than a lot of paraplegics, but it was still something the doctors couldn't fix. They pointed to stem cell research as a possibility for the future, but Gabe couldn't count on anything so uncertain and far away. He had to take matters into his own hands, overcome the effects of the accident with hard work and positive thinking. That's how he'd always handled everything else.

"I'm sure you didn't come all the way out here just to talk about my carpet," he said.

Mike fidgeted with his hat, bending the rim and sliding it through his curled fingers in a circular motion. "No."

Again, their eyes met and Gabe had the uncomfortable feeling that Mike was about to ask for something he couldn't give. But they'd been friends too long. Gabe couldn't see any way to avoid hearing Mike out.

"Have a seat." He motioned to the couch, which was about the only piece of furniture in the cabin Gabe hadn't made. Working with wood—and recently experimenting with other materials like metal—gave him purpose beyond his therapy. But spending so much time at it made for an odd collection of furnishings. Not that he particularly cared. Very few people came to visit. His old football buddies used to call and want to drop by, but he'd turned them away so consistently that most eventually gave up. They didn't like seeing the league's MVP reduced to half a man, and Gabe hated how uncomfortable they felt in his presence. He couldn't help resenting their pity.

"What's with the table?" Mike asked as Gabe wheeled over and grabbed a paper towel to wipe the blood off his arm.

Gabe considered the piece he was currently creating. Eight feet by six feet, it was made in mission style, but the sheen of the metal and the large rivets gave it a very urban feel. Gabe had seen something similar in a magazine once. "I'm branching out."

"It's unusual, but…nice. In a creative sort of way."

Gabe chuckled at Mike's diplomacy. He missed the old days when they'd been close. Before the NFL. Before the accident. Before Mike had married Lucky.

"We'll see how it turns out." Pushing himself back into the living room, he studied his friend's face. He could tell by the lines of fatigue around Mike's eyes and mouth that the past ten days had been hard on him. It was nothing more than Gabe had expected. Coach Hill's heart attack had come out of nowhere.

"I'm sorry about your dad," he said, and meant it. Coach Hill had been like a second father to him. Because Gabe had skipped both fifth and eighth grade, he'd been two years younger than the other boys in his class, which put him at a disadvantage athletically. It was Coach Hill who recognized his talent and refused to let the other coaches cut him from the team when he went out for football his freshman year. It was Coach Hill who dared to start him as a senior. Without Mike's father's influence, Gabe never would have played for UCLA, which was where he really matured and began to excel.

A muscle flexed in Mike's cheek, revealing his deep emotion. "Thanks for coming to the funeral. It was the first most folks have seen of you in a long time."

Gabe didn't respond to Mike's subtle jab. He was too busy wondering how he'd feel if it had been his dad who died. He'd barely spoken to his father since last year, when Senator Garth Holbrook had ruined his bid for Congress by announcing something he'd managed to keep secret for twenty-four years….

"I've been busy," he said, yanking his thoughts away from that dark moment. "So…what can I do for you?"

"I think you know why I'm here."

Gabe combed his fingers through his hair, which fell in layered waves almost to his shoulders. He rarely bothered to have it cut anymore—having it cut required a trip into town, a trip that wasn't rewarded with food or the prospect of seeing a football game. "And I think you know what kind of answer you're going to get."

"It'd be good for you, Gabe."

Gabe scowled. *Everyone* thought they knew what he needed. "Don't tell me what's good for me, Mike."

"Then do it for the town. The season starts in two weeks. The school board's frantic, wondering who they're going to hire as a replacement. I know they'd go with you in a heartbeat, if only you'd take the job."

"I don't want the job." If he wanted to work, he had plenty of other opportunities. Someone from ESPN called him nearly every month, begging him to co-host *NFL Sunday Countdown.* But he couldn't settle for less than the brass ring—the Super Bowl ring he'd been denied. He couldn't let anything get in the way of his focus, least of all coaching a small high-school football team. "Why can't one of your father's assistants take over?"

"Who? Owens?"

"No. His arthritis is getting too bad."

"So you're suggesting Melvin Blaine?"

Gabe squared his jaw at the challenge in Mike's voice. "I guess I am, if there's no one else."

"That's who the board will probably choose if you don't step up. But you played for Dundee High, Gabe. You remember Blaine's temper. I don't want him to have any more power over those boys than he already has. My father wouldn't have wanted that, either."

"But I've never coached before!"

Mike set his hat next to him and leaned forward, propping his elbows on his knees. "No one knows football better than you do."

"There's more to the job than knowing the game. Coaching is about…getting a bunch of individuals to play as a team. It's about…inspiration."

"You can inspire. Hell, most of those boys worship you already. You're a local hero."

Gabe felt a headache coming on and began to rub his temples. "They worship what I used to be."

"You're still the same man."

He wasn't the same at all. The accident had cost him more than his ability to play ball. It had stripped him of his identity. He wasn't even sure what was important to him anymore. He'd thought it was his family, until he'd learned about his father's deception. He had to find his way back to the man he used to be. Coaching would only get in the way. "It'd be a huge undertaking. Every coach's style is different and with only two weeks to get ready for the first game—"

"You could handle it."

Maybe he could. But he refused to let himself be distracted. He had to hang on to who he used to be since he didn't know who he was now. And there was another problem….

"Won't Kenny Price be playing on varsity this year?"

At last, Mike began to look a little uncomfortable. "He doesn't have to. He's only a sophomore."

"But he's good." Gabe knew how good because he'd seen him play. Since he'd lost the ability to walk, it was always a bittersweet experience to visit the stadium, but he hadn't been able to stay away. When football season rolled around, he drove into town to watch both the junior varsity and varsity games. Besides an occasional trip to the grocery store, it was one of the few places Gabe still bothered to go.

"I know you've got to feel strange toward his mother. If you don't think you can live with having him on your team, it's no big deal," Mike insisted. "Let him play JV another year."

Strange didn't begin to describe how Gabe felt toward Hannah Price. But even at sixteen, Kenny was a better quarterback than senior Jonathon Greer or junior Buck Weaver. "I wouldn't play a kid based on his age. I'd go by talent. And from what I've seen, keeping Kenny on JV wouldn't be fair to him or the team."

"Gabe, unless you take over as coach, Melvin Blaine's going to get the job."

If he could turn down a multimillion-dollar contract with ESPN, he could certainly reject this opportunity, he told himself. "So maybe it's a throwaway year. Replace Blaine after the season's over, when the board is able to find someone better suited to the job."

Mike looked at him as if he had to be crazy. "A throwaway year? You think *that's* fair to the boys? Would you have wanted to bust your ass for a team with no promise?"

Gabe was far too competitive for that, and Mike knew it.

"Besides, it won't be that easy to replace Blaine," Mike went on. "If he gets in, he'll stay until he does something stupid. Something like he did to you. You really want to give him that opportunity?"

Gabe continued to rub his temples but said nothing.

"Come on, it's only for one season."

Wadding up the paper towel he'd used to wipe the blood from his arm, Gabe banked it off the wall, into the kitchen wastebasket. "I loved your dad, Mike. I owe him a lot. But—"

"Then do it for him, Gabe."

Shit… The memories Gabe had been fighting finally intruded, and he pictured Coach Hill asking to meet with him at the beginning of his junior year, just after he'd been caught ditching school. Because he was so much younger than the other guys, he'd been trying to prove himself, which at that age meant drinking and being careless about grades and rules in general. He'd never dreamed Coach Hill would notice or care about a fifteen-year-old junior. Until Duane Steggo blew out his knee a month later, Gabe hadn't even been on varsity.

But Coach Hill did more than notice. Late one afternoon, he called him in and sat him down in an otherwise empty locker room. Then they had the *talk*. Coach Hill explained that there were two kinds of men: strong men, who remained true to their internal compasses regardless of all else; and weak men who were easily misled and wound up cheating themselves of all they could be. He'd told Gabe he only wanted strong men on his team, and asked which kind of man Gabe wanted to be. That's when Gabe quit worrying about fitting in and decided to put his energy toward being the best—at everything—and wound up graduating with a 4.0 grade point average and a football scholarship to UCLA.

He wasn't sure he would've turned around without Coach Hill. His own father had tried to motivate him in many ways. But somehow it was Coach Hill who'd made the difference.

"Gabe?" Mike pressed.

Gabe scrubbed a hand over his face, then frowned when Lazarus laid his snout in Gabe's lap and stared up at him as though pleading Mike's case.

Maybe Gabe could turn down a national sports show but, given what Coach Hill had meant to him—what *Mike* meant to him—he couldn't turn down his best friend or his old alma mater. "Fine," he said at last. "But tell the school board to find a replacement for me as soon as possible because one year's the most they're gonna get."

Grabbing his hat, Mike stood and clasped Gabe's hand. "Thanks, buddy. I knew I could count on you." He strode to the door but hesitated there. Predictably, his visit wasn't over yet. "Don't suppose you'd consider coming to my house and letting Lucky make you dinner in the next week or two," he said.

Gabe clenched his jaw. Mike extended an invitation like this almost every time they saw each other. But Gabe couldn't really hold it against him. Mike loved Lucky. Of course he'd try to get her whatever she wanted, and ever since Gabe's father had taken that paternity test, it was no secret that she was eager to become friends with the family she'd so recently discovered.

"Maybe sometime," he said.

Mike sighed. "The old 'Don't call me, I'll call you,' huh?"

"You got me to coach. Be happy with that."

"I *am* happy with that."

From his friend's sudden smile, Gabe suspected Mike was secretly congratulating himself despite the failed dinner invitation. He'd just handpicked his father's successor and dragged Gabe back into society at the same time.

But coaching was a concession Gabe had to make. He owed Coach Hill. And he hated Melvin Blaine.

"MOM, WHERE ARE YOU?" The front door slammed shut behind Hannah Price's oldest son, and his footfalls landed heavy on the stairs as he took them two or three at once. "Mom!"

A chill of apprehension swept down Hannah's spine at the distress in the sixteen-year-old's voice. It had already been a rough week. What was wrong now?

"In my office," she called and set aside the frame she'd been examining. One of the manufacturers she'd been working with for the past several months was starting to send her substandard material. She had to put a stop to it—but that could wait.

Kenny charged into the room wearing gym shorts, a cut-off T-shirt that was soaked with sweat, and a pair of muddy cleats. He'd obviously come straight from practice, but she didn't scold him for tracking mud into the house. She was too worried about the pained expression on his face.

"What's the matter?"

He slumped onto the step stool Hannah used to reach her office supplies on the top shelves of the closet, and for probably the hundredth time this summer, Hannah realized just how tall he was getting. He'd been stocky as a young child—like Brent, her seven-year-old, who'd come as a complete surprise long after she'd decided not to have another kid. But over the past few years Kenny's baby fat had melted away. With his thick brown hair and brown eyes, he looked so much like her she sometimes resented it. Too many people told him he was almost as pretty as his mother.

"Why did Coach Hill have to die?" he asked, sounding more like the little boy he used to be than the man he was becoming.

She smiled sadly at him. "You're missing him, huh?"

The news of Larry Hill's passing had moved her son to tears even though he considered himself too old for crying. And he hadn't been alone. The entire football team had wept through the funeral. Hannah was grieving, too. As a single mother, she was especially grateful to Dundee's football coach for taking an interest in Kenny and for being such a good role model. Especially because owning her own business—a photography studio, which she ran out of her renovated garage and spare bedroom—meant she couldn't always be available to her son.

"The guys are saying I won't get to play this season," he said.

She shoved some of the files she had stacked on the floor to the side so she could scoot her chair closer to him. She was tempted to go into her "don't worry, it's just a game" speech, but didn't. Russ, her ex-husband and Kenny's father, cared more about Kenny's football career than Kenny did. Five minutes with him would wipe out all her attempts to bring football into perspective. It always did. "Of course you'll get to play. You started every game last year."

"That was JV, Mom. Coach Blaine called me up to varsity yesterday. And now that Coach Hill is gone—"

"Whoa." She squeezed one of the overlarge hands dangling between his knees. If Kenny ever grew into his hands and feet, he'd be a very tall man indeed. "Whoever they find to replace him will recognize your talent."

"They've already found someone," he said glumly.

"Who?"

"Gabriel Holbrook."

Hannah jerked back at the name. "What?"

"You heard me." Kenny blinked rapidly, as if he was close to tears again, and she could understand why. In her mind, she heard the collision that still haunted her dreams, felt that weightless, ominous tumbling....

"The guys are right, aren't they?" he added, head and shoulders drooping. "He's gonna hate my guts."

"Of course he won't hate you," she said, but in her heart she wasn't sure. How would Gabe feel toward her son? Would he really want to see Kenny excel at a sport he could no longer play *because of her?*

Kenny kicked a brightly colored ball she used when photographing babies. It hit the wall with a sharp *smack.* "I wish that accident never happened."

If only she could turn back the calendar.... Hannah had regretted leaving the house that night every minute of her life since.

Her son looked at her imploringly. "Maybe it wasn't totally your fault. Maybe he was driving too fast and—"

"No, it was me." Of course, she wouldn't have been on the road, driving like a maniac if not for Russ and the panic she'd felt for her children's safety. But Hannah knew it wouldn't do any good to point that out. She was the one who'd hit Gabe head-on as he was coming home for the Christmas holidays. With a tragedy like that, reasons and explanations didn't help.

Kenny shoved the hair out of his troubled eyes. "I've heard what everyone else has to say about the accident. But you never talk about it. What happened, Mom?"

Hannah shook her head. She couldn't give him the details. The repercussions of that night made her too heartsick. She'd grown up knowing Gabe. He'd been larger than life, talented, charismatic, the guy who had it all.

In the space of a heartbeat, she'd changed everything. The new Gabe hid a world of hurt behind his blue eyes, kept to himself and rarely ventured into public. But he was still strikingly handsome. Besides eyes that seemed deeper than the ocean, he had wavy black hair, a lean, chiseled face and a rock-hard body. "The guy I know wouldn't hold what I did against you."

"How can he help it?" Kenny asked. "He can't even walk because of you." Drawing up his knees, he rested his chin on his arms. "Did you ever apologize to him?"

"Of course."

"Did he accept it?"

"I think so," she said, but she couldn't be too confident about that, either. The face Gabe showed the world these days, if he showed himself at all, seemed like some sort of mask. She didn't know what was going on underneath it. When she tried to tell him how sorry she was, he either acted as though he wasn't interested enough to listen. Or he gave her a gorgeous smile and told her it was fate.

His generous attitude only made her feel worse. As late as a few months ago, after they'd bumped into each other at Finley's Grocery on one of his rare appearances in town, he'd even sent her a brief note telling her to stop apologizing, that there wasn't any need to think of him again.

She didn't *want* to think of him. But guilt made that impossible. Besides, they lived in too small a town for her to avoid mention of him. She was quite aware that she was now better known for ruining the career and the life of Dundee's only hero than she was for her photography.

"I don't think Coach Blaine's any happier than I am about Gabe taking over as head coach," Kenny said.

"Why not?"

"He thought *he* was getting the job."

"Did he say something about it at practice today?"

"Nothing to the whole team. But his face went red when Mike Hill showed up to make the announcement. And I heard him mumble to Coach Owens that if they think a crippled, washed-up football player can coach better than he can, they've got another think coming."

Hannah pressed a hand to her chest. "He called Gabe a crippled, washed-up football player?"

"Yeah."

A hard knot lodged in Hannah's stomach. She'd already done enough to make Gabe's life miserable. She didn't want her son involved in the drama at the high school. "Kenny?"

He was still wearing a sullen expression when he glanced up at her.

"You give Coach Holbrook everything you've got, you hear me? You play hard. You do what he says. And you don't complain."

"What if he benches me because I'm related to you?"

"Regardless."

"But Mom—"

"He's head coach, Kenny. He should have your loyalty, your respect and your support."

"What about Coach Blaine?"

"What about him? You never liked him much before now."

"He's okay to certain players."

"He has his favorites, and he has his scapegoats. Just because you might have become one of his favorites doesn't mean I like his methods. Stay away from him as much as possible," she said, but as her son stood to leave, she had no idea whether or not he'd listen to her. Especially considering that Russ had lost his starting position to Gabe in high school and was likely to give Kenny conflicting advice.

CHAPTER TWO

BECAUSE GABE HAD BECOME such a recluse, Hannah had imagined his remote cabin as the stereotypical small shack with an overgrown yard, barrels filled with drinking water off to the side and a collection of beer bottles or hubcaps cluttering the front porch. What she saw as she parked behind his truck was a rather large, honey-colored two-story cabin with a neatly tended yard. Ivy climbed the stone chimney, a hammock swung gently in the breeze, and the porch didn't have a single beer bottle or hubcap—it had unusual, attractive furniture made of tree branches.

The scent of rich earth and pine filled her nostrils as she got out of her car. Although it would be plenty warm later in the day, it was still chilly in the mountains, and she could see smoke streaming from Gabe's chimney.

Obviously, he was home—but she'd expected him to be. Football practice wasn't for another two hours.

Fidgeting nervously with her keys, she finally shoved them into her purse as she approached the house. After his note telling her not to apologize anymore, Hannah knew Gabe would rather she leave him alone. In fact, he'd made it pretty clear he wanted *everyone* to leave him alone. But now that he'd decided to coach the Dundee High varsity football team, Hannah needed to talk to him.

A classic rock station played inside the house, so she knocked loudly to compensate. Gabe's dog, Lazarus, whom most people had met—Gabe never left the cabin without him—started barking, but Gabe didn't appear.

Was he working on something in back? She'd heard he built furniture. Now that she'd seen the chairs on his porch, she knew he was no amateur. Perhaps he'd sell her one. She could take some great photographs of children seated in a chair like that, holding a bunny or a dog....

She knocked again.

Nothing, except more barking from Lazarus.

There was a wooden gate on the side of the house. She walked around and, calling to announce her presence, let herself into the backyard, where she found a deeper porch with more eclectic patio furniture. A set of wind chimes rang as she followed a concrete path that weaved through a spectacular garden toward a large workshop, the door of which stood open.

"Gabe?" When she stuck her head inside, she couldn't see him, but she saw lots of other interesting things. There was a carved mahogany armoire that still needed to be stained, a metal dinosaur that looked as if it belonged in a garden as elegant as his, a grandfather clock, several other clocks and parts of clocks, a sea chest, and three rocking chairs in different sizes.

Hannah doubted she'd ever seen more beautiful work. The hand-carved rocking chairs were fabulous. They reminded her of her favorite childhood story, *The Three Bears*. Just as she decided to try one out, she heard Gabe's voice at the door.

"Is there something I can do for you, Hannah?"

Someone's been sitting in my chair.... She jumped up as he rolled across the threshold—and fought the urge to dash around him and run off. He was wearing jeans and a white golf shirt that showed off the depth of his tan and made her suspect he did a lot of his sanding and staining outdoors without a shirt. And his hair was wet.

"Sorry to intrude," she said. "I knocked at the house but no one answered. I thought maybe I'd find you back here."

Lazarus trotted forward to welcome her with a sniff and a lick on the hand.

"I was in the shower."

Hannah couldn't read his expression very well, but she thought she detected a hint of curiosity in his eyes. "You're probably wondering why I'm here."

"I'm guessing it has something to do with Kenny." Lazarus licked her again, but when Gabe whistled and snapped his fingers, the dog immediately moved back to his side. "He'll be on my team this year, won't he?"

She could smell turpentine in the shop, the scent of tomato plants drifting in from the garden. "Yes."

"From what I've seen, he's pretty good."

"Football means a lot to him."

She clasped her hands nervously behind her back. Football had meant a lot to Gabe, too.

Suddenly it seemed stupid for her to have come out to his cabin. She wasn't the right person to help him. Gabe might be in a wheelchair, but he still had a powerful presence. She knew from everything she'd seen so far that he could compensate for his handicap. Blaine probably wouldn't pose any problem for him.

But she was already here. It was too late to back out.

"Actually, I didn't come to talk about Kenny. I wanted to warn you that you might run into a little resentment from Coach Blaine."

He rubbed his chin with his knuckles. "What makes you think so?"

Gabe had kissed her once, at a high-school graduation party. For some reason, Hannah couldn't help thinking of that now. His mouth had been soft and commanding, his hands firm on her back as he pressed her against him. He'd been the boy "Most Likely to Succeed," if not by actual vote by common understanding, and she'd gone home with a huge crush....

"Hannah?"

She was staring at the shape of his lips, which, like his thick-lashed eyes and the rest of his deeply tanned face, was something to be admired.

Clearing her throat, she felt her cheeks warm as she scrambled to remind herself of his question—why did she think he might have trouble with Coach Blaine? "Something Kenny mentioned to me when he came home from practice yesterday," she said.

"What was that?"

No way was she going to tell Gabe what Blaine had called him. "Basically, he's jealous that you got the position he wanted."

He didn't seem impressed that she'd driven so far to warn him. "So?"

She blinked in surprise. "I'm afraid he might work against you, try to make you look bad somehow, make you feel unwelcome."

"So?" he repeated.

"So…I wanted to tell you to watch your back."

Lazarus barked, but Gabe quickly and easily silenced him by putting a hand on his head. "I can take care of myself, Hannah," he said. "I don't need you to protect me."

"I know. I just…" Her words faltered. He was right. If he weren't in a wheelchair, she wouldn't have come out here. She would have known he could handle Coach Blaine.

All the regret she'd felt since the accident caused a painful ache in her chest. She wanted to redeem herself somehow. Make things right. But there wasn't any way to do that. "I'm sorry," she said.

Tears burned behind her eyes. She fought them as she tried to skirt past him, but he caught her wrist before she could clear the workshop door. "Hannah?"

The warmth of his touch seemed to wrap around her like a blanket. Again she remembered that night twenty years ago when he'd kissed her. She wished he'd kiss her now, wished he could be the man he used to be. She had walked away from that accident with only a broken arm and a gash on the forehead, but she wasn't sure she'd ever recover from the remorse.

"I'm fine," he said firmly. "You have to forgive yourself, okay?"

He let go, but she didn't move away. She wanted to throw her arms around him so she could feel his heart beating. She knew he was right. They both needed to get over the accident and move on. Only he *wasn't* fine. He was sitting in a wheelchair, and he was angry and bitter, even if he was trying not to direct those emotions at her. "Gabe…"

"What?"

She didn't have the right to ask him for anything, but that ache in her chest made it impossible to walk away. Unable to find words, she ran two tentative fingers down the side of his face.

His eyes immediately riveted on hers. She recognized the raw need that flared inside them and was so surprised to see his defenses slipping, she couldn't breathe. He looked as if he was starved for human touch, and it was little wonder. He'd lost so much. And what he hadn't lost, he'd rejected.

The dog whined and suddenly, the mask of indifference Gabe usually wore snapped into place. "Don't do me any favors," he said gruffly, rolling back several inches. "Forget about me and go on with your life."

She let her hand fall to her side. "I can't forget you," she admitted. But before he could respond, Lazarus tore off, barking, and Mike Hill strode into the backyard.

STRUGGLING TO COPE with the powerful emotions that had come out of nowhere, Gabe whistled for Lazarus and focused on Mike's approach. Hannah would leave soon and his pulse would settle. He just needed to bide his time, ignore the sudden yearning, stick with his therapy so he could eventually reclaim his life. Since the accident, he'd withdrawn from everyone, even his family. It was only natural he'd miss the closeness and the physical interaction.

"There you are." Mike wore a congenial smile as he petted Lazarus, but Gabe recognized the surprise running underneath that smile. Hannah would be about the last person Mike would expect to find here. Gabe sighed. What had happened to his blessed solitude? He'd moved thirty miles from town and built his cabin on a hundred acres of forested mountaintop. Evidently, he hadn't gone to *enough* trouble. Without outside interference, he could deal with his problems in his own way—could even remain oblivious to the exact depth of some of his more poignant losses. But when Mike talked about horses or football or even marriage and family, Gabe realized how much he missed his old life. And when Hannah touched him, he realized how badly he craved the smell, taste and feel of a woman.

Someday, he told himself. When he recovered....

Gabe quickly schooled his expression to hide his irritation at yet another intrusion into his private domain. "What brings you all the way out here *again,* Mike?" He knew his voice fell a little short of welcoming, but Mike didn't seem to notice.

"I brought you the team roster." He handed Gabe the clipboard he was carrying, then tipped his hat at Hannah. "I thought I recognized your Volvo, Hannah. How are you?"

"Fine, thanks," she murmured, and Gabe hoped he was the only one who noticed the blush creeping up her neck. He didn't want her to give away the fact that Mike had interrupted them at an awkward moment. Mike would probably have enough questions about Hannah's presence as it was.

"How's business?" Mike asked her.

Gabe knew Hannah worked hard to support her two boys. He also knew she had no choice if she wanted to see them fed and clothed. It was common knowledge that Russ Price certainly didn't contribute much to the family. He didn't have a job half the time.

"Pretty good," she said. "Now that summer's almost over, things are starting to slow down, which is good because I need to get Kenny and Brent ready for school."

"Is Kenny playing on JV again this year?" Mike asked.

Gabe gave Mike a look he hoped would get him to shut up and back off. He knew what Mike was doing. Mike was trying to set Hannah's expectations low, just in case Gabe decided to leave Kenny where he was.

"Coach Blaine brought him up to varsity last week," she said.

Mike's gaze flicked toward Gabe. "I hadn't heard."

"I hadn't heard either," Gabe said, and made a point of adding, "But that's perfect, since I was planning on doing it myself."

"Kenny will be glad to hear you think he belongs on varsity." Picking up a tennis ball, she threw it for Lazarus. "I've got to do some shopping. I'd better go."

Mike watched her leave, but Gabe turned his attention to a game of fetch with Lazarus. He didn't see any point in admiring Hannah's trim figure, her long dark hair, olive complexion or wide brown eyes. His libido was on hold indef- initely.

"Why was Hannah here?" Mike asked when she was gone.

Gabe called out to quiet Lazarus, who'd gotten distracted by a squirrel and was barking up a tree. "No reason."

Mike challenged this response by cocking one eyebrow.

"It's the first time she's ever been out here. She came to tell me that Coach Blaine isn't happy."

"How does she know? Did she get specific?"

"No." Gabe accepted the tennis ball Lazarus dropped in his lap. "I'm guessing Kenny overheard something at practice. That's all."

Mike frowned. "I could feel Blaine's anger when I delivered the news," he said, sounding almost as concerned as Hannah.

Gabe hated being treated so differently than before. "Is that why you drove thirty miles instead of delivering the roster to the field?" he asked, throwing the ball again. "To warn the poor cripple?"

Mike disarmed him with a slow smile. "Sorry, man. I didn't expect to interrupt anything important—especially with Hannah Price."

"Mike…" Gabe warned.

Turning his palms up in mock innocence, Mike shrugged. "I'm just glad to see you don't blame her for the accident. What happened was Russ's fault."

Except that it wasn't Russ who'd crashed into him. Had Hannah been two minutes earlier or two minutes later—or simply waited for Russ to bring the boys back…

"Any caring mother would go after her kids," Mike said.

Sometimes Gabe agreed; sometimes he didn't. Generally, he tried not to think of Hannah, or any other woman for that matter. "Why do I get the feeling you're trying to drive that point home?"

His friend's grin grew more meaningful. "Maybe it's because I saw the way she was looking at you."

Mike was always quick to point out when Gabe turned a pretty woman's head, but Gabe had no patience for it. Regardless of the sudden awareness he'd felt a moment ago, that part of his life was in cold storage and would be until he could walk again. "Can we get back to football?"

"You have a lot of years ahead of you, Gabe. There's no need to live them alone, especially because you're the only thing stopping you from finding someone to share them with."

Mike sounded like an echo of Gabe's sister, Reenie. Everyone thought he should settle for what he could get out of life in a wheelchair. But Gabe had never been one to settle for anything. Walking again was his only priority. "In case I haven't made myself clear enough in the past, I don't want to hear your take on the situation, Mike," he said.

Lazarus had dropped the ball in Gabe's lap a few seconds earlier. Now he barked to get Gabe to respond. "Here you go, boy," Gabe said and lobbed the ball into the air.

The dog took off after it as Mike walked up the ramp Gabe had installed on his deck and took a seat in a chair that hung from the rafters. Made of rattan, it was shaped like a bowl—another of Gabe's recent experiments. "I'm just saying you should ask

Hannah out, that's all. What's one date? I'm sure she'd go out with you."

Gabe was sure of it, too. She felt so guilt-ridden about the accident she'd probably do almost anything he asked of her. But he wasn't the slightest bit interested in exploiting her pity or anyone else's. He hated pity. "Forget it."

"Come on. Grab a movie with her or something. Lord knows she could use the break. It's not easy raising those kids on her own."

"I don't think she's raising them on her own."

"For all intents and purposes she is. Russ's involvement only makes things harder," Mike said.

"And you know this, how?"

"It's Dundee, Gabe. Everyone knows everyone else's business." He hesitated. "Except maybe yours."

Gabe recovered the ball, but Mike's statement about Russ making Hannah's life more difficult had piqued his curiosity enough that he forgot to throw it. He wheeled a little closer. "He's still giving her trouble?"

"He'll always give her trouble. A week or so ago when Russ had the boys, Kenny caught Brent watching a porn video."

"How'd he get hold of it?"

Lazarus barked, Gabe threw, and the dog took off again.

"It was called *My Little Pussy*," Mike said. "He thought it was about a kitten."

"God." Gabe grimaced.

"You got it."

"Did Kenny see the video, too?"

"I don't think so."

"How'd you hear about it?"

"Russ told half the people at the Honky Tonk last Monday. He found Brent's questions about what he'd seen hilarious."

"What an idiot." Gabe shook his head in disgust. "How'd she end up with a guy like him?"

When Mike propped his arms behind his head and put his feet

up on a nearby footrest, Gabe almost regretted asking. It looked as if his friend was planning to stay awhile, and having company wasn't in keeping with Gabe's plans. He needed to mentally prepare himself for his first practice with the team. After being out of circulation for three years, he'd be dealing with a lot of people. He'd face an onslaught of questions, an avalanche of curiosity, and plenty of rude, blatant stares. Being famous made him an attraction already. Now that he was crippled *and* famous, he couldn't go anywhere without conversations falling to a hush and people whispering behind their hands.

But he suspected Mike knew it wouldn't be an easy day for him and had come over to keep him company—probably so Gabe wouldn't back out. And as long as they were talking about Hannah, Mike was unlikely to bring up Lucky.

"You don't remember what happened between her and Russ?" Mike asked.

"I'm not sure I ever knew." He'd been away at college, too busy making his dream come true to pay much attention to what was happening in Dundee.

"They got married a few months after she graduated from high school. She was pregnant."

Gabe glanced across the lawn, expecting Lazarus to come charging back to him, and saw him chasing another squirrel. "I can't see her sleeping with Russ in the first place."

Mike shrugged. "Who knows how it happened? She couldn't go away to college like the rest of us. She had to stay and take care of her mother, and Russ lived right next door."

A few weeds had infiltrated one of the garden boxes Gabe had built up off the ground. He bent forward to take care of the problem. "What was wrong with her mother?"

"Cancer."

Gabe tossed the weed he'd pulled on top of the pile he was making. He'd heard about her mother; he remembered now. "Where was her father?"

"Died in a plane crash when Hannah was little. I know they got some sort of settlement, but it was just her and her mom until her mother died."

Gabe smoothed the soil he'd disturbed and stretched to reach around another plant. Hannah must've been lonely....

"My mother thinks she was after his family," Mike added.

Brushing the dirt from his hands, Gabe glanced up in surprise. "I've heard of a woman being after a guy's money, but never his family."

"When Hannah's mother got sick, it was Violet Price who helped her deal with the situation. After her mother died, Hannah might've been trying to cement those relationships, to hang on to the people she already cared about."

That sounded reasonable to Gabe—but the years didn't match up. "Kenny's only sixteen years old," he said. "If she got pregnant right out of high school—"

"She miscarried." Mike gave him a sidelong look. "Any other questions I can answer for you about Hannah Price?"

Gabe scowled. "We're just talking, Mike. There's nothing wrong with talking, is there?"

Mike's lips curved in a broad smile. "Not a thing, buddy. You need someone to fill you in on what you missed all those years you were busy showing off on national television."

Showing off... Mike had always teased him about his fame.

Gabe smiled in spite of himself as he rolled over to the toolshed to retrieve his small pruning shears. He'd spotted some dead blooms on his roses. "Considering the gap between Kenny and Brent, she must've stayed with Russ a long time."

Mike didn't comment. He leaned his head back, closed his eyes and tilted his hat to shade his face.

"Mike?"

"What?"

Gabe knew he was stupid to press the issue, but he was probably never going to hear the end of Hannah, anyway. So he risked one more question. "Why didn't she leave him after the miscarriage?"

"If you're not interested in Hannah, why do you want to know so much about her?"

"I'm familiarizing myself with the family situation of my starting quarterback. Coaches do that sort of thing."

Putting his feet down, Mike sat forward and nudged his hat up. "So Kenny's the attraction?"

"Of course."

Mike hardly looked convinced, but he shrugged. "Well then, for *coaching's* sake, I'll tell you this. I don't know why she stayed as long as she did. Especially because Russ was a lousy husband. He went from one job to another, hung out at the Honky Tonk every weekend, went home drunk more times than not, and bought things they couldn't afford, even when he wasn't earning any money. My mother's been a good friend of Violet's for years and shakes her head whenever Russ's name is mentioned."

Gabe lifted his gaze as Mike stood. "Was Hannah supporting the family with her photography way back then?"

"Not in the early years. She worked at the diner, remember?"

"No." For more than a decade Gabe had been living out-of-state and hadn't paid attention to anything beyond his career and his immediate circle of family and friends. "So when did she start taking pictures?"

Mike crossed the deck. "Beats me. Must've been before the divorce, though, because I heard Russ went after her for spousal maintenance."

That statement made Gabe prick himself on a thorn. Mumbling a curse, he shook the sting out of his finger. "Tell me he didn't win. Certainly she's not supporting him…."

Mike's teeth flashed in another smile. "You'll have to ask her."

"What?"

His friend strode down the ramp and sauntered toward the gate. "Call her," he said.

"I'm not going to call her!"

"Why not? Take her out to a movie."

"No way."

"You might have a good time, Gabe. Would that be so bad?"

"Yes!"

The gate clicked shut, and Gabe threw his pruning shears in the opposite direction. They arced, like a perfectly thrown football, imbedding themselves in the fence with a vibrating *thwack* that made Lazarus freeze near the trees and prick his ears forward. Having a good time with Hannah *would* be bad, Gabe thought. Because then he might want to see her again. And he couldn't let himself get too comfortable. He had a long fight ahead of him. He couldn't afford to bow beneath the odds and settle for spending the rest of his days in a wheelchair.

"I'm not going to ask her out," he called. But Mike was long gone, and only the deep *bong* of the wind chimes and Lazarus's howl answered back.

CHAPTER THREE

THE DAY HAD TURNED HOT and dry. The heat blasted into Gabe's truck as he opened the door, lifted his wheelchair to the pavement and swung into it. Already he could feel the attention of those on the football field. Even the cheerleaders practicing stunts in front of the gym stopped to watch as he got out.

It wasn't difficult to imagine what they were thinking: *He's here... That's his truck... How does he drive without using his feet? How does he get into his chair? Oh, look at that...*

He'd been MVP of the National Football League for two years running. The last thing Gabe ever thought he'd become was a freak show.

Taking the roster from the back seat of his extended cab, he hooked it on the handle of his wheelchair, whistled for Lazarus and started pushing for the gate.

Excited by the promise of a new activity, Lazarus trotted circles around him. Gabe was fairly sure Coach Hill had never brought a dog to practice. He knew Lazarus might raise a few eyebrows, but Gabe didn't really care. If the school board didn't like it, they could fire him. He hadn't asked for this job in the first place.

Coach Owens immediately spotted him and hurried over. They met up just as Gabe rolled onto the track surrounding the field. "Hello, Coach. Good to see you again. It's been a while."

Coach... Gabe wondered how long it'd take him to get used to his new title. "Thanks. Good to see you, too."

Owen's arthritis had taken more ground, distorting his hands, but his smile revealed no animosity, even when he glanced at Lazarus. Gabe decided Coach Owens was as good-natured and open as he'd always been.

Blaine, of course, was a different story. He stood on the far edge of the field with a whistle in his mouth, his hands propped on his hips in a classic stance of "I'm the boss here." He glared at Gabe for several long seconds, making Gabe feel even more self-conscious about getting his damn chair down onto the field. But Gabe refused to be intimidated by a man who couldn't even manage his own temper. Gabe had seen Blaine toss players into lockers, throw a football at the back of a guy's head, chuck a clipboard across the room. He'd even held Gabe's head under water once, when Gabe had called an audible instead of running the play Blaine had sent out to him. It didn't matter that Gabe had read the defense and knew Blaine's play wouldn't work. It didn't matter that the change resulted in a touchdown pass that won the game and secured the team a spot in the play-offs. Everyone knew Blaine hadn't called what Gabe ran, and Blaine didn't like being upstaged.

Considering Blaine's lack of control, it was a miracle he still worked at Dundee High. Anywhere else in America he would have been sacked long ago. But his more violent outbursts had occurred back when teachers had a great deal more latitude. And he'd coached at Dundee High so long he seemed like a permanent fixture. In a town where everyone knew everyone else, firing Blaine felt too much like firing family.

Gabe squinted against the sun to see the boys who had all turned expectantly toward him. Oddly enough, their faces were already streaked with dirt and sweat as if they'd been practicing for some time. "Am I late?" he asked, checking his watch, which indicated he wasn't.

Owens shifted from foot to foot and clasped his gnarled hands behind his back. "No, not really. It's just that...well, Coach Blaine wanted to get an early start."

Gabe surveyed the forty or more athletes staring curiously back at him. "He called all these boys and told them to come to practice early?"

Mopping the perspiration on his brow with the towel that hung around his neck, Owens cleared his throat. "Actually, we have a phone tree. He…um…had me start the phone tree."

"And no one thought to notify me?"

Owens glanced across the field as if he wanted to ask Blaine what to say now. "I guess you're not on the list yet."

"Put me on it," Gabe said. "Put me right on top, because I'll be the one to start the phone tree in the future."

"Sure, okay, Coach. Anything you say."

Evidently Blaine was already pushing to see what he could get away with. Gabe couldn't give an inch, or he'd be looking at twice as much resistance later on.

"Would you mind telling Coach Blaine I'd like a word with him, please?"

Gabe could almost read Owens's mind as his eyes once again darted toward the man in question. No doubt Owens was more than a little hesitant to become a target of Blaine's temper. If Gabe quit or wound up fired, Blaine would most likely take over as head coach. Then Owens would be in a very difficult position.

"Is there a problem, Coach?" Gabe asked when Owens didn't move.

"No, ah, no, of course not," he said. "I'll get him."

Along with the entire football team and several parents who were sitting in the stands, Gabe watched Owens jog over to Blaine. They exchanged a few words. Then Blaine made his way slowly across the field, seemingly unconcerned.

"You wanted to see me, Gabe?" he said when they were finally within speaking distance.

Gabe knew Blaine had purposely used his first name to avoid giving him the respect of his new title but said nothing. He waited for Blaine to get a little closer. He had no intention of broadcasting the fact that they were having a problem with each other on the very first day. That would only boost gossip and start folks choosing sides, and Gabe drew enough attention as it was. He preferred to keep a low profile, if only Blaine would let him.

"What is it?" Blaine prompted.

"Well, *Melvin,* it seems I wasn't notified of a change in the practice schedule."

Blaine's lip curled in a poor approximation of a smile. "I didn't see any need to make you come in early. I wasn't sure how flexible you could be with…" His gaze dropped to Gabe's chair. "Well, let's just say I wasn't sure of your schedule, and I knew Owens and I could handle it."

Gabe's hands tightened on his wheels. Blaine had coached him; he knew how driven Gabe was, knew what being in a chair cost him. Blaine was trying to make him feel like less of a man because of his handicap, and it angered Gabe that his insecurities allowed Blaine to hit the target so perfectly.

The memory of Blaine's hand on the back of his head, forcing him under water played again in Gabe's mind. He was only sixteen at the time, and Blaine must've been forty. But once panic set in, Gabe had come up swinging and knocked his coach to the ground. He'd been ready to do more, if necessary. He *still* wondered what might have happened if Coach Hill hadn't walked into the locker room at that moment.

Taking a deep, calming breath, Gabe said, "Making that change on your own is fine for today. But it had better never happen again. Do I make myself clear?"

Gabe had kept his tone and his expression so pleasant that it took a moment for his words to register. "It's just practice, Gabe," Blaine said. "I thought—"

"Next time you won't need to think. You'll know better."

A muscle jumped in Blaine's jaw. Except for the color of his hair, which had turned gray, he looked exactly like he had the night he'd nearly drowned Gabe in the team's water cooler.

"Owens and I have been doing this since you were in diapers," Blaine hissed.

"And now I'm in a wheelchair," Gabe said calmly. "And that isn't going to change anything either."

Blaine said nothing. Neither did Gabe. It was a silent contest of wills. Blaine needed to understand that, wheelchair or no, Gabe was as competitive as ever. He hadn't asked for this job, but now that he was here, he wasn't going to let Coach Blaine run him off.

"I'm sure having a dog at practice is against school policy," Blaine said at last, obviously grappling for whatever ammunition he could use.

Gabe shrugged. "So file a complaint."

"It's distracting to the boys," he persisted.

"They'll get used to it."

Blaine's lips blanched white but he held his tongue.

"Unless you have further questions, I think that about covers it," Gabe said. "Call the team together. I'd like to talk to them."

KENNY HAD BEEN looking forward to football since the end of last season. It gave him something to focus on that had nothing to do with his personal life. But today's practice had been tense. Kenny hadn't seen Blaine so pissed off since last year, when the varsity front line let the starting quarterback get sacked five times in one game.

"You need a ride, man?" Senior Matt Rodriguez nudged Kenny in the shoulder as he passed, his cleats clicking on the cement.

"No thanks." Kenny put his gear, which he'd carried out of the locker room with him, on the ground and sat down at the curb by the fence surrounding the field.

"Your mother coming?" Matt asked.

"My dad," he said, which meant he'd have a wait. His dad was always late.

Matt dug his keys out of his football bag. "See you tomorrow, then."

"Yeah, you too." Kenny watched enviously as his friend pulled out of the lot in a beat-up red truck. Kenny had his license but no car to drive. Because his mother occasionally had to travel to different shoots, she couldn't loan him her Volvo, at least not very often. And he knew better than to hope his dad might help him buy a car—even an old junker. Russ Price was lucky to have wheels of his own. What he drove usually ran worse than Matt's truck.

Tossing a rock across the parking lot, Kenny leaned against the fence and considered the coming weekend. The prospect of spending another few days at his father's trailer wasn't particularly appealing. Kenny was still angry about Brent getting hold of that porn video. What kind of father kept that shit in the house where a little boy could reach it?

The sound of a car made him glance up.

"You need a ride, Kenny?" Tiffany Wheeler smiled prettily at him from inside her green bug. The cheerleaders were usually gone when football practice let out. Evidently they'd stayed late.

"No, I'm covered," he said. "Thanks."

"You goin' to the dance tonight?"

Tempted by the promise in her voice, he hesitated. He was almost positive Tiffany liked him, which was quite a compliment since she was a year older and so many of the other boys admired her. But he couldn't go to the dance. After the lack of remorse Russ had shown over that video incident, Kenny didn't want to leave his little brother with their father. Kenny wouldn't put it past Russ to go out drinking and leave Brent home alone. "Not this time."

"Oh." Her expression revealed her disappointment. Kenny feared she'd simply set her heart on someone else, but he couldn't change his mind.

"Okay. Have fun whatever you do," she said.

He'd be baby-sitting, which didn't sound like fun at all. He did a lot of it. But he was Brent's only protection when they weren't with their mother. If Kenny told Hannah half the stuff that went on at his father's place, she'd sue Russ for full custody *again,* and Kenny didn't want that to happen. The court battles freaked everyone out. Especially Brent, who loved Russ regardless.

Kenny loved their father, too. He just wished Russ could pull his life together and take some pride in himself for a change. "See you around," he said as Tiffany drove off.

Car doors slammed, engines rumbled and parent after parent came by for those who didn't drive.

At least half an hour later, Coach Blaine stalked past Kenny, but didn't say anything. A few minutes after that, Coach Owens mumbled goodbye.

Even Owens seemed worried about the recent changes, Kenny realized, and cursed under his breath. He missed Coach Hill. Everything was cool when Coach Hill was around. Gabe had given them a stern lecture about persistence and determination. He'd talked about all-for-one and one-for-all, personal excellence and self-discipline, and he'd said that only those guys who played with heart would play for him. Then, he'd instituted a few new drills that were guaranteed to make them too sore to move tomorrow. The speech was good, and the drills might prove helpful, but with the coaching staff fighting amongst themselves, Kenny wasn't sure any amount of motivation or hard work would make enough difference. Coach Hill always said they had to be unified or they wouldn't win a single game. *Football is a team sport, my friends....*

"Kenny?"

He scrambled to his feet when he saw Coach Holbrook and his dog coming toward him from the locker room. Kenny wasn't surprised Gabe was still around—Gabe's truck was one of the few vehicles remaining in the lot—but Kenny was more than a little self-conscious about facing his new coach alone. The wheelchair made him nervous. The fact that his mother was to blame for the wheelchair made it even worse. "Yes, sir?"

Holbrook studied him for a moment. "You need a ride?"

Kenny glanced at the entrance to the lot, hoping to see Russ's old Jeep. But the drive was empty and so was the street.

"Um, my dad's probably on his way."

Gabe arched his eyebrows. "The 'probably' part has me a little worried."

Kenny tried to pump some conviction into his voice. "I mean, I'm sure he'll be here any minute."

"What if he doesn't come?"

"I'll walk." Kenny shrugged as if it was no big deal, but his mother lived more than three miles away, he was already exhausted and it was hotter than hell. Besides, if he showed up at her place, she'd know Russ had forgotten him again and his parents would end up in another huge fight.

Holbrook consulted his watch. "Did you tell him when practice would be over?"

Kenny had actually told Russ it ended half an hour earlier than it did. That strategy sometimes cut down on the waiting. But he wasn't going to admit that to Gabe. It made his father look pathetic. "Yeah."

"He's nearly an hour late."

"He's busy, I guess."

Gabe's lips formed a grim line. "Come on, I'll drop you off."

Kenny didn't know what to do. He didn't feel like waiting for his father any longer. But he didn't want to get into Gabe's truck. What would they talk about?

Reluctantly, he gathered his stuff and trailed his new coach across the lot. When Gabe started to get out of his wheelchair, Kenny hesitated. Should he offer to help? Should he be the one to load the wheelchair?

Gabe didn't turn but he must've felt Kenny's hesitancy because he said, "I've got it," sharply enough that Kenny knew offering to assist him would not be a good thing.

Kenny had just rounded the truck and climbed in beside

Gabe's dog when his father finally pulled up next to the passenger side. Brent was in the back seat, without a seat belt.

"There you are," Russ called out from the Jeep. "What, did practice let out early today?"

His dad was so full of crap. Kenny didn't respond. Grabbing his shoulder pads and helmet, he scrambled out. "I guess my ride's here," he mumbled. "Thanks, Coach."

"Hey, Brent, see that? It's Gabe Holbrook," Russ said. "Did you know he was MVP two years in a row?"

Even Brent looked like he was afraid their father would embarrass them. "Get your seat belt on," Kenny grumbled to him.

"Are *you* coaching the team now?" Russ asked as Brent buckled up.

Holbrook situated himself behind the wheel before answering. "That's the latest."

"No one told me." Russ glanced accusingly at Kenny. "Why didn't you tell me?"

"I haven't seen you since it happened," he said and silently begged his father to drive off.

Unfortunately, they didn't move. "I have to admit that makes me a little nervous," he said. "I mean, this kid's got real talent. You won't…you know, hold Kenny back for what Hannah did, will you? Kenny had nothing to do with putting you in that chair. And he's the best quarterback you've got. He should definitely start."

Kenny felt his face flash hot. Thanks to his father, he was going to be benched for sure. *Why* did Russ have to get involved?

When Gabe's gaze cut from his instrument panel to Kenny's father, the expression in his eyes was glacial enough to remind Kenny of a character he'd once seen in a cartoon strip. Iceman could freeze people to the spot with one glance…. "You worry about your job as Kenny's father, I'll worry about my job as Kenny's coach," he said. Then he turned some knobs and flipped some switches and roared out of the lot.

Russ shook his head. "Oh boy," he said. "Gabe's going to be a problem, I can tell already. We need to take Coach Blaine out for a drink."

GABE GLANCED at his watch. Before he drove all the way home from practice, he thought he should probably stop by and see his mother. He didn't do that very often because he didn't want to run into his father. But the state senate was in session, so Gabe was fairly confident Garth wouldn't be around.

He cruised past his parents house, checking for his father's Lincoln. When he didn't see it in the open garage, or find his sister's van in the drive, he pulled to the curb. His mother wasn't to blame for the mess that had resulted in a half sister Gabe didn't want. But it bothered him that Celeste persisted in being so understanding about the whole thing. How could she welcome Lucky into the family after what Garth had done?

Gabe's mother never ceased to amaze him. She was unfailingly kind, eternally patient and always engaged in a worthy cause. He wondered how much money she'd raised for the various charities she'd supported over the years....

"Gabe!" she said, flinging open the door while he was still rolling up the walk.

Lazarus shot out ahead of him, and she gave him a good pat.

After the accident, his parents had hired a contractor to install a ramp. She placed a kiss on Gabe's forehead as soon as he reached the top of it.

"Hi, Mom," he responded. "How are you?" She looked great. She'd put on a few pounds in recent months. And her dark hair had begun to thin. But the sparkle in her blue eyes would always make her pretty.

"I'm fine. What a nice surprise to see you."

"I was in town. Thought I'd drop by."

"I'm glad you did. Come in and have some iced tea. Your father will be so disappointed that he missed you."

Gabe halted before crossing the threshold. His mother was always trying to patch things up between him and his father, but Gabe wasn't in the mood to put up with any coaxing. "Don't start, Mom."

She held the door expectantly and Lazarus trotted inside, his toenails clicking on the marble floor. "Start what?" she said.

"You know what I'm talking about," he said, following his dog.

She led them into the kitchen and poured him a glass of iced tea, but she didn't drop the subject, as he wanted her to. "Gabe, when are you going to put this thing with Lucky behind you?" she asked. "I can't stand what it's doing to you or your father. I want my family back."

"A family that includes Lucky?"

"Why not? She's just as innocent as you are."

On one level, Gabe understood that and agreed. But the whole Lucky situation was simply too overwhelming to deal with right now. "I'm not trying to hurt her. I just want to be left alone. Live and let live."

"She asks about you all the time."

"Mom—"

"And your father—"

Gabe's glass sounded as though it might break when he slammed it down on the tile countertop. "You're worried about *Dad?* He's the one to blame for all this."

She usually backed off when he grew angry. But that wasn't the case today. "You have to weigh a man by his whole life, Gabe," she said gently. "Not one mistake. Anyone can make a mistake."

No kidding. Had Gabe not been living with Hannah's mistake, he probably could've taken his father's in stride, the way his mother and sister seemed to have done. But he'd learned about his father's affair, and the existence of his half sister, when the foundation of his life was already crumbling beneath him. He'd thought his father was the one thing—the one person—he could always rely on. Then Garth had made his shocking confession and Gabe had realized he couldn't take anything for granted.

"He had an affair with the most notorious prostitute in town, Mom. Worse, that affair resulted in a child. How can you accept what he's done?" He scowled. "God, I was out there campaigning for him, raising money by telling everyone that he has integrity and would make a solid congressman."

He thought she'd argue that Garth *would* make a solid congressman. Deep down, Gabe really believed that, too. But she didn't bother. "So this is about embarrassment?"

"Of course not. Public humiliation is only part of it," Gabe said. "Anyway, I don't want to talk about Lucky anymore. I came here to tell you I've got a job."

"Really? Where?"

"Here. I'm taking over the Spartans."

"That's wonderful! Your father will be so—" She caught herself. "Even Reenie will be pleased to hear it."

"Yeah, well." He shrugged. "We'll see how it goes."

The phone rang. She raised one hand in a gesture that said she'd only be a minute and answered it. "Hello?… Yes, dear, I've heard. It is good news. I'm glad you're happy about it. I know… He'll be fantastic… Actually, he's sitting right here so I'd better… Well—" she glanced at him and frowned "—actually, he's in the restroom right now. Maybe he could call you later?… Right. See you on Thursday… We'll have a good time… I always love shopping for antiques… Okay, then. I'll talk to you soon…"

Gabe's mood darkened as he watched her disconnect. "Who was that?"

She hesitated, obviously leery.

"Mom?" he pressed.

"It was Lucky."

Lucky again. The most important people in his life had all grown close to *her*. With a sigh, he pushed his iced tea away. "I gotta go."

"Gabe, don't leave yet," she said. But his sister came through the front door at that precise moment.

"Hey, I thought that was your truck Decided to act a little human and actually leave the cabin today, huh?"

Gabe didn't respond. With a whistle, he called Lazarus and left.

So where was Kenny?

Hannah sat at her desk staring at the phone, a victim to the same nail-biting, stomach-knotting anxiety she felt almost every time Russ took the boys. She was afraid that her ex would get drunk and drive with Brent and Kenny in the car, fall asleep with a lit cigarette and burn down the trailer, or bring home a couple of vagrants who couldn't be trusted around kids. There was no telling what Russ might do. He'd done plenty of questionable things in the past, some she knew about and probably lots she didn't. Kenny and Brent and Russ's family, especially his sister Patti, tried to cover for him, but Hannah had lived with Russ for twelve years. She knew what he was like. And she knew he'd gone downhill since the divorce. It was a travesty that the courts had made it impossible for her to protect the boys.

The phone rang and she snapped it up. "Hello?"

"Hannah?" It wasn't Kenny. It was Betsy Mann, the woman who'd called nearly two hours ago to complain that Russ had been terribly late picking up Brent from his play date with her grandson, which made her miss her voice lessons. Hannah found it irritating that folks still expected her to apologize for Russ's shortcomings. She and Russ had been divorced for nearly six years. But life in Dundee changed slowly, if at all, and today she was far more worried about the fact that Betsy hadn't seen Kenny in the Jeep when Russ finally arrived. Had he forgotten Kenny or dropped him off somewhere? Hannah was betting on the former. Russ forgot the boys, or simply blew them off, all the time.

"Have you found Kenny?" Betsy asked.

Leaning forward at her desk, Hannah rested her forehead on the butt of her hand. "No. Russ isn't answering. I haven't been able to reach Coach Blaine, either. But Coach Owens told me Kenny was still waiting on the curb when he left."

"Did you go over to the school?"

"Of course. I didn't see him."

"Maybe he tried to walk home."

"There was no sign of him on the streets."

Kenny was not a little boy. And Dundee wasn't exactly a high-crime district. But an accident could happen anywhere. What concerned Hannah was that she knew he wouldn't call her if his father didn't show up. He tried to keep that sort of thing quiet so he wouldn't stir up trouble.

"Marge over at Finley's Grocery said that Gabe Holbrook's the new head coach now that Larry's passed away, God rest his soul," Betsy said. "Have you tried him?"

"Not yet."

"Do you have his number?"

"No."

"Don't worry. I called Celeste, Gabe's mother, and got it for you, just in case."

Sometimes people in Dundee were a little *too* helpful. But with Kenny's welfare hanging in the balance, Hannah didn't mind.

"He's unlisted, you know," Betsy was saying as Hannah rummaged through the drawer, looking for a pen. "Gabe's such a big star he can't publish his phone number for anyone to find. I happen to be good friends with Celeste, so she gave it to me the moment I asked. I help her with the crab feed for Safe & Sober Grad Night every year, you know."

What Hannah knew was that Gabe wanted to avoid his old acquaintances as much as his adoring fans—and she suspected he wanted to avoid her more than anyone else. Especially after what had passed between them this morning. But she found a pen and took down his number. Maybe he'd seen Kenny get into a car with one of the other players. If so, at least she'd have somewhere else to look.

"Thanks," she said and hung up. Then she traced the numerals of his number several times while working up the nerve to call him.

GABE SET his staining brush aside, used the remote to turn down the stereo in his workshop and leaned over to reach the phone. It had been a long day, filled with more interruptions than he'd had in the past year. It seemed like half the town had contacted him since practice. Some had questions about whether or not he was planning to significantly change the football program at DHS. Some put in a plug for one player or another, or wanted to analyze this year's talent. Others simply called to say how grateful they were that he was stepping in for Coach Hill. After his little confrontation with Blaine, Gabe was grateful for the support. But he'd kept to himself for so long, he also felt bombarded, overwhelmed and more than a little rusty on the social skills.

"Hello?"

"Gabe?"

In the corner, Lazarus sat up.

"Yes?" It was Hannah. Gabe knew it instantly, and immediately feared that Mike had called her and made some type of suggestion that they get together.

He was considering breaking his best friend's nose when she asked if he'd seen Kenny, and he realized he'd jumped to the wrong conclusion.

Letting a sigh slip silently between his lips, he remembered the way Russ had acted when he'd pulled up that afternoon, and his anger turned to disgust. "His father picked him up at practice," he said.

"Oh, he did?" He heard her relief. "I haven't been able to reach them, so I wasn't sure."

Taking advantage of the fact that Gabe had stopped working, Lazarus walked over and nudged him. "He was pretty late, but he finally came," he said, scratching his dog behind the ears.

"That's good."

"Glad I could help." Gabe was eager to get off the phone. He'd dealt with enough people for one day—and he didn't want whatever had happened between them this morning to raise its head again. He could already feel some kind of tension humming through the line. But she spoke before he could hang up.

"Marissa asked about you the other day."

"Marissa?"

"My friend? The one I hung out with all the time in high school?"

That Marissa. How could he have forgotten her? She'd been one of the more determined girls-in-pursuit he'd known at Dundee High. Even the groupies who'd followed him around once he started playing in the NFL hadn't had her perseverance. She'd asked him to the prom, after he already had a date, called him incessantly, sent him love letters, drove past his house three or four times a night. Once she even decorated his truck with hundreds of lipstick kisses interspersed with chocolate kisses. It had taken him hours to clean it off. "I remember... How is she?" he added when he realized his response had been a little too deadpan to be polite.

If Hannah noticed, she didn't let on. "She's living in Boise, married with five kids."

"I'm happy for her," he said. But he was even happier for himself now that he knew there was little chance of running into her, or once again becoming the object of her adoration. He'd expected his wheelchair to deter some of the women who'd chased him so brazenly, but the numbers hadn't dropped significantly until he'd bought his cabin and disappeared from public view. He wasn't sure what drew them. Maybe it was sympathy, the compulsion to feel needed, a craving for attention. Or maybe they simply saw dollar signs.

Fortunately—or unfortunately, depending on how he looked at it—he'd known since the accident that he wasn't interested in a romantic relationship. He especially didn't want to keep company with a woman who sought him out because of pity or greed.

"She's doing well," Hannah said.

There was an awkward lull in the conversation, but instead of saying goodbye, Gabe hesitated, thinking of what Mike had told him earlier. He wanted to ask Hannah if Russ had won any spousal maintenance. The idea of an able-bodied man like Russ living off Hannah really bothered him. But what had happened between her and Russ was none of his business.

"Well, have a nice weekend," he said.

"Gabe?"

Lazarus yawned as Gabe brought the phone back to his ear. "Yeah?"

"I was wondering…"

Gabe's muscles nearly cramped while he waited. What was she going to ask? Had Mike spoken to her after all? From the temerity in her voice, it certainly sounded that way. "What?"

"Is there any chance you'd—"

"No."

Lazarus barked, probably in response to the tension he sensed in Gabe. Then there was a long silence during which Gabe wondered how to smooth over the rejection that had just shot out of his mouth.

"But you don't even know what I was going to ask," she said at last. "I mean, you make so much furniture. One chair can't be all that important to you. Or, if it is, maybe you could make me one like it."

That took him aback. "What are you talking about?" he asked.

"The chair on your front porch. I was hoping you'd sell it to me."

Gabe blinked in surprise—and felt more than a little foolish. "You want my *chair?*"

"If I can afford it," she said.

Smiling at Lazarus, as if his dog could share his embarrassment, he shook his head. He had Mike to blame for his false assumption. Maybe his vanity had something to do with it, too, but it wouldn't have been the first time a woman had asked him out. "You can have it," he said.

"No…I wouldn't feel good about that. I'd rather…can you name a price?"

Gabe had no idea what to charge her. He'd never sold any of his furniture before. And he didn't need the money. He thought giving her the chair was a great idea. It could stand as a token of his goodwill, so she could go on with her life without carrying any baggage from the accident. Then, whatever happened—whether he walked or he didn't—it would be his problem exclusively.

"It's no big deal," he said. "Really. I'll drop it by tomorrow after practice."

"Now I'm embarrassed I even asked."

"Why?" He began scratching Lazarus again.

"Because I can't take it unless you let me give you something in return. What if we worked out a trade?"

His hand stilled. The suggestion piqued his interest, if only to see what she might offer him. "What kind of trade?"

"I don't know… Do I have anything you want?"

Gabe waved Lazarus away and straightened in his chair. Was he the only one whose mind was suddenly painting erotic pictures? "Give me some suggestions," he said. Since the accident, he'd tried very hard to cram his sex drive and anything related to male/female intimacy into a single compartment in his brain, a compartment he no longer used. Yet that innocent question from Hannah had his heart pounding as he imagined her naked beneath him, his lips gliding down her flat stomach….

She seemed to realize that what she'd just said could be misinterpreted and sounded embarrassed when she scrambled to clarify. "I mean, I'm a pretty good photographer. I could do some portraits of you."

"Of *me?*"

"Why not? You could use them as Christmas gifts for your folks, or put them inside Christmas cards."

Now that he had allowed the sexy images in his mind to take shape, he was having difficulty brushing them aside. Certainly, getting his picture taken sounded like a poor substitute for what he'd been thinking. He didn't send out Christmas cards, and he wasn't sure he'd be spending the holidays with this folks this year. Even if he changed his mind, a portrait was about the last thing he wanted to give them. "No thanks."

"I could photograph Lazarus."

"Uh…" He arched a questioning eyebrow at his dog, who'd returned to his favorite corner and was yawning again, then chuckled softly. "I love Lazarus, but I'm not really the type to hang up a big photograph of my dog."

She didn't try to talk him into it. She immediately moved on to something else, which strengthened his suspicion that she was working hard to compensate for the "Do I have anything you want?" blunder. "Then maybe I can cook for you. You'll be busy now that you're coaching, right? If you like, you could swing by and pick up your dinner after practice each day, then heat it up when you're ready to eat."

Gabe didn't want to be distracted from the life he'd plotted out for himself—especially by the type of images he'd just entertained. But he knew Hannah's offer wasn't really about a chair. Despite the years that had passed, she was still looking for some way to feel better about her part in the accident. "I guess we could try it," he said. "I could give Kenny a ride at the same time if you like."

Hannah quickly agreed and seemed eager to discuss the details. But Gabe knew almost instantly that he'd made a mistake. He might have given way to Mike's pressure to take over the Spartans, but that didn't mean he had to let other people intrude in his life.

"Gabe?" she said when the conversation began to wind down.

"What?"

"What did you think I was asking for earlier?"

"When?" He already knew the answer—when he'd given her a resounding "no" before she could even finish the question—but he hoped to buy himself some time.

"When I was asking about the chair."

No good answer presented itself. "Oh, something else," he said vaguely, then added a quick, "I gotta go." He hung up before she could press him, but the memory of her voice lingered in his mind as Lazarus followed him into the house. He'd let her cook for a week or so, he decided, as he changed into his T-shirt and shorts so he could work out. Then he'd thank her, insist it was enough and get back to growing his wheatgrass.

CHAPTER FOUR

GENERALLY HANNAH DUCKED her head and tried to go unnoticed whenever anyone mentioned Gabe Holbrook. There were too many folks in town who hadn't yet forgiven her for destroying their favorite football star. She suspected they were more upset that they could no longer bask in his reflected glory than they were about *his* loss. But they often shook their heads and *tsked* when she passed by, especially at the beginning of football season and in the weeks leading up to the Super Bowl.

Today, the mention of Gabe's name made Hannah as self-conscious as ever. When Trudy Johnson started talking about the new coach at the high school, Hannah cursed silently and raised the cookbook she'd brought into the hair salon. She should've expected the town to be buzzing with the latest news. Folks in Dundee took school sports very seriously. Here, the high school coach possessed almost as much clout as the mayor.

"I never dreamed he'd accept the position," Trudy was saying.

"I know!" Over the top of her book, Hannah saw thirtyish Shirley Erman crane her head around even though Ashleigh Evans was trying to put perm rods in her hair. Saturdays were always busy at the beauty shop. "He's been living like a hermit for three years," she said. "Then, suddenly, he's the new coach of the varsity football team? I mean, I hate that Coach Hill passed away, but I think it's great Gabe's willing to take over."

Hannah agreed. In her opinion, Gabe needed to feel passionate about something again, to regain his zest for life. But she didn't say anything. She wasn't sure she wanted to draw attention to herself and suffer through that awkward moment when the others realized that she—the person who'd ended his career—was sitting only a few feet away.

"He'll do a good job." Rebecca Hill was giving Trudy a short jagged cut that looked far too *Vogue* for a little town in Idaho, but that was the beauty of Rebecca. She was artistic and dramatic, and she followed her heart. Since marrying Mike's brother a few years ago, she'd grown slightly more conservative, especially since the birth of their baby. But she'd never be plain or boring. And her salon reflected that. Gone was the faded candy-cane-striped wallpaper and pale pink vinyl of the beauty parlor Hannah remembered from her childhood. Now the salon was decorated in black and white and chrome, had a checkered floor, sleek, contemporary lighting, and vases filled with exotic flowers. Recently, Rebecca had even changed the name. After she'd remodeled and expanded to include facials, electrolysis, massage and aromatherapy, Hair and Now had become Shear Temptation. Located next to an old-fashioned drugstore on one side, and a redbrick bank on the other, Shear Temptation looked like a spaceship parked between two Model T's.

"Being a good player doesn't make someone a good coach," a voice nearby responded.

A quick peek around her book told Hannah that Deborah Wheeler, one of Coach Blaine's daughters, had made that comment from a seat in the waiting area closer to the front desk.

Hannah had been so absorbed in trying to go unnoticed that she hadn't seen Deborah come in. She lowered her cookbook. "Being a good player doesn't make someone a bad coach," she said, rushing to Gabe's defense in spite of herself. Now that he was venturing back into society, she wanted to make sure he received the support he deserved.

Everyone's gaze momentarily fixed on her. She waited for someone to mention the accident but, thankfully, nobody did.

"I just want what's good for Gabe," Shirley said, turning back to Deborah. "If coaching will give him fresh purpose, I'm all for it."

"Even if he's not cut out for the job?" Deborah countered.

"Even if he doesn't win very much," Shirley said. "My husband might disagree, but I say we can't expect every season to be as good as the last few. Gabe needs this."

Deborah had a thin, angular face. Now she pursed her lips as though it tried her patience to deal with folks obviously less educated than herself. She taught Honors English at the high school and acted as if she knew everything. Some of the ladies in town made fun of her, but she had her admirers. "Gabe doesn't *need* this job," she said. "He made millions while he was playing football. And anyway, no one should get a coaching position out of pity."

Hannah opened her mouth to say that with a record like Gabe's he'd hardly landed the job on pity, but Rebecca answered before she could. "Pity has nothing to do with it! Gabe's well-qualified."

Deborah shook her head. "You don't understand."

"What's not to understand?" Hannah asked.

"Think about it." She set her magazine on the table. "Making Gabe head coach places him in a position where he has everything to lose and nothing to gain. He doesn't need the money from the job—"

"This isn't about money," Rebecca interrupted.

"—and if the team wins, so what? We've won plenty of times in the past without him." She tilted her head at a jaunty angle. "But let's look at what happens if the Spartans have a bad season. Now there's a story. Poor, crippled Gabe Holbrook takes on his old high school team, a team with a winning season nearly twenty years in a row," she was careful to emphasize, "only to watch them lose again and again. Which could happen. He's an untried entity. So my question is this—do we really want to risk seeing Gabe fall any farther off his pedestal? The accident nearly destroyed him. What's he going to do if he fails at this?"

Hannah suspected Deborah was actually more afraid Gabe would succeed. "He won't fail," she said.

Deborah folded her arms across her nearly flat chest. "You don't know that."

"I, for one, am proud of him for trying," Shirley said. "People who won't attempt something for fear of failing, cripple themselves. At least Gabe's not doing that. His handicap was caused by an outside source."

Deborah's eyes seemed to slice right through Hannah. "You should know all about that, right, Hannah?"

Hannah clenched her jaw. Deborah certainly wasn't perfect. She'd had an affair with the band teacher at Dundee High four years ago, which had caused a small scandal and broken up two marriages. From what Hannah had heard, Deborah had regretted her actions almost immediately and tried to win her husband back, but he'd refused to reconcile. Hannah knew she could point to that mistake and say, "Everyone lives with some regret, Deborah."

But what was the point? Deborah hadn't stripped a man of his ability to *walk*. Hannah's sin was far worse, and the guilt she felt wouldn't allow her to defend herself. If only she hadn't tried to pass on that curve....

Rebecca spoke up. "That was beneath even you, Deborah."

"This isn't about the past," Shirley added in a conciliatory tone. "It's about the future. We, as a community, need to stand behind Gabe."

"Why?" Deborah cried, jumping to her feet. "Why is he any different from the rest of us? If I got in a car accident and was put in a wheelchair, do you think this community would do anything for me? No! Because I'm not some hotshot football player. Just because he can throw a ball eighty yards doesn't make him any better than anyone else," she said and stormed out.

Hannah turned to watch Deborah flounce down the street toward her car. Shirley joined her at the window. "I heard she wanted Gabe," she mused. "But I didn't believe it until now."

"Do you think he rejected her?" Ashleigh asked. Still unmarried, Ashleigh generally kept tabs on every available man in town and sounded put out that something might have occurred that she didn't know about.

Trudy rolled her eyes. "Ya think?"

Shirley ignored Trudy's sarcasm. "He must have."

Hannah set the cookbook on the seat next to her. "Deborah was in my graduating class. She had a crush on him way back then, but so did a lot of girls."

"I bet he's never even looked at her," Shirley said. "Probably the only thing that made her think she finally had a chance with him was that wheelchair. Otherwise, he'd be so out of reach it'd be like crying for the moon."

Hannah wasn't sure that rejection was the reason for Deborah's sniping. Probably had more to do with her father not getting the position as head coach. But Hannah could certainly understand why Blaine's daughter might find Gabe attractive. There probably wasn't a woman in town who hadn't fantasized about him. He was strong, talented, intelligent and handsome. *Really* handsome.

Remembering the look in his eyes yesterday, that brief flash of something powerful and erotic, gave Hannah the same fluttery expectation she felt on a roller coaster as it climbed the highest hill.

There were times she wanted him herself.

But even if he could forgive her, she doubted he'd ever be able to forget what she'd cost him.

SHOVING HIS EMPTY plate away, Kenny shifted uncomfortably in the booth at Jerry's Diner and told Brent to eat the rest of his hash browns. Their dad had finally rolled out of bed at eleven-thirty, so they were having more of an early lunch than a late breakfast. But missing breakfast wasn't anything unusual when they stayed with Russ. This Sunday morning had gone pretty much like all

the others—except that Kenny had dragged himself out of bed
the moment Brent had gotten up to watch cartoons. Kenny hadn't
intervened when his little brother helped himself to a candy bar
first thing, but no way was he going to allow Brent to get hold
of another porn video.

Brent pushed his potatoes around on his plate. "I'm stuffed,"
he complained. "I can't eat another bite."

Looking immediately to their father, who'd recently started
growing a goatee to compensate for his thinning hair, Kenny said,
"He's done. Can we go?"

Russ hooked an arm over the back of the booth and waved
for the waitress to come round with the coffee. "Of course not.
Coach Blaine hasn't arrived yet."

Kenny wasn't sure if Blaine would show. Kenny couldn't see
a man like him having much to do with Russ, even if they both
wanted to see Gabe Holbrook give up the job he'd just taken.

"He should've been here half an hour ago," Kenny said.
"Something must've come up."

"We're in no hurry. We can wait."

His father was never in any hurry. But Kenny didn't want to
wait. He didn't really want to see Blaine. Growing anxious, he
started bouncing his knee.

His father scowled at the movement. "Jeez you've got a lot
of energy. Has your mother ever had you tested for ADHD?"

Russ had only recently learned of ADHD—and instantly decided he had it. He saw symptoms in everyone else, too, and was
quick to suggest medication. Left to him, more than half the town
would be on Ritalin.

"I don't have ADHD, Dad."

"Coulda fooled me." He added cream to his coffee. "You
fidget more than Brent does."

That was an exaggeration if Kenny had ever heard one. Brent
was pouring sugar onto the table right now. His father had to take
the sugar dispenser away from him in order to sweeten his cof-

fee, but he handed it back as soon as he was done. Russ let Brent do just about anything.

"Don't you care that he's making a mess?" Kenny asked, irritated that his father didn't act more like…well, a father.

Russ shrugged. "I don't have to clean it up."

"*Someone* does."

His father grimaced. "You're sounding more like your mother every day, you know that?"

Russ accused him of that a lot, probably because Kenny couldn't come up with a good answer.

"Anyway, he probably has ADHD, too," his father said, jerking his head toward Brent.

Ignoring them both, Brent squeezed ketchup all over the sugar volcano he was building on the table. The mess bugged Kenny enough that he would have stopped his brother, but after what his father had said, he couldn't—not without sounding more like Hannah than ever. "He doesn't have ADHD, Dad. People with ADHD have trouble focusing."

"I know," his father replied, nodding emphatically. "I've been struggling with it since I was a kid."

Kenny wished he could believe that. But it sounded like another convenient excuse —the latest in a long line of excuses. "Brent focuses fine. And so do I."

His father leaned forward. "Then, why don't you focus on having a cup of coffee and quit bitching at me for a damn minute?"

Kenny wasn't particularly sensitive to bad language. He could swear with the best of them. But he didn't understand why their father had to cuss so much in front of Brent.

He shot a quick glance at his little brother to see if Brent had marked it, and knew he had when Brent shot him a mischievous grin. "Dad—" Kenny started, but fell silent when Russ's eyebrows clashed, making a solid slash of brown above his golden eyes.

"What now?"

Kenny stared down at his plate. "Never mind." It wasn't any use asking Russ to quit with the bad language. His father would only do it more, or say that he and Brent needed to come live with him before their mother turned them into complete pussies.

The waitress came around, but Kenny refused coffee. While she filled his father's cup, he glanced at the other tables, and froze when he spotted Josh and Rebecca Hill seated in the far corner with Booker and Katie Robinson. Like his brother Mike, Josh was a good friend of Gabe Holbrook's, and Booker owned the only automotive repair shop in town, so he probably serviced Gabe's truck. Which meant, if Coach Blaine showed up and Kenny sat talking with him for any length of time, Coach Holbrook would probably hear about it. Because his father and Blaine acted as though they had some problem with Holbrook, Kenny didn't want that. His mother had told him to give Holbrook his loyalty and, despite his worries about getting to play, he wanted to. Maybe Hannah had put Gabe Holbrook in a wheelchair, but the coach was still a man who could command respect regardless of what the accident had cost him.

Keeping his eye on the clock, Kenny forced himself to sit still for another five minutes. Then he appealed to his father once again. "Blaine's late, Dad. I don't think he's coming. Can we go? Please?"

His father glared at him. Then, muttering, "I'll bet my ass you do have ADHD," he finally tossed twenty bucks on the table.

Briefly, Kenny wondered how his father had twenty bucks for breakfast when he couldn't pay his child support this month—he'd heard his parents arguing over it just last week. But he didn't want to think about any of the stuff that made him angry. He'd learned early on when it came to his father he had only two choices—he could cut Russ out of his life, or he could put up with him. There was no other alternative, and therefore no way to win. It was important to take his father moment by moment.

At least they were leaving the diner now. At least Kenny

wouldn't have to face Coach Holbrook at practice on Monday knowing—

"Sorry I'm late." Coach Blaine loomed over them before they could even stand all the way.

Swallowing a groan, Kenny flopped back into his seat. Russ did the same as Blaine slid into the booth next to him, wearing a muscle shirt and a pair of jogging shorts. Although Blaine was probably in his fifties, he was a stickler for physical fitness. Today he was sweating badly enough that Kenny knew he hadn't been late for any reason other than a morning jog. Obviously Blaine didn't think this meeting was important.

"I'm glad you could come, Coach," Russ said eagerly.

Blaine waved for the waitress to bring him coffee. "What'd you want to talk to me about?"

Russ blinked as if surprised by the question. "I'm concerned, of course. Aren't you?"

"About what?"

Most folks in town didn't take his father too seriously. Blaine was clearly one of them.

"What do you think?" Russ replied. "The recent changes at the high school. I mean, you've given that team thirty years of your life. You can't tell me you're happy to be overlooked now that Coach Hill has passed on."

A tightening around Blaine's lips proved that he wasn't happy about it at all. "They say it's only for one year."

"Well, if I know Gabe, he'll decide to stay. What else is he gonna do now that he's in that chair? And, if he does decide to stay, who in this town is gonna tell him no?"

Wiping away the perspiration rolling from his temple, Blaine attempted a shrug, but it didn't come off as casual as he'd probably intended. "He won't stay."

"How do you know?" Kenny was unable to hold the question back.

Blaine seemed in no hurry to answer. The waitress had arrived with his coffee, and he waited for her to move away. "We probably have the weakest team we've had in over a decade. And now we've got a head coach with absolutely no experience." His spoon clinked as he stirred cream into his coffee. "Add to that the fact that we're all used to the Spartans coming out on top, and we'll see how excited everyone is when we start losing our games."

Kenny heard the eagerness in Blaine's voice. "You *want* us to lose?"

"It has nothing to do with what I want," he said shortly. "It's what's going to happen."

If Kenny had his guess, it was *exactly* what Blaine wanted.

"You seem pretty sure of it," Russ said.

"Maybe I wouldn't be so sure if Gabe would listen to me. But I called him just this morning to tell him how things are normally run."

"And?" Russ prompted.

"He said not to worry about the past. He'll be making some changes." Blaine grimaced at the sugar, ketchup and water mess Brent had created on the table. Grabbing the sugar container, he sweetened his coffee, then set it well outside Brent's reach. "Coaching isn't as easy as Gabe seems to think."

"We've only had one practice," Kenny said, wondering how Blaine could already be so convinced of their failure. Sure, they didn't have the strongest team. Several of their best players had graduated last spring. But Kenny was still hopeful they could pull off a winning season.

"It's Holbrook's attitude," Blaine explained. "He isn't willing to learn from those who've been doing this far longer than he has."

"So what do *we* do?" Russ asked.

"We wait, I guess. When the Spartans begin to lose, the school board will eventually step in and beg me to take over." His long nose disappeared in his cup while he drank.

"I was going to ask you to look out for Kenny," Russ said. "You know how Gabe must feel toward Hannah. I don't want to let him take his resentment out on my boy."

Blaine's eyes flicked over Kenny's face. He obviously wanted to say something, but he hesitated.

Kenny leaned closer. "What is it?"

"For God's sake, if you think that might happen, use your heads."

"How?" Russ asked.

"I'll say it one more time. The more games we lose, the quicker Gabe will find himself back at his cabin, where he belongs."

"Where he belongs?" Kenny echoed.

"He sure as hell doesn't belong on the sidelines with me. And neither does that damn dog of his."

"But will you take care of those who stick by you?" Russ asked.

Blaine wouldn't look at him, but his words were decisive enough. "Of course."

Kenny wasn't sure he understood this exchange—wasn't sure he wanted to understand it. He frowned as Blaine said, "Stay in touch," and left without bothering to pay for his coffee.

Russ said nothing, and suddenly the clack of dishes, the tingle of silverware, the voice of the waitresses calling to the cooks and the hum of conversation at the crowded booths surrounding them seemed unnaturally loud to Kenny. At last, with a sigh, his father stood. "Well, you heard him."

"I heard him say we were going to lose," Kenny said glumly.

Russ lowered his voice. "I heard him say you'd better make sure of it."

Kenny backed up as though he'd just encountered poison. "You can't really expect me to do that?"

His father glanced furtively around, then shuttled him outside. Brent was still lingering in the booth, tearing up strips of napkin—but at this point, Kenny didn't much care about the lack of parental intervention.

"It's better to lose a few games in the beginning than to give up the entire season, and maybe next year as well," Russ said, when the door closed behind them.

Kenny squinted against the sudden brightness of the sun. "But I can't do less than my best!"

"I'm sure you won't be alone. Blaine has two nephews and a second cousin on the team."

Kenny knew that. The twins had necks almost as thick as Kenny's waist and were part of the offensive line. Their cousin, with a much lighter build, was the kicker. "You're saying Blaine and some of the guys are going to sabotage our games?"

"What do you *think* Blaine was talking about?"

"I don't know, but I can't do that," Kenny said, shaking his head emphatically. "I'd let everyone down. I'd—"

"Do you want to play in the NFL someday?" his father snapped.

Kenny was so shocked at what his father had suggested, that he paid no mind to Tiffany Wheeler, who honked as she drove by. "You know I do."

"Then you have to think past three or four games. Gabe won't want to see you succeed. He's never liked me, and you know what your mother did. Blaine's our only hope. He'll probably be taking over soon—next year if not this year. You scratch his back, he'll scratch yours."

The bell jingled over the door as Brent finally joined them, his shirt smeared with ketchup.

"But we haven't given Coach Holbrook a chance," Kenny replied.

Russ's movements were jerky as he opened the door of the Jeep for Brent. "Coach Hill didn't give me much of a chance when he handed my position to Gabe."

Kenny remained rooted to the cracking blacktop. "What's that got to do with anything?"

His father climbed behind the wheel. "Gabe's already had his share of lucky breaks."

"And unlucky ones," Brent piped up, out of nowhere.

Sometimes Brent surprised Kenny. He was getting so big, catching on to more and more. But it was their father who surprised Kenny the most. "That's life," Russ said and waved for Kenny to get in.

CHAPTER FIVE

EARLY MONDAY morning, Hannah pulled herself away from her work to drive Kenny to the high school for football practice.

"Coach Holbrook will bring you home," she told him.

"Coach *Holbrook?*" he echoed in surprise. "Why?"

"Because he's coming by to pick up one of the dinners I'm trading him for a chair."

Brent, her younger son, stretched his seatbelt so he could lean closer to her. "Isn't that the guy in the wheelchair?"

Hannah hated to hear Gabe referred to by his handicap. "Yes. But he's also the guy who won Most Valuable Player in the NFL two years in a row. Maybe we could use that to set him apart instead, huh?"

"How does he drive?" he asked as though she hadn't said anything.

"With his hands." She looked over at Kenny, who was sitting in the passenger seat. His reticence seemed a little unnatural. "You don't mind riding with him, do you?"

"No," he grumbled.

"Kenny?"

"That's fine."

When they arrived at the high school, Hannah saw Gabe's truck parked in the lot and was tempted to linger. She wanted to see how Gabe managed his wheelchair on the field. Did he allow anyone to help him? How did he move on the thick turf?

She wondered but didn't find out because Coach Blaine arrived a moment later, and she didn't want him or anyone else to see her hanging around. Someone might interpret her interest as doubt in Gabe's ability. Judging by the cars filling the lot, there were more than enough parents in the stands already. The last thing he needed was a bunch of gawkers.

As she drove toward the exit, she tried to concentrate on other things. It was good to have the boys back. She always breathed easier once they were home. Fortunately, this weekend seemed to have gone smoother than the last time Kenny and Brent were with their father. The news about Brent and the porn movie had upset her so much she'd decided to take her ex back to court. But Kenny insisted that Brent had only seen the cover of the video before Russ whisked it away from both of them.

Hannah suspected that wasn't the case, but without Kenny's support, she knew her petition would end in joint custody, like all the others before it. For the moment, she seemed to have no choice but to let the incident go.

Pulling into the lot of the grocery store, Hannah parked, found her list and did her shopping. Then she hurried home.

"Where do you want me to put this?" Brent asked, helping her unload the van.

She glanced at his round face, which was turning red beneath his thick strawberry-blond hair because he'd insisted on carrying the watermelon.

"Over there." She motioned to the sink, figuring she'd make room for it in the refrigerator after she unloaded the bags of groceries waiting on her counter. Considering the busy day she had ahead of her, she should've done her shopping over the weekend. But she'd had trouble deciding on the menu. Gabe was wealthy and famous enough that he'd probably eaten at some of the best restaurants in the world. How would her cooking ever compare? What had she been thinking, offering meals to a man like that?

She'd been thinking of the cleverly-crafted chair on his porch, she reminded herself. But she knew her suggestion had more to do with her conscience than anything else. She was hoping that making his life a little easier would take some of the sting out her regret.

But cooking for him wasn't as easy as it had sounded when she'd volunteered to do it. She'd already spent two days poring through every cookbook she could find. Nothing seemed good enough. Finally, she'd bought the ingredients to make a rice and lemon chicken dinner for Monday, her own special recipe of beef stroganoff for Tuesday, shrimp shishkabobs on Wednesday, and green chili enchiladas on Thursday. Friday was still a question mark. When they'd made the arrangements, Gabe had insisted anything would do, but she'd heard he'd become a bit of a health nut. She wanted to see which type of meal went over best—fancy and exotic, low-fat, low-carb or the more standard Dundee fare of meat and potatoes—before planning any more menus.

"Jeez, do you have company coming or what?"

Hannah turned from the cupboard where she was putting away the cold cereal to see Patti, her ex-sister-in-law, come in through the garage. Although on the surface, Hannah's friendship with members of Russ's family remained intact, they weren't nearly as close as they used to be. The court battles between her and Russ had forced the Prices to choose sides. Hannah had known in advance that her divorce would ripple through every relationship that really mattered to her. That was why she'd hung on for so long.

"No company," she responded. "Just stocking up for the coming week."

"I'm glad I have girls." She tossed her keys and her purse on the only bare spot of counter space available and peeked into a sack. "These boys must be eating you out of house and home."

Patti's statement could easily have led to a conversation about Russ, and the fact that he was only paying his child support in fits and starts. Hannah craved a friend with whom she could discuss such things. But Patti was Russ's sister. Since the divorce, they'd had an unspoken agreement not to discuss him at any length. The Prices didn't like to face unpleasant realities and pretty much bought into Russ's excuses and ignored his short-comings. They'd done the same thing when she was married to him, but they'd also tried to support her as much as their loyalty would allow.

"Hi, Aunt Patti!" Brent slipped into her arms for a big hug.

"How's my favorite nephew?" she asked.

He angled his head to look up at her. "I *knew* you liked me better than Kenny."

"You're my favorite nephew *under ten*," she clarified.

He grimaced. "I'm your *only* nephew under ten."

"You're still my favorite," she said with a chuckle. "You gettin' tired of summer, kid?"

"No way. I like being out of school." He gave her a gap-toothed smile. "Will you take me swimming today? Since I'm your *favorite?*"

She tweaked his nose, which was covered with a light dusting of golden freckles that would probably disappear the way Kenny's had. "I guess I could drive you and the girls over to the high school for an hour or so."

As a stay-at-home mom, Patti had much more opportunity to be spontaneous than Hannah did. At times Hannah envied the support Patti received from her husband and Violet, her mother, but not enough to wish her any less happiness.

"Get your swimsuit," Patti told him. "You can go home with me in a few minutes."

Brent hesitated. "Do you think we could go after lunch?"

"Why? Is your schedule so busy that you can't squeeze me in?"

"My schedule?" he repeated, obviously surprised by the adult-like question.

She chuckled. "What are you doing this morning?"

"I'm gonna help my mom make dinner for Coach Holbrook."

Patti's head jerked up. "Coach *Holbrook?*"

Hannah put the bottle of wine she'd bought for one of Gabe's dinners in her rack. "Haven't you heard? Gabe's taking over for Coach Hill."

Patti blinked. "Gabe, the football star turned recluse?"

"He's not really a recluse."

"He barely leaves his cabin."

"He's coming to town every day for practice."

"No kidding." Her brow creased thoughtfully. "Can he get around well enough in that wheelchair?"

"I guess so."

Patti pulled a crusty loaf of sourdough bread and a tub of cheese spread out of a grocery sack and stared down at them. "Wine. Sourdough bread. Fancy cheese. Looks like you've got something romantic going on."

"No, nothing like that." Hannah dug through another sack to avoid Patti's probing gaze.

"How'd this come about?" Patti asked.

"He makes furniture."

"I've heard."

"There's a chair I want," Hannah said. "So I offered to trade him some meals for it."

"Really." Patti said the word with a heavy emphasis on the first syllable.

Hannah buried her head in yet another sack. "It'll make a good prop for my pictures."

"And how'd you see this chair in the first place?"

Remembering her trip to Gabe's cabin and her initial glimpse of him rolling toward her, freshly showered, the white of his shirt stark against the golden-bronze of his skin, his eyes the aquamarine of a Caribbean sea, Hannah felt a nervous excitement and whirled to put some frozen corn in the freezer. "I drove out to his cabin to tell him Coach Blaine isn't happy about being nudged out of the coaching position he's coveted for so many years."

Patti slowly folded an empty sack. "You drove all the way out there just for that?"

"Why wouldn't I?"

"Because Gabe had to have expected as much. Blaine's been waiting for a chance to be head coach since we were in the sixth grade. The Spartans are everything to him."

"I know, but Gabe has a lot on his mind. I wasn't sure he considered Blaine when he took the job. This is the first time since the accident that he's shown an interest in anything—at least that I know of. I didn't want him to be disillusioned on his first day."

Patti set a few more grocery items on the counter. "Okay… So, how'd he treat you?"

"Mom, where does this go?" Brent held a sack of rice in the crook of his arms, like a baby.

"In the pantry, bottom shelf." She put the salad makings into the produce drawer and returned to her conversation with Patti. "He was nice. Gabe's always nice," she said. But she knew that wasn't *strictly* true, at least not anymore. Gabe's parents had been in the public eye forever—his father was currently serving in the state senate and his mother led the charge for every charitable cause in Dundee. They'd raised their two children, especially their son, to be unfailingly polite and that hadn't changed with his fame. It had taken the accident to make him standoffish and morose.

"What about Kenny?" Patti shoved the sack she'd already folded under the sink with the others. "Is he happy about this development?"

Hannah blocked out the distress she'd seen in her son's face when he first gave her the news. "He'll live with it."

"Do you think Gabe will be as supportive of Kenny as Coach Hill was?"

Hannah couldn't help wondering if Patti blamed her entirely for what had happened to Gabe, or whether she held her brother at least partially responsible. Hannah wanted to believe that Patti, of all people, would consider the mitigating circumstances. "I don't know," she said. "But we'd be facing the same question no matter who took over for Coach Hill, right?"

Brent tapped her on the arm. "Mom, can I have some yogurt?"

Hannah nodded as Patti pulled tomatoes from one of the remaining sacks and headed around the kitchen's small island to the fridge. "Not necessarily. Blaine, or even Owens, would be much more familiar with Kenny's abilities."

"If they can spot Kenny's talent, Gabe will be able to see it, too," Hannah said, filling the basket on her kitchen table with apples.

Patti turned to face her, one hand still on the refrigerator door. "I think maybe you're being just a little too trusting, Hannah. I'm sorry for Gabe, but I can't say I'm happy about having him coach Kenny. It's only natural that he'd resent you, and—"

"He wouldn't hold what I did against Kenny."

"Don't let all that mysterious charisma of his fool you. He's not a saint."

"I know, but—"

"He already got in the way of Russ and a career in the NFL. I don't want him to ruin Kenny's future as well."

Gabe had gotten in Russ's way? Hannah almost laughed out loud as she imagined her ex-husband's thickening middle and the way he used to lie on the couch for hours in front of the television when he should've been out looking for a job. A man had to have drive and ambition to get ahead in professional sports. At the very least, he needed to stay in shape. It wasn't a year after she'd married Russ that she realized he had very little motivation and would happily stay at home indefinitely while she worked to pay the rent.

His talk about football was just that—*talk*. "Russ didn't really try for a football career," she pointed out.

"Because Coach Hill decided he preferred Gabe and gave him all the playing time. That demoralized Russ before he ever had a chance."

Hannah stopped unpacking. "Coach Hill was a good coach, Patti. I don't think he based his decisions on personal bias."

"At that age, Gabe was no better than Russ."

"Coach Hill must've thought so."

"I don't care. It was opportunity that built Gabe into what he became," she argued. "If Russ had had the same chance—"

Irritation welled up so quickly, Hannah spoke before she could check herself. "You know what? Whether you want to admit it or not, Russ is responsible for his own failures."

Patti opened her mouth as though she had a hot and ready response, then clamped it firmly closed again, and Hannah cursed herself for landing them in another of those awkward impasses that never used to exist. Not many years ago, she and Patti could talk about almost anything—but that was before she'd crossed the line and filed for divorce.

"Gabe's already had his chance in the sun," Patti finally said, her words clipped. "It's Kenny's turn, and I don't want anyone screwing that up for him."

"Neither do I," Hannah agreed. "But let's make sure there's going to be a problem before we jump to any conclusions."

"Fine." She shrugged, but the stiff set of her shoulders told Hannah she wasn't letting go that easily.

"So what's up? Where're the girls?" Hannah asked, hoping a change of subject might smooth things over.

Her movements quick, Patti put the avocados on the windowsill above Hannah's kitchen sink. "At Mom's. I'm on my way there. I just came by to tell you that Donny and Jamie are getting a divorce."

Donny was Russ's younger brother by two years. Although he and Jamie had been married for at least twelve years and had a ten-year-old daughter, Kara, this news came as no surprise to Hannah. When Hannah was still married to Russ, Jamie used to complain about her own husband all the time.

Hannah put a six-pack of soda in the fridge. "Is Kara going to stay with her mother?"

"Looks that way."

"What about Donny?"

"He'll be getting his own place."

Too bad he wouldn't be rooming with Russ, Hannah thought. Donny had his share of problems, but he owned a construction company and he worked hard. Maybe, under Donny's influence, Russ would finally seek a steady paycheck....

"What's going to happen to Aunt Jamie?" There was a tinge of panic in Brent's voice at the prospect of yet another big change in his life.

Patti must've heard it, too, because she seemed to soften. "She'll be around, kiddo. Don't worry." She scooped up her keys and purse. "I'd better go."

Hannah followed her to the door, feeling bad about the tension between them. "Patti…"

Patti glanced over her shoulder and shook her head. "Life sucks sometimes, doesn't it?"

Hannah knew she was talking about the loss of the relationship they once knew, and nodded. They both felt the same way. They just didn't know how to reclaim the closeness they'd shared.

"I'll pick up pip-squeak this afternoon and take him swimming. Have fun cooking dinner for Mr. Unreachable."

"Mr. Unreachable?" Hannah said. "Why do you call him that?"

Patti tossed her purse inside the car and turned back. "Because even when he could walk, he'd never emotionally engage. There was no penetrating that sexy smile, no getting under his skin and really making his heart pound, you know?"

"He's been with some very beautiful women," Hannah said. "I'm sure they made his heart pound."

Patti arched her eyebrows. "Maybe his heart was pounding when he was—" she glanced meaningfully at Brent "—physically engaged. But certainly not before or afterward."

"You don't know that."

She singled out her ignition key. "Yes, I do. Just ask Deborah Wheeler."

"You're friends with Deborah Wheeler?"

"We talk now and then, since she moved in down the street from me."

That explained some of Patti's prejudice, considering Deborah's connection to Coach Blaine. "And she's an expert on Gabe?"

"She told me when he was playing ball he never brought the same woman home twice."

"He was living in California, so how would she know?"

"He never brought the same woman *to town* twice. She said that even when he used to show up with one of the tall, leggy blondes he seemed to prefer, he was always amiable, always entertaining, but you could tell that if the woman waved goodbye and walked out the door he wouldn't think twice about her."

"That's a lot for Deborah to assume, Patti. I don't think she saw him that often."

"Has he ever had a steady girlfriend?"

"Maybe. It's tough to say. Like I said, for a long time, he didn't even live here."

"If he'd been with someone, word would have gotten around. He couldn't buy a new *car* without everyone talking about it."

Crossing her arms, Hannah leaned against the lintel. "A lot of professional athletes play fast and loose with women. Maybe it's not right, but it's partly a factor of how aggressively they're pursued. And Gabe had legions after him."

"What about now?"

"Dating is probably the last thing on his mind. He's still dealing with what's happened to him."

"It's been three years, Hannah. It's like Deborah said to me the other day. He's already passed the crossroads."

"What crossroads?"

"If he was going to adjust and move on, he would have done it by now."

Those words terrified Hannah, probably because, on some level, she feared they were true. Gabe was letting his handicap limit more than his body. He was letting it take control of his life. "It takes time to recover," she said, but not very convincingly.

"Where women are concerned, he hasn't changed." With a parting wave, Patti got in the car.

Hannah watched her drive off, picturing the tortured look in Gabe's eyes when she'd touched his face. He'd tried to remain true to his unaffected public persona, but he'd slipped for a moment, and she'd caught a glimpse of the real man.

Patti might be right about some things, but she was wrong about Gabe being unreachable. The heart that beat beneath his muscled chest wasn't too hard. If Hannah had her guess, it was too soft.

Otherwise, he wouldn't have to protect it so well.

KENNY BLINKED FAST and wiped the sweat from his brow. They'd been practicing for two hours already. The past fifteen minutes had been spent running a new play Coach Holbrook had designed. Two receivers crossed in the middle, then headed down opposite sides of the field. Kenny was supposed to roll out to his left and throw a long diagonal bomb, which would hopefully turn into a touchdown pass. But he couldn't get it right. He was too upset by the conspiratorial look Coach Blaine had given him a few minutes earlier.

While waiting for the front line to return to their formation, Kenny tried to stretch the tension out of the muscles in his neck. What was he going to do? He didn't want to be a traitor to his own team. But he didn't want to ruin his chances to play college or professional ball, either. Everyone was saying Coach Holbrook had only stepped in for one year. If Holbrook wasn't making any type of long-term commitment to the team, how could Kenny risk his future by remaining loyal to him? Even if they had a winning season, chances were good Blaine would take over next year. And he was one coach who wouldn't forgive or forget if Kenny didn't do exactly as he said.

Gabe's whistle sounded. "Again!"

They ran the play, but Kenny's pass wobbled weakly and fell short for the third time in a row. Finally, Holbrook pulled him out and replaced him with senior Jonathon Greer.

Jonathon gave Kenny a triumphant smile before slipping on his helmet and running onto the field, but Kenny pretended not to notice. His stomach hurt. He wanted to go home.

"Thirty-four, twenty-eight, sixteen, hut, hut." Jonathon's voice carried easily through air that smelled sharply of dust and sweat. Dropping back in the pocket, he cocked his arm to throw but hesitated, waiting…waiting…

The crack of shoulder pads and the thud of bodies rang in Kenny's ears as the defense tried to reach the quarterback. Then Jonathon loosed a perfect spiral, which sailed through the air and landed easily in receiver Brandon Joseph's arms.

Kenny could have done that. He could have done it easily if he wasn't so damned upset….

"That's what I want to see," Gabe said. "Let's do it again."

They ran the play four more times. Jonathon missed only once.

A cold shower and some dry clothes were growing more appealing to Kenny by the minute. Yanking off his helmet, he tucked it under his arm, feeling humiliated and eager to be alone. If he didn't improve his play, he wouldn't have to worry about double-crossing the team. He'd be sitting on the bench with the other two sophomores.

"Hey, what's wrong with you, man?" Sly, the kicker who was also Blaine's cousin, sidled up to him.

"Nothing." Kenny cast Sly a sideways glance and scowled. "What's wrong with *you?*" he said darkly.

Sly lifted his hands. "I'm chillin', dude. You're the one who's chokin' out there."

Kenny said nothing. He had no desire to talk to Sly. They'd

never been friends before, and Kenny didn't want what his father had arranged at the diner to change that.

"The point is to win a starting position *before* you play like shit," Sly whispered, then chuckled and spat at the ground.

Kenny glanced furtively at the other boys, all crowded so close. "Keep your mouth shut."

Sobering, Sly straightened and eyed him doubtfully. "My uncle said you were in."

Kenny refused to look at him.

"You're in, right?" he pressed. But Gabe had just called an end to practice and, pivoting abruptly, Kenny stalked off.

CHAPTER SIX

THE RICE WAS TOO STICKY. Hannah glanced nervously at the clock and wondered if she'd have fifteen minutes to make more. She'd never had her rice cooker fail her before. The rice was supposed to be the easiest part....

At least the chicken tasted good. And the steamed vegetables and coffee cake. She'd decided long ago that a woman couldn't go wrong with coffee cake. She'd never met a man who didn't like her mother's special recipe, especially when she went heavy on the chocolate chip and brown sugar crumble topping.

She was just adding extra to Gabe's half of the cake when she heard a car pull into the drive and knew she was out of time. That would be him, bringing Kenny home and expecting his dinner.

Tossing her mushy rice a final grimace, she hurried to the front window. Sure enough, Kenny was climbing out of Gabe's truck. She'd been hoping practice would go well so that public interest in Gabe's taking the job would soon wane, but judging by the frown on Kenny's face, that wasn't the case. Slinging his bag over one shoulder, her son kept his head down as he made his way toward the house.

"What's wrong?" she asked as soon as he came in.

"Nothing." His glower indicated otherwise, but she didn't have time to question him. Gabe was waiting.

"You got Coach Holbrook's dinner ready?" he asked.

"I just need to pack it up." Hurrying into the kitchen, she settled everything into a grocery sack. Kenny had followed her and stood ready to take the food, but she skirted past him. "I've got it."

"Good," he grumbled and shuffled down the hall toward his room.

His door slammed as she stepped outside. The sudden bang took Hannah by surprise. Her step faltered, but she could feel Gabe's eyes on her so she continued around his truck. She was wearing a short denim skirt with a Bebe tank top and flip-flops—something casual and comfortable in the warm weather because she wasn't meeting with any clients until later. But she suddenly wished she'd put on something a little more attractive. Considering the sophisticated, model-perfect women he used to date, she probably looked like a country bumpkin.

He rolled down the window when she reached his side of the truck, and Lazarus leaned his head over the side of the bed, obviously interested in the food he smelled coming from her bag.

"Tonight's menu is lemon chicken and rice," she announced, handing the meal up to him. "But I'm afraid the rice didn't turn out too good."

"It'll be fine. Thanks." He set the sack on the seat next to him.

She gave Lazarus a scratch, then raised a hand to shade her face. Gabe's shirt was damp. It was easy to tell he'd been outdoors. But he didn't smell bad. The heat seemed to enhance the soaplike scent of his warm skin. Even the inside of his truck smelled clean and nice—like the pine trees surrounding his cabin. "How'd practice go today?"

"Okay, I guess."

She admired his strong jaw and straight nose, the long, black eyelashes that framed his light eyes. He'd been nominated as one of *People*'s most beautiful men a few years ago—and she could see why. For a moment, she felt dazzled to have his full attention.

But concern for Kenny quickly overtook her appreciation of Gabe's good looks. "Kenny's upset?"

"He had a bad day."

"In what way?"

"His aim was a little off."

"I'll talk to him about his attitude."

Gabe shrugged. "Don't be too hard on him. It's tough for a team to lose its coach. I'm sure he and the other boys will be fine once they've had a chance to adjust."

She glanced back at the house. "If you say so."

He rested his arm over the steering wheel. "I meant to bring your chair today, but I got started late. I'll drop it by tomorrow."

"Or the next day," she said. "There's no hurry."

"Okay. Thanks for dinner." He flashed her a smile, and she found herself imagining him as he used to be—possessing all the confidence and swagger of youth and more talent and success than he knew what to do with. What had happened to him was a tragedy, but it was an even greater tragedy that he now held himself so aloof from others.

Hannah stepped back so he could leave, thinking of Patti's words. *If he was going to adjust and move on, he would have done it by now....* Could that be true? She hoped not. Mike Hill had managed to get Gabe involved with the Spartans, hadn't he? Maybe she could do something to help him, too. She owed it to Gabe, after all.

"Gabe?"

He was backing toward the street, but he stopped at the end of the drive and poked his head out his open window. "Yeah?"

"Um, I just realized I need to take your picture for the school yearbook." She'd been planning to go to the field tomorrow, but now she was hoping to use the assignment to better advantage.

"When we were in school, the students always handled the yearbook," he said.

"I take the team photos," she explained. "Anyway, I'm busy in the morning, so I was hoping I could cook in the afternoon and bring dinner out to your place afterwards. I'll take your picture while I'm there."

"Don't you want a team photo?"

"Actually, I took one before Coach Hill died. As a tribute, I think they're going to leave that as is. But they want to include a picture of you, along with an introductory paragraph or two about your accomplishments."

"So you're finished with everyone else?"

"You're the last one." Her heart beat at least twenty times before he said anything else.

"You don't want to drive all the way out to the cabin if we can do it at—"

"Actually, I'd enjoy the scenery," she said, cutting him off.

"Can't you use an old picture? I haven't gotten around to getting my hair cut in a while."

"If you have one you'd rather use, you can give it to me when I come. But I'd like to get the football pictures turned in this week, if that's okay. The guy making the program needs them."

He hesitated for another few seconds. She could tell he was reluctant to let her return to his cabin and wasn't happy about the idea of having his picture taken. But she was betting he'd be too polite to refuse, and she was right.

"Okay," he said at last. "But if the drive becomes a problem for you, let me know. I can take a rain check on dinner and see if I can dig up a picture to send home with Kenny tomorrow after practice."

"The drive won't bother me. I'll bring my camera, just in case."

Hannah waved as he drove off, then headed toward the house. She wanted to contemplate how she could build on what Mike Hill had accomplished with Gabe. But she needed to deal with Kenny first.

Hoping for a good heart-to-heart, she hurried across the threshold—and nearly ran into him.

"I'm taking off for a little while, Mom," he said, circumventing her.

"Where are you going?"

He jogged down the front steps. "I don't know. Maybe to the swimming hole with Tuck."

"You're not wearing a swimsuit."

"I'm not going swimming."

Worry gnawed at Hannah's stomach. Kenny's whole demeanor had changed over the weekend. "Kenny—"

"Cut me some slack, okay, Mom? I just need to be alone for a while," he said and stalked off down the street.

"Kenny!" she called after him.

He turned.

"It's only a game, okay?"

He shook his head as if she'd never understand. "Yeah, right. Tell Dad that," he said and was gone.

KENNY'S BEST FRIEND Tuck sat slouching against a stump, dangling the keys to his mother's old Mustang, while Kenny skipped rock after rock across the small pond everyone called The Old Swimming Hole. Technically, the property was part of the Running Y Resort owned by Conner Armstrong, but all the high school kids came out here to swim. No one bothered to stop them—unless they were drinking. The police had broken up more than a few weekend parties at the hole. There was always the fear someone might fall in and drown.

"So what are you going to do?" Tuck asked.

Kenny shrugged. He didn't have any answers. He simply wanted to play football, but it wasn't that easy anymore.

"Maybe you should quit the team," Tuck said. "Go out again next year, when the whole coaching thing has been resolved."

Resolved. Tuck had to be the only teenager who talked like that. But then, Tuck was different. His IQ fell somewhere in the range of genius; the teachers at school called him gifted. "I've thought about it."

"And?"

"If I quit this year, they'll never let me start next year."

Tuck brushed his flyaway brown hair back from his Harry-Potter-like face. "So start your senior year."

"My junior year is most important. That's when all the colleges look at you."

"What about choosing a different sport? You could always be a track star like me."

A smile tugged at Kenny's lips despite his current dilemma. Tuck had narrow shoulders and little muscle. He wasn't much of an athlete. The track team only took him because he had a lot of heart and would never quit in the middle of a race, no matter how far behind he fell—and the faster, stronger boys played baseball during track season. "I'll be busy with baseball, remember?"

"So stick with baseball. You're a great catcher."

"Not great enough to get a scholarship. And if I don't get a scholarship, I'll never be able to go to Stanford with you. We have plans, remember? Who's going to room with you if I'm not there?"

"Maybe I won't end up getting in, either," Tuck said.

Tuck never took anything for granted. But Kenny knew Stanford would be lucky to get his friend. Tuck was going places. He could be the next Albert Einstein. "Tuck, your test scores are so high, they're sending you Stanford key chains and shit."

Tuck removed his glasses and cleaned them on his plain white T-shirt. It had taken some doing, but Kenny had finally convinced his buddy to stick with T-shirts and jeans and to forget the old man clothes his mother bought for him.

"Okay. Why not make your mark in something unrelated to sports?" Tuck asked.

This was certainly a new idea. "Like?"

Tuck blinked at him. "You could join the debate team."

"Except that I can't debate."

"I could teach you." Tuck settled his glasses back over the bridge of his nose. "I'll be captain of the team this year."

Kenny knew Tuck *would* put him on the team, and then try to cover for him when he couldn't argue anything. He wasn't interested in the political issues that excited Tuck, but he appreciated his friend's loyalty. He'd thought about trying to get Tuck on the football team somehow, just so he'd have better luck with the girls. But Tuck didn't understand the thrill of knocking other guys down. The whole track thing was, according to him, "simply an attempt to be well-rounded."

Kenny shook his head at the term "well-rounded," but Tuck's uniqueness was part of the reason Kenny liked him so much. Tuck had things to say that really mattered. And despite his small size, he had more guts than anyone Kenny had ever met. Kenny would never forget seeing Tuck stand up to his father when Mr. Mills was hitting his wife. The boys had been only twelve years old at the time. Tuck and his mom had gotten pummeled pretty good before Kenny could bring help, but he'd calmly wiped away the blood on his mouth, taped his broken glasses back together and explained that some people weren't emotionally mature enough to deal with their inadequacies in an effective way.

Fortunately, Mr. Mills was gone now. No one knew where. Tuck and his mother had had to sell their house in Kenny's neighborhood and move across town into a small duplex. But at least no one was beating on them anymore.

The keys to the Mustang they'd parked a few feet away jingled as Tuck shifted position. When Kenny glanced back, he found his friend frowning and staring at the ground.

"What is it?"

"I was just thinking…."

"About what?"

"About how this is the kind of decision that can define a person for life."

Tuck was always saying Yoda crap like that. Half the time, Kenny didn't know what he meant. But judging by Tuck's somber expression, he was putting a lot of brainpower toward

Kenny's problem and, if it would bring a solution, Kenny wanted to hear about it. "How?"

"Well, what kind of person do you want to be?"

"I want to be a professional football player."

Tuck's hazel eyes lifted to Kenny's. "I'm talking about character traits. Do you want to have honor?"

"Of course."

"Do you want to earn what you get with courage and determination?"

Kenny scowled. "Come on, Tuck. You know I do."

His friend draped one arm over a bony knee. "Then the answer's simple. Be true to yourself."

Kenny threw a twig at him. "Damn it, Tuck. Why don't you just tell me to use the force?"

Predictably, Tuck didn't duck fast enough. The twig caught in his hair, but he calmly pulled it out and tossed it aside. "That's what it comes down to," he said. "Either you sell out or you don't."

"There are consequences. The consequences are the problem. If I don't fall in line with Blaine, it could affect my whole career."

"Your whole *life*," Tuck agreed.

Kenny gaped at him. "Right. So why do you sound so excited?"

"Don't you get it? If you want to be the kind of man you just told me you want to be, you have to hold fast to your ideals even when it requires a sacrifice. This is an opportunity to prove yourself."

An *opportunity?* Had Tuck finally wigged out? "Prove myself to who?"

"To the only person that really counts—you. Think of that movie we saw in English class."

Kenny grasped at the first one that came to mind. *"All The President's Men?"*

"A Man for All Seasons."

"God, you're talking about Thomas More again." Tuck had been going on and on about More for the past two weeks.

"He chose to die rather than sacrifice his ideals."

"Which didn't make his wife and children very happy," Kenny pointed out.

"If he would've given in, I don't think anyone would've blamed him. But there wouldn't have been anything remarkable about it, either."

Kenny tossed another rock into the lake, creating a big splash because he hadn't bothered to throw it at a slant. "No one will be making a movie about this, Tuck. Especially when I get booted off the team."

Tuck's voice was soft when he responded. "If you get booted off for doing the right thing, it'll be something you can proud of whether they make a movie out of it or not."

HANNAH SAT at her desk, staring at the phone. She was supposed to be framing some portraits that had just come in, but the hot summer sun streaming through her office window was making her sluggish. And she couldn't quit thinking about Kenny…and Gabe. She wanted to follow Mike's lead and draw Gabe out of his cabin once in awhile. But how?

Tapping her fingernails on her blotter, she decided her best chance would be to get him dating and socializing again. Now all she needed was the right woman. Dundee wasn't exactly New York City or Los Angeles, but it had several single women. Who was available, attractive and fun enough to appeal to him?

An image of Ashleigh Evans immediately popped into Hannah's mind. Ashleigh was perfect. She possessed a body that rivaled Pamela Anderson's, so she had a good chance of enticing an ex-football player, who'd been out of circulation far too long, into having dinner with her once or twice. And she seemed to like everyone without getting too attached, so she was unlikely to get hurt. Besides, Ashleigh cut hair for a living, which gave Hannah a good excuse to bring her out to Gabe's cabin.

Smiling, she looked up the number and dialed.

Someone else answered, probably her roommate. "Is Ashleigh there?" Hannah asked.

"Just a minute."

Despite the hip-hop music playing in the background, Hannah could hear Ashleigh talking and laughing in the room before finally coming to the phone. "Hello?"

Hannah started doodling on a sticky pad. "Ashleigh?"

"Yes?"

"This is Hannah Price."

"Hi, Hannah. What's up?"

"I'm calling to see if you might be available to go to Gabe Holbrook's cabin with me tomorrow night."

There was a surprised silence, then, *"You're* going to Gabe Holbrook's cabin?"

Hannah ignored the unspoken "But he hardly talks to anyone, and *you're* the one who put him in that wheelchair." "He's hired me to make him a few meals now that he's busy coaching," she said, to keep things simple.

Ashleigh hesitated as she absorbed the news, then continued hopefully, "And he asked you to bring me along?"

Hannah definitely didn't want to mislead Ashleigh. She wasn't trying to get Gabe into a steamy physical relationship; she only wanted to generate enough interest to coax him back to a more normal life. "No, I just thought it would be nice. He needs a haircut."

"Oh, for a haircut. Now I get it. I mean, he's gorgeous, but he's never been particularly friendly to me. Usually, he has Rebecca cut his hair and barely even looks at me."

Hannah heard the deflation in her voice and struggled to steer Ashleigh somewhere in the middle of "no hope there" and "hot pursuit." "He doesn't look at anyone these days, Ash. But he needs friends. Distractions. Social engagements. And you're pretty connected to the social scene around here, right?"

"I guess. And I'd be willing to help him. But he doesn't give anyone anything to hang on to, you know? He's not…responsive."

"Maybe, for right now, we need to lower our expectations," she said. "He needs people who are fun and outgoing. We've all stood back, sort of shocked and uncomfortable with what happened to him. Especially me, since I caused the whole thing. But I think it's time to quit apologizing and feeling bad and *waiting* for him to recover. I think it's time to be proactive."

"I like that," Ashleigh said. "*Proactive.* Sounds modern and bold."

"Exactly. We're going to help him."

Ashleigh didn't even hesitate. "Okay. When will you pick me up?"

Hannah made a mental note to add the wine she'd bought to tomorrow's dinner. "Five-thirty. We'll see you then, okay?"

"Hannah?" Ashleigh said, catching her before she could hang up.

"What?"

"Do you think…"

"What?" Hannah prompted when her words fell off.

"Do you think Gabe can still make love?"

The thought that she wouldn't mind finding out firsthand flitted through Hannah's mind, but she quickly squashed it. It had been six years since she'd slept with Russ, with anyone. She was beginning to feel old already. But she had her boys to think about. The risks of getting involved with another man were too great. If she wound up pregnant or made another bad decision…

"I don't know," she said, but she could have added that one night, not long after the accident, she'd actually searched the Internet and learned that a male's ability to have an erection depended on the level of the spinal cord injury. She'd also learned that the nerves that controlled an erection are located in the sacral segments. According to the newspapers and talk around town, Gabe's spine wasn't completely severed, and his injury was low enough that it was possible he could make love the same way as other men. But there was also the chance he couldn't. "We're not shooting for that level of intimacy, Ashleigh."

"I was just wondering."

"Well, if it ever comes to that, he's got plenty of parts that do work, and work well. I'm sure he can figure out how to use them."

Ashleigh giggled. "I guess that's true, huh?"

Hannah pictured the beautiful blondes she'd seen on Gabe's arm in the past and wondered how he'd react to Ashleigh. "Don't forget your clippers, okay?"

Gabe's hair actually looked pretty good long. Hannah wouldn't have minded photographing him just the way he was. But leaving him as he was didn't mesh with her new plan. Maybe she couldn't help him walk again, or return to the NFL, but she was going to do her damnedest to see him live a happier life.

"This is going to be great," Ashleigh said. "I love a challenge."

Hannah felt the same excitement. She only hoped they'd be as optimistic tomorrow night. It wasn't going to be easy to break through Gabe's defenses.

CHAPTER SEVEN

THE DINNER HANNAH HAD COOKED for him looked delicious. Gabe heated it up early, around four o'clock, and sat down to watch the various tapes Owens had given him. He had several pieces of furniture in different stages of completion, but the hobby that had diverted him since the accident didn't appeal to him half as much as studying clips of the teams the Spartans would play this year. Maybe he'd taken on coaching a little grudgingly, but he was already beginning to feel exhilarated by the challenge. He loved the strategy and skill involved in football. And he wanted to win. Which made him particularly interested in the footage of Oakridge High's last season. The Wildcats had been Dundee High's rivals for as long as Gabe could remember, and the Spartans were going to have to play them first this year.

He lowered his gaze to the food on his plate and couldn't help smiling. He'd been disgruntled about coaching *and* letting Hannah cook for him, but he didn't regret either right now. Her food tasted better than anything he'd had in a long time—since he'd stopped visiting his parents.

Turning his attention back to the television, he saw senior Val Newcomber, quarterback for the Wildcats, fill the screen. Because Val had already played two years on varsity, Gabe knew there'd be plenty of tape on him.

For the next twenty minutes, he examined the way the Wildcats ran their offense, then checked the details he'd jotted down while speaking to Owens on the phone earlier. Owens had said—

and Gabe could see—that Newcomber had a strong arm. The boy was also capable of stunning accuracy. But he was more of a Dan Marino than a Steve Young. He couldn't scramble if the pocket began to collapse, and he didn't make the best decisions under pressure....

So the Spartans would blitz often and hard, Gabe decided. If they could penetrate the Wildcats' offensive line at least once every set of downs, maybe get a few sacks, they could rattle Newcomber, make him hear footsteps even when there weren't any coming. With so much pressure on their quarterback, the Wildcats would have to go to their running game, which would be easier to defend against because they didn't have much of a runningback.

Gabe rubbed the stubble on his chin as he watched another impressive pass. The only other way to compensate for Newcomber would be to cover the Wildcats' receivers and try to pick off a few passes. Interceptions could turn a game around quicker than anything. But—he used his remote to rewind the tape so he could take another look at a leaping catch by Wildcats' receiver Luke Friedman—their receivers had too much speed. The Spartans didn't have what it'd take to shut them down. Not from what Gabe had seen of his defensive backs. He was better off working with the weak side defensive end—

The telephone rang. Gabe gave it a quick, impatient glance. He didn't want to be disturbed right now. But he thought Mike might be trying to reach him, and consoled himself with the fact that they could strategize together.

Pausing the tape, he rolled over to the counter. "Hello?"

"Hi, son."

His father. Gabe dropped his head in one hand and pinched the bridge of his nose. He would have been more careful about snatching up the handset if he'd anticipated a call from Garth. Several months ago, Garth had promised to give Gabe time to adjust to the recent changes in their family. Other than a few messages relayed through his mother, he'd respected that promise. Until now.

"Sir."

His father hesitated, as if disappointed by Gabe's formality. But, a heartbeat later, he recovered and barreled into a conversation. "Your mother told me the good news."

"What good news?"

"That you're coaching the Spartans."

Since the accident, Gabe had heard a great deal of false cheer in his father's voice. After the pride that had always been there before, he hated it. But today Garth seemed genuinely pleased.

"It's only for one season," Gabe said.

His father didn't let that dampen his enthusiasm. "So what's the team like this year? You got any talent to work with?"

In the past, Gabe would have told Garth about Kenny Price's raw ability. He would've mentioned that they had a strong offensive line, not much in the way of defensive backs, a runningback that could be faster with some practice, and a few good receivers. But he and his father weren't close anymore. After what Gabe had learned nearly a year ago, he didn't even want to talk to Garth. "A little."

At his short, abrupt answer, an awkward silence ensued.

"Gabe, please," his father said at last. "Isn't there some way we can put the past behind us?"

"The past, Dad? The past is now part of the present and the future, isn't it? I take the chance of running into Lucky every time I drive into town. Through her, I have a new niece. She's also married to my best friend. How do I put that behind me?"

"Accept her and adjust!"

Unfortunately, that was easier said than done. "I prefer to mind my own business and stay away from the mess you've created."

"Come on, Gabe."

"It's my problem, Dad," he said. "Forget about it."

"I can't forget about it. You're still angry."

His father had that right. Gabe knew he'd probably be angry for the rest of his days—angry with Russ for sending Hannah into such a panic the night she crashed into him, angry at Hannah for passing that damn truck on a curve in a snowstorm, angry with his father for hiding his secret for so long then letting it out when Gabe needed him most. Gabe had gone from MVP of the NFL to a crippled man living in a cabin; his father had gone from someone who'd been admired and respected by the whole community to just another schmuck who'd cheated on his family.

"Can't you forgive me?" Garth asked.

"I forgive you," Gabe said immediately. He had no desire to hurt his father. But his trust was destroyed and he no longer had anything to give. He was struggling too hard to hang on to the hope that he'd walk again, when he'd seen so little progress over the past three years.

"Then, will you come to dinner on Sunday night?"

Gabe envisioned sitting at the table with Reenie shooting meaningful glances his way and pointing out all the things he could still do, even in a wheelchair. His mother, at the other extreme, waiting on him hand and foot as if he could no longer do anything. His father pretending that life was good now that the family was complete again. Hell, maybe Lucky would even show up.

The thought of facing that situation made despair inch closer—and Gabe immediately shied away. "Sorry, I'll be busy getting ready for our first game. It's in a little more than a week."

His father didn't respond for several seconds. "I miss you," he said at last.

Suddenly, Gabe's chest constricted and his eyes burned. He missed his dad, too, but he missed the Garth he used to know. He missed striding up to his sister and throwing her over his shoulder to swat her butt when she provoked him too much. He missed his mother calling to let him know when she needed something in the house repaired and his father was too busy to do it.

He missed the world as it used be. And he didn't know how

to find his way back to the happiness he'd once known. He wasn't even sure it was possible.

He glanced down at his legs. "I'm afraid some things are irreversible," he said and hung up. He refused to think any longer about his father, or Lucky, or the accident. He had things to do.

But as Gabe rolled back to the living room, he realized he'd lost his appetite and wasn't interested in watching tapes of high school football anymore.

Turning off the television, he headed outside to his shop, where he blasted his stereo and poured all his energy into sanding a cedar chest. By the time he quit, it was getting dark, and he was almost too exhausted to wheel himself into the cabin.

The telephone woke Gabe just as the sun was coming up. He squinted against the light streaming through the window above him and looked around to discover that he'd slept on the couch last night.

"Shit." He hated waking up this way. After he'd been released from the hospital, he'd seen little point in living, much less performing the daily conventions of living. He hadn't bothered to shave, change his clothes, clean his cabin, or do anything else, really, except lie in front of the television. Once in a while, he'd open a can so he could eat, but he hadn't even done that with any regularity.

Once he started losing weight, his family realized how badly off he was and Reenie came to stay with him for a few weeks. She goaded him and challenged him—even physically wrestled with him on occasion—to get him to bounce back. When he finally started to respond, he let her believe it was because she'd made his life unbearable. But that wasn't the truth. Life had already become unbearable. He let her help him because, for a while there, he'd needed her strength to prevent himself from sinking into the dark pit of depression.

Once he'd gotten a hold of himself, however, he'd gone in the opposite direction. Now he was almost militant about his daily hygiene, his fitness, the cleanliness of his house, his yard, his shop.

He frowned at his rumpled clothes. Until last night.

The phone rang again. Remembering the call from his father, he didn't make any effort to answer.

A few seconds later, the machine picked up. "Gabe, where are you? I need to talk to you."

Mike. It sounded serious.

"Give me a call when you get this—"

Gabe reached above his head for the cordless phone he kept on the side table. "What is it?" he said, but he wasn't sure he really wanted to know. Ever since he'd agreed to coach the Spartans—ever since he'd started associating with people again—his emotions seemed so much more extreme than before. He felt excitement, stimulation, hope. He also felt discouragement, embarrassment, fear and despair.

He wasn't sure the trade-off was worth it.

"I just got a call from Dale Lindley's mother," Mike said.

Dale was on the football team, but he wasn't a good player. Unless the Spartans were winning by a wide margin, Gabe knew Dale probably wouldn't play. Fortunately, the boy was happy just to wear the uniform, practice with the team, and help the coaches.

"What did she want?" he asked.

"Dale woke her up to tell her something he overheard in the locker room yesterday after practice."

"This early?" Gabe glanced at the clock above his television. It was barely six.

"He didn't sleep well."

"Evidently not. What's going on?"

"I guess Sly Reed was bragging to Tiger Shipley that he could predict the outcome of the game next Friday. He said the Spartans are going to lose."

Gabe let his eyes drift closed again. "So? Sly's a loudmouth." And he wasn't one of Gabe's favorite players. Sly needed to be in the limelight and often did stupid things to get there. Coach Owens had mentioned that he'd been suspended last year for drinking at a school dance.

"Evidently, there's a little more to it than that," Mike said.

At this, Gabe opened his eyes to stare at the ceiling. "What more could there be?"

"He was willing to put a hundred bucks on it."

"Sly's dad is the school janitor. He doesn't make a lot of money. Where would Sly get a hundred bucks?"

"Beats me."

"How did Tiger respond?"

"He got mad and stormed out."

Gabe covered his face with his arm. "Good for Tiger."

"I'm not finished yet. After Tiger left, the twins cornered Sly in the locker room and warned him to keep his mouth shut. Then Dale heard them say Blaine would take it out of Sly's hide if anyone found out."

At the mention of Blaine's name, Gabe shoved himself into a sitting position. "Blaine's involved?"

"Looks that way."

"You think he's trying to sabotage the team?"

"What else could it be?"

Gabe pictured Blaine, with his bladelike nose and cool gray eyes. Did he want Gabe's job badly enough to risk his reputation and his future at Dundee High? He'd built his career with the Spartans. Gabe couldn't imagine him doing anything so blatantly wrong. Maybe he let his temper get the best of him on occasion. But what Mike was suggesting took planning and forethought and collusion with others. If word ever got out, the boys who were involved would be kicked off the team for good.

And Blaine would be fired....

Gabe shook his head. "Blaine's feeling some resentment right now, but he wouldn't take it that far."

"Do you have another explanation?"

"Maybe it's nothing. Sly's always trying to stir the shit. You know how he is."

"I know he's related to Blaine. I know the twins are, too. If Blaine was going to split the loyalties of the team, he'd start there."

Gabe used his hand to move one foot and then the other to the ground. "High school boys don't give a damn about the politics involved in football on a coaching level. They just want to win."

"They care about positions and play time and lettering," Mike argued. "Who knows what Blaine might be promising them?"

Pulling his wheelchair closer to the couch, Gabe lifted himself into it so he could head to the bathroom. "Whatever this is, I'm not worried about it," he said.

"You're not?"

"No," Gabe lied. "And you're not my big brother, so quit trying to look after me, okay? You have enough to worry about over there at the ranch."

Gabe heard Mike sigh. "Whatever you say, Coach."

"I'll talk to you later, Mike." Gabe hoped he'd convinced his friend that he wasn't going to think twice about it. But the situation remained on his mind through his shower, his breakfast and the long drive to town. He knew Blaine would feel pretty vindicated if the Spartans went into a slump. And he couldn't help thinking how easy it'd be to throw a game—or two or three.

All it would take is the cooperation of a few key players.

AT EIGHT-FORTY-FIVE, Hannah poked her head into Kenny's room to find him still in bed. Yesterday, he'd spent the entire day with Tuck and hadn't come home until just minutes before his midnight curfew. She'd been waiting up for him, but she'd been exhausted and he'd been morose, so they'd gone straight to bed. She was hoping he'd feel better today, that maybe they'd finally have a chance to talk. "Kenny, your alarm went off over a half hour ago. You're going to be late for practice if you don't get up."

No answer.

She sat next to him and shook his shoulder. "Kenny?"

"I don't want to go to practice," he mumbled.

Hannah blinked in surprise. "Practices are mandatory. You know that."

"So?"

"You'll be benched. If you miss too many, you'll be kicked off the team."

He rolled over and buried his head beneath the covers. "I don't care anymore."

He didn't *care*? About *football*?

She pulled the blanket down to reveal his dark head. "You've never complained about practice before. What's going on?"

"Nothing." He scowled, his hair rumpled, his eyelids still heavy with sleep. He yanked at the covers, but she didn't let go.

"Coach Holbrook said you had a bad day yesterday, but he sounded as though he still has a lot of confidence in you."

No response.

She remembered their exchange after Gabe left, *It's only a game...Tell Dad that!* "Is this really about football? Or does it have something to do with your father?"

Kenny's scowl deepened. "Dad thinks I have ADHD."

"He thinks everyone has ADHD, including me."

"Does *he* have it? Is that why he's...the way he is?"

If Russ had ADHD, it wasn't the worst of his problems. But Hannah tried not to denigrate him in front of the boys. "I'm not familiar enough with ADHD to say," she said, smoothing the hair out of his eyes.

Kenny was generally a loving person, but he was going through those typical teenage years when displays of affection were considered embarrassing. Knowing the mood he was in, she thought he might become irritated with her for treating him like a little boy. But he didn't. He seemed to need the gentle caress.

"What's going on, honey?"

He didn't answer. He stared toward his window, where the sun glimmered between the slats of the blind. "What was Dad like in high school?"

Hannah remembered the days when she and Marissa had spent so much time getting ready for dances and talking about boys. Russ had been interested in her ever since the eighth grade, but she'd grown up next door to him and had never considered him boyfriend material. Like most girls her age, she'd idolized Gabe Holbrook and Mike Hill's younger brother, Josh, and even shy, creative Randy Nunez, who'd gone on to become an artist.

But when her mother fell ill, her whole world had changed. She'd gone through her senior year in a daze, stubbornly believing Fiona would survive. Russ's mother had provided Hannah with a warm kitchen and an occasional home-cooked meal. She sometimes sat with Fiona, so Hannah could take a break and go to a movie. She even volunteered to drive Fiona to Boise for chemotherapy.

Russ's mother had given Hannah a place to belong, but as the days passed, Hannah soon realized that belonging came at a price. Violet, Patti, the whole family knew how much Russ admired her. They kept pushing them together. Inviting her over and placing her next to Russ at the dinner table. Suggesting a movie, then tossing only one blanket over for her and Russ to share. Sending Russ to help her with the yard work or to spend the night so she wouldn't have to be alone with her mother in those last weeks. It wasn't long before Russ was attaching his own price to his friendship and support.

The helplessness Hannah had felt when she was young seemed to suck at her energy like quicksand. She wished she'd known then what she knew now, wished she would've been more assertive and taken a different path. After her mother died, she should've gone on to college or seen something of the world. But by the time she recovered from the loss, she was already married to Russ. Then she was part of a family again, was creating a family of her own, and divorce was unthinkable.

"He was strong and handsome, just like you," she said with a smile. "It took me a while to notice him because he'd lived next door all my life and, at some point, I'd quit really looking at him, but—"

"How old were you when you started dating?"

Hannah didn't remember dating Russ. They did things with his family but rarely ventured out alone. For one, Russ had never had the money. "I guess I was about seventeen."

"And when did you get married?"

"When I was eighteen."

"Jeez, that's only two years older than me!"

She'd been so young…. "That's true."

"How did you know you were in love?" he asked.

Where were these questions coming from? Hannah wondered. She studied her son curiously, trying to figure it out. When he turned red, she realized he was probably interested in a girl. "Why? Have you met someone you think is cute?"

His blush deepened, and she knew she'd been right. Kenny was starting to think about girls.

"What's her name?" she pressed.

"Tiffany Wheeler."

"The church chorister's daughter?"

He nodded. "I'm thinking of asking her to Homecoming."

"That'd be fun."

"Yeah. I like her, but…I can't imagine falling in love."

"That's good," she said. "I wouldn't advise it for several years to come. Give yourself time to get an education."

"Will *you* ever get married again?" he asked.

Hannah felt her eyebrows notch up. "Who would you have me marry?"

"That's a question, not an answer," he said.

He'd recognized her dodge. He was growing up so quickly. "Maybe." And maybe—no, definitely—not.

"So you think about it sometimes?"

"Not really." Not if she could help it. But there were times when she couldn't.

"It wouldn't be hard for you to meet someone," he said. "All my friends think you're hot."

She laughed. "I'm flattered, but they're a little young for me."

"I don't want you to be lonely, Mom."

Hannah was touched by his concern. "You have a kind, generous soul, Kenny. I'm proud of that. But you don't have to worry about me. I'm too busy to be lonely," she said, but she knew that, too, was a lie. Sometimes she watched Rebecca with Josh—the way they touched, stood close, looked at each other—and envied them. She was happier without Russ than she was with him, but she still wished she could've had a marriage like Josh and Rebecca's.

"Loneliness doesn't have anything to do with how busy you are," Kenny said.

When had her sixteen-year-old become such a sage? "Perhaps." She rose to her feet. "But we don't have time to talk about my love life right now. We can discuss this again later, when you're willing to tell me more about *yours.*"

"Not a fair trade," he said. "You don't have a love life."

"And you do?"

He grinned.

"All right, wise guy. Hurry and get ready or you'll be late for practice."

He caught her at the door. "Mom?"

When she turned back, she saw that his grin was gone. "What?"

"What if I said I wasn't going to practice?"

Was he testing her? Seeing if she meant what she always said about football? "I'd tell you it's early enough in the season that you can quit if you want to. Do you want to?"

"Dad would hate it if I did."

"It's not his choice."

"He'd still hate it."

Because he was living vicariously through Kenny instead of doing something with his own life. "He'd have to accept it. But I'm surprised you're even talking like this. You used to love football."

"I still do," he said.

"Then, what's wrong?"

For a moment, it looked as if he might have something to tell her. But then his expression changed, and he kicked off his blankets. "Nothing," he said gloomily. "I'll be ready in fifteen minutes."

AT PRACTICE, Kenny was careful to avoid Sly and the twins. He didn't want to be connected to them, didn't want to see them wearing secretive smiles that said, "You're one of us." Minding his own business seemed to work pretty well—until it was time to go and he made the mistake of hurrying out of the locker room. He was hoping to catch a glimpse of Tiffany before she left cheer practice but ran into Coach Blaine instead.

"You played better today, Price," he said.

Kenny glanced behind him. Coach Holbrook wasn't driving him home today but he could still come rolling toward them at any moment. Fortunately the sidewalk was empty, except for a couple of guys over by the drinking fountain. "I did okay."

"Better than okay."

Only because he'd managed to block out everything else and simply play the game. But one good practice didn't mean his problem was gone. It had only gotten worse, because he'd just moved closer to a starting position, where he could actually make an impact on the outcome of a game. "Thanks."

Blaine stepped toward him and lowered his voice. "Sly said you were acting a little funny at practice yesterday. Everything okay?"

"Sure, Coach. Everything's fine," he mumbled, but he continued to stare at the ground, wishing Matt would hurry so they could leave.

"I hear Tiffany Wheeler's got her eye on you."

Kenny looked up in surprise. "How—"

"Word gets around, and I generally hear it. I've worked at this high school a lot of years, Kenny. And I'm going to work here a lot more."

Kenny had no idea how to respond, so he said nothing.

His coach stuck his hands in his pockets and jingled his change. "If she likes you already, she'll really be impressed next year, when you're the star of the team, huh?"

Something about Blaine's smile told Kenny they were talking about more than Tiffany. Blaine was painting a picture of how it could be in the future...if Kenny didn't disappoint him.

"She won't be too impressed when we lose against Oakridge," he said. "Everyone's going to hate that."

Blaine opened his mouth to reply, but Boo Taylor came out of the locker room. The moment Blaine saw they had company, he started moving away as if they hadn't exchanged anything except a "See ya later."

When Boo got in his car and shut the door, Blaine turned back. "Have you ever played chess, Kenny?" he asked.

Kenny played chess with Tuck now and then. He generally lost, but he didn't really expect to win. The teachers at school couldn't win against Tuck. "A few times."

"Then you understand that occasionally you have to sacrifice a few pawns."

Blaine was trying to be clever using a line he'd probably picked up from some movie. Kenny wasn't impressed. But one word stood out: *sacrifice.* Blaine wanted him to sacrifice his integrity. Tuck wanted him to sacrifice his career.

Kenny didn't want to sacrifice anything. But, thanks to Coach Hill's heart attack, that was no longer an option.

"I understand," he mumbled and breathed a sigh of relief when Blaine finally walked away.

CHAPTER EIGHT

As THEY TURNED in to the drive that wound through the trees to Gabe's cabin, Hannah took one last look at Ashleigh and wondered if this idea was a mistake. She'd been hoping to set Gabe up with an attractive woman who could befriend him and draw him out. That was it. But Ashleigh looked as though she had bigger plans, and it was difficult not to feel a little jealous. Wearing a tight black miniskirt with a low-cut blouse that made the most of her impressive bustline, she was definitely registering a "ten" on the "hot pursuit" side of the scale.

Gabe wouldn't know what hit him, Hannah thought. But maybe that was okay. This wasn't about what Hannah wanted. It was about what would be best for him. At the very least, Ashleigh would remind him of the women he'd hung on his arm in the past. Maybe he'd even realize he could have those women flocking around him again, if he'd just let his life resume a more natural course.

"I think I'll ask him to dinner on Saturday," Ashleigh announced, checking her lipstick in the mirror above the sun visor.

Hannah tried to imagine how Gabe might respond to such an invitation. Personally, she thought it premature. "I don't know, Ashleigh...."

"You said you wanted me to get him out of the cabin, right?"

"Right," she said. "But..."

"What?"

"You might first try getting him to join you and a group of

people. You know, so it's not like a date. It'll seem more casual that way." *And somehow it would be easier on me....*

"What do you suggest?"

"I don't know. Tell him you and a few friends are going to dinner in Boise on Saturday night or something."

"But we're not," Ashleigh replied. "Mostly, my friends and I hang out at the Honky Tonk on weekends."

Hannah had bad memories of the Honky Tonk. Russ had spent far too much time there when they were married. She didn't want to see Gabe frequenting a bar. She'd driven him into seclusion; she didn't want to drive him to drink.

"Dinner or a movie would be better. You could always get a group together, right? Especially if Gabe's going. Everyone's curious about him. Just make sure the people you take don't come on too strong—" here, she hoped her hint penetrated but feared it did not "—and be careful not to overwhelm him."

"If you ask me, a party of *three* would be too many," Ashleigh muttered, but Hannah didn't have a chance to comment because Ashleigh immediately turned to her window.

"This is nice," she breathed as they finally drove into the clearing that revealed Gabe's large cabin with its quaint porch, detached garage and natural landscaping. "He must have a housekeeper *and* a gardener, huh?"

"As far as I know, he doesn't have either."

"He takes care of this place himself?"

"I think so."

"But why? It's got to be difficult in that wheelchair. And he's rich."

"He must prefer to do the work himself."

Ashleigh shot her a quick grin. "Further proof that he has plenty of working parts."

Hannah didn't want to talk about Gabe's sexual abilities again. This week she'd already spent too much time daydreaming about the man—and they were not her usual dreams of discovering some medical breakthrough that would fix what she'd broken. She'd imagined him kissing her and touching her until she moaned his name…. Then she'd imagined him satisfying her so completely that she didn't think real life could ever match it.

Her cheeks burned just thinking about the images she'd entertained, but she told herself to stop being silly. Everyone had fantasies—and hers had probably imbued Gabe with more sensitivity and responsiveness than he really possessed. Certainly they had imbued him with more than Russ had ever shown her.

Still, she knew she was going to have a difficult time looking Gabe in the eye today without feeling a little embarrassed.

She studied Ashleigh again. With such a tall, beautiful blonde around, he probably wouldn't spare Hannah a glance.

She tried to convince herself that this was a *good* thing as they parked behind his Ford F-150, which he'd left in the drive near the garage, and got out. Tonight, she'd packed his dinner in a basket, thinking it'd be easier to transport. Each day, he could bring her the basket with the dishes from the previous night, and she could refill it with his new dinner.

"How long has he lived here?" Ashleigh asked as Hannah slung her camera over her neck.

It wasn't difficult for Hannah to calculate. After the accident, she'd followed his progress day by day, hoping and praying for a full recovery. "He was in the hospital for thirteen days after the accident. Then he went into therapy at a clinic in Boise for two months. After that he lived with his folks until summer. So it's been about two and a half years."

"I could never live out here by myself," Ashleigh said. "I'd be bored stiff in two days. And I'd be terrified about the possibility of running into a bear."

Hannah suspected Gabe was more afraid of the things he confronted in town. The people who'd invariably bring up his lost career or press him for an autograph. The stares and curiosity he'd encounter as he tried to maneuver in his chair. His father and the scandal that had chased him even farther into seclusion. "I can see why he likes it," she said. "It's beautiful and it's quiet."

They reached the porch. Once again, Hannah could hear rock music playing inside the cabin, so even though Lazarus barked a couple of times, she assumed Gabe wasn't waiting for them at the door and allowed herself a brief moment to admire the chair that would soon be sitting in her studio.

"Isn't this the coolest chair you've ever seen?" she asked, putting her picnic basket on the porch and settling into it.

Ashleigh shrugged. "I guess. If you like the natural look."

Obviously, Ashleigh didn't have an eye for furniture. But she had an eye for men. Hopefully, she wouldn't—

Suddenly, the door swung open and Lazarus came charging outside, wagging his tail in excitement.

"Hello?" Gabe's voice was filled with surprise to see Ashleigh standing on his front mat.

Hannah scrambled to her feet and hurried over to her friend's side. "Hi Gabe. This is Ashleigh Evans."

"We've met." His eyes lifted to Ashleigh's generous display of cleavage, and Hannah began to wonder if Ashleigh had done the right thing in wearing that tight blouse, after all. She'd certainly gained his attention. Men were so predictable….

"You mentioned that you needed to get a haircut, so Ashleigh agreed to come with me and give you one." Hannah smiled brightly as Lazarus circled around her, obviously interested in the food she'd brought. "This is dinner, by the way. Beef Stroganoff."

Gabe's expression remained pleasant, but as he told Lazarus to sit, she sensed he was none too pleased. She supposed it was possible he hated beef Stroganoff—but guessed it had more to do with the license she'd taken in bringing Ashleigh to his house when he'd already been reluctant to let *her* come. "Thanks," he said. Another brief pause, then, "Would you like to come in?"

"Actually, we could do the cut right here on the porch," Ashleigh said. "It'd save the clippings from getting into your house. And the weather's so nice."

He hesitated. "Okay. But...don't you need me to wet my hair first?"

Brandishing her big bag, Ashleigh pulled out a spray bottle and a pair of clipping shears. "I've got everything I need right here. You have a beautiful dog, by the way."

"Thanks." He considered her shears and water, then shrugged and pushed himself outside.

Ashleigh raked her long nails through Gabe's hair. "Wow, you've got great hair."

Hannah's fingers itched to feel it, too, so she sunk them into Lazarus's fur and cleared her throat to help get her mind back on the right track. She was the one who'd set up this whole thing. Maybe Ashleigh had taken it a little farther than Hannah had anticipated, but it was silly to feel such envy. "Do you mind if I heat up your dinner so it'll be ready for you when we're finished?" she asked him.

"Go ahead," he said as Ashleigh pulled out a plastic cape, and Hannah left Lazarus to play in the yard while she carried the food inside.

She'd expected Gabe's house to contain more of the furniture she'd seen in the workshop, but there was an even bigger variety than she'd anticipated. The triangular accent tables in his living room drew her eye first. There were three, two side tables and a coffee table, and they were all made of a smooth, light-colored wood with a darker inlay. They were beautiful; she'd never seen anything quite like them.

Feeling the weight of the camera hanging around her neck, she longed to photograph the exquisite tables. But first she'd replace the more practical items he had on top of those tables—a remote control for his television, some *Sports Illustrated* magazines, a telephone and perpetual-motion clock—with a hand-blown glass vase and some exotic flowers.

She wondered if he'd ever thought about getting his furniture into decorator magazines.

Circling an unusual metal table that was as interesting as everything else, she moved into a kitchen that had blue marble countertops, white cupboards and a hardwood floor. Copper pots hung on hooks above an island, a wheat grinder was affixed to the counter, and a string of garlic hung from the ceiling along with baskets of fresh herbs and vegetables.

She liked it here, she realized. Maybe Gabe was closeting himself away, but he seemed to be handling the basics of life quite well. The only thing that made her uncomfortable was the absence of football plaques, trophies and pictures. Gabe had risen to heights most men only dreamed about. She should have found evidence of it here. But, so far, she'd seen only his exquisite collection of furniture and, on the walls, paintings of mountains, lakes and animals.

Why didn't Gabe hang up anything to remind him of his incredible achievements? Did the contrast of what he'd once been make the present too painful?

With a sigh, she set the food on the metal table so she could rub her temples. If only she hadn't tried to overtake…

"Hannah?"

Ashleigh's voice carried easily through the screen door.

"What?"

"I was just telling Gabe about the stuffed mushrooms you made. Any chance you could bring us a couple?"

"Sure. Let me heat them up. They'll be better that way."

Hannah put the Stroganoff on the stove to simmer, then used the microwave to warm the mushrooms. She was tempted to explore the rest of the house, but she knew he valued his privacy and she needed to respect that.

She did allow herself a quick peek into the room off the kitchen, though. It had a high ceiling and one whole wall of windows, and was completely filled with exercise equipment. Obviously, Gabe worked out often. She knew that from looking at him, but—

The microwave beeped. She ducked back into the kitchen, grabbed the mushrooms and three glasses of wine and carried everything outside on a tray she found hanging just inside a large pantry.

Ashleigh paused from her work long enough to let Gabe try a mushroom and have a sip of wine. Then Hannah took his glass and set it on the ground next to her chair, away from the hair falling from the clippers.

"It's incredible up here," she said.

Gabe's eyes darted her way, but he didn't say anything. She suspected he was still a little put out by his surprise visitor and impromptu haircut. But she didn't care. She had to push him. Someone had to push him.

"What do you think?" Ashleigh asked her several minutes later.

Hannah considered what Ashleigh had done to Gabe's hair, and felt the same fluttery feeling she'd experienced when she'd stared up at him in his truck yesterday. The back was very short, but Ashleigh had left the front long enough to fall across his brow. The style seemed careless enough to fit his bad-boy image. It also emphasized the slight cleft in his chin, the five-o'clock shadow that darkened his jaw, and the pretty blue of his eyes.

"It's...nice," Hannah said simply, although "nice" didn't begin to describe how good he looked.

Ashleigh dug a mirror out of her bag. "And you, sir? What do you think?"

He gave her a winning smile, but Hannah felt certain it was forced. They were dealing with the public, charming Gabe right now. He was on stage, doing his show. The real Gabe probably wanted to choke them for bothering him.

"I appreciate the house call," he said. "How much do I owe you?"

"Nothing." Ashleigh glanced at Hannah. "But I was hoping that maybe… Well, Hannah mentioned that you might like to go out with me on Saturday night. To dinner and a movie. Right, Hannah?"

Hannah had mentioned? Hannah had told her to ask him to join a *group!* But now that the subject of a date had been broached, she had no choice except to lend her support. "Right, uh…" She pasted a bright smile on her face. "Actually it's a group thing. Ashleigh and a few friends are going to Boise for dinner and want you to join them."

Gabe's pleasant expression never wavered, but Hannah felt a distinct undercurrent. He blamed her for getting him into this awkward situation, and he wasn't happy. "Really."

"Right. It's a group," Hannah added.

"I think you mentioned that."

"It'll be just a few friends, having fun." She waved toward Ashleigh, hoping to remind him of the appeal of those breasts he'd admired not too long ago. "All the girls look like she does. Well, not *exactly* like she does, of course, but young, beautiful—" she scrambled for other descriptors that might appeal to him "—blond."

"Blond?" he repeated with an arch of one eyebrow.

Hannah stifled a groan. *Blond?* Was she an idiot? She needed to calm down. "Mostly," she said, hoping to smooth over her blunder. "Right, Ash?"

Ashleigh looked as though she was about to say something else. Knowing it probably wouldn't be helpful, Hannah held her breath but, finally, Ashleigh nodded. "Uh…yeah, I guess."

"Are *you* going?" he asked pointedly.

Hannah's nails dug into her palms. "Me? No."

"Why not? I'm sure Ashleigh wouldn't mind if you joined us." He looked to Ashleigh for confirmation.

"Of course not," she said, but slowly enough to let Hannah know she wasn't particularly excited about the idea.

"That's sweet of you both," Hannah said, ignoring the delay in Ashleigh's response. "But I'm busy that night."

"Doing what?" he prompted.

"I have to work." She figured that was a pretty safe excuse because it was true. She always worked on the weekends—after the boys went to bed.

"Surely, you can miss one night. There'll be a *group* going," he said, throwing her words back at her. "And I might even be able to come up with someone blond, for you."

She made a face at his sarcasm. "Right. Well, I don't think blond hair appeals to me quite as much as it appeals to you, so maybe I'll take a rain check—"

"Are you kidding?" he interrupted. "It wouldn't be the same without you. I'll pick you up at six, and we'll meet Ashleigh and her friends at—" he turned to Ashleigh "—where?"

"Asiago's?" she said uncertainly.

"Perfect." He flashed them the toothy smile Hannah had seen splashed on so many magazine covers, but a muscle twitched in his cheek, confirming that he wasn't as pleased as he pretended.

She straightened her spine. Maybe Gabe wasn't happy to have her interfering in his life, but someone had to take him on, damn it. He'd been living like a hermit long enough.

She gave him a glacial smile. "Sounds great."

"Then we're equally excited." He removed a twenty from his wallet and handed it to Ashleigh. "Here, you did such a nice job, I insist on paying you a little something."

Ashleigh beamed at the compliment and took the money. "Thanks. It was easy. You have such nice hair," she gushed.

"Too bad his hair doesn't match his disposition," Hannah muttered.

Ashleigh's jaw dropped in surprise, but Gabe acted as if he didn't hear her. "Thanks for coming, ladies," he said. Then he whistled for Lazarus, rolled into the cabin and shut the door, leaving Hannah standing on the porch with no basket filled with dishes from the night before, and no yearbook picture.

GABE NARROWED HIS EYES as he watched Hannah's taillights disappear into the trees. What the hell had she been trying to do, bringing Ashleigh out here to run her fingers through his hair and rub her chest in his face? Obviously, Hannah Price had plans to get him involved with her little friend. But he wasn't interested in Ashleigh. And he sure as hell wasn't interested in having Hannah meddle in his love life. He'd dealt with enough interference over the past few years. If Reenie couldn't railroad him into dating again, nobody could. Evidently Hannah didn't understand that she was out of her league when it came to stubbornness.

Dropping the blind, he turned back to the kitchen and the beef Stroganoff she'd made for him, wondering why he'd handled Ashleigh's invitation the way he had. He could have told her no and sent them both on their way. Instead, he'd derived some kind of perverse pleasure in turning the tables on Hannah, who probably needed to get out more than he did.

He thought of the plain slacks and shirt she'd been wearing and nearly chuckled. With a little help in the clothing department and a new hairstyle, he believed she could come pretty darn close to stunning. But he doubted she'd ever go to the expense of a makeover. She probably skimped on herself to provide for her children—and somehow her sacrifice was ten times sexier to him than Ashleigh's low shirt and short skirt.

So where did that leave him?

With the vague memory of how sweetly she'd let him kiss her twenty years ago—and an ill-advised date for Saturday night.

But trying to avoid Hannah wasn't working. She wouldn't forget about the accident and move on. Maybe she *couldn't*. Her sense of justice seemed to dictate she pay a price for her mistake. So maybe, for his sake as well as hers, he needed to let her.

If he exacted a little retribution, allowed her to atone in some way, maybe she could finally put the whole thing behind her.

It was an interesting thought—seemed to make sense. But what could he have her do for him?

He piled his plate high, added the steamed vegetables she'd brought and a homemade roll and turned on his football tapes. But his mind remained on Hannah. She seemed to like cooking well enough. He supposed he could have her continue to make him dinner until she tired of it. Maybe he'd even have her clean his house, his truck, weed his garden, run his errands. Coaching was already causing him to slack off the rigid schedule he'd designed for himself....

He supposed life could be worse than having someone look after his every need. Especially because he'd be doing her a favor....

He grinned. A favor—to take on so much extra work. Poor Hannah. Some people just couldn't do things the easy way.

"SO...WHAT DO YOU THINK?" Ashleigh twisted in her seat to face Hannah as they drove the windy road that led down the mountain and back to town. "That seemed to go okay, didn't it? I mean, at least he agreed to go out with us on Saturday."

The sun was sinking behind the trees, casting long shadows across the pavement. Hannah flipped on her headlights in preparation for the darkness that would soon follow and pictured the challenge in Gabe's eyes when he'd pressed her to join them on Saturday. Although well-meaning, Ashleigh had botched everything. Hannah just didn't want to say so. He'd agreed to go, but something behind his acceptance made Hannah nervous. Surely when he'd mentioned setting her up, he'd been joking....

"It went great. Thanks for coming with me," she said. Then she glanced at Ashleigh's chest and wanted to groan. She was going to look like a donkey amid racehorses. She'd probably be ten years older than anyone else in the group and the only woman with no medical enhancements. She worked hard and sometimes she didn't pause to eat, so she was a little too thin. She didn't even have tips on her nails. They got in her way when she tried to frame her photographs and, in the months that Russ didn't pay his child support, she couldn't afford the maintenance.

Had she done enough to keep herself up?

She imagined herself naked and wondered what a man, someone besides Russ, might think of her. She exercised every day, but she had a stretch mark low on her stomach from her last pregnancy, and her tan came from working in her small garden. As a single mother, she had different priorities than Ashleigh and her single friends. Hannah wasn't concerned with buying lingerie and bringing a man home on a Saturday night. She was happy with a terry-cloth robe, a good book and hearing Kenny come in before his curfew.

She feared that made her frumpy, boring…

"What's wrong?" Ashleigh asked, her forehead rumpling.

Hannah realized she was going too slow and sped up. "Nothing, why?"

"You had a funny expression on your face."

"Oh…I was just thinking."

"About what?"

Hannah considered telling Ashleigh the truth. She could've used a second opinion. But she didn't want Ashleigh to think she had designs on Gabe. And anyway, voicing her insecurities would probably be a waste of breath, since Ashleigh would be too nice to be honest with her. "Nothing."

"What are you going to wear on Saturday night?"

Hannah frowned. That was another problem. The past few years, she hadn't spent much money on her own wardrobe. The boys and her business had needed too many things. "I'm not sure. How dressy is Asiago's?"

"You've never been?"

Hannah shook her head.

"It's nice. You'll want to go sort of…classy and chic."

"We live in Dundee, remember?"

"You don't have anything dressy?"

"I have current casual and dated casual. Unless you want me to wear my old prom dress."

Ashleigh laughed. "At least it says something that you can still fit into your old prom dress."

"Stress has a way of taking its toll."

Ashleigh eyed Hannah carefully. "You know, you're about the same size as my little sister. I bet she'd have something you could borrow."

"Tell me she's over twelve."

"She's twenty-four, and until a few weeks ago, she was living in California."

"And that's significant, why?"

"The people in California have taste, style."

"That depends. From what I've heard, Bakersfield isn't much of a fashion center," she said, navigating another tight turn.

"She's been living in L.A., silly. And she's got some beautiful clothes. Why don't you leave what you're going to wear Saturday night up to me?"

Hannah glanced skeptically at Ashleigh's miniskirt and tight-fitting blouse. Considering the fact that Ashleigh hadn't wanted anyone else around when she went out with Gabe, she was being a pretty good sport about the whole thing. "You'll be conservative, though, right? I mean, I don't have the boobs for a shirt like that." *Or the guts.*

Ashleigh made a noise of irritation. "Would you quit worrying? You're going to look great. Trust me."

CHAPTER NINE

TRUST ME...

Ashleigh's words rang through Hannah's mind as she stared in the mirror at six o'clock Saturday evening. Ashleigh had been running late, so she'd finally sent her brother to deliver the outfit Hannah was supposed to wear. But, if Hannah hadn't known better, she might've believed there'd been some sort of mix-up. She'd asked for something conservative—and gotten *this?*

She couldn't wear these clothes in public. The coral-colored blouse was definitely pretty, but it was almost sheer, revealing a lace-covered push-up bra of the same color that went underneath. And the narrow black skirt, which hit her at midcalf, had a slit that went all the way up to her thigh. A matching necklace, bracelet and earrings completed the ensemble.

Taken as a whole, she looked stylish, daring and impulsive. The thought of going out on the town like this made her blood race with an excitement she hadn't felt in years. But she didn't recognize herself and she wasn't sure she could trust the stranger in the mirror to remember that she was a mother of two, a woman with Responsibilities.

The doorbell rang. Kenny was with Tuck, and Brent was spending the night with Patti and his cousins. Hannah was the only one around. But she needed to change before she let Gabe in.

"Just a minute," she called and began digging through her closet. She had plenty of shorts and denim skirts and khaki capris, but nothing as elegant as what she was wearing.

The bell rang again.

"Not very patient, are you," she muttered, and pulled out a plain white blouse, some black slacks and a pair of sandals. This was the best she could do, she decided. Maybe she'd be mistaken for one of the waitresses, but—

"Hannah? Are you hoping I'll give up and go away?" Gabe had opened the door.

She froze with her blouse halfway unbuttoned and one spiky heel tossed aside. "No, of course not. I'm looking forward to tonight," she called down the hall.

"I'm hungry. Are you almost ready?"

She fingered the soft fabric of her blouse. She would never let her boys see her wearing such a thing. But they weren't here. Maybe it wouldn't hurt to climb out on a limb for one night. Ashleigh and her friends would probably be dressed much more provocatively....

In any case, Gabe was in her living room, anxious to leave. It was too late to change.

Buttoning her blouse, she slipped on her shoes and headed down the hallway. Better to stop quibbling over clothes and get the evening over with, she decided. Hopefully, Gabe would connect with Ashleigh or one of Ashleigh's friends and be whisked into the social scene for good.

GABE WASN'T SURE WHAT he'd been expecting, but he knew it wasn't what he saw. When Hannah emerged from the back of the house dressed in a sheer blouse that revealed a lacy bra, he couldn't look away. She wasn't as big-busted as Ashleigh, but there was something stimulating about the way the soft fabric revealed more than it concealed. He could see the slight, feminine indentations below her collarbone, the muscle tone in her upper arms, the small swell of her breasts above her bra—and felt a sudden jolt of testosterone.

This was the second time Hannah had affected him on such

a basic level, he realized. Ashleigh had thrust her breasts right in his face when she'd cut his hair the other night. He'd noticed, even taken a moment to admire what he'd seen, but the sight hadn't hit him nearly as hard as Hannah standing there in that sexy blouse.

Maybe it was her manner that appealed to him. She didn't act as blatantly sexual or as experienced as Ashleigh. Despite what she was wearing, she appeared soft and reserved, almost inno-cent—peaches and cream instead of sugar and spice.

"Hello." Her voice was open and friendly, but she immedi-ately folded her arms across her chest as if she wanted to shield herself from his view.

He let his gaze sweep over her anyway. "You look nice."

He could tell by the tone of her response that she thought he was only being polite. "Thanks. So do you. Royal blue brings out the color of your eyes." She cleared her throat. "I mean, I'm sure Ashleigh will like it."

Ashleigh? Evidently, she was still trying to play Cupid. But he had something to teach her about meddling…. "What do *you* think?" he asked.

She hesitated only briefly. "I like it," she said, but her words didn't reveal how much. He found it interesting that she'd obvi-ously excluded herself from whatever group of women she'd se-lected to catch his eye.

"Are you going to cover up like that all night?" he asked.

"Like what?"

He indicated the arms that guarded her chest.

"No…"

"Then, put your arms down."

She pulled her bottom lip between her teeth and blinked sev-eral times.

"Well?" he prompted. "If you can't wear that in front of me, how do you expect to wear it in front of the friend I've invited to meet us tonight?"

"You invited someone?"

He grinned. "Don't worry. He's young and good-looking. And this is a group activity, remember? That should bring you some comfort."

Her face fell. "You're not joking."

"Of course not. What's sauce for the goose is sauce for the gander. I'm sure you've heard the saying."

He could tell she didn't know quite what to think about this turn of events, and immediately decided he'd been right to accept her invitation for tonight. This was going to be fun. "I met him at a photo shoot I did for *Sports Illustrated* a few years ago. He lives in Boise. When I called, he said he'd love to hook up with us."

"Great," she grumbled.

"Come on, show a little more enthusiasm. He's blond, after all." He waved to her defensive posture. "So, if you don't mind…."

She didn't move. "What does the color of his hair have to do with anything?"

"You're the one who's fixated on hair color. You tell me." He winked at her.

"Fine," she said. "I *do* prefer blondes," and studied his dark hair with a glint in her eyes before slowly lowering her arms.

Since she was willing to meet his challenge, Gabe took several seconds to absorb the details of what he'd already glimpsed. He could tell she was self-conscious, but keeping her off-balance was part of the fun. He loved the blush creeping up her neck, the way her tongue darted out to nervously wet her lips.

"Where're the boys?" he asked, finally meeting her gaze.

She cleared her throat and started to cross her arms again—then seemed to catch herself. "Brent's with his father's family, and Kenny's running around with Tuck."

They were alone. For some reason, Gabe remembered all the times he'd gone to pick up a woman for dinner or some other event, and ended up in bed with her before they ever left the house. The NFL had been a real eye-opener for a country boy like him, who'd been a virgin until halfway through college. His father had always been ferociously protective of women, had drilled it into him that a real man never broke a woman's heart.

Gabe could still remember being grounded for two whole weeks because he'd been rude to a girl who'd called him. It hadn't mattered that she'd called him every day for weeks and he was tired of her unwanted overtures. Whether the concept was old-fashioned or not, his father demanded he be a gentleman, and Gabe had taken that to heart. Because he'd never fallen in love deeply enough to make any promises, he'd mostly kept his hands to himself.

But then he'd entered the NFL and his first brush with fame and too much money had tumbled him like wet cement in a mixer. The women seemed to come from everywhere. They were aggressive beyond anything he'd ever experienced and frankly admitted that they didn't care if he offered them anything more than a one-night stand—they just wanted him between their legs. They'd tuck notes in his pocket, send him nude pictures, whisper lewd promises in his ear, follow him back to wherever he was staying, appear at all hours of the night with an offering of wine, or even drugs. He ended up sleeping with so many women during those first few years, he wasn't sure he could count them all. There'd seemed no point in saying no. They didn't care if he was sensitive, generous or kind. They cared only for peeling off his clothes so they could brag about it later.

But it didn't take long for the influence of his upbringing to finally reassert itself. Gabe began to long for a deeper, more stable relationship. Eventually he hoped to find a wife and settle down. But he never met the right woman. He suspected he'd gone from one extreme to the other and become *too* adept at avoiding the hands that were always clutching at him. In any case, he'd accumulated enough experience through those early years in the

NFL to know what it felt like to forego a date and head straight to bed.

I prefer blondes. He was tempted to throw that taunt right back in Hannah's face, show her that the color of his hair had nothing to do with what he could or couldn't do for her. He suspected it had been a long time since she'd entertained a man in her bed and wondered if she missed it.

But he hadn't made love to anyone since the accident and knew it would never be the same.

Thinking about the changes helped him rein in his libido—that and the fact that this was Hannah, the woman who'd *caused* the accident. Getting involved with her would be far too complicated, especially now that he was Kenny's coach.

Forcing his mind to the mundane and practical, he shook off the first real excitement he'd known in almost three years. He had no business thinking about sex until he was back on his feet. He had enough challenges ahead without bringing a woman into his life.

"I'm returning your dishes from the past couple nights," he said.

She crossed to the basket he'd put inside the door. "Thanks. I'll take them into the kitchen and grab my house keys so we can go."

When she didn't come back right away, he wondered where she'd gone. Then she appeared in a plain white shirt instead of that semisheer blouse and the mystery was solved.

"Lost your nerve?" he teased.

She knew immediately what he was talking about. "I decided it might get too chilly."

He laughed softly. "I think you're afraid it'll get too hot."

"I don't know what you're talking about."

"Yes, you do. You're nervous about my friend."

"No, I'm not."

"You expect me to take the risk of opening myself up to new relationships, but you're not willing to do the same."

"This isn't what you seem to think," she argued. "It's just a night out with friends."

"Right." He rolled his eyes. "It's venturing into the singles scene, and if I'm going, you're coming with me."

Her forehead gathered into a V. "Why?"

"Why not? Don't you want to date, have fun...maybe even make love again?"

She turned a deeper shade of red than before. "I have kids."

The way she said it told Gabe more than she probably wanted him to know. It *had* been a long time since she'd felt a man's hands on her body—and, yes, she missed it.

He fought off a fresh wave of desire. "Some people don't think having kids and an active social life are mutually exclusive."

"In Dundee they are. There's no way to have a relationship without word spreading all over town. I'm beginning to think the bigger gossips actually troll the neighborhoods at night, hoping to find someone's car in the wrong drive."

"The gossips are still that hungry after all I've offered them over the years?"

She propped a hand on her hip. "You haven't been doing your part lately."

He chuckled. "Okay, I'll give you that. But you have to meet men somehow. Don't you plan to remarry someday?"

"No."

She didn't qualify her response, which surprised him. He rolled back several feet. "It was that bad with Russ?"

"It was that bad."

He felt a flicker of sympathy for her, but he knew he couldn't give in to it. He had to push her the same way she was pushing him or she'd spend the next six years like the last. Maybe, because she didn't live in a remote cabin, no one else noticed, but she was isolating herself almost as much as he was. "Not every guy is like Russ."

She didn't respond, so he went for his ace in the hole. "And the way I figure it, you owe it to me to do pretty much whatever I ask."

She folded her arms—which wasn't too lamentable in that white shirt—and leaned against the wall. "I *owe* you?"

He struggled against a smile and indicated his wheelchair. "Look what you've done to me. It's tragic."

She pursed her lips together. "Somehow it's more tragic when you're not trying to capitalize on it."

He couldn't help laughing. "Can you really begrudge me a little fun?"

"Fun? At my expense? You told me I should forget you and move on with my life. You told me to forgive myself. What happened to that?"

"You didn't do it," he said with a shrug. "You decided to stick your nose in my business instead. Now I'm doing you the same favor."

She stared at her feet for a few seconds before looking up at him again. "So this...revenge of yours. It's essentially a blind date?"

"More or less," he said brightly. "Now go put that blouse back on so we can leave."

She shoved off the wall. "You don't think your friend will like me in this?"

He let his lips curve into a slow, crooked grin. He suspected she was still wearing the bra he'd seen earlier and he enjoyed the contrast of daring and sexy hidden beneath the almost-puritanical white shirt she had on now. He liked thinking he'd be the only one who knew the color and texture of that skimpy bra. But he was pretty sure Hannah needed some sexual experience beyond Russ, and as much as he wanted to do the honors, he knew he wasn't the right man for the job. "I think it's safe to assume he'd prefer Option A."

RACE, THE MAN Gabe had set Hannah up with, was nothing short of gorgeous. He had blond hair, of course, just as Gabe had promised, a tall, muscular body, a perfect tan, and large white teeth he often revealed in a gleaming smile. When Gabe first introduced his friend, he announced that Race had been part of a male revue in Vegas. That information certainly didn't impress Hannah, but she would have been okay with it if subsequent conversation hadn't revealed the guy to be immature and egotistical.

He was the male version of the stereotypical blond bimbo, she decided as she watched him talk, and knew by the devilish smile Gabe cast her every once in a while that, not only did he agree, he'd invited Race for that very reason. He was playing with her—and seemed to be enjoying it.

While watching her, he entertained Ashleigh and her two girl-friends, Michelle and Jessica, so well they worshipped him with their eyes and hung on his every word—while she struggled to keep from yawning as Race regaled her with his latest modeling exploits. He'd just received a call from someone at Calvin Klein, he said, and was ninety-nine percent sure he'd be their next underwear model.

She was a thirty-seven-year-old mother of two, and he was a twenty-four-year-old model with his sights set on New York and Paris. They were worlds apart, but she was determined to prove to Gabe that she could have as much fun tonight as he was. She told Race he was perfect for billboards across America and Europe, and of course the job would be offered to him because…gosh, he was so darn handsome. Then she told everyone she wanted to wash her hands and excused herself from the table so she could manage a brief respite in the bathroom.

At least she no longer felt self-conscious about her blouse, she thought as she crossed the small, trendy restaurant. Race didn't even seem to be aware of what she was wearing. Of course, Ashleigh had squeezed into a tiny black dress cut so low she nearly spilled out of it, so Hannah looked tame by comparison. It did seem a little odd, however, that the only person who really seemed to notice her, at least at their table, was Gabe. His eyes lit on her every few minutes and drank in what her blouse revealed, causing a sudden rush of heat to pool low in her belly.

Then he'd give her a mysterious smile, and she'd respond by throwing herself into her role as the ideal date for Race with renewed enthusiasm.

If he was trying to teach her a lesson, it was working. Setting him up with Ashleigh had been a bad idea. Wearing this outfit had been a bad idea. Spending the past two hours driving to Boise with him, talking comfortably about their days at Dundee High, the football team, her hopes for Kenny and Brent, and her photography business was a bad idea. Now all she wanted to do was ignore everyone else and draw him away.

"Isn't this a blast?" Ashleigh said.

Turning in surprise, Hannah swallowed a sigh of disappointment to see that her friend had followed her into the bathroom. So much for finding solitude.

"Yeah, a blast," she said.

If her tone fell a little flat, Ashleigh didn't seem to notice. She was too busy gushing about Gabe. "I didn't know he could be so friendly. He's always been sort of…remote in the past, you know? But he's actually very funny and nice and…well, I already knew he was one of the handsomest men alive."

When she spotted the mirror, Ashleigh immediately pulled out a small cosmetics pouch and began dusting her cleavage with powdery glitter. "And he brought that gorgeous friend for you," she added. "Wasn't that sweet of him?"

Hannah started washing her hands. "You honestly think Gabe believes Race and I are a good match?"

"Of course." Ashleigh blinked innocently back at her in the mirror. "Why else would he bring him along?"

To throw me out of my element, she thought. But she didn't say that. "I don't know," she mumbled.

Predictably, Ashleigh didn't press her. She was in too much of a hurry to get back to Gabe. "The food will be ready soon, so don't take long," she said and rushed out of the room.

Hannah slumped against the wall. The rest room smelled too

strongly of deodorizer and was small enough to make her slightly claustrophobic, but a little discomfort was worth a few seconds alone. She wasn't sure how much more of Race she could endure. Or was it the way Ashleigh and her friends fawned over Gabe that bothered her? She suspected, even if they didn't, that he wasn't particularly interested in them. But that didn't mean he wouldn't end up taking one of them home with him for the night….

She felt depression set in at that thought, then stood up straight. *Wait a second!* That was what she *wanted* to have happen, remember? She was doing this for Gabe, to interest him in life again, to get him acting like himself, to see him dating and enjoying the company of others. So what if he took a girl home? So what if he forced her to put up with a man like Race for a few hours as penance for pressing him a little? She'd gotten him out of his cabin, hadn't she? She could be the victor here, if only she didn't lose heart and let him beat her at her own game.

Taking a deep breath, she marched out of the rest room—and nearly collided with a waitress delivering food to a nearby table. She jerked back to keep from knocking the poor woman's tray to the ground, but her narrow heels slipped on the marble floor, and she gave a startled cry as she started to fall. She expected to hit the floor and embarrass herself in front of everyone, and would have if not for a strong pair of hands. Somehow Gabe was there at the right moment to pull her into his lap before the worst could happen.

The waitress shot her a condemning look, righted her tray and scooted past them, leaving Hannah clinging, for a moment, to the man who'd caught her.

"You're okay," Gabe murmured.

"Where'd you come from?" she asked.

"Race went to the bathroom right after you did. I was coming to tell you both that our food has arrived."

They'd all had a glass of wine while waiting for dinner. She could smell a hint of it on Gabe's breath. "You smell good," she said, out of nowhere, then cursed herself for not guarding her tongue.

His eyes lowered to her lips, then dipped to the blouse he seemed to like so well, and she realized that she hadn't come face to face with him like this since they were in high school. The kiss they'd shared twenty years ago flashed through her mind, raising her heart rate and tempting her to lean closer. It had been so long since she'd really kissed a man. She wanted one more taste of Gabe, one more good kiss to erase all the ones in between.

If they'd been alone, she might have gone for it. Where he was concerned, she didn't have much to lose. And he owed her *something* after setting her up with Race. The little pep talk she'd given herself in the bathroom had left her feeling feisty again. But they were surrounded by people who'd turned to stare when she nearly fell.

"Thanks for catching me," she said and quickly climbed out of his lap.

"Too bad Race wasn't around to do the honors," he drawled.

She knew he was teasing her, but she refused to acknowledge it. She was too embarrassed by the scene she'd created. Taking her seat as demurely as possible, she proceeded to push the pasta primavera she'd ordered around her plate while folks began to recognize Gabe. A man and two women approached him, asking for his autograph. Then his circle of admirers quickly grew.

Race returned from the bathroom a few minutes later and continued talking about himself while eating his steak and shrimp. He seemed oblivious to the fact that Gabe wasn't at the table. But Ashleigh, Michelle and Jessica obviously missed the man they'd been drooling over all evening. They seemed to like Race well enough, but it was Gabe they wanted to be with.

They kept grumbling about the people who detained Gabe, but it was Hannah who finally got up to intervene. She could tell by the tension in Gabe's shoulders that he wasn't enjoying himself. The strangers were imposing on him, and they didn't care that they were being rude. No wonder he insisted on keeping such a low profile.

"Excuse me, but I'm afraid Gabe's food is getting cold. Would you mind giving him a chance to eat?" She spoke with a sweet, warm smile, but looked at each one pointedly.

"Oh, no, of course not…. Please, go ahead and eat," they muttered.

Gabe took hold of his wheels. "I wouldn't want to be accused of neglecting my friends. Have a nice evening," he said and wheeled back to their table.

When she caught the expression on his face, Hannah feared she might have been too assertive. But she wasn't about to let a bunch of insensitive people ruin his first night out. If that happened, maybe he wouldn't accept another invitation.

"You don't have to be so nice," she whispered to him as she passed by on her way to her own seat. "You've got a right to eat, too."

Ashleigh, Jessica and Michelle had watched the whole thing with their mouths hanging open. "Wow, Hannah," Ashleigh said, recovering first. "Way to go."

Hannah was fairly certain Gabe wasn't impressed. He insisted on taking care of himself, didn't like being helped. So why had she let her protectiveness motivate her to interfere where she probably wasn't wanted? If she hadn't already been in the habit of looking out for her boys, she probably wouldn't have done anything.

Gabe might not have approved, but he didn't seem too angry. In fact, when she caught his eye, he laughed and shook his head. "Did you have to do that?"

With a meaningful glance at Race, she smiled brightly. "One good turn deserves another."

"We'll see," he said softly.

Hannah had no way of guessing his intentions, but the promise in his voice definitely had her worried.

CHAPTER TEN

"I'VE DECIDED what you can do to make it up to me."

They were on their way home from Asiago's, and Hannah was feeling full from the meal and relaxed from the wine. When Gabe spoke, she turned away from watching the highway rush under their tires. "Make what up to you?"

Oncoming headlights momentarily lit his face, making his eyes shine like pieces of cobalt. "The accident."

Where was he going with this? "There *isn't* any way to make it up to you," she said. "Therein lies the problem."

"Doesn't mean you shouldn't try."

As angry and bitter as she suspected Gabe was, he'd gone from ignoring her and trying to shut her out of his life to setting her up with a male model. Why hadn't he rejected her and Ashleigh's invitation? "You like toying with me, don't you?"

"Of course. Your crushing guilt makes you easy to bait."

"Not *that* easy," she said. She didn't bother denying the crushing guilt part. Sometimes she felt so bad about what she'd done she wanted to wake up in someone else's skin. "Anyway, you've piqued my curiosity. How can I make it up to you?"

He turned down the radio, which was playing Shania Twain's "She's Not Just a Pretty Face." "I need my windows cleaned," he said. "Since I started coaching, I can't get around to it."

She blinked at him. "You want me to wash your windows?"

"Only if it'd make you feel better."

She could tell he was fighting a smile. "What if it wouldn't?" she asked bluntly.

He let go of an exaggerated sigh. "I guess I'll just have to keep struggling along on my own."

She laughed out loud at his martyr act. "You don't seem to struggle too much," she said. "Except maybe when it comes to interpersonal relationships. Closeting yourself away for months on end isn't exactly healthy behavior."

"I'm great at relationships," he countered. "Look at how good we're getting along."

When he ignored her reference to his seclusion, she figured he didn't want to talk about the past three years.

She wondered if he'd ever open up and share his pain with her or anyone else. He wasn't an easy man to get to know; he had too many layers. She seemed to have peeled away the top one—the social persona he showed the outside world—but there were depths to him she knew she'd probably never see.

Patti's comments came to mind, and Hannah briefly wondered what it'd take to reach the very heart of him. She wanted to get to know the real Gabe. But she figured she should be grateful for the progress she'd made and, taking her cue from him, kept the conversation light.

"Revenge is hardly a good basis for friendship," she observed, raking her fingers through her hair.

"Most women would consider being set up with a guy like Race a real treat."

"Sorry, but I have trouble devoting much time to a conversation about whether or not someone is losing their tan."

He shot her another glance. "Boy, are you picky. Now you're looking for someone who's young, blond, handsome *and* a good conversationalist?"

"I'm not looking for anyone!" she said.

"Race isn't my only friend, you know."

"Stop right there." She raised her hands. "No more blind

dates. I already told you, I don't want to remarry, so there's no reason for me to go out with your friends."

"What about sex?"

She refused to look at him. "What about it?"

"You're willing to give up that kind of intimacy for the rest of your life?"

She almost said that his lifestyle suggested he was giving up that kind of intimacy, too. But this time she managed to curb her tongue. Although his amazement indicated otherwise, she wasn't positive he *could* make love. "This night, this crazy conversation—it's my fault, isn't it? I couldn't walk away three years ago, couldn't say, 'Sorry Gabe, better luck next time.'"

The teasing glint in his eyes disappeared. "You couldn't walk away three *days* ago," he said, "but—" his full lips curved into a crooked grin "—I like that about you."

She felt unexpected warmth coming from him and knew she'd just peeled back another layer of his personality. That she was somehow getting closer to him made her feel…breathless. It had to be his smile, she decided. He'd never smiled at her like that before.

"Considering what happened three years ago, it's amazing you can like anything about me," she said, trying to interest herself in the dark trees flying past her window instead of his far-too-handsome profile.

"See? There you go with the accident again." He slung an arm over the steering wheel, driving as comfortably as any other man. "You definitely need to do my windows."

She pictured him laughing and smiling at dinner, remembered the covert glances he'd shot her way—and how they'd made her skin tingle as if he'd touched her. She had an inkling that her plan to draw him out was backfiring, but he'd gone out tonight, hadn't he? She wasn't going to argue with success. "*If* I wash the windows, when would you like them done?"

"What's your schedule like tomorrow? Will the boys be home?"

"It's my weekend, but Russ called earlier, wanting to take them to a car show."

"And being the nice person that you are, you said yes, right?"

His tone made her scowl. "I'm not a pushover," she said. "At least not anymore."

A logging truck rumbled past going the opposite direction, making it difficult for her to hear Gabe's response. "If you say so."

"It's just that the boys were pretty excited," she explained, feeling defensive. "How could I say no?"

"You couldn't," he agreed, but she suspected he was teasing her and wasn't happy that he'd pegged her as such a softie. She *wasn't* weak. She couldn't be. She'd endured the loss of her father, the death of her mother, the disillusionment of divorce. Yet she'd taught herself a trade, established a business and made a home for her boys. She'd built a good life, even if it was a little lonely. "Weak women get no respect."

"I didn't say you were weak."

"You *intimated* that I was too weak to say no."

"I intimated that you're too *nice* to say no," he said. "There's a difference. Anyway, it sounds like you're free tomorrow."

"I have to work."

"You can't afford to give me a couple hours?"

She knew she could; she even knew she would. But he'd just accused her of being a pushover. She didn't want to give in too easily. "Maybe."

"Great." His self-satisfied smile would have irritated her—except she was determined to keep her priorities straight. Seeing Gabe smile was always a good thing. How many times had she laid awake at night, hoping to see that very thing?

"Any chance you'll bring me a piece of apple pie from the diner when you come out?" he asked.

"I said *maybe* I'd come," she reiterated.

"I know you're a tough, modern woman and everything, but something tells me 'maybe' with you always means 'yes'."

She glowered at him. "That's it."

"You're not coming?"

"No pie."

His teeth showed as his grin turned slightly wicked. "You're drawing a hard line."

"My guilt has its limits."

"I'll remember that." They drove in silence for a few seconds, then Gabe glanced over at her again. "What do you like to eat?"

"Why?"

"Because, if you do the windows, I'll make dinner."

Was he serious? He'd gone out with a group and now he was inviting her to his place for dinner? Of course, *she* was the woman who'd put him in a wheelchair, so it was only because he wanted her to wash his windows, or because he was finally craving a little casual company. Either way, progress was progress. "I like champagne, caviar, bacon-wrapped filet mignon, garlic mashed potatoes, maybe some chocolate-covered strawberries for dessert," she said, going all out to get back at him for seeing through her so easily.

"Champagne?" he said.

She shrugged. "If I'm asking for too much, you could always find someone else to do your windows…."

"But I'm only trying to do what's best for *you*," he said.

She couldn't help laughing as she rolled her eyes. "Right!"

His lips tilted on one side. "Someday you'll thank me."

"Gabe?" Hannah said when they were almost home.

"Hmm?"

"Why aren't you more interested in Ashleigh? Or one of her friends?"

"Who said I wasn't interested?"

"You put on a good act back there, but I can tell it was for their benefit, not yours."

"They're too young for me."

"It's not often you hear a man say something like that," she said wryly.

"*And* there wasn't any chemistry," he added.

"I think *they* felt some chemistry."

"So did Race. He was hoping to go home with you tonight."

This information succeeded in surprising Hannah. "No, he wasn't."

"Yes, he was."

"How do you know?"

"He asked me what I thought his chances were."

"What'd you tell him?"

"That you have two kids."

She pretended to dust off her hands. "And that probably took care of that."

"Actually, he said he wasn't looking for a long-term relationship so kids didn't matter."

"What? How shallow can you be? See? I'm better off on my own."

"Haven't you ever had a one-night stand, Hannah?"

She knew she should've been offended by the personal nature of the question, but for some reason she wasn't. "No."

"Ever slept with anyone besides Russ?"

"Are you gathering this information for Race?" she countered.

"I'm curious," he admitted.

She crossed her arms over her chest because she was suddenly feeling self-conscious again. "What do you think?"

"From what you said earlier, I'm guessing no."

"No doubt Oakridge will be a challenge next week," she said, making a point of changing the subject.

He laughed softly. "It's nothing to be ashamed of."

She wasn't ashamed. She'd married young and given Russ everything she had, even though she'd never really loved him. But talking about such intimacies with Gabe made her feel strange, unsettled. She missed having a sex life more when she was with him than at any other time.

Of course, it could be her age, and not Gabe at all that had her in such a state, she told herself. Some people claimed a woman didn't come into her sexual prime until she hit her thirties. Maybe she was a late bloomer, and hormones—not the man sitting next to her—were to blame for her recent awakening.

Hannah wasn't sure she believed that but she was willing to give herself the benefit of the doubt. "Don't you think this is a dangerous subject for a man who guards his own privacy as fiercely as you do?" she asked.

He shrugged. "Why?"

"What if I were to ask *you* something you'd rather not answer?"

"What do you want to know?"

She'd expected to scare him off, not have him challenge her in turn.

Clearing her throat, she looked away. She wanted to know the obvious—could he still make love? But she couldn't bring herself to ask. She was too afraid the answer would be no. She didn't want to risk humiliating him. And she didn't want to have to assume responsibility for causing him that loss as well as all the others. "Never mind."

"Hannah?"

She looked at him again. "What?"

"The important parts still work."

This was good news indeed. At least she hadn't robbed him of that.

She smiled. "I'm so glad."

His eyebrows lifted at her enthusiasm. "So am I."

THE FOLLOWING MORNING, Hannah hummed as she made breakfast. She felt more carefree than she had in a long time.

"Hi Mom!" Brent burst into the house with his usual exuberance.

She tucked her sleep-tousled hair behind her ears and set aside the spatula she was using to turn the eggs. "Hi, baby," she said, giving him a hug. "Is Patti still here? Do you want to see if she'd like to come in for breakfast?"

"She already left. She said she had to hurry or she'd be late for church."

Patti didn't usually go to church. Hannah wondered if she was really in that big of a rush, or if she'd simply chosen not to come in. "Did you have fun last night?"

"Yeah. Uncle Joseph played me in Battleship and I won!"

"Good for you, sweetheart." Hannah covered a yawn. She'd gotten little sleep last night. Even after Gabe had dropped her off, she'd lain awake in bed, thinking about him. "Go tell your brother it's time to get up, okay?"

"He won't listen to me," Brent complained.

"Tell him he's going to miss the car show if he doesn't get a move on."

Brent started from the room, but his footsteps went only halfway down the hall before his voice came back to her. "He's up, Mom—but there's something wrong with his face."

"Shut up, you little mutant."

Something was wrong with his *face?* Hannah was so surprised by this comment she didn't react to Kenny's less than kind response to his brother. She glanced over her shoulder as they both entered the kitchen—and dropped the egg she'd been about to crack. "Kenny, what happened to you?"

He slumped into a chair at the table. "Nothing. When's Dad coming?"

Russ was supposed to arrive any minute, but Hannah didn't pass the information along. She was too shocked to see her son's fat lip and black eye. "How'd you get hurt?"

"How do you think?" he said. "I was in a fight."

She'd checked on him when she came in last night, found him already sleeping in his bed. She hadn't noticed the injuries, but with his blinds drawn, it had been dark in his room, and she never would have thought to look that closely. "You haven't been in a fight since third grade, when Chris Amberzini stole the cupcake out of your lunchbox."

He said nothing.

"Who were you fighting with?"

"Some jerk on the team."

"What's this jerk's name?" In a town as small as Dundee, she was almost guaranteed to know him or his parents, maybe both.

"Sly Reed."

"Coach Blaine's nephew?"

"Yeah."

"Sly's always fighting," Brent volunteered. "He's mean."

Hannah was too interested in getting to the bottom of the story to pay any attention to the peanut gallery. "Did he attack you?" she asked Kenny.

"No." Kenny scowled. "Can we just forget about it?"

"Of course not!" she said. "Tell me what happened."

He folded his arms and glared up at her. "Fine. Tuck and I went to the Arctic Flyer. Sly was there. He started getting in my face, saying some stupid shi—stuff," he quickly corrected. "So I hit him. That's all."

Hannah covered her mouth. This wasn't what she'd been expecting. *Sly* was the bully. "*You* started the fight? Kenny, how could you? You know better than that."

Between his glower and his injuries, Kenny looked awful. "Sly deserved it, Mom," he said, and she was grateful to hear a flicker of the sweet Kenny she'd raised come through in his voice.

Knowing her son, Sly must've done *something* to provoke him. Kenny wasn't easily angered and had never been a problem child. He was popular, well-liked. But she hadn't heard anything yet that would warrant the use of violence. Why wasn't he coming forward with a clear explanation? "This happened in the lobby of the Arctic Flyer?" she clarified, still grappling to get the facts straight.

"In the parking lot, behind the building."

"Did someone stop the fight, or…."

"Mr. Campbell came out and said he was going to call the police."

Harvey Campbell owned the Arctic Flyer restaurant and often complained about the number of teenagers who hung out there on weekends. They made a mess, distracted the workers and spent precious little money. Hannah could easily imagine how well a fight in the parking lot must've gone over with him. "So you ran off?"

"Are you kidding? Tiffany Wheeler was there. I wasn't about to run anywhere."

So this had something to do with salvaging his pride?

"How did it end?"

"Booker Robinson pulled me off Sly and gave me a ride home."

"Booker Robinson was there?"

"He and his wife were in line at the drive-through."

Thank goodness, or Hannah might have had to pick her son up from the police station. "I don't believe this, Kenny," she said, no longer sleepy in the least. "Did you hurt him?"

"He definitely took the worst of it," he said triumphantly.

"Kenny got in a fi-ght...Kenny got in a fi-ght," Brent chanted.

"Shut up," Kenny growled.

Hannah pressed a hand to her suddenly aching head. "Brent, please."

Brent gave her a sheepish look and stopped taunting. Hannah turned back to Kenny. "What did Sly say that got you so mad, honey?"

"He told Tiffany we were going to lose next Friday."

"That's all?"

"He told her we were going to lose because of me, that I was going to play a sucky game."

"I can see where that wouldn't make you happy, Kenny. But I can't see why you'd get mad enough to hit him. Just prove him wrong."

Kenny's shoulders rounded and he stared at the floor. "You don't understand."

She didn't deny it. "Let me see your hands."

Grudgingly, he held them out to her, and she made a note of the nicks, gouges and swollen knuckles. "Do you think you might have broken anything? Do we need to get X-rays?" Money was tight this month. If he needed X-rays, she wasn't sure how she was going to pay for them. Because medical insurance was so expensive for the self-employed, she carried a policy with a high deductible.

He flexed his battered fingers. "No."

That was good news, at least. But she was willing to bet that what had happened last night wasn't over yet. There'd be some fallout from it, most likely in the form of a call from Sly's mother. "What am I supposed to say when Sandy Reed contacts me?"

"Tell her I want her son to stay out of my face and leave me alone," Kenny said.

Hannah went to the cupboard for some Tylenol—for both of them. "What did Tuck do while this was going on?"

"Tuck thinks Sly's a loser," Brent volunteered.

"Sly *is* a loser," Kenny concurred.

Hannah set a glass of water and two capsules on the table. "That isn't what I asked."

Kenny swallowed the medication, then downed the rest of the water. "He tried to stop it. But you know Tuck. He's not the strongest guy in the world."

"Mom, you're burning the eggs!" Brent cried.

The acrid smell finally registered in Hannah's brain. Whirling, she snatched up the spatula and tried to save the eggs she'd managed to get into the frying pan before Kenny appeared. But it was too late—they were already black. With a sigh, she dumped them down the garbage disposal, set the pan aside and opened a window. But before she could return to her discussion with Kenny, the doorbell rang.

"If that's Dad, tell him I don't want to go anymore," Kenny said.

Hannah hoped it'd be that easy. She'd rather handle this latest development without Russ's involvement, because no matter what she said, she knew her ex would take the other side. If she punished Kenny for fighting, Russ would praise him for being a man's man and tell her she was trying to turn him into a mama's boy. If she supported Kenny in what he'd done, he'd accuse her of trying to win points with their son at the expense of being a good parent.

After the positive emotions she'd experienced last night, and the dreams she'd entertained afterward, it was too soon to deal with such a large dose of reality.

"Stay here," she said. "I'm sure he'll hear about the fight, but maybe this will buy us a couple days."

"Where's my lunch?" Brent asked, bending to tie his shoes.

"On the counter." Hannah doubled back to get it for him. Brent was all ready. Maybe she could send him off without having to invite Russ into the house. Then she could figure out what she needed to do about Kenny.

"Thanks, Mom!" Brent took the paper sack and started to race out of the kitchen, but Kenny snagged him by the back of the shirt before he could clear the door. "Wait a second. Where do you think you're going?"

Brent scowled and tried to jerk away. "To the car show."

"Not without me, you're not."

"I'm not going to miss it just because you don't want to go," he said, yanking on his shirt.

"Kenny, let him go," Hannah said.

"Why? It won't be any fun for him." Kenny's glower darkened. "You know Dad. He'll be with his buddies, talking and drinking beer. He'll basically ignore Brent."

Hannah gave him a meaningful look. "Are you telling me it's not safe?"

Kenny didn't answer.

The doorbell sounded again, followed by a rapid knock. "Hey, you guys up?" Russ called from outside.

"Kenny?" Hannah prompted.

Reluctantly, her son met her eyes. "No, but…why can't he stay here with us?"

"Because I want to see the cars," Brent said. He'd finally wiggled loose from Kenny's grasp and was attempting to slip around Hannah, but she held him off.

"I already told him he could go, Kenny. Is there some specific reason I should change my mind?"

Hannah thought he might come clean about the porn video. She could tell he wanted to. But she knew he'd decided against it when his gaze slid to the floor again. "Never mind. Give me a minute to change and I'll go, too."

"Kenny—"

He shoved to his feet. "It's fine, Mom. Everything's fine. Just answer the door before Dad loses it and starts shouting."

CHAPTER ELEVEN

HANNAH TOOK A DEEP BREATH and tightened her robe before answering the door.

"They ready?" Russ asked without so much as a greeting.

Hannah's eyes scaled the man she'd lived with and slept with for twelve years. Russ's lifestyle was taking a toll. He was growing a goatee, which helped to hide the bloat in his face. But it made him appear mean instead of just derelict. Today she thought he might even be hung-over. "Brent is."

As if her words had been his cue, Brent shot around her and headed straight for his father's Jeep. But Kenny wasn't dressed yet. Russ wouldn't be leaving right away, as Hannah would've preferred.

Russ looked her up and down. "Where's Kenny?"

"Changing."

"Tell him to get his ass out here."

"Give him a minute."

"We're gonna be late," he complained. "I told you to have them ready."

"You're lucky I'm letting them go," she pointed out, taking exception to his imperious tone. "It's *my* weekend."

It was a good thing she didn't expect any gratitude for the small sacrifices she made for the boys' sake, because Russ was still so bitter over the divorce he vacillated between begging her to come back to him and making sure she never would. "Right. You're a saint, much too good for me. I remember."

She bit her tongue, knowing the antagonism between them would only get worse once he saw Kenny's face. "If you'd like to wait in the Jeep, I'll send him out when he's finished," she said, hoping to avoid the whole exchange.

"I'm here," Kenny called from halfway down the hall, and Hannah braced herself with a deep breath.

"What the hell happened to you?" Russ bellowed as soon as Kenny appeared.

Mr. McDermott, her neighbor across the street, was outside watering his lawn. He glanced up, but Hannah pretended she didn't see him. Curving her fingernails into her palms, she focused on Russ, being careful to keep her voice low. "He got into a fight last night."

"With who?"

"Sly Reed."

"Sly?" Russ blinked several times, then his eyebrows drew together and his mouth clamped shut. "Get in the Jeep," he told Kenny and stalked away.

Hannah straightened in surprise. He was leaving? That easily?

Suddenly, she realized that she must be missing a piece of information. Kenny had never been in a serious fight before, yet Russ's emotions seemed to have skipped shock and worry and gone straight to anger. *Why?*

Kenny cast her a sideways glance before climbing into the Jeep. She lifted her hand to wave, but his stark expression made her freeze midmotion. Earlier she'd assumed he'd wanted to stay home because he didn't relish the thought of hearing his father's reaction to the fight—and maybe he was hesitant to be seen in public with a black eye and a busted lip. Now she wondered if there might be more to it.

Regretting her decision to let Russ take the boys, she stepped forward to stop him. But he acted as if he didn't hear her calling his name. Blasting his stereo, he peeled out of the drive.

Hannah was tempted to get in her car and chase him down. But she'd tried that once, and paid a heavy price for it.

They stayed with their father every other weekend, she told herself. Certainly one extra day wasn't going to matter. It was just a car show, and Brent was excited to go. They'd be back tonight.

She managed to let them drive away. But no amount of self-talk could shake her worry over Kenny. Kenny hadn't been himself for more than a week, and she was fairly certain Russ had something to do with it.

WHEN GABE WENT into town for groceries and dog food, it usually didn't take long to get what he needed. He bought a side of beef once a year, which he had the butcher cut up and package for his freezer. He grew most of his own fruits and vegetables in his garden, and he didn't eat a lot of processed foods. But Hannah had asked for some items that weren't easy to come by. Like caviar.

He doubted she'd ever tasted caviar. He was willing to bet she wouldn't like it when she did—it certainly wasn't a personal favorite of his—but he still thought it'd be fun to call her bluff. Again.

Because he didn't know where to look for the caviar, he went to the champagne section at Finley's Grocery, and began studying the labels. He had plenty of wine at the cabin. Wine seemed to be his friends' gifts of choice at Christmas. But no one had ever sent him a bottle of champagne. Considering what had happened to him, he supposed they thought it'd be in bad taste—and they were probably right.

"Can I find something for you?" Marge Finley asked amid small puffs for air. She'd been trotting after him ever since he'd entered the store, but she was significantly overweight and had a difficult time keeping up with his chair. He'd been hoping to lose her. She'd already asked, repeatedly, if she could help him, but he wanted to shop by himself.

"No, thanks." Selecting a bottle of the best champagne there, he put it in the basket he carried on his lap. Then he pivoted away from her and started down the aisle to search for the caviar.

"Nice choice," she said, at his elbow once again.

He turned the corner and gathered speed, but she continued to follow. When she began to hum along with the Celine Dion song being piped through the store's sound system, Gabe finally admitted to himself that he'd be smarter to let her help him. At least then she'd have to leave his side. "Actually…"

When he stopped, she nearly ran into the back of him. "Oops, I guess you need some brake lights on that thing, huh?" She laughed, knocking into a display while trying to stop her forward motion.

Gabe eyed the teetering soup cans to be sure they weren't going to fall, then forced a smile. Marge was trying to be nice; she wasn't *intending* to drive him crazy. "Could you tell me if you carry Beluga caviar?"

She quickly stabilized the display she'd nearly demolished. "We don't have any, but we can order some, if you like. It won't take more than a few days to come in. Would you like me to check the price?"

"No, I need it today. What about chocolate-covered strawberries? Could you get me some of those?"

Marge didn't bother hiding her surprise. She propped her hands on her wide hips. "Gee, what's the occasion? You generally buy nuts and trail mix."

"I've got a sweet tooth."

She tucked the wisps of hair coming loose from her long braid behind her ears. "Well, I'm afraid we don't have any chocolate-covered strawberries, either. They go bad too fast."

At this point, he was grateful he had the steaks in his freezer. "No problem. Thanks, anyway."

"You could always make them yourself," she said, coming after him again.

"How?"

She motioned with her arms as she explained. "Wash and dry your berries first. Then melt a bag of milk-chocolate chips with a dab of Crisco—maybe a tablespoon or so—in the microwave. Don't leave it in too long, mind you, or your chocolate's gonna burn. After that, stir the chocolate until it's smooth, then go ahead and dip. Remember to put the covered berries on greased waxed paper when you're done. And if you're gonna add anything fancy, do it before they set up."

"Fancy, like what?" he asked.

"Oh, you could sprinkle them with nuts or coconut or crushed candy, or drizzle white chocolate over the top. Anything, really."

Marge looked like a woman who knew what she was talking about when it came to desserts. And, considering the level of difficulty involved in some of the furniture he made, Gabe thought he could handle a few chocolate-dipped strawberries. "Do you have the big kind of berries?"

"Not the ones with the stems, like they sell in those expensive boutiques and such. But we can certainly round up a few baskets of berries that'll work nicely."

"Sounds good." He started down the aisle toward the produce section, but she surprised him with a burst of speed.

"I'll get everything for you."

If people didn't stand back and stare as if they were afraid his wheelchair might bite them, they tried to do too much for him. But at least she couldn't be in two places at one time. Instead of rejecting her offer yet again, he waited at the front register, nodding and smiling at everyone who turned to gawk at him as they passed by.

When she returned, she was breathing as if she'd run a mile, but she was smiling broadly. "This should do it."

"Thanks," he said, hoping he was the only one who heard the dry note to his voice.

As she headed behind the register to ring him up, Gabe glanced at the small cooler of flowers he'd noticed while waiting. He wondered how long it had been since anyone had bought Hannah flowers, doubted Russ had been the type. But he wasn't sure he wanted to add a bouquet to his purchases. He was only trying to help Hannah get past the accident, not set the entire town abuzz with gossip.

"Will there be anything else?" Marge asked as she scanned his items.

A package of condoms caught his eye. Most stores sold birth control from a regular, easily accessible shelf. But a couple of years ago, Finley's had taken to locking it in a case behind the counter. They were trying to protect the morals of Dundee's youth, but teen pregnancies had soared ever since—and Gabe found it quite curious that no one seemed to be able to figure out why.

"That'll be seventy-eight dollars and fourteen cents," she said, hitting the total button even though he hadn't yet responded to her question.

Gabe's attention returned to the condoms. For the first time in three years, he wanted to buy some. But he'd just rejected a bouquet of flowers because of the potential for gossip. Surely he'd be a fool to buy condoms here. Marge would be on the phone before he could leave the store...,

He could go over to the drugstore. But the situation wouldn't be any different there.

God, he was tired of the unrelenting interest of everyone around him. At times he was tempted to move away from Dundee, but where would he go? After the fame he'd known, he'd have to leave the country to escape recognition. And he wasn't about to do that. Since the accident, there was definitely something comforting about home.

He considered his recent restlessness, how often he'd thought about sex this week....

It was just a passing mood, he decided. Nothing he needed to act on. His body was starting to adjust to his condition. But that frightened him more than anything. He couldn't accept what had happened, couldn't adapt too much—or twenty years from now he'd still be rolling around in a damn wheelchair.

Forget the condoms.

"Give me the purple hydrangea plant you have right there next to the cooler," he said.

A hydrangea plant wasn't like a dozen roses. Still, Marge's eyebrows, which looked like they'd been drawn on with a pencil, lifted almost to her hairline. "You want to buy *flowers?*"

Good thing he hadn't asked for the condoms. "Isn't that what hydrangeas are?"

"Yes, but I…sure, okay." Marge's shoes squished as she walked to the cooler and back. "That'll be a hundred and twenty-three dollars and sixty cents," she said, giving him his new total as she set the pot of flowers with his other purchases.

He pulled out his wallet and handed her two crisp one-hundred-dollar bills. But the damn condoms seemed to be calling his name…. He resented the craving that prompted the purchase. But he resented even more the fact that he couldn't ask for them as casually as the next guy.

Screw it, he thought. *Let 'em talk.* They did anyway. "And I'll take a package of those," he added.

Marge hesitated, money in hand, and turned to look where he was pointing. When she realized what he wanted, her eyes nearly popped out of her head, and he halfway expected her to blurt out, "I didn't know you could still do that!"

"I'm over eighteen," he said when she didn't react right away. "I'd be happy to show you my ID if you'd like."

"What?" she gasped. "ID? Oh, no. I don't need that." Her face flushed bright red as she withdrew a ring of keys from the pocket of her smock and started sorting through them. "Do you want the—the Trojans or…"

As long as he was thumbing his nose at the gossips, he figured he might as well do it right. "Give me a size large in the natural sheepskin."

She set the box on the counter, then fumbled to get the case locked up again. He was about to ask her if she could do that later when he heard a voice he recognized. "Looks like you've got a hot date, Gabe."

Deborah Wheeler was just getting in line behind him. When he saw her, he nearly cursed out loud. Six months or so ago, he'd run into her at the gas station. She'd approached him to say she'd gone to school with him. He barely remembered her, but for the sake of being polite, he didn't say so. They'd talked a little about football, then he'd left with a polite thank-you for the compliments she'd paid him. He'd never dreamed that simple exchange would give her the encouragement to call him. But it did. Her calls and invitations had continued, unrelenting, for several weeks.

Finally, he'd had to tell her he wasn't interested in pursuing a relationship with her—and she hadn't taken the news very well. She'd hung up on him, and followed that up with a couple of scathing letters, accusing him of thinking he was better than everyone else and telling him that rejecting her was probably the biggest mistake of his life.

She was not the kind of person he wanted to see him buy condoms for the first time since suffering a major spinal cord injury....

"Or, considering your condition..." Her eyes swept over his legs, which, for the most part, he couldn't feel, and focused on his groin, "Those must be for a few of the boys on the football team, huh?"

He knew what she was suggesting—that he couldn't get enough of an erection to make a condom worthwhile. He could tell by the way she looked at him. Ever since he'd made it clear he wasn't interested in her, she'd been absolutely vindictive.

Anger and humiliation ripped through Gabe with a vengeance, but he refused to give her the reaction she obviously wanted. "It's nice to see you again, too, Deborah."

Marge frowned. "You wouldn't give these to the boys, would

you? I mean…they're not old enough. That's why we put them in the case."

A triumphant smile lit Deborah's face when Marge followed her lead but, although Gabe's blood raced with fury, he kept his expression perfectly pleasant. "No worries about that," he said. "This box won't last me through the weekend."

Marge blushed and giggled, obviously relishing his response. Deborah's mouth formed a surprised *O*.

Taking his change and his groceries, he started wheeling away. "Have a nice day, ladies."

"Who are the flowers for?" Deborah called after him, but he didn't respond. He'd been stupid to buy them in the first place.

HANNAH WAS LOOKING FORWARD to helping Gabe. Washing windows was one more thing she could do to improve his life in some small way. But she was torn about leaving the house. Sly's mother had called earlier, claiming Kenny had attacked her son without provocation and saying Hannah would have to pay the medical bills for Sly's stitches. Hannah was worried about the money, but she was even more concerned about Kenny. What had made him hurt Sly? She'd called Tuck's house several times already, hoping Kenny's best friend could explain the mystery, but Tuck and his mother had been gone all day.

As Hannah rounded the final bend in the road before the turnoff to Gabe's driveway, the clock on her dashboard read three-thirty. There was a possibility that Kenny and Brent might beat her home tonight, she realized. She didn't want that, but she knew Russ was just as likely to keep them out late as bring them home early. He was so unpredictable.

Her tires crushed several pinecones as she turned into Gabe's drive and headed through the trees that towered along both sides. She loved the dappled sunshine and the scents she encountered up here, even the ones associated with Gabe—especially the ones associated with Gabe. He was the kind of man who never smelled distinctly of cologne. She doubted he wore any. Generally, he smelled of freshly laundered clothes, warm skin, cool air and fresh-cut wood.

Spotting that handcrafted chair on his porch again, she smiled. He could do anything. She'd never seen furniture so—

Suddenly her smile faded. What was she thinking? He couldn't walk or play football, which were the two things he wanted to do more than anything else. And he couldn't do them because of her....

With a sigh, she cut the engine and got out. She should've moved away when her mother died. She should have gone to college somehow. She could have searched for grants, explored the possibility of student loans. She could have done any number of things.

Instead, she'd married Russ.

When she reached Gabe's front door, she knocked loudly, then turned to gaze out over the yard. Because of a slight breeze, the weather was cooler today than it had been for the past week. She imagined Christmas here at the cabin, knew it'd look like a winter wonderland.

The minutes stretched, but she couldn't hear Lazarus inside and no one came to the door. Where was Gabe? He knew she was coming and she could see his truck in the drive.

After another quick knock, she finally went around to the gate. Sure enough, as she drew closer, she could hear the grating of an electric saw. He was working in his shop.

She let herself into the backyard, where she found Lazarus lying on the porch at a relatively safe distance from the noise. He stood as though he wanted to greet her but didn't approach when she veered toward the workshop, where Gabe was sitting, wearing a pair of goggles and cutting a thick piece of wood.

"Hello!" Hannah called out but he couldn't hear her. When she deemed it safe, she touched his shoulder.

The sudden silence rang in her ears when he turned off the

saw and lifted his goggles. He twisted to look up at her, but he didn't smile. There was a hard edge to the set of his jaw, and she could see lines of tension in his face.

"Cleaning stuff's in the house," he said. "Door's open."

Hannah hesitated. Something was obviously wrong. After seeing him in such good humor last night, after talking freely with him and having him taunt her and tease her, this turn of mood stole all the warmth from the day.

"Are you okay?" she asked.

"Of course. I'm always okay."

But he wasn't. Hannah could tell he was trying for his usual façade of indifference, but for some reason he was struggling to pull it off today. The tension humming through him was almost palpable.

She certainly hadn't expected such a drastic change in him. But emotion was normal, she reminded herself. This was what she wanted from him. Something real, even if it wasn't nice. "You're upset."

He started to put his goggles back on, but she stopped him with a hand on his arm. "Why, Gabe?"

His eyes narrowed. "I can't imagine."

"You were fine last night. What happened?"

"Nothing new."

"Does it have to do with your father?"

She felt the muscles of his arm bunch beneath her hand—right before he shook her off. "You might as well go home. The window thing…and dinner. It's not going to work out today."

"Maybe dinner's not going to work out, but I can still do the windows," she said.

"I don't want you to."

"Why not?"

No answer.

"Gabe, quit shutting me out," she said gently. "We all hurt once in a while."

The scowl that marred his good looks deepened. "I didn't have time to make dinner." He dug a twenty out of his wallet and tried giving it to her. "Here, get something in town."

She batted his hand away. "I don't want your money."

"Fine." He tossed the bill on a nearby table and started the saw again.

Despite the noise, Lazarus slunk closer. His wet nose nudged her palm, and he watched Gabe as though he sensed his master's pain.

Hannah wanted to help Gabe. She just didn't know how. He'd asked her to leave, but she knew if she did she'd probably never hear from him again, except maybe in the capacity of Kenny's coach. He was trying to regroup, put the distance back into their relationship.

"Gabe."

His dark head whipped around to look up at her. "Damn it, I said—"

"I know what you said," she shouted because he hadn't stopped the saw. "But I'm not leaving. I'm asking you not to make me suffer through any more of your unhappiness."

The saw stopped.

Hannah's heart pounded as Gabe stared up at her with a scorching anger in his eyes. But she didn't regret what she'd said. If he wouldn't pull out of his emotional nosedive for his own sake, maybe he'd do it for someone else. "Please?" she added softly.

He shook his head as if what she asked was too much for him.

Hannah meant to soothe him in a way she might have soothed Kenny or Brent. She needed to reassure him, to reassure herself that they could get through the aftermath of that damn accident. If only he'd open up, they could do it together. But when she bent forward to press her lips lightly to his forehead, she suddenly found his mouth instead. She wasn't sure if she'd changed targets or he'd moved, but the next thing she knew, she was kissing him as though she'd rather die than stop.

CHAPTER TWELVE

IT HAD BEEN AGES since Gabe had kissed a woman. And it felt even longer. Almost at first contact, the anger that had simmered inside him since he'd left Finley's Grocery rose up like a great tidal wave. As she parted her lips and welcomed the eager onslaught of his tongue, that anger seemed to crash into and ignite with the surprising passion of her response. For one fleeting second, he wanted to bite her, to hurt her the way he was hurting, to maim, to punish, to strike out. But that passed almost immediately. Then the anger and everything else distilled into one very primitive urge, and all he could think about was burying himself inside her. He imagined driving into her again and again, could almost feel his muscles shake with the strain, his nerves tense with the anticipation....

Somewhere in his mind, dimly, he knew his reaction was half-wild. Even Lazarus, who stood barking at them, seemed to feel it. But Gabe was looking through a different window on the world than ever before. He could no longer treat a woman as casually as he once had or take making love, or any of the other good things in life, for granted. *Breathing* meant more than ever before. Hell, all the simple things he'd barely noticed for more than thirty years suddenly held significant meaning.

Hannah's fingers delved into his hair, pulling tight as she made a fist. The abandon he sensed in her as her tongue met and moved with his tempted him to let go of all restraint. She tasted like a bubblegum-flavored snow cone, and she kissed far better than he would have imagined—had he ever allowed himself to imagine kissing the adult Hannah Price. He wanted to suckle the breasts he'd studied at every opportunity through her shirt last night, take her in to his room....

But he knew she'd do anything to absolve her conscience. And having sex with him was one thing he would never ask.

WHEN GABE PULLED AWAY, Hannah grabbed for the support beam. She felt almost too weak to remain standing on her own power. She also felt robbed. She wanted to draw him back to her, to touch him everywhere, to feel his breath on her skin as his lips moved down her neck.... She didn't know how much of her response had to do with her need for reassurance that he was going to be okay, but she knew she'd never kissed a man like that before. And yet, she was far from satisfied.

"I—" She felt compelled to break the awkward silence but didn't know what to say. "I didn't mean to do that. I'm sorry if it made you uncomfortable."

"Uncomfortable?" He chuckled humorlessly. "Hannah..."

"What?"

"Uncomfortable is definitely not the right word."

She was having a difficult time catching her breath, slowing her racing pulse. "What then?"

"Bottom line, I don't think it's smart for you to be out here. You shouldn't be cooking my meals or doing my windows—"

"Why not? You're trading me a chair that would probably cost two thousand dollars in a gallery. I'm coming out way ahead. And the windows...I don't mind helping out."

"But you don't owe me anything. Do you think I've never passed a car by crossing a double line? It was an accident. It could have happened to anyone. Why don't you understand that?"

"Maybe I'm here because I want to be, Gabe. With all the women who've thrown themselves at you in the past, certainly that shouldn't come as a surprise."

"Bullshit. You're here because of the accident."

Right now, she wasn't so sure. The accident, his injury…it definitely figured into her emotions. But she was certain there were other issues at play. "I don't think… It's not that simple."

"Exactly. Nothing's simple anymore. My emotions are all over the place. One minute I'm mad as hell. The next…" He shoved a hand through his hair. "What if I hadn't stopped just now?"

Hearing the challenge in his voice, she met his gaze squarely. "What if?"

"We'd be inside, *in my bed.*"

His comment nearly stole her breath. "Making love?" she said softly.

His eyes swept over her as though her words brought back the hunger of their kiss. "We sure as hell wouldn't be sleeping."

"Would that be so bad?"

He gaped at her. "Hannah, you don't know what you're getting into. You don't really know me."

Maybe they hadn't spent much time together. But Hannah's crush on Gabe after high school had lasted for years. And he'd been on her mind almost every waking moment since the accident. She followed anything anyone ever said about him, prayed for him daily, worried about him constantly. She even remembered cringing for him when she'd learned about Garth and the affair. Somehow he was as much a part of her life as Kenny and Brent. "We grew up in the same small town, went to high school together, kissed at a graduation party twenty years ago. I know your family, many of your friends. I know you better than you think."

"I'm getting out of this chair someday, Hannah," he said. "I'm not looking for a comfy relationship where I can sit back and lick my wounds or let someone else take care of me."

"I won't offer to take care of you. I don't plan on introducing another man into my family life. There's too much to consider."

From his expression, she couldn't tell if he was happy about this or not. "You're making yet another sacrifice for Kenny and Brent?"

"I'm making a safe, well-informed decision."

"Well, while you're making well-informed decisions, there's something else you should know," he said.

"What's that?"

"My body could fail me. Making love could turn out to be ugly, humiliating, frustrating. You'd be a fool to get involved. And I'd be a fool to let you. Hell," he said, rubbing his jaw, "I haven't even touched a woman since the accident. I have no idea what might happen."

"That doesn't scare me, Gabe." Dimly, she thought it probably would if all she felt for him was regret and pity. But she didn't want to isolate and identify her other emotions. Falling in love was not an option.

His Adam's apple bobbed as he swallowed. He seemed about to override all his objections. But then he shook his head. "Stop. You don't know what you're asking for."

There was a dangerous quality about Gabe after the accident that hadn't been there before. Despite her brave words and her desire to help him, he made her a little nervous. If she was finally going to sleep with someone, she thought she could probably find a lover with whom she could maintain some objectivity. But no one excited her like Gabe did. The jittery, out-of-control feelings he elicited were part of his allure. "Who are you afraid can't handle what might happen, Gabe? Me? *Or you?*"

The frankness of her question seemed to surprise him. He stared at her for several seconds, then a gleam she wasn't quite sure she could trust came into his eyes. "That's it," he said. "Come here."

Oh boy.... Hannah's heart hammered against her ribs as she stepped forward. At least neither one of them could find a partner more discreet, she told herself. She wouldn't have to worry about her boys finding out; he wouldn't have to worry about seeing the details of their encounter splashed on the cover of the latest tabloid.

They'd have one mutually beneficial romantic encounter out here, where they were isolated. She'd feel young again, like a woman instead of just a mother. And he'd learn what his body could and couldn't do. Knowledge was power. With knowledge he could adjust and take it from there....

"Hannah?"

She didn't realize she'd been holding her breath until she needed to speak. "What?"

"Unbutton your blouse."

She glanced at Lazarus, who sat expectantly at Gabe's knee. "Here?"

He nodded.

"You don't think Mike will surprise us again, do you?"

"It's Saturday night. He's with his wife. No one else ever comes up here."

"Right." She swallowed to ease her dry throat. Obviously, he didn't realize that it had been forever and a day since she'd done anything like this. She needed a dark room and his hands doing all the work, not full daylight with him staring at her as if she was about to unveil the most beautiful thing in the world.

She tried to unbutton the top button on her blouse, but her hands were shaking too badly to do it as smoothly and enticingly as she wanted. "I guess I'm a little nervous," she admitted. "I—I have a stretch mark."

His eyebrows lifted. "A stretch mark? I'm sitting here in a wheelchair, and you're worried about a stretch mark?"

"But you've been with so many women, and I'm sure they all looked like models. Actually, they probably *were* models."

"I think you're beautiful," he said. "It doesn't matter what came before. I'm not even the same man."

Catching her lip between her teeth, she nodded and started unbuttoning her blouse again. He rolled closer, but he didn't touch her, and she couldn't bear to meet his eyes. She was afraid she'd lose her nerve. Maybe it had been a long time for him, too, but he had to know he could have Ashleigh or Michelle or Jessica up here stripping for him instead. They all had perfect figures and knew a lot more about seducing a man than she did. She had to be crazy to be doing this. Especially now, when she was having problems with Kenny and had so many other things on her mind….

She needed to leave. She pulled her shirt back together and opened her mouth to tell Gabe she'd changed her mind. But he chose that moment to finally touch her. The warmth of his large hands covered hers, steadying them. "Hannah?"

Blinking rapidly, she stared down into his face. "What?"

"Relax, okay?" He gently coaxed her to let go, and undid the last button himself.

She was still considering backing out—until he nudged her blouse open. Then the appreciation she read in his reaction sent a deluge of hormones to her rescue and she couldn't walk away. She'd never seen a man look at her like this before.

"Last chance to reconsider," he murmured. But his hands circled her waist as though he'd hang on to her if she tried to leave.

By way of answer, she let her blouse fall off and kissed the top of his head. Slipping her arms around his neck, she rested them on his broad shoulders, marveling at how many times she'd longed to do this.

He responded by rubbing his lips against her bare stomach and sliding his hands slowly up her rib cage.

He must've heard her quick intake of breath when he reached her breasts because he leaned back to give her the most radiant smile she'd ever seen from him. Fleetingly, she wished she could photograph it, capture that very expression, so the memory of this moment would never fade.

"I don't want you to have any regrets," he said, running his fingers lightly, teasingly over the silky fabric of her bra. "You'll be okay if we do this, right?"

She was tingling all over. "Is that thing you're doing with your fingers just to hedge your bets?"

His grin slanted to one side. "I think of it more as a nonrefundable deposit."

"What if I require a bigger deposit than that?" she asked and ran her mouth lightly over his, teasing him by giving him only the very tip of her tongue.

"I'm negotiable," he said and caught her mouth more securely, joining them deeply, hungrily.

She groaned at the sensations he evoked. "You're talented at this," she whispered breathlessly.

"Good thing you know where I live."

She might have told him she wouldn't be coming back, at least for this, but he'd pulled her into his lap and was running his lips down her neck to the swell of her breasts. She couldn't think of anything except the goose bumps he was leaving in his wake—and peeling off his clothes.

"Let's get rid of your shirt," she said and sat up straighter so he could use both arms to pull it over his head. Lazarus followed the shirt with his eyes as Gabe tossed it carelessly aside, then whined and barked in an encouraging fashion, and Hannah couldn't help laughing.

"What?" Gabe murmured.

"Your dog is watching us."

"Don't let him bother you. If he's half as turned on as I am, he's having a good time."

She laughed, feeling small in contrast to Gabe's powerful chest and shoulders. His body was even more beautiful than she'd expected. She kissed his collarbone, ran her fingers over his warm skin. "Nice…"

He unclasped her bra, and Lazarus gave another encouraging whine as it landed next to Gabe's shirt. This time Hannah barely noticed. She was too focused on the man who sat back to examine what his hands had revealed.

A cool wind cascaded over Hannah's sensitized skin as she waited nervously for his reaction. The daring of being naked in his yard instead of in his house added a certain element of fear to the experience, but it might have been even more erotic to her if she hadn't been terrified already. Certainly she'd never forget this moment.

"You look exactly as I imagined," he finally said with a smile.

"Imagined, when?" she asked.

"In your house, in the restaurant, in the truck, and whenever I closed my eyes after I got home last night."

Maybe she would have admitted to dreaming about him, too. But he'd already lowered his head to her breast.

She jumped as his mouth closed over her nipple. "Wow, it really has been a while."

He chuckled and tickled her with his tongue. "Some things are worth waiting for," he said. "I have a feeling this is one of them."

Hannah checked his expression to see if he'd just given her a line, but he seemed sincere. At least the mask she hated was gone. If Gabe was shielding himself in any way, she couldn't feel it. He seemed vulnerable yet trusting, completely open to her for the first time. And she was going to make sure he never regretted it. This was a start for him. If things went well, there was a chance he'd take the next step and the next until he was back to his old self, socializing and dating....

The thought of him moving on to make love to someone else sent an unexpected stab of pain through Hannah, but she told herself his health and happiness was all that mattered. Gabe Holbrook was never meant to belong to her. He was like a rare, injured bird. Once she nursed him back to health, she'd have to set him free. She didn't deserve him after what she'd done to him.

She couldn't imagine how cold and empty her life was going to seem when he was no longer part of it. He was the sun, the warmth streaming through her blood, the air she was dragging into her lungs...

Misunderstanding her little shiver, Gabe pulled her to him,

chest to chest, and she decided that had to be the best sensation of all. "You're getting cold. Let's go in the house."

GABE HAD TAKEN PLENTY of painkillers right after the accident. He'd even abused them for a few months, when he realized he wasn't going to bounce back from his injury as quickly as he'd hoped. But he'd never experienced the kind of high he felt when he made love to Hannah. Despite the potential difficulties he'd envisioned, they quickly learned what positions were easiest and most comfortable. Maybe it wasn't quite as smooth and effort-less as when he could use his legs, but he loved looking up at her as she straddled him, watching the emotion on her face.

Hannah made love with her heart more than she did her body, which changed the experience somehow, made it more meaning-ful. And although he couldn't feel much of his legs, the rest of his body compensated by becoming more sensitive to the touch. He could feel every whisper of her hand, lips or tongue on his skin as if he'd taken some sort of nerve-enhancing drug.

He'd heard Viagra helped some paraplegics. His doctor had tactfully mentioned it at one of his checkups. But Gabe hadn't been planning on making love to anyone so he'd never ordered any. Fortunately, he'd been able to do what he wanted for Han-nah without it—but he was certainly glad he'd bought condoms. They'd needed only one, but their lovemaking had lasted a long time and satisfied them both.

Watching the sun go down, he ran his fingers along Hannah's arm as she dozed contentedly next to him in bed. He hated to see the days grow shorter as fall approached. Getting around was more difficult in winter, but he enjoyed the turning of the leaves, the smells associated with the season. For some reason, autumn always evoked fresh hope that maybe, if he worked hard enough through the winter, he'd be back on his feet by spring.

Hannah shifted, bringing more of her bare back in contact with his chest. The softness of her, the promise of more companionship like he'd known today—maybe that was all he needed. Maybe it was time to be realistic about his chance of a full recovery.

You've been fooling yourself, a voice in his head seemed to whisper. *It's over. The chair is all you'll know. Better find someone who can tolerate living with half a man. Someone who can deal with having everyone stare at her just because she's at your side. Someone who can tolerate the whispers about whether or not you can get it up for her. And settle down before you have nothing….*

Blocking out those insidious voices, he covered Hannah with the sheet and slid to the edge of the bed, where he'd left his chair. He'd always been praised for his athletic prowess and wasn't sure, even at this late date, how to change his own measure of success. He couldn't even think of getting into a relationship when he had so little of himself to give, could he?

"Gabe?" Hannah muttered sleepily as he moved toward the door.

"Go ahead and sleep," he said. "I'm going to make dinner."

"That was great," she said softly.

She was talking about their lovemaking. He grinned. It *had* been great. As a matter of fact, this afternoon they'd created the only memory of the past three years that he wanted to carry with him.

CHAPTER THIRTEEN

IT WAS COMPLETELY DARK when Hannah opened her eyes. For a moment, she was so disoriented she couldn't remember where she was. She wasn't used to waking up in strange places. Her stomach tensed with apprehension—until she turned her face into her pillow and smelled Gabe. Then she realized she was in his bed and would have smiled and stretched languidly, except that her next thought was for her boys.

What time was it? She had to get home.

Scrambling to her feet, she pulled on her underwear and shorts, but her blouse was still on the floor of the workshop. She and Gabe had been in too much of a hurry to bother picking anything up. So, unless she wanted to stride into the front of the house half-naked, she had no choice except to borrow something of his.

She found a white cotton T-shirt bearing the logo Hawaii Surf & Sun on top of his hamper and slipped it on before hurrying down the hall. "Gabe?"

"There you are." He looked up when she entered the kitchen and smiled, and her heart skipped a beat as her mind showed her several intimate pictures of him in various stages of making love—poised above her, his gaze intense and locked on to hers, lying on his side, watching her with heavy-lidded eyes as he used his hands in the most incredible way she could imagine, laughing at her giggles when he pinned her hands above her head so she couldn't cover up against his slow, burning perusal....

She cleared her throat because she wasn't quite sure how familiar she should be. Should she walk over and kiss him like she wanted to, or were things back to the way they'd been before?

"Hungry?" he said, his expression turning slightly perplexed when she held back.

She could smell the food cooking, hear the sizzle of meat on the grill through the door that stood open to the back porch. Surely, if he was still cooking dinner, she couldn't have slept too long. She hoped. "What time is it?"

"Nearly nine-thirty."

"I've got to go."

His eyebrows shot up. "Before you eat?"

"Russ might've dropped the boys off at home already."

"Kenny's sixteen. Can't he baby-sit Brent for a little while?"

"Normally, he could, but—" She noticed Lazarus sitting at attention in the living room, following her every move. "Your dog's staring at me as if he knows all my dirty secrets."

"That's because he does."

"I don't see why he has to taunt me about it," she said with a grin.

"He's not taunting. Lazarus just knows a good thing when he sees it."

"That dog's like a canine extension of you," she grumbled.

"I'll take that as a compliment. Alaskan Malamutes are smart. But you have to train them when they're young or you'll never gain control."

"I'm sure your mother once said something similar about a little boy named Gabriel."

"Wrong. I was as angelic as my name."

"I bet."

He laughed and moved to the sink to wash his hands, and she realized he'd been working on something.

"What are you doing?"

"Making a mess."

It certainly looked that way, but when she moved closer, she could see that he'd actually been dipping strawberries. Instantly, her mind reverted to the menu she'd given him for dinner tonight. Evidently, he'd gone to some effort to deliver. "Those are for *me?*"

He frowned at the results of his labor. "Well, they didn't turn out quite as pretty as the ones you might see at Godiva's, but—" he licked his fingers "—they taste almost as good as you do."

She couldn't help smiling at him. "Do you have champagne and caviar around here somewhere, too?"

He cocked an eyebrow at her. "Don't you think you're asking for a little much, considering you haven't washed one window?"

"You had your chance for windows," she said flippantly. "You chose an alternate activity. Ask Lazarus."

Gabe's gaze fixed on her chest. "No regrets on my part. We can save the windows for another time."

She could tell he was testing her to see what to expect from her in the future and knew she had to speak up. If she continued to visit Gabe's cabin, what happened today would turn into a full-blown affair and one of them would wind up getting hurt. Namely her. She was in love with him already. The current of her desire had pulled her in deep—too deep. "Actually, I probably won't be coming back, Gabe."

The smile fled his face. "Seriously?"

"I think it'll be easier to cut things off now, don't you? We both know what happened today can't go anywhere. Neither of us is in a good position for a relationship, so there's no need to cause a big stir."

"What constitutes a 'big stir'? We're both single. We're both adults."

"And we both live in a close community. If word got out… Well, I'm sure my boys would hear about it, and Russ and his family, and—"

"You're afraid of the gossip?"

No, she was afraid of getting too attached, too used to feeling his hands on her body. She didn't want to see him with another woman after their affair ended and feel the kind of kick-in-the-gut jealousy she knew she'd feel if she hung on to him too long. She preferred to cherish this brief interlude and move on while she could do so with some dignity. "Look on the bright side, Gabe. Now you won't have to let me down gently in a few weeks."

"I've told you before I can take care of myself, Hannah. I don't need you to walk away today so I won't have to do it later. Just like I didn't need you to run interference for me last night at the restaurant," he added as an afterthought.

She ignored the first part because it was easier to argue about the second. "If you didn't need me to intercede, why did you let those people monopolize your time? You weren't enjoying yourself."

"How do you know?"

"I could tell. I know your expressions, your…smiles," she finally finished.

"My smiles. God, you're so…"

"What?" she prompted.

"Frustrating!" he said, but she got the impression he meant "endearing." They weren't really fighting. They were trying to adjust to the rapid changes in their relationship, and she knew it.

Lazarus barked and hurried to the side of his master the moment Gabe raised his voice. But Gabe shot him a scowl, and he immediately quieted and sat down.

"Because I'm wrong?" Hannah said. "You were having fun signing your name on napkins at the restaurant while your food turned cold?"

He didn't answer.

"You more or less told me you didn't want a relationship. Now you're saying you do?" she said.

"God." He rubbed his eyes. "I'm not sure what I want. You come out here and…and things get wild, hot. Then you get up and say you're not coming back. What am I supposed to make of that?"

She'd rejected him before he could reject her. This had to be pride talking. But now that he knew his body probably wasn't going to fail him at a critical juncture in some future relationship, he didn't need her anymore. He could proceed with confidence. "You'll be fine from here on out," she said. "Just…"

"What?"

She wanted to say, "Just know that this day meant a lot to me," but that was far too revealing. "Be happy."

"Great, thanks for the 'see ya later'."

She ignored his sarcasm. "I'm sorry. I wish I could at least stay for dinner."

"But you're in too big a hurry to slam the door in my face."

"That's not it."

"You've got to be hungry, Hannah. Sit down and eat with me."

"I'd like to. It smells good. But I slept too long and now I have to run. Kenny got in a fight last night, and—"

"What?"

For the moment, she'd succeeded in shocking him out of the surliness she'd caused with her "no strings attached" response to today. "I know," she said. "It came as a surprise to me, too. You should've seen him when he got up this morning."

"Is he hurt?"

She shrugged. "He has a black eye and a busted lip."

"Who hit him?"

Hannah sensed the same protectiveness in Gabe she'd felt when she'd first seen Kenny's face. But she didn't want to acknowledge his support. She didn't need any more reason to love him. "That's the problem. From what I can tell, *he* started the fight."

Gabe looked doubtful. "I can't see Kenny doing that. He's not the type."

"No, but he's been acting strange lately. All of a sudden,

he doesn't want to go to football practice. This morning he didn't want to go to the car show with his dad after being excited about it for the past couple of days. And the only thing he'd really tell me about the fight was that Sly deserved what he got."

"Sly was involved?" Gabe asked.

"Yeah, you know him, right?"

"Of course. He's on the team."

"Well, now I have to pay for Sly's stitches, and decide whether or not to punish Kenny, and whether or not to make him go over and apologize. But first I have to get to the bottom of whatever is bothering my son." She started for the back door.

"Where're you going?"

"To get my blouse."

"I already brought it in. It's on the arm of the couch."

Switching directions, she scooped up the clothes she hadn't seen until he pointed them out to her.

"Why change?" he said. "Just bring my shirt to me later."

Evidently he didn't believe she wasn't coming back, but she didn't want to bring it up again.

"Going home in your shirt would give us away." She moved toward the hall, but he rolled in front of her before she could reach it.

"Where are you going now?"

"To your bedroom."

"Why not put on your shirt right here? We're alone."

"No, I… *No!*" she said.

"You're kidding me, right?"

"About what?"

"I just made love to you a couple of hours ago. Now I can't even see you change your shirt?"

She let go of a dramatic sigh. "Gabe, you're not making this any easier."

"You're the one who's being difficult." He centered himself in the hallway. "You're in a hurry, remember? Better start stripping."

"Get of my way!" She tried to dart around him, but he caught her and pulled her easily into his lap.

They wrestled, gently nipping each other's lips as they fought. She'd thought she might have a chance of overpowering him because of the wheelchair, but she'd underestimated his strength. He easily subdued her, mostly because she was laughing too hard to continue the struggle. Then he held her hands behind her back at the wrists and reached boldly under her shirt, as if he had a right to.

"You're *so* bad," she said as their eyes met.

"And you're so good. I think that's part of the attraction. You know what they say about opposites." He kissed her, but this time it was a soft, sweet kiss that made her melt. When she responded by nestling closer to him, he grinned down at her. "You'll be coming back," he said confidently and let her go.

"Don't count on it," she said. She gave up trying to gain some privacy in which to change, but after she whipped off his shirt, she didn't hand it back to him. She stuffed it in her purse.

"Hey, what's up with that?" he asked, but she could tell he didn't really care. He was too preoccupied with the show.

She put on her bra, then shoved her arms into her blouse. "I'm taking it home."

"Why?"

"It's a souvenir."

"Not you, too," he said dryly. "Want me to autograph it?"

"No, thanks. I'm not likely to forget where it came from." She knew he had to be wondering at her motivation. But all she cared about was that the shirt smelled like him. *He* meant something to her, not his fame.

When he immediately sobered, she thought maybe he understood. "Be careful driving back."

She nodded, grabbed one of his chocolate-covered strawberries, and rushed out the door. She regretted having to miss Gabe's dinner. After what they'd shared, it seemed sad to cut the evening short. But as much as she knew she'd always treasure the memory, she was a little apprehensive about what she'd done. Had she started some irreversible chain of events that would come back to haunt her later—the way her involvement with Russ had?

She started her car, did a three-point turn and tried to reassure herself as she headed down Gabe's long drive. She and Gabe had used a condom. No one knew she was coming out here. Even if they did, they'd never expect the woman who'd injured him to become his lover. And he'd certainly never tell anyone. She could go back to her life and her kids as if it had never happened and—

Hannah slammed on her brakes. Just as she was about to turn onto the road, a car came barreling around the curve.

The driver honked impatiently, as if the near-collision was her fault, then the car continued on its way, but for a second, Hannah thought she recognized the person behind the wheel. Leaning as far forward as possible, she tried to get a better view, but it was too dark. She saw only the back of a generic white sedan before the taillights disappeared.

Maybe she was imagining things. It probably wasn't anyone she knew.

THE CABIN SEEMED TOO QUIET after Hannah left. Gabe turned on some jazz to fill the silence while he finished cooking dinner. Then he gave Lazarus Hannah's steak so he wouldn't have to eat alone. Since the accident, the cabin had been his haven. It was the only place that provided the privacy he craved. But, suddenly, it seemed far too isolated.

Could one afternoon with Hannah really have made that much difference? Sure there'd been times over the past three years when he'd felt bored or restless. But all he'd had to do was think about playing football again. Then the stubborn competitor in him would take over and weight training or therapy would fill the void. If that didn't work, he'd mow the yard, weed the garden, or make a new clock, rocker or cabinet.

None of those activities appealed to him tonight, however. The hours stretched before him, endless and empty. Hannah had simply left too soon. He wanted her to come back, take off her clothes and curl up with him again. Watching a movie in bed sounded like fun. Heck, as long as she was with him, *sleeping* sounded like fun.

He wondered what she'd say if he called her and suggested she drive out after the boys were asleep. For most of his life, he'd never had to worry about rejection. Woman always said yes to him.

But Hannah was different. She cared about him, or she never would have slept with him. He knew that. He could tell by the way she'd kissed him, the way she'd touched him. Problem was, she had this image of what she needed to be in order to be a good mother to Kenny and Brent, and it completely precluded having any fun herself. She'd shut down that portion of her life just as absolutely as he had.

As if that wasn't enough, she was also pretty worried about Kenny. Gabe was concerned about him, too. He was concerned about the whole team. He hadn't wanted to believe that Blaine would take the kind of risks Mike had intimated he might be taking, but now Gabe wasn't so sure. Kenny wasn't typically violent. The fact that he'd hurt Sly so badly could indicate a lot of things. It could simply be a coincidence that he'd had trouble with Blaine's nephew. It could indicate that Kenny had been approached by Sly on behalf of Blaine and reacted negatively, which was a happy thought. Or, not so happy, it could mean that he and Sly were involved in some way. Bottom line, the fight lent credence to what Dale Lindley had overheard in the locker room, what he'd told his mother. It connected Kenny and Sly. Gabe just didn't know how.

Maybe he needed to find out. Gabe liked Kenny, didn't want to see him get swept up in something that could hurt his chances of future success and ruin his reputation as a player. Gabe didn't want to see that happen to any of the kids on the team. And he wouldn't stand for having his own assistant working against him. If he couldn't win a football game by playing on the field, he'd do it by coaching on the sidelines. No one was going to stand in his way, least of all Melvin Blaine.

When Gabe started to wheel away from the table, Lazarus assumed he was going to work out and trotted expectantly in the direction of the gym. His dog knew the routine. But Gabe couldn't bring himself to work on his range and coordination right now. He felt as if he'd been beating his head against a wall for the past three years, chasing a dream he was never going to catch while letting other things, possibly just as important, slip right past him.

But that was a subject he'd have to contemplate later. Right now he needed to figure out what was going on with his assistant coach—which meant he had to make some phone calls.

Taking out the team roster, Gabe sat it beside him on the counter and dialed the first number. Coach Blaine.

Blaine lived alone. His wife had died nearly a decade ago, and all his children were grown and out on their own. He answered almost immediately. "'Lo?"

"It's Holbrook."

Blaine's voice grew instantly leery. "What can I do for you, Gabe?"

Lazarus sat at Gabe's feet, watching him curiously, his ears perked forward.

"You can start by telling me if we have a problem."

"With what?"

"The team."

There was a significant pause. "We have a lot of problems. Our defensive backs are weak, we have a young, rather inexperienced quarterback, we're giving too much ground on the front line. Maybe you could be more specific."

"Kenny Price got into a fight with your nephew last night."

"I heard. My sister called me about it earlier. What does that have to do with me?"

"That's what I'd like to know."

"Nothing."

Was he lying? "You don't have any idea why there might be friction between them?"

"Absolutely none."

Gabe was surprised by how badly he wanted to believe Blaine. As much as he disliked his assistant coach, he didn't want to see the football program at Dundee High suffer from the actions of one overly ambitious and far too selfish man. "I'm glad to hear that," he said. "Because if any of my boys—"

"*Your* boys?" Blaine interrupted.

"*My* boys," Gabe repeated. "Whether you like it or not, this is my team now. And if you take advantage of your position by getting any of the players involved in something that might hurt them or the program, you'll be a very sorry man. Do you understand?"

"You have a lot of nerve, calling me up and threatening me like this," Blaine growled.

"If you're screwing up, you should be grateful I'm giving you the chance to change direction."

"We haven't even played our first game, Gabe. Are you looking for a scapegoat already?"

Gabe chuckled and shook his head. "I'm not going to need a scapegoat, Melvin. We're going to win. You can either help me do that or get out of my way."

"You think your big head will be enough to pull this team through?"

"Still dealing with some residual envy?" Gabe said.

"What's to envy?" Blaine replied. "*I* can walk."

CHAPTER FOURTEEN

HANNAH sat in her driveway, staring at the light gleaming through the window of her own living room. Russ's Jeep was parked at the curb. She knew he had to be waiting for her and didn't want to talk to him, not with Gabe's T-shirt stuffed in her purse and her skin still sensitive and tingly from his touch.

She hoped her ex-husband would give up and leave, but as the minutes dragged by, she knew that wasn't going to happen. Unless she was willing to drive off for a while, he'd see her the second he stepped outside, anyway.

Taking a deep breath, she dropped her keys in her purse, forced the zipper to close despite Gabe's shirt and got out. Somehow she had to get through the next few minutes. But she knew it wasn't going to be easy. She could still smell Gabe on her skin and clothes. Surely everyone in the room would know by the guilt on her face exactly how she'd spent her afternoon the moment she tried to explain that she'd gone out to Gabe's cabin to wash windows.

How long had Russ and the boys been home? Maybe she could say she went for a long drive. That was sort of true. No one needed to know she'd even seen Gabe.

"There you are," Russ said as soon as she walked through the door. He was sitting on her couch, which was pretty much where he'd spent most their married life, drinking one of the beers she kept in the fridge for Patti.

"Sorry I'm home so late," she said. "I wasn't sure when to expect you back."

"We didn't know we had to submit a schedule if we wanted to find you again. Where the hell have you been?"

"Hi, Mommy." Brent hurried over to give her a hug as she put her purse on the small table inside the front door.

"You don't have the right to ask me that, remember?" she said to Russ while giving her son a squeeze. "We're not married anymore."

"I have a right to know where you are when I'm trying to return the boys."

"Why? Obviously, Kenny had his key to the house, or you wouldn't be here, drinking my beer and watching my TV. He's old enough to sit with Brent until I get home." She glanced around, looking for her oldest son, but didn't see him. "Where is Kenny?"

"In his room."

"Is he okay?"

Russ shrugged. "He's fine. Just mad."

Hannah walked over and turned off the television. Finding Russ on her couch was bringing back some of the old helpless, I-can't-escape feelings she'd had during her marriage. "Why?"

"Mom, I was watching that," Brent complained.

"It's getting late," she told him. "Go take your bath and get in bed. I'll tuck you in later."

Brent grumbled some more but finally left, and Hannah turned back to Russ. "Why's Kenny upset?"

"Because I made him go over to Sly's house and apologize."

Hannah stiffened, but quickly reminded herself that as Kenny's father, Russ had the right to get involved. Still, it was difficult not to resent the fact that she hadn't been consulted when she typically took care of Kenny's every need and had already been dealing with Sly's mother. "You *know* it was his fault?" she asked.

"Of course. He hit first, didn't he?"

Russ finished his beer, then belched and crushed the can.

When he set it on the accent table next to her couch, Hannah almost snapped at him to get up and throw it away instead of leaving it there. But she wanted him to leave as soon as possible, preferably without an argument, so she bit her tongue. The less said, the better.

"I wasn't sure how it happened," she said. "Did Kenny explain it to you?"

"He wouldn't say much. But he admits to throwing the first punch, and I won't have a son of mine—"

For a split second, Hannah thought he was going to say, "picking fights," and was prepared to be mildly impressed. But she should've known better.

"—doing anything that could hurt his chances to play football."

"You're teaching him to take care of number one, I see."

"Sly is Blaine's nephew," he said, as if that somehow justified his behavior.

"So? There're more important issues at hand here, Russ. Dealing with anger and feelings of aggression. Solving problems in a constructive manner. *Character* issues Kenny could carry with him into adulthood."

"Yeah, well, I want to see him carry a football into adulthood."

Hannah's mind reached for the memory of Gabe's kiss as she strived for patience—positive to balance the negative. "You need to quit pushing him, Russ. If he continues with football, it has to be his dream, not yours. Kenny has a great mind. There're a lot of paths for him to choose from."

"He wants to play football, and you know it."

"Why are you here?" she asked. "So we can have the same tired argument we have all the time?"

He shoved a hand through his thinning hair. "No, I..." He seemed to struggle for words, which wasn't something he did very often.

"What?"

"I wanted to ask you to stand by me for a change."

Stand by him? She'd stood by him for twelve years—until he'd completely annihilated all the positive feelings she'd ever had toward him. But…he looked pretty sincere today and, for her boys' sake, she couldn't give up hope that he might change. She didn't want to let Brent and Kenny down if her cooperation might make a difference. "How?"

"Tell Kenny that I'm only trying to help him. I'm his old man, I love him."

"He knows you love him, Russ."

"But I don't have any credibility when it comes to him. He…he pays more attention to what you tell him. He…respects you."

Maybe Russ was reaping the rewards of his own actions, but Hannah couldn't help feeling sorry for him. She would be heartbroken to think that her sons didn't respect her. "What do you want me to say to him?"

"Tell him I know what I'm talking about when it comes to football."

Football again. Hannah didn't like the importance Russ placed on this one issue, but she supposed supporting him when it came to sports wasn't too much to ask. He knew more about football than she did. "I'll tell him you have his best interests at heart," she said.

"That's not exactly what I meant."

"Sorry, no blanket endorsements."

"What happened to that soft heart of yours?"

"You took advantage of it."

He grabbed the ball cap he'd left on the arm of the couch. "Where were you today?"

She cleared her throat as guilt washed over her again. She wanted to believe she'd done what she'd done for Gabe's sake. But deep down she knew making love with Gabe was *exactly* what she'd wanted for a long time, and the fact that she hadn't been disappointed somehow made it worse. "I went for a drive."

"Where?"

"Up in the mountains. It was nice, refreshing."

"Must've been. I've never seen you look prettier."

Hannah's cheeks burned. "Thanks."

"Any chance you might like to—"

"No, I'm sorry," she said before he could even finish. She knew he was going to ask her out. He still did that, occasionally. But she had no desire to be with him and knew better than to give him, or their boys, any false hope.

"Right." He nodded. "Okay, well, I'd better go."

He crossed the room and stepped outside. She followed to say goodbye and lock up, but he came to a sudden stop. "What's Gabe doing here?" he asked.

Hannah's jaw dropped as she leaned around Russ to see that Gabe had pulled into her drive. Lazarus was in the back of his truck—along with the chair she wanted.

GABE HAD SEEN Russ's car, knew Hannah's ex-husband was at her house and that meeting up with him might not be the most comfortable of moments. But he wasn't about to turn around without fulfilling the reason he'd driven all the way to town. After speaking to Blaine, he'd called Mike—and learned that Josh and Rebecca had spotted Blaine having breakfast with Kenny and Russ at the diner a week ago. He needed to warn Kenny not to get involved with Blaine, just in case.

Lazarus jumped out as soon as Gabe released the tailgate. Then Gabe started pulling the chair he'd brought for Hannah toward him by the legs, so he could lift it to the ground.

Russ reached him before he could manage it. "What's this?"

Gabe didn't answer. He didn't owe Hannah's ex any explanation.

Hannah glanced up from where she'd knelt to pet Lazarus. "It's a chair."

"I can see it's *a chair*," Russ said. "What's it doing here?"

"It's mine."

"You bought this and had *Gabe* pick it up for you?"

Hannah stood up and moved closer. "He built it. He makes all kinds of furniture. Isn't it great?"

Gabe nearly smiled at the enthusiasm in her voice. She *really* liked the chair. He'd caught her sitting in it on his porch, had even heard her tell Ashleigh how cool she thought it was.

Russ stepped forward as Gabe lifted it over his head. "Looks like you need some help with that."

"I've got it," Gabe said.

"But—"

Gabe shimmied his hands up the frame of the chair to lower it.

"Okay." Russ backed up a step as Gabe set it on the ground. "So you can move furniture. Great. Is this a gift or…or what?"

The jealousy in Russ's voice and posture wasn't difficult to detect. Gabe looked to Hannah. This was her ex-husband; he wanted to let her handle the situation.

"It's a trade," she said.

"What kind of trade?"

"Just a *trade*." She stepped toward Russ's Jeep. "Thanks for taking the boys today."

Ignoring her broad hint that he leave, he glanced at Gabe. "It's been a long time since Gabe and I have had a chance to talk. Mind if I come inside so we can catch up?"

"Not tonight," Hannah said. "I'll see you next week when you pick up the boys."

Hearing this dismissal, Gabe lifted the chair and held it upside down on his head with one hand while pushing his wheelchair up the drive with the other.

"Want me to—" Russ started to skirt past Hannah, but she caught his arm and drew him even more pointedly toward his Jeep.

"Gabe's got it."

A few seconds later, Gabe heard the engine start. Then, Russ tossed him a frown and pulled away.

When Hannah came up the walk, Gabe couldn't help running

his eyes over her and remembering what a sweet, sensitive lover she'd been. He knew that what had happened today had changed him, stolen some of the drive he'd been fighting to keep. But he couldn't regret it. Yet. Maybe he would tomorrow, when the memories weren't quite so fresh.

"Is this where you want it?" he asked, indicating the spot by her front door where he'd put the chair.

She smiled. "For now. When the weather gets colder, I'll probably move it into the studio. I'm going to take bunny pictures with it next spring."

"For *Playboy?*" he teased. "Make sure you send me one of those."

"I'm talking about *kids!*"

"Oh, real bunnies."

She chuckled at the disappointment he'd injected into his voice, then sobered when their eyes met. "You probably shouldn't have brought it here yet," she said.

"Why not?"

"I've only made you two meals."

He straightened the chair a little, then shrugged. "You'll make more."

"Actually, I'm not sure that'd be too smart."

Only the shadow of the porch light fell on her face, but he could tell she looked troubled. "Why not?"

She cleared her throat. "I might want dessert."

He grinned. "Something tells me you're not talking about chocolate-covered strawberries."

"No."

He pretended to put some thought into her response. "Personally, I like plenty of dessert."

"But I can't afford it in my life right now," she whispered.

She was scared. Hell, so was he. They were both feeling vulnerable. But he knew, after what had happened, they probably wouldn't be able to stop seeing each other anytime soon. Once

those barriers came down—and they were certainly down now—
it was too hard to prop them up again.

"Okay," he said simply. He wasn't going to push her. She
needed time to work through her reservations.

Once he gave in, she didn't seem to know how to respond.
"So…do you still want to come in?"

"If you don't mind. I actually came over to talk to Kenny."

"Kenny?" She blushed. "You let me go through that whole
thing thinking—you let me make a fool of myself!"

"You didn't make a fool of yourself. I enjoyed what happened today, too."

"I didn't enjoy it *that* much," she said, but he knew it was only
to get back at him.

He cocked his head to the side as he looked up at her. "You
called it *dessert*."

"I know, but…" She laughed and shook her head. "God,
you're…"

"Bad?"

"Cocky!"

"Fortunately, you don't mind."

She rolled her eyes. "Just tell me you're not having a problem with Kenny. Why do you want to talk to him?"

"It's probably nothing to worry about," he said, hoping that was
true. They lived in such a small town it wasn't inconceivable that
Russ and Blaine would meet for breakfast as friends. And maybe
the fight between Sly and Kenny simply stemmed from the usual
teenager-type angst. Neither event proved anything. "I want to discuss last night's fight. We're going into our first game in a few days.
I need to make sure the team puts their personal squabbles aside."

"Right. Okay. Well, Russ made Kenny go over to Sly's and
apologize today. That should help."

"Maybe," he said.

"Mommy?" Hannah's youngest son had opened the screen
door and poked his head out. "Who's here?"

Hannah gave him the evil eye. "Brent, aren't you supposed to be in bed?"

"But who's here?"

"It's Coach Holbrook."

"Kenny's football coach?"

"Yes. Can you please remember your manners and say, 'It's nice to meet you?'"

Brent didn't respond because he'd spotted Lazarus at the edge of the yard. "Is that your dog?" he asked excitedly.

Gabe nodded, and Brent burst out onto the porch. "Can I pet him? Please?"

Lazarus was busy marking the trees and bushes. When Gabe whistled, the dog hurried over, and Brent immediately went down on his knees.

"He's big!" he squealed, then fell over giggling as Lazarus proceeded to lick his cheeks.

"I want a dog," Brent said, only halfheartedly protecting his face.

"You have a rat," Hannah said.

"A rat isn't as good as a dog. *Look,* Mom! He loves me."

"You can have a dog when you get a couple years older."

"Kenny's older," Brent said.

Gabe thought Brent had a pretty good point, but Hannah had an answer for that, too.

"Kenny's a teenager. He's gone a lot."

Brent rolled away and tried to get up, but Lazarus wasn't finished with him yet. A moment later, he fell down laughing again. "How old...do I have...to be?"

"At least ten," she replied.

Gabe called Lazarus off, and Brent finally sat up. "Then can I have a big dog like Coach Holbrook's? Please, Mom? This is the *best* dog I ever saw."

Gabe couldn't help smiling at the grass in the boy's mussed hair—and feeling a little sorry for Hannah. She cared so much about her kids, she'd probably break down and get Brent a dog before another week was out, even though she had too much on her plate already. "Dogs are a lot of work," he said, trying to throw a little support her way. "Especially Alaskan Malamutes. They're typically friendly, but they're pack animals. You have to establish yourself right away as the dominant figure in their life."

"I could be a—a—what is it?" Brent said.

Gabe chuckled. "A dominant figure."

"I could be one of those," Brent said with more confidence than Gabe had expected.

"When you're ten or so, it'll be easier," he insisted.

"Can I take him inside, to my room?"

"For a few minutes, if it's okay with your mom."

Brent checked with Hannah, and she nodded. "Come on, boy," he said.

Lazarus followed Brent as far as the door, then paused to look back at Gabe. When Gabe nodded, the dog disappeared inside the house with his new friend.

"I wish my boys were as obedient as your dog," Hannah said.

"Boys are a little harder to train."

She gave him half a smile before opening the door. "I'll see if Kenny's still awake. Are you coming in?"

Gabe pictured trying to talk to Kenny with her possibly overhearing the entire conversation and decided to stay where he was. "Actually, maybe Kenny and I could have a few minutes alone out here on the porch."

She hesitated. "You're sure everything's okay?"

He could tell that she was used to carrying the whole load when it came to the worry and care of her boys. He sympathized and tried to reassure her. "He's a good boy. He'll be fine."

"Okay." She slipped inside, and he felt some concern of his own. She'd trusted him that easily—but if Kenny let him down...

It was only a couple of minutes before Kenny shuffled out onto the porch, wearing a muscle shirt, a pair of holey jeans and no shoes. "Coach," he said, his voice sullen.

Gabe rolled back and motioned for Kenny to sit in the chair he'd just brought. Kenny's eyebrows lifted when he saw it, but he didn't ask where it had come from. "Something wrong?" he asked.

Gabe indicated his face. "Looks that way."

Kenny's chin came up. "He got the worst of it."

"That's what I hear. But you could have broken a hand last night. Do you realize that?"

He didn't answer.

"Where would the team be if our starting quarterback broke his hand before the season began?"

He shrugged. "Maybe the team would be better off."

"How?"

"Jonathon Greer could play."

"He could, but you're better at avoiding a sack. You know that, right? You know our chances of winning go down if you don't play?"

"No."

Gabe waited for him to say more, but he didn't. "What was the fight with Sly all about, Kenny?"

Kenny seemed to be studying his bare feet. "Nothing."

"You banged him up that bad without a reason?"

"He's got a big mouth, that's all. He doesn't know when to leave me alone."

"You've never had a problem with Sly before."

"I've never liked him," Kenny said.

"But you've never had a problem with him."

No response.

"Is there anything going on with the team that I should know about?"

He rubbed his neck but continued to avoid Gabe's eyes. "No, Coach. Not that I know of."

Gabe wished Kenny's body language was half as convincing as his words. He decided to be more direct. "Coach Blaine hasn't contacted you, has he?"

His eyes darted up. "About what?"

"About anything."

He blinked several times, and his Adam's apple bobbed. "No, sir."

Kenny had spoken so softly Gabe could scarcely hear him. "What?"

"I said no."

"Then, we're all set for our first game this week?"

Kenny's gaze fell again, but he nodded.

"You don't seem too excited."

He didn't say anything.

"You're going to play your heart out during that game, right?"

Kenny's shoulders rounded a little more. "Yes, sir."

Gabe put a hand on his arm. Finally, Kenny looked up. "I'm counting on you."

He nodded.

"Will you get my dog and tell your mother good-night for me?"

"Sure." He started into the house but paused on the doorstep. "Coach?"

"Yes?"

"I—I think you're doing a good job. With the team, I mean."

"Thanks," Gabe said, wishing Kenny would open up to him. Gabe had been hoping that Mike was wrong. But after talking to Hannah's son, he was more convinced than ever that something was going on.

So what did he do about it? Did he save Kenny from himself by pulling him from the game? Did he pull other key starters, as well? Did he complain about Blaine to the school board and try to get him fired?

No, he couldn't do any of that. He had no proof. Blaine might not be his favorite person, but the guy deserved the chance to prove himself one way or the other.

The proof would be in the game. On Friday, Gabe would know who was really on his team—and who wasn't.

CHAPTER FIFTEEN

HANNAH PULLED ON HER NIGHTGOWN and washed her face before knocking softly on Kenny's door. She hadn't wanted to pounce on him the second he came in from outside. When she'd summoned him to speak to Gabe, he'd looked pretty beleaguered. Considering how sore he must be from the fight, and the way Russ was behaving, suddenly taking a stand against something he normally would have applauded as a healthy display of masculinity, Kenny's day had probably not been a very good one.

"What did Gabe have to say?" she asked when her son told her to come in.

"Just the usual," he muttered. In bed with the lights off, he had Sheryl Crow on the stereo.

Hannah could smell a hint of the sweaty socks and T-shirts he tossed in the hamper instead of the basket on the washing machine, and the dirt on the tennis shoes and cleats that were supposed to be left in the garage but were in the middle of his floor. Both smells reminded her of Kenny as a little boy. But she could also detect the Abercrombie & Fitch cologne her son had wanted for his birthday and ordered through the Internet. He only wore it when he went out on the weekends, but it was that particular scent that made her realize how soon he'd be an adult. In three years he'd graduate from high school and head off to college. It was hard to believe.

Then it'd be just her and Brent.

"What's the usual?" she asked. "Surely the head coach doesn't visit every player before a big game."

"I'm the quarterback, Mom. Coach Holbrook wanted to know if I was ready to play on Friday, that's all."

She moved away from the door frame and sat on the foot of his bed. "So not only are you getting to play, you're starting."

"I guess."

"Doesn't that make you happy?"

"Yeah," he said, but he didn't *sound* too happy.

"Are you ready?"

He sighed heavily. "As ready as I'm ever going to be."

"Your father seemed a little upset tonight."

Kenny shoved up onto his elbows. "What does *he* have to be upset about? I apologized to Sly, like he wanted me to."

"He's afraid you're mad at him for forcing the issue."

"I am!"

"I think he was trying to do the right thing, Kenny. Fighting isn't any way to resolve a problem."

"Dad doesn't care about fighting, Mom. If I would have hit someone else, he would have been fine with it."

So much for supporting Russ. Hannah bit her lip for a moment, then tried again. "I know, but…in his own way, I think your dad is trying to take care of you. He loves you."

"He's confusing me," Kenny said.

"About what?"

"About a lot of things. Doesn't he think I'm good enough to make it in football without…kissing up to the coaches?"

She straightened his blankets. "He thinks he was robbed of certain opportunities. He doesn't want the same thing to happen to you."

"I wish he'd just stay out of my business."

Taking his chin, she forced him to look at her. "Do you want to tell me what's going on, with your father, the fight, football? You've been acting so strange lately."

"It's nothing." He fell back and covered his eyes with his arm for a few seconds, then peeked at her again. "Do you like Coach Holbrook, Mom?"

Hannah's heart skipped a beat. She liked Coach Holbrook, all right. She liked him a lot. Too much. But a second later, she realized Kenny wasn't asking about that kind of like. "I, um, do. He's—" *drop-dead gorgeous, a skillful lover, and infuriatingly complex* "—a good guy." She moved Kenny's alarm clock over on his nightstand because it gave her something to do with her hands. "What about you? Do you like him?" She told herself it didn't matter, that she wasn't going to get involved with Gabe romantically again, but she couldn't help wanting her sons to think well of him.

He nodded. "Every play has to be absolutely perfect before we leave practice, but…he seems cool, you know? Except when he looks at me with those sharp eyes."

"*Sharp* eyes?"

"It's like they're sending a message—'Come on, you can do it.' It makes me want to be sure I don't let him down, you know?"

"Mom?" Brent's voice reached her from down the hall.

"What?" Hannah called.

"Can I have the two dollars you owe me?"

"For what?"

"Weeding the yard."

"When did you weed the yard?"

"When we got home today."

"That's fine." She turned back to Kenny. "Sounds like Gabe has a lot of confidence in you."

"Maybe too much," Kenny grumbled.

"Mom?" Brent again.

"What?"

"Can I go ahead and get the money?"

"Sure." Hannah bent to pick up the basketball shorts Kenny had obviously dropped on the floor just prior to climbing into bed. "Sly had to get stitches last night, you know," she said, folding the shorts.

"I heard."

She arched an eyebrow at him. "His mother expects me to pay the doctor bill."

"I'll pay it," he said. "Or work the money off somehow."

"That's exactly what I was going to suggest." She held up the folded shorts. "Clean or dirty?"

"Clean."

Moving across the room, she put them in a drawer. "Well, I'm sure you're tired. I'll let you—"

She didn't finish because Brent startled them both by suddenly barging into the room and flipping on the light.

Hannah opened her mouth to tell him to turn it off. He'd just blinded her and Kenny. But then she felt her stomach drop to her knees. She wasn't so blind that she couldn't see Brent had a hold of Gabe's T-shirt.

"What's this?" he asked, holding it up in apparent confusion.

For a moment, Hannah's mind raced. How was she going to explain having a man's shirt in her purse? Especially Gabe's? "A...T-shirt."

"Whose is it?" Kenny asked his brother.

"How should I know? I just pulled it out of Mom's purse."

"I found it," Hannah said because she couldn't come up with anything more plausible.

Kenny sat up to get a better look. "Where?"

On top of Gabe's hamper... "On my drive."

"You found a shirt while you were driving?" Kenny's expression reflected his confusion. "Was it lying on the side of the road or something?"

Or something... Hannah quickly crossed the room and snatched the shirt away. "It's just a shirt I found, nothing to worry about. Time for bed, you two."

"But I didn't get my money," Brent complained.

"I'll get it for you." Hannah shooed her youngest from the room and closed the door behind her—before Kenny could recognize the shirt as one Gabe might have worn to practice.

WHEN THE HOUSE FELL QUIET, Hannah headed to the kitchen for a glass of wine, where she gazed at Gabe's Hawaii T-shirt. If not for that piece of proof, she might have convinced herself that today hadn't been real—that it had been just another one of her Gabe Holbrook fantasies.

The memory of Gabe pulling her into his lap and kissing her deeply caused excitement to sweep through her again. She was *so* infatuated with him....

The phone rang. Straightening, she glanced at the clock. It was nearly midnight on a Saturday, which meant Russ was probably calling her from the Honky Tonk. Sometimes when he got drunk, he called to cuss her out for leaving him. Other times, he cried and begged her to come back to him.

Tonight she wasn't sure she could deal with either extreme, especially because he was sure to have something to say about Gabe dropping by. But if she didn't answer, he might drive over. Then they'd fight, possibly wake the boys and disturb the neighbors.... She definitely didn't want that.

"Hello?"

"Did I wake you?"

It was Gabe. Relief, surprise and awareness assaulted Hannah all at once. "No, I'm not in bed yet."

He said nothing.

Wetting her lips, she held the phone to her ear with her shoulder and instinctively tightened the drawstring on her pajama pants. "But Kenny's asleep, if you called to talk to him."

He chuckled softly. "No, I've got the right person."

More silence.

"Gabe?"

"What?"

"Are you going to tell me why you called?"

"I need someone to come over and help me eat all these strawberries."

Hannah pressed his T-shirt to her face as she imagined his strong arms going around her....

"Hannah?"

She lifted her head. "Sounds like an emergency."

"It is. Can you come tonight?"

"Tonight?"

"They go bad fast."

She could hear the teasing in his voice and laughed. "Not *that* fast."

"Ask Marge over at Finley's if you don't believe me."

"Finley's is closed."

He sighed, no doubt for her benefit. "I guess you'll just have to trust me, then."

She squeezed her eyes shut, fighting the urge to drop the phone, scoop up her keys and dash off to his place. It had been three hours since she'd been with him and already she was dying to touch him again. This wasn't good.... "I—I can't come over."

"Why not?" he said.

"I already told you I won't be coming back."

"Fortunately, you didn't mean it."

She shook her head at his response. "How do you know?"

"I was there, too, remember? I heard how you said my name when I slipped my—"

"Gabe!"

Another soft laugh. "Okay," he said. "Call me when you're ready."

A second later, the dial tone hummed in Hannah's ear. He'd hung up—but not before making a significant dent in her defenses. Hannah didn't know whether to be relieved that she'd held tough or disappointed. She supposed she felt a little of both. She also suspected Gabe had only been testing her resistance, letting her know his door was still open so the temptation could continue to work on her long after he hung up.

He was so arrogant, she thought. But she was relieved to find all his former confidence hadn't really deserted him. He was regaining his balance....

She smiled as she finished her wine. Ever since the accident, she'd been praying for Gabe to get back on his feet, figuratively if not literally. She always hoped her prayers would be answered. But she never imagined she'd have a front-row seat to his recovery.

She was just gathering his shirt when the doorbell sounded.

"Not now," she muttered.

Dropping Gabe's shirt on the table, she padded through the living room and checked the peephole to find Russ on her porch. Summoning patience, she opened the door. "Did you forget something, Russ?"

He ignored the question and stabbed a finger at the chair Gabe had made. "What the hell's up with that?"

"What?"

"You know what! And where did those damn flowers come from?"

Flowers? Hannah leaned outside to see a small, potted hydrangea bush on the other side of her door. "I don't know," she said. But, although she hadn't seen Gabe bring them, she knew they'd come from him. She'd seen a pot of flowers like them at his house, on the counter.

"They have to be from Gabe, right? Why is he bringing you gifts?" Russ asked.

"They're not gifts. I mean, the chair's not a gift. I—I don't know about the flowers."

"They're from him. I know they are."

"Russ, do me a favor and go home, okay?" she said.

"We might be divorced, Hannah, but you're still the mother of my children. I have a right to know what's going on."

"No, you don't. You have no right to come knocking on my door in the middle of the night."

He scowled and shifted on his feet. "Your lights were on already. Don't pretend I'm making trouble."

"The lights were about to go off. I'm tired, and you *are* making trouble. Now, if you'll excuse me…"

He put a hand on the door to stop her from closing it. "You're not seeing him, are you, Hannah? I mean, not Gabe. Anyone but Gabe, okay? Will you promise me that much?"

Hannah knew Russ would have a problem with her seeing *anyone*. He was as possessive now as he'd been six years ago. "I won't promise you anything."

"He might be rich and famous, but he's crippled. You don't want to take care of a cripple for the rest of your life, do you?"

"Gabe doesn't need anyone to take care of him. He can take care of himself," she said.

"So you *are* seeing him?"

"No…I…leave me alone, Russ. Just go."

"You can't walk out on me for a damn cripple, Hannah!"

"I walked out on you for other reasons." She tried to close the door, but he was pushing the opposite way, forcing his way in. "Russ, get out," she said between gritted teeth. "Before you wake the boys."

"If you want to see someone, see me. I'm the one you should be with. I've changed. Give me another chance."

She pushed harder, but it didn't help. He was too strong. "I don't want to be with you, Russ. Ever. Do you understand?"

"You'd rather be with Gabe?"

She finally released the door, letting it swing wide. "What do you think?"

He stopped trying to get in and blanched so white Hannah couldn't help reaching out to comfort him. "Russ, I'm not trying to be unkind but you—"

She didn't get to finish because he belted her across the face.

The blow came with such force that she staggered back several feet and almost lost her footing.

Grabbing the door for support, she gaped up at him, tasting blood where her teeth had cut her lip, and he immediately crumpled.

"I'm sorry, Hannah. Oh God, I didn't mean to do that. You…you make me crazy. Sometimes I…I think I'll die if you don't come back to me." His hands clenched and unclenched. "This was your fault. Do you understand? I've never hit you before. I didn't mean to do it now."

Hannah raised her fingers to her stinging cheek. "Go away."

"Please, Hannah. Don't be angry. It…it was the back of my hand. I didn't use my fist. I—I didn't hit you that hard."

Whether he'd used the back of his hand or not, the blow had rattled her teeth. Tears filled her eyes, and her lip and cheek grew numb and swollen.

"Don't ever come here again, unless it's to pick up or drop off the boys," she said. "Or I swear I'll get a restraining order."

She shut the door, then locked it and leaned her forehead against the wood as tears rolled down her cheeks. Sometimes, she hated Russ so much she could hardly contain the emotion. Why had she ever gotten involved with him? Why had she ever succumbed to the pressure? If not for Kenny and Brent, she'd curse the day her mother had ever moved next door to the Prices'….

She listened, wondering if he'd bang on the door again, wanting to continue his apology. But what had happened must've shocked him as badly as it did her because he didn't even try. A few minutes later, she heard the Jeep start up and the engine noise dim as he drove away.

He's gone, she told herself, sagging against the door in relief. *He's gone.* But the pain from his visit wasn't.

Using the walls to help fight the dizziness, she cleaned her mouth and retrieved some ice. Then she carried Gabe's shirt into her room and curled up in bed, blocking out everything except the smell of Gabe on soft cotton.

THE NEXT MORNING, Hannah had a fat lip and bruised face to rival Kenny's. When she first got up, she stared disconsolately at herself in the mirror, wondering what to do about Russ. He'd never struck her before, and he'd seemed sincerely contrite the second after it happened. But she needed to document the incident in case he wouldn't leave her alone in the future. With a sigh, she decided to go to the police station later and file a police report.

Making her way through the quiet house, she checked on Brent to see that he was still sleeping, then headed outside to turn on the sprinklers. The sun was just beginning to rise, casting the world in a promising pink glow. She loved this time of morning—but today she wasn't quite sure what to think of anything. Her life had definitely taken an unexpected twist since she'd started seeing Gabe. Part of her wanted to embrace the change. The other part wanted to hang on to the relative safety of the life she'd built since the divorce. For one thing, Russ had never resorted to violence until Gabe came on the scene.

Hannah picked up the newspaper lying on her walkway, but instead of opening it, she sat in her new chair and stared at the flowers that had surprised her so much last night. Gabe must've brought them to the door after she'd said good-night to him—

"There you are." Kenny opened the screen door.

"You're up early," she mused.

"I couldn't sleep any longer." He stepped out to join her but froze the moment he got a good look at her face. "What happened to you?"

"I got into a fight with Sly's mom," she said.

"*What?*"

She attempted a chuckle, even though her split lip resisted a smile. "I'm kidding. I got up to go to the bathroom in the middle of the night and accidentally ran into the door." She didn't want Kenny to know what had happened with his father. Because of what Tuck had gone through when he was little, Kenny was particularly sensitive to domestic violence. And she didn't want to drag her sons through any more of her and Russ's problems.

"I guess now you know how I feel, huh?" he said.

She adopted a rueful expression, which at this point came naturally enough. "I guess."

"We'd better lay low. We don't look so good today."

"No kidding."

He sat on the porch railing, watching the sprinklers. "I can't believe school starts tomorrow."

She snuggled deeper into the big sweatshirt she'd pulled on over her pajamas. "Neither can I. It seems like only yesterday that I was sending you off to kindergarten."

The phone rang.

"Who'd be calling this early?" he asked.

Hannah doubted it was Gabe, but she hopped up, just in case. "I'll get it."

Slipping into the house, she jogged across the living room to the kitchen, where she snatched up the cordless phone. "Hello?"

"Hannah?"

It was Patti, but her voice sounded unusually harsh. "Hi, Patti. Is something wrong?"

"Is it true?" she demanded.

Hannah searched her mind, hoping to grasp what her ex-sister-in-law could be talking about. "Is *what* true?"

"Are you sleeping with Gabe Holbrook?"

CHAPTER SIXTEEN

HANNAH'S HEART POUNDED as she searched for an answer to Patti's frank question. How could her sister-in-law know? Especially so soon? She and Gabe had been together only *yesterday!*

"No," she said out of stubborn resistance. She didn't care if it was a lie. She resented the intrusion. Russ certainly had his nerve calling Patti after what he'd done last night. Fortunately, Hannah knew he didn't really have any proof, except that Gabe had visited with a pot of flowers.

"Gabe dropped by to talk to Kenny about the game on Friday. The flowers are a simple thank you for cooking for him," she explained. "They don't hold any special significance. Whatever else Russ told you—"

"I haven't talked to Russ," Patti interrupted. "Deborah Wheeler and I walk together every morning. She just said—"

Suddenly, Hannah knew that the car she'd almost hit coming out of Gabe's driveway yesterday belonged to Deborah. That was why Hannah had felt a spark of recognition even though she hadn't seen the driver's face.

Dropping her head in her hand, she rubbed her temples while Patti finished exactly as she expected "—she saw you at Gabe's cabin yesterday."

Hannah remembered what Shirley and the others had said about Deborah in the beauty shop and knew it had to be true. Why else would Deborah be skulking around Gabe's remote cabin? "I went to pick up my dishes."

"Hannah, she saw you in Gabe's backyard without a shirt."

Oh God... "She must be mistaken. That... She couldn't have—"

"She did."

The front door slammed and Kenny appeared. "Who is it?" he said curiously.

"Patti." Hannah kept her tone as light as possible, but her stomach had tightened into a hard ball.

"Is that Brent?" Patti asked.

"Kenny."

"Does he know?"

Recognizing the futility of trying to keep up the charade, Hannah closed her eyes and let her breath seep through her lips. "No."

"I take it you don't want him to know."

"Of course not." Clearing her throat, Hannah looked up at Kenny again. "Would you mind turning off the sprinklers for me?"

"You're done watering? Already?"

She wasn't, but she needed another moment alone, so she nodded.

"Okay," he said and left.

She turned her back to the rest of the house and lowered her voice, just in case Brent was starting to stir in his room down the hall. "Gabe and I are adults, Patti. What we do isn't anyone's business, least of all Deborah Wheeler's."

"I agree. What she did was nasty, horrible. But she saw him buy condoms yesterday, Hannah. He's famous and he's crippled and he's been out of circulation for three years. Of course a purchase like that would grab her attention."

"She didn't go out to his place because of mere curiosity, Patti. She went there because she has a crush on him."

"So?" Patti responded. "Most of the women in this town have fantasized about Gabe at some point. It's not Deborah I'm worried about. I don't want you to be hurt."

"You don't need to worry about *me*."

"Hannah, I know things have been…strained between us since the divorce. Because I care about you *and* my brother, I sometimes feel torn in two. I can't help wishing you could patch up your differences and be a family again."

Hannah ran her tongue over her swollen lip. "I can't, Patti. I don't love him." She could have added that she'd never loved him, that he'd hit her across the face just last night. But she swallowed the words. It wouldn't matter. Patti would find some way to excuse him.

"At least he's willing to love you, Hannah," she said. "At least he's willing to be a husband and a father."

"Some love," Hannah grumbled, but Patti didn't seem to hear her. She was too busy making her point.

"Gabe's not the type to settle down. He was aloof before the injury—now he's even worse. Besides, he could have almost anyone—despite the wheelchair."

"You're saying he would never settle for me." Patti's words hurt almost as much as her brother's blow.

"It's not you, Hannah. You're a wonderful woman, and you're very attractive. Almost any single man in this town would be happy to be with you—any regular guy, that is. But this is Gabe we're talking about. You're a thirty-seven-year-old divorcée with two children. And have you forgotten that you're the one who put him in that chair?"

"How could I ever forget that?"

"Exactly. Do you think, even if you got together with him, that it would last? Resentment would *have* to crop up at some point. What are the chances that you'd be able to hold on to him?"

Next to nil, Hannah thought. She doubted she could catch him in the first place. But that didn't stop her heart from wanting…

"Hannah?" Patti said when she didn't respond.

"I'm still here," she replied.

"I'm sorry to be so blunt, but I don't want to see you suffer. And I don't want Russ or Kenny and Brent to suffer."

"Right."

Kenny came back in and stood in the doorway, watching her curiously.

"I've got to go," Hannah said numbly.

"That's it?" Patti asked.

"What else can I say?"

There was a long silence. "I'll call you later."

Hannah wished she wouldn't. She didn't want to talk to Patti or Russ or even Violet. "Okay."

"What did Aunt Patti want?" Kenny asked as she hung up the phone.

Hannah studied the marks the fight had left on her son's young, handsome face. "She thinks I should get back with your father."

"Why?"

"So everyone can be happy again, I guess."

He frowned at her response.

"Don't you agree with her?" she asked. She knew in the past Kenny and Brent had both hoped she and Russ would reconcile and thought he'd probably tell her the same thing.

But Kenny surprised her. "No," he said softly. "You deserve to be happy, too."

WHEN GABE HEARD the bell, he flipped off the football tapes he'd been watching and followed a barking Lazarus to the door. It had to be Hannah. He hadn't heard from her all day.

But he should've checked the window. When he opened the door, he found a woman on his front porch, but it wasn't Hannah—it was his sister, Reenie.

"I need to talk to you," she announced without preamble.

Lazarus slipped around him to lick Reenie's fingers. "You couldn't have called?"

She didn't flinch at his sarcasm; Reenie didn't flinch easily. "Are you kidding? With what I have to say, you'd only hang up on me."

"Oh, boy. Now I know I really have something to look forward to."

"Nothing more than the hard truth."

She patted Lazarus, then brushed past him the second he gave her enough room and, not for the first time, Gabe decided that his sister reminded him of a Chihuahua. Only five foot two and *maybe* one hundred pounds, she was petite and attractive and younger than him by nearly a decade. But nothing intimidated her. Occasionally, he grudgingly admitted that she had a generous heart and enough drive to accomplish almost anything; more often he complained of her bossy nature and sharp tongue. She was determined to carry the world on her shoulders—and God help anyone who stood in her way.

Which was where Gabe came in. Besides Keith, her husband, he was one of the few people in her life who still offered her some resistance. He supposed it was because he was just as hard-headed as she was. Whatever the reason, he felt it was his duty to keep the force of his sister's personality from leveling everything and everyone in its path.

"Is there anything I can do to avoid this little confrontation?" he asked. He had too much on his mind right now, didn't want to argue with his little sister.

She arched her dark eyebrows, and he looked into blue eyes that were almost a mirror image of his own. "No, but I'm willing to start with the positive."

"Which is…"

"I'm glad to hear you're finally coming to your senses."

This certainly wasn't what Gabe had expected to hear. "About—"

"Letting go of the past and embracing the future."

"What are you talking about?"

"Hannah Price, of course. I think it's wonderful that you're seeing her."

He thought of Hannah's reluctance to draw public attention. "I'm not sure I'd call it that," he said.

"You'd better be calling it that," she snapped indignantly. "You slept with her yesterday, didn't you?"

Gabe sat up taller. "Whoa, wait a second. Where are you getting your information?"

"It's all over town. When Shirley Erman rang me up at the Gas-N-Go this morning, she told me Deborah Wheeler told her that Hannah was half-naked in your yard yesterday afternoon."

Gabe's muscles bunched as anger flooded through him. "How would Deborah Wheeler know that?"

Lazarus was wagging his tail and watching her expectantly, hoping for another crumb of attention. "I called her to ask the same thing," she said, absently petting him again.

"And she said…"

"She just happened to be in the area."

He grimaced. "God, she's even worse than I thought."

"She's not the only one who's spreading rumors. Marge over at Finley's said you bought champagne, chocolate-covered strawberries and flowers. She added, with a wink, that you also bought condoms and told her you were planning to use the whole box this weekend. With all of that, did you think you were keeping your relationship with Hannah a secret?"

He hadn't been planning to sleep with Hannah when he'd bought the damn condoms! But now he could see that his subconscious had been working against him all along. "Shit," he said, shoving a hand through his hair.

"So, do you think this thing between you and Hannah might be serious?" Reenie asked.

Serious? Gabe had no clue. His attraction to Kenny's mother had taken him by surprise, and now she was running scared, and having the whole town talking about them wasn't going to help. Surely word would get back to her boys, which he knew she didn't want…. "If this is the positive side to your visit, what's the negative?" he asked to avoid his sister's question.

"I want to talk about Dad."

"Not now," Gabe said.

"Gabe, this thing between the two of you has gone on long enough."

"It's none of your business, Reenie."

"It *is* my business. He's my father. You're my brother. I love you both, and I'm tired of having this division in the family."

"Maybe Dad should've thought about how it might divide the family before—"

"He had the affair twenty-four years ago, Gabe. That's a long time. Can't you cut him a little slack?"

"Cut him some *slack?* We have a half sister because of him!"

"And she's a wonderful person. I like her. I think you would, too, if only you'd give her a chance."

He didn't know what to say. He *wanted* to let go of the past. But whenever he pictured his father with Lucky's mother, that terrible sense of betrayal welled up inside him and nearly choked him.

"Maybe there are things you're not taking into consideration, Gabe," she said when he didn't reply.

"Like what?"

"Like the fact that marriage isn't always easy, even when both parties are basically good people."

Something about the tone of her voice told Gabe she was talking about more than their parents. "What do you mean?"

She knelt in front of Lazarus and scratched him as if she really didn't want to look Gabe in the eye. "Exactly what I said."

"No, there's more. You're not having trouble with Keith, are you?"

"Of course not," she said, but she spoke too quickly to convince him.

"Something's going on. I know you too well to buy into that stiff-upper-lip thing, Reenie."

"It's nothing," she said, straightening. "Keith's a good father."

"And he's a good husband, right?"

"I love him. I love him more than anything in the world."

"But…"

She stared down at the keys she held in one hand. "He's changing."

Her expression grew so troubled Gabe couldn't feel any animosity toward her at all. Despite the discord that had existed between them for the past couple of years, she was still his little sister and he'd do anything to protect her. "How?"

"He's…preoccupied or…or something."

"Since when?"

"I don't know. It's happened gradually, I guess."

"Having him gone almost a week out of every month can't help."

"He's gone more than that. Softscape decided that three weeks of telecommuting in one month was too much. For the past year, he's been gone half the time."

Gabe had been so involved in recuperating that he hadn't paid any attention. "It's not good for you to be apart so much."

She chuckled humorlessly. "No kidding. I'm beginning to feel like a…a divorcée or a widow. But…never mind." She acknowledged Lazarus again when he gave a short whine. "None of this has anything to do with you."

Gabe knew she was afraid she was indulging in self-pity, which is something she'd accused him of doing often enough. But he couldn't hold what she'd said in the past against her. "Why not have him quit his job? Do something else?"

"I've asked him to."

"What does he say?"

"He says okay but never gives notice. It's always going to happen *next* week or *next* month or *next* year."

"Why don't you push the issue?"

"Because I'm not sure he'll be able to find something better around here. There aren't many options for a computer programmer in such a small town."

"Have you thought about moving to L.A. to be with him?" Gabe asked.

"I've mentioned it, but he won't even entertain the idea. He says he doesn't want to be responsible for taking me and the kids away from our friends and family."

"Well, if it's about money, Reenie—"

She held up her hand. "Don't even offer, Gabe. We won't let you support us. We have too much self-respect for that." Squaring her shoulders, she slipped back into her tougher self. "I'm just saying that marriage can be difficult and…and maybe you should think about that and let bygones be bygones with Dad. We don't know what he was going through at the time he had the affair. At least he was always there for us. I've never doubted his love for us. Have you?"

Gabe's problem with his father wasn't about love; it was about hypocrisy. But maybe Reenie was right. Gabe had never been married, didn't know how difficult it could be. Look at Reenie. His sister usually had an answer to everything, and a clear path before her, but even she seemed a little lost right now.

"I'll try," he said.

"Will you come to dinner next Sunday? I know it'd mean a lot to him. He hardly said a word when I was there today. He just ate quietly and kept looking at your empty chair."

Gabe gazed at his dog, who sat watching them both, tail thumping the floor. Dinner at his folks' house. Coaching for the high school. Sleeping with Hannah. His life was getting far too complicated. "I'll think about it."

This response must've pleased her because she put a hand on his arm. For a moment, he thought she was going to hug him and actually hoped she would. She seemed so small, even defenseless for a change.

But she didn't. Instead, she gave him a brief smile and slipped out.

Gabe whistled for Lazarus not to follow her, then watched from the porch as she walked to her car. "Call me if you need anything," he hollered. "I don't like the idea of you and the kids being alone days on end."

She tossed him a smile. "I'm okay. Just come to dinner next Sunday. That's all I ask." She got in the car and rolled down her window. "You can bring Hannah, if you want."

"Thanks," he said dryly, but he was fairly certain Hannah wouldn't want to give folks anything more to talk about. *I don't plan on introducing another man into my family life...*

As his sister drove away, the phone rang, jerking him away from his thoughts. He wondered if it might be Hannah, wanting to know why he'd bought condoms at Finley's. And why he'd then announced to the woman with the biggest mouth in town that he planned to use the whole box.

He should've said no to Mike when his best friend appeared that day, pleading for Gabe to take over the Spartans. This all stemmed from that one small concession....

"Come on, boy," he said to Lazarus and went in to answer the phone. But he didn't immediately recognize the caller.

"Hello, Gabe. How the hell are ya?"

"Fine," he replied. "Who's this?"

"Phil Hunt, ESPN."

The producer of *NFL Sunday Countdown*. Gabe had heard from him before. He normally cut Phil off right away, but today he was glad for the diversion. "What's going on, Phil?"

"I'll tell you what's going on. We need a color commentator, and we need one badly."

"I thought you already found someone."

"Have you watched the show lately, Gabe?"

"No." He typically avoided it. Hearing the hosts predict which team would win which game and listening to them discuss the players, all of whom, except for the rookies, had been Gabe's peers, made him miss football like nothing else.

"Why not?"

Unless he wanted to drive himself crazy, a man on a diet didn't hang out at a bakery. "I've been busy."

"Well, let's just say that Norm Bolitzer has yet to overcome his stage fright. He was a great runningback—don't get me wrong. But he's too stiff as a color man. He's not letting his personality come through, if you know what I mean."

"Does *he* know he's not working out?"

"Fortunately, he came to us before we had to go to him. He's like you. He doesn't need the money. When he realized he wasn't having fun, he didn't want to do it anymore."

"What makes you think I'd be any better?"

"Are you kidding? We've had you on the show enough to know. You think fast and speak well in front of people. That's what it takes."

"Phil—"

"Wait a minute, Gabe. At least hear me out. This is an offer even you can't refuse."

Gabe opened his mouth to say there wasn't enough money in the world. But Phil's call had come at an interesting time—right when he was beginning to realize that he couldn't put his life on hold any longer. He had to start living again, either in Dundee or somewhere else. And in Dundee, there was no "start slow, gather speed" option. There was Blaine and the trouble he was causing with the team. Hannah and the fact that he'd managed to land her exactly where she didn't want to be—in the thick of town gossip. Reenie and the strain between her and Keith, and finally, his relationship with his father. He couldn't stall Reenie indefinitely. If he stayed, he'd have to reconcile with his father. It wouldn't be more than a few more weeks before he'd be sitting at Sunday dinner.

He wasn't ready, he decided. He'd only just begun to accept the fact that he'd never walk again, that the short window of opportunity for a full recovery had already disappeared. Maybe New York would provide him with a transition period—a year or two to ease into his new reality.

"Gabe? Are you still there?" Phil asked when he finally stopped for breath. He'd been reeling off details of a compensation package, but Gabe hadn't been listening carefully.

"I'm here," he said.

"Impressive, huh? What do you say? Will you come to New York for the season?"

New York. The Big Apple. It was so different from Dundee. But if he couldn't gain the anonymity he craved at home, he might as well go public in a big way, see if he could develop a career that might be half as fulfilling as the one he'd lost. He'd be stupid not to check it out, wouldn't he?

"I'll give it a try," he heard himself say.

"What? You'll do it?" The squeak in Phil Hunt's voice gave away the fact that he hadn't really expected to meet with success.

"Why not?" Gabe said.

"When can you come?"

Gabe glanced over at Lazarus. The dog had gone to lie down on his favorite rug in front of the fireplace. When he realized he had Gabe's attention, he cocked his head, and his expression seemed to say, "No way. Don't go."

But Lazarus was just a dog. Maybe a dog wouldn't like the big city as well as the mountains, but Gabe had to find himself again, figure out where he really belonged now that football was no longer an option. "When would you like me?" he said into the phone.

"Yesterday."

Gabe thought of the game on Friday. "I can't fly out until Saturday."

"That'll work. We'll make it work. I'll have my secretary schedule your flight and get back to you."

"And I'll probably have to be here during the week for awhile, until I can find someone to take over the high school team I'm coaching." Gabe hated to leave the Spartans, but he figured it was better to do it now, before the season progressed any further.

"Don't you worry about that. We'll replace you with the best coach Dundee has ever seen. We'll fly him there and pay him enough that he won't mind staying through the season. Everyone will be happy."

Even with their connections and money, Gabe doubted ESPN could find a better coach than Mike's father had been. But they could certainly come up with someone who had a hell of a lot more experience than Gabe did, which would solve everything.

"I'd want to meet him before he officially takes over."

"Done."

"Fine," Gabe said and hung up. Soon the Deborah Wheelers and the Melvin Blaines of Dundee would be too far away to have the slightest impact on his life, he told himself. He'd be raking in millions once again. He'd have a high-profile job that would put his mug on TV and maybe even on the cover of a few magazines. Certainly that was a semblance of what he'd lost, wasn't it?

No, a voice in his head whispered. He could deal with Melvin Blaine and Deborah Wheeler. Compared to the weightier issues he faced, they were minor irritants. And the money and fame had never meant much to him. It was the accomplishment. It was about being *the best.*

But he was broken now. He didn't know what his life was about, what *did* matter to him. So he blocked out the nagging feeling that he was making a mistake. It was time to force a change.

CHAPTER SEVENTEEN

THE NEXT FEW DAYS DRAGGED by like the slow drip of a faucet, maddeningly repetitive yet inexorable. Because of the gossip and the constant threat of Kenny or Brent overhearing it, Hannah felt a mounting tension. But she went about her business, ignoring the murmuring that seemed to accompany her wherever she went. She heard Marge whisper about her when she went to Finley's Grocery to pick up some milk—*Can you believe Deborah saw...* Marge's voice lowered at that point, but Hannah knew she was saying that Deborah had seen her half-naked—or fully naked as the story was now going—in Gabe's yard.

Shirley's grin when Hannah stopped to buy gas indicated she'd heard the news, too. Even Lula and Evelyn Bell, who suddenly appeared at her door to pick up the pictures they'd let languish in her studio for three weeks, made a reference to Gabe. They said they were willing to bet a hundred bucks that, crippled or not, he was better in bed than their own husbands, then giggled behind their hands when Hannah refused to comment.

Although the details were becoming exaggerated, Hannah figured the furor would die down much sooner if she didn't respond. She definitely wanted life to return to normal before Russ had anything more to say about Gabe, or before her boys caught on to what was happening around them. Fortunately, Kenny seemed preoccupied with his own life.

Four days later, she thought there might still be a chance the uproar would simply fade away, like the bruise on her face, which was turning yellow. But she was beginning to fear that the desire to be with Gabe again would *never* disappear. He'd called her Sunday night to tell her what she already knew, that their little secret was no longer a secret, but they hadn't talked long. The conversation had been stilted, full of pauses that indicated too many things were being left unsaid. They'd finished with a quick agreement to suspend their dinner arrangement—even though Gabe's chair already sat on her porch, marking her house like a giant scarlet letter.

By Thursday Hannah felt as if she'd been walking a tightrope all week. Fortunately, as far as she knew, she still had several things in her favor. Her boys continued to be oblivious to the subtle changes around them. Owing, no doubt, to the fact that it had never happened before, everyone seemed to accept without question her "I ran into the door" explanation for her bruised lip and face. She'd filed a police report, but she hadn't pressed charges. Guilt for what Russ had done seemed to be working well enough to keep him away. And she'd managed, despite unrelenting temptation, not to call Gabe.

So far her luck seemed to be holding. But she couldn't imagine that her errand this morning would help matters. The guy who was in charge of the yearbook had called her twice this week, asking for the photographs she was supposed to have delivered last Monday. She had to finish them up right away, which meant she had to visit Gabe's cabin and photograph the man she undressed in her mind every time she closed her eyes.

"Should be fun," she muttered sarcastically, wondering how her innocent, well-meaning plan to get Gabe back into circulation could have dragged her into such a tailspin.

"Did you say something, Mom?"

Hannah hadn't realized that Kenny was within hearing distance. "No, nothing important," she said, packing up her camera bag.

He gathered his backpack from the kitchen table. She was

planning to drop both boys off at school on her way. "Do we have to go to Dad's this weekend?" he asked.

"You don't want to?"

A quick shake of his head answered that question.

"I haven't heard from your father in a few days, but…I'll call him after school and find out what his plans are."

"Okay."

Hannah hollered for Brent to hurry, then put the bag with her camera and film over her shoulder and held the front open.

"You look nice," Kenny said as he passed her.

She'd dressed up in a skirt and blouse. "Thanks."

"You're going out on location today?"

Brent finally came running down the hall. Obviously, he'd attempted to wet his hair down, but he hadn't bothered with a comb. Hannah did her best to improve the situation with her fingers but didn't have time to do much more.

"I have to finish taking the football pictures," she told Kenny as she locked the door.

"Didn't you already finish?"

Her heels clicked on the cement as she hurried down the walkway. "Not with Coach Holbrook. I'm driving out to his cabin this morning."

Brent shot her a grin, which she caught out of the corner of her eye just before she opened the door. "What?"

"Are you gonna kiss him, Mommy?" he asked.

Hannah's heart jumped into her throat as Kenny's gaze flew first to her, then to his brother. "What are you talking about, dweeb?" he said.

Refusing to be intimidated, Brent glared up at him. "Coach Holbrook is Mommy's boyfriend."

"No, he's not," Kenny said, but he didn't sound very certain and immediately looked to her for confirmation.

Hannah had frozen at Brent's question. "Who told you that, Brent?"

"I heard my teacher talking to Lindsay's mom about it. She said you were the luckiest woman in the world to be with Gabe Holbrook."

Before Hannah could respond, Kenny spoke up. "You're not seeing Coach Holbrook, are you, Mom?"

Hannah didn't know what to say. She'd hoped her boys would remain oblivious, but now that they'd clued in, she wanted to be as honest with them as possible. "I like him," she admitted. "I like him a lot."

Kenny's expression grew guarded. "That T-shirt the other night…"

Panic crawled a little higher in Hannah's throat. "Is his," she admitted. He—" here she decided to fudge "—he loaned it to me so I wouldn't get my blouse dirty while we played with Lazarus in his backyard."

Letting go of the car door he hadn't opened yet, Kenny hiked his backpack a little higher. "But you're not…a *couple* or anything."

"No. I…we went out Friday night and spent the afternoon together on Saturday, that's all."

Kenny turned to glance at the porch. "*That's* why he brought that chair and those flowers. He likes you, too."

"I don't think he likes me that much," Hannah said, putting her bag in the car.

For a moment, Kenny seemed deep in thought. "So, if he thought I was connected to something bad—"

"What are you talking about?" she asked.

"I'm saying it probably wouldn't be good for you if Coach decided he didn't like me."

They were going to be late, but she didn't want to rush this. "There's no reason he wouldn't like you. You're not involved in anything you shouldn't be, are you?"

"No, but—"

"Then don't worry. Gabe and I are only friends. I'm not really his type."

The frown didn't completely disappear from Kenny's face but, checking his watch, he got in. "Why not?"

Hannah laughed self-consciously as she slid behind the wheel. "He's sort of a confirmed bachelor. And, as one of the greatest quarterbacks who ever lived, he's out of my league, wouldn't you say?" She could have added that the accident would most likely become an issue at some point. As early as their first argument, accusations over what she'd done to him would surely come up. But she decided to keep it simple.

Kenny looked directly at her. "*No one's* out of your league, Mom."

Touched by the conviction in his voice, Hannah reached across the seat to squeeze his arm. "Thanks, honey."

"If you marry him, maybe he'll share Lazarus with me!" Brent said, piping up from the back seat.

Hannah smiled as she started the engine. Somehow she'd thought it'd be difficult for her children to imagine their mother with a man other than their father, but Brent certainly didn't seem to object to the idea of her being with Gabe. Kenny was another story. She couldn't tell what he was thinking. He seemed sort of...brooding.

"I told you, Coach Holbrook and I are only friends," she said, backing into the street. "So don't make any plans to take over his dog."

"I'll share my room with Lazarus," Brent went on, as if she hadn't spoken. "He can even *sleep* with me. It'll be too crowded in your room, what with Coach Holbrook and his wheelchair and all of his clothes in there." He rubbed his hands in excitement. "Just wait till I tell the kids at school that I'm going to have Coach Holbrook's dog!"

Kenny turned in his seat. "Don't mention Mom and Coach Holbrook to anyone."

"Why not?"

"You have to give them some time to work things out."

"I don't think an eternity would help," Hannah said flippantly as they left their little neighborhood. "There's nothing to work out."

Kenny turned to look at her. "Don't underestimate Coach Holbrook, Mom. He's smart, like Tuck. He'll know what you're worth," he said, but he wasn't smiling and she still couldn't guess at his thoughts.

GABE HAD BEEN lifting weights. Hannah could see that as soon as he opened the door. He wore fingerless gloves, a pair of gym shorts and a sleeveless T-shirt. Sweat glistened on his smooth skin and, as usual, Lazarus was right beside him.

She supposed she should've called to give him some warning that she was coming. She wasn't sure exactly why she hadn't. Maybe she was afraid he'd act as if he didn't want to see her after all the gossip.

"Sorry to bother you," she said. "But James Deerborn—"

His eyebrows lifted in surprise. "Who?"

She took a deep breath because her heart was hammering so hard she could hardly speak above it. "The yearbook guy. He's been bugging me to finish up the pictures I was supposed to give him last week, so…I was hoping I could take that photograph we talked about the other day." The day she'd brought Ashleigh to his house. The day he'd insisted she join the party on Saturday and everything between them had changed….

Gabe studied her for several seconds but didn't move back or invite her in. "What happened to your cheek?"

"Oh." She laughed, hoping he wouldn't press. "I ran into the door in the middle of the night. It was dark," she added quickly.

He didn't smile in return. "When?"

"Sunday."

"After you left here."

She nodded.

"Let me look at it." He motioned for her to lean closer.

After a moment's hesitation, Hannah bent down so that they

were at eye level. Lazarus tried to lick her face, but Gabe nudged him away and held her chin firmly as he examined her injury. Meanwhile, she could see the long sweep of his dark lashes, the soft lips that had grazed her skin in so many places....

"It's almost gone," she said, pulling back before the longing could grow any worse.

He seemed oblivious to the instant arousal flooding her. "You want to tell me again how you got it?"

What did he mean? She just had! "It was stupid, really. I—"

"Didn't walk into a door," he finished for her.

She wasn't sure how to respond. No one else had challenged her story. "Well..."

"Well?" he repeated.

She swallowed hard and knelt to pet Lazarus. "I need to take your picture, Gabe."

"Was it Russ?" he asked.

"It doesn't matter," she said. "It's not going to happen again."

The line of his jaw hardened. "Why didn't you tell me?"

"Because I have the situation under control."

"Do the boys know?"

When she stood, Lazarus whined as though disappointed to lose her attention. "Of course not. No one knows. It wouldn't matter anyway. I could announce it from the rooftops right now and no one would even notice. The only thing anyone seems to care about is the fact that we slept together last weekend."

At her reference to what had happened between them, his gaze swept over her, letting her know that the arousal she'd experienced wasn't as one-sided as she'd thought. Still, he wasn't willing to let the subject go. "Is that why he hit you? Because he found out about us?"

It hadn't taken even that much. The flowers had done it. But she didn't want to spell out the details. "He got jealous, that's all."

"I think he and I need to have a talk."

"It's fine, Gabe. I filed a police report."

"Good. So you're going to press charges?"

"No. At this point, taking it that far would only succeed in making the boys and everyone else feel sorry for him. I can already hear what he'd say. *I barely hit her. It only happened once. She threw Gabe in my face.* I only wanted to document the incident in case I need to go back to court someday."

"You're considering filing for full custody of the boys?"

"I've tried that several times already, but it never works. Russ's family always marches into court and makes it sound as though I'm uptight and worried about nothing. It's frustrating for me, and all the anxiety and fighting only makes life more difficult for the boys."

"Having this on record should help."

"Russ took one impulsive swipe. Because he's never done it before, the court might decide I provoked him. Bottom line, I doubt it'll be enough. But I'm ready, just in case it happens again. One isolated incident he might be able to explain away; two, he wouldn't."

Suddenly Lazarus barked and tore off in pursuit of some small furry animal. Hannah caught only a brief glimpse of it as it scampered into the trees, but she thought it might be a skunk.

When Gabe whistled, the dog immediately halted, but he swung his head between his target and his master as though he was still tempted—until Gabe added a sharp command to the whistle. Then Lazarus reluctantly returned. "He could hurt you a lot worse next time," Gabe said, looking back at her.

"I honestly don't think there'll be a next time," she said. "He seemed pretty upset by what he did."

Gabe rubbed his chin for several seconds, then finally rolled back. "Want to come in?"

She nodded and stepped past him. Lazarus followed her inside and cocked his head curiously as she started retrieving the camera from her bag.

"You're not going to take a picture of me like this, are you?" Gabe asked.

"Why not?"

"Because I need to shower first."

"Oh, right." To her, he looked good just the way he was. "You want me to wait here?"

"Is it my choice?" he asked.

Too late, Hannah realized how he'd interpreted her question. Their gazes met and held, and she knew things between them could never be the way they used to be. She knew too much. She knew the salty taste of his skin, the woodsy scent of his body, the gentle play of his hands when he touched her in places only Russ had touched her before. She even knew the intimate sounds he made when he abandoned all restraint and drew her as close to him as a woman could get....

"Hannah?" he prompted when she didn't respond right away.

She knew she should still be fighting the good fight, for self-preservation if nothing else. She was going to be destroyed when he finally broke things off with her. But her boys didn't seem to object to her seeing Gabe, and the entire town was already buzzing with the news. She had nothing else to cling to. Her attraction to him seemed bigger than she was, almost beyond her control. In any case, deep down, she knew it was no use fighting—she'd already lost the battle.

Setting her camera aside, she knelt between Gabe's legs, lifted his shirt and pressed her lips to his warm, flat stomach.

Gently pushing Lazarus away, Gabe took hold of her upper arms and lifted her enough that he could reach her mouth. Then he kissed her as though she'd break if he pressed too hard, coaxing her lips open and her tongue into a rapid response until they were kissing as hungrily and breathlessly as last Sunday.

"There you are," he breathed, rubbing his thumb over her wet bottom lip. "Welcome back."

GABE KNEW he should've told Hannah that his days in Dundee were numbered. He'd meant to. But their lovemaking had progressed too fast and become too powerful to think of anything else. They'd started in the shower before moving to the bed. The past hour had been a heady experience, almost better than before, because of the relief he felt at having her with him again, responding so readily, so eagerly.

He supposed he could tell her about New York now that she was lying, completely spent, across him. He had to do it sometime. But Lazarus had finally quit whining at the door, and he didn't want to break the contented silence.

Unfortunately, the phone intruded.

When he didn't move, Hannah lifted her head to look at him. "Aren't you going to answer it?"

He gave her a challenging grin. "Why don't you?"

Her eyes darted to the phone, and he knew she had to be thinking of the big stir they'd already caused. Obviously, if she answered his phone, they'd be making a statement. "You don't think I'll do it," she said.

"I think you should. People lose their power if we don't care about their opinion. If they say we're sleeping together, we say, 'Damn right, as often as possible.' Where can they go after a response like that?"

It was bold, she had to give him that. But Gabe had always been larger than life. "True," she mused and returned his smile as she reached for the handset. "Hello?"

Gabe could tell she'd tried to clear the sleep from her voice, but he thought the person on the other end would have to be deaf not to hear the huskiness in it.

"No, it's Hannah." She made a face to indicate she didn't like whoever it was, which piqued Gabe's curiosity. "What did you say? Yes, he's here. Just a minute."

"Deborah Wheeler wants to talk to you." She handed him the phone, then licked his nipples to distract him when he tried to answer.

Laughing, he hooked his arm around her neck and pulled her

down on top of him so she couldn't torture him anymore, reveling in the feel of her breasts as they pressed up against him. He should have gotten to know Hannah much sooner, he decided. "Hello?"

Deborah didn't answer for a moment.

"Hello?" he said again. He was about to hang up when she finally spoke.

"If you can pull yourself away from your new lover for a few seconds, I've got something to tell you."

"I'm not sure I want to hear it," he said frankly.

"I'm pretty sure you do."

He frowned as he ran his fingers through Hannah's silky hair. "What?"

She hesitated, but when she spoke again the tone of her voice had changed. "Never mind," she said briskly and hung up.

"What did she want?" Hannah asked in surprise.

Gabe stared at the receiver for a few seconds, then slid over to return it to its base. "I don't know. She never said."

"I guess she wasn't too happy to find me here."

"Evidently."

"She's a pretty devoted admirer."

He grimaced. "Are you kidding? She hates my guts."

"Only because she can't have you."

He didn't want to talk about Deborah. "You hungry?" he asked, rolling her onto her back and leaning over her to nuzzle her neck.

"A little. What've you got?"

"Champagne and sandwiches."

She grinned as he rubbed his nose against hers, butterfly fashion. "Nice combination."

"I'm thinking if I can get you drunk, I might be able to take advantage of you again."

"Yeah, I put up such a good fight last time," she said sarcastically.

He smoothed the hair off her face. "Maybe not, but you didn't come here planning to sleep with me. And you didn't call me all week," he added sulkily.

"I told you I wasn't going to."

"You knew I wanted you to come back."

"I was still trying to save myself."

"What's that supposed to mean?"

"Nothing."

He kissed the tip of her nose. "Good thing you needed that picture, or I might have had to stoop to drastic measures to get you out here."

"Such as…"

"Such as offering you another piece of furniture."

"I like your furniture."

"I know."

"I like you, too," she said. "A lot."

He could tell by her expression that the words had slipped out, that she wasn't sure whether she should've made the admission. "But as far as bribes go, your furniture will always work," she added quickly.

A fissure of guilt made Gabe uncomfortable enough that he started moving away from her, so he could get dressed. "I'll give you your choice of it all before I leave for New York, okay?"

"Leave for New York?" she echoed, leaning up on her elbows. He'd thought he might be uncomfortable around a woman, especially in such an intimate situation, having to maneuver the way he did. But he saw nothing in Hannah's face that led him to believe his handicap bothered her.

"I have to fly out on Saturday," he said.

She sat up, but he felt the sudden strain between them when she pulled the sheet up to cover herself. "What for?"

"A job offer."

"Oh." She sucked her bottom lip between her teeth as she absorbed this news, then, "Is it a good one?"

"Most people would think so."

"What is it?"

He felt reluctant to tell her. "ESPN wants me to host their *NFL Sunday Countdown.*"

"What?" Her jaw dropped before she could recover and clamp her mouth closed. Then, "That's *huge,* Gabe. How…how exciting for you."

The false cheer in her voice told him she was putting a lot of effort into acting pleased.

"So will you be moving to New York for good?" she asked.

Lazarus started whining again at the door.

"Not for good," he said. "Just for a year or so."

She slipped out of bed and began pulling on her clothes. "A year or so," she echoed.

"I'll go make some sandwiches," he said.

"Actually, that's okay. I've got to leave."

He scowled, cursing his conscience for making him speak up when he did. "What, do you have something against eating with me?"

She kept her focus elsewhere, mostly on her clothes. "No, of course not. I just, I need to take your picture and get it back to Mr. Deerborn for the yearbook. And I have some appointments this afternoon."

"Russ pays you child support, doesn't he?" he asked. He didn't care if the question came out of nowhere; he had to know she'd be okay when he left.

"Oh, yeah, of course," she said. "He…he's really good about it."

"Do you mind if I have a talk with him before I go?"

Her delicate eyebrows drew together. "Please don't. There's no need. Aside from the incident on Sunday, we've been getting by on our own for years. I'm sure I'll manage."

Finally dressed, he shifted into his chair, and she put her back to him. He suspected it was so that he couldn't see her expression.

"What about the team?" she asked as she pulled her light-weight sweater over her head.

"Their new coach arrived yesterday and attended practice. His name is Buzz Smith. I think you'll like him. He's a great guy, has coached a lot of college ball."

"So the players know?"

"Not yet. I told everyone Buzz was a consultant. I haven't de-cided for sure that I'll take the job."

She turned, but a brittle smile had replaced all the warmth and happiness that had shown in her face a few minutes earlier. "Of course you'll take the job. I *want* you to take the job. How do you turn away an opportunity like that? It's perfect for you."

"It's not completely about the opportunity, Hannah. It's more like—" he took a deep breath and shoved a hand through his hair "—I'm trying to figure out where I belong in the world now that…things have changed, you know?" He wished he could ex-plain it better, but he wasn't sure how to tell her that he'd lost part of himself when the accident injured his back and the rest when he realized he couldn't overcome it. He certainly didn't want to make her feel any worse about the accident. "I hope you understand."

She nodded. "Of course. I—I knew it'd come to this sooner or later. I guess…today…I just let myself believe—" she shrugged and gave a humorless laugh "—that it would happen later."

"Do you want me to put them off?" he asked.

"No, never. I—I want whatever's going to make you happy."

He believed that. Hannah was one of the few people he'd met who didn't ask for anything. "Will you have dinner with me to-morrow night, after the game?"

"If I can," she said with a noncommittal air. "I don't know what Russ has planned for the boys."

"Isn't it his weekend?"

"It is, but I haven't heard from him since…" she finished with, "since last weekend," but Gabe knew she'd been about to say, "since he hit me."

"I wish you'd let me talk to him," he said because he knew he was going to do it anyway and would prefer to gain her permission. He couldn't leave without putting Russ on notice that there'd be serious trouble if he ever hurt Hannah again.

She opened the door to the bedroom, and Lazarus rushed inside, acting as though he hadn't seen Gabe for several weeks. "You have enough to handle," she said, giving Lazarus a preoccupied pat as she headed past him. "Your first game is tomorrow, you're heading to New York after that. I've already dealt with Russ. Everything is under control."

He followed her into the living room, where she grabbed her bag and started outside.

"What about the picture?"

"Oh, right."

She paused long enough to remove her camera. He whistled for Lazarus to calm down and sit still, and she snapped a few shots.

Gabe wasn't certain what he looked like. He knew his hair had to be rumpled after their lovemaking, but he didn't really care. Hannah had distanced herself from him again, thrown up that protective shield she'd tried to use on Sunday. But this time he couldn't blame her.

"I'll call you later," he said.

She nodded and managed a brief smile as she put away her camera and hurried out.

CHAPTER EIGHTEEN

HANNAH PULLED OFF the road as soon as she was out of sight of Gabe's cabin. She was shaking too badly to continue driving. God, she was a fool. First she let herself get involved with Russ, a man she didn't love who would never go away. Because of her boys, she couldn't even allow herself to hope for his disappearance from her life. Then she'd let herself fall in love with a man who was bound from the beginning to leave her.

What was her problem? Was she one of those women who purposefully sabotaged her own happiness?

She glanced at her camera bag, remembered seeing Gabe through her lens, with his hair mussed from her hands and his smile still making her heart thump, and groaned. She'd never be able to look at that picture without thinking of today.

Once again, she had no one to blame but herself. And she had no choice but to live with the consequences. She'd made love with Gabe knowing she could never hold him. *He's a rare, injured bird, remember?* The fact that she was responsible for his being in a wheelchair would have torn them apart eventually. She just couldn't believe that it was already time to let him go.

The pain doesn't matter. Ignore it. She'd survived Russ; she'd survive Gabe. She had to. She couldn't let anything beat her because she had two boys who were counting on her to be the mother they'd always known.

Taking a deep, soothing breath, she waited for the truck coming up on her left to pass by, then headed home.

ON FRIDAY MORNING, Kenny was sure he was going to be sick. He almost wished the flu *would* strike, so he'd have a good excuse to stay home and miss the game. But he knew skipping out wouldn't solve anything for him in the long run. He had to let his father and Coach Blaine know where he stood, once and for all.

He rolled over and glanced at the clock. It was time to get up. He could hear his mother in the kitchen, making breakfast. She always made pancakes on Friday. She thought the carbohydrates would be a good start for game day.

The telephone rang. Kenny snagged it before his mother could, knowing it'd be Tuck. Tuck usually drove on Fridays because it was the only day his mother could spare the car.

"You going to school?" Tuck said.

"Yeah."

"Are you playing tonight?"

"I guess."

"Have you decided what you're going to do about Blaine and your father and all that?"

"Kenny, Brent! Breakfast is ready!" his mother called.

Kenny kicked off the covers and sat up. "Yeah."

"And?"

Kenny thought of his mother and the way she'd said, "I like him. I like him a lot" about Coach Holbrook. "I'm going to do my best."

"I was afraid of that."

Kenny scowled at his own rumpled image in the mirror above his dresser. "Why? I thought that's what you wanted me to do."

"Well, I've been thinking. Maybe what I said at the Old Swimming Hole was a little too…idealistic."

"*Idealistic?* How about we talk my language, Tuck?"

"I don't want to see you lose your shot at being a big football star in the NFL because of me, okay? Maybe you should do what your father told you to do. Who am I to tell you different? This situation is his and Coach Blaine's fault. It's *their* defining moment, not yours."

Scenes from *A Man For All Seasons* played in Kenny's mind. Thomas More could have given in and blamed it on the fact that his life was being threatened—but he didn't. Kenny knew Tuck, of all people, had to see the similarities. Tuck had certainly spent enough time thinking about Thomas More. But Kenny didn't want to point that out just in case he couldn't really kiss his football career goodbye. "I know."

"So you want me to pick you up for school?"

"Can we take Brent?" he asked. Hannah had been a little quiet last night. She insisted that there wasn't anything wrong, but Kenny was worried about her. He wanted to help out with his younger brother, if possible.

"Sure."

"See you in thirty minutes or so."

"Kenny, are you coming?" Hannah called as he hung up.

"Give me a minute."

"Are you ready for the game tonight?"

"Yeah," he called back but he knew in his heart that remained to be seen.

THE SCHOOL BAND PLAYED the Fight Song as Hannah parked and made her way to the football field. Just about everyone in Dundee turned out at these events, so she and Brent had to wait in line to get in, but she didn't mind. They had a few minutes until kickoff, and she liked the atmosphere. The smell of hot dogs and nachos permeated the air, and the cheerleaders danced in their flashy red-and-gold uniforms on the other side of the chain-link fence. Tiffany Wheeler stood out front. Hannah could see why Kenny would have his eye on her. She had a nice tan, plenty of long, curly blond hair and beautiful legs.

Hannah hoped he hadn't noticed the legs. She wasn't ready to think about girlfriends and future daughters-in-law.

Shifting the lap blanket she'd brought to her other arm, she reached into her purse to pay for their admittance. Then she took Brent's hand and started pressing through the crowd toward the stands, smiling and nodding at everyone she knew. She hadn't gone very far when she heard a voice that affected her very much like nails screeching down a chalkboard.

"Hannah, Brent. Up here!"

Hannah glanced into the stands to see her ex-husband sitting with Patti and her family and Donny. Donny's estranged wife wasn't around and neither was his daughter. Violet and Pug, Hannah's ex in-laws, used to come to the games, but they were getting old, and the noise and cooler weather bothered Violet.

"Can we sit with Dad?" Brent asked.

Hannah couldn't believe it, but Russ was acting as if what he'd done last Sunday had never happened. She didn't know how he could so easily disregard the bruise on her face, but she supposed she shouldn't be surprised. He'd probably convinced himself that he wasn't to blame. *I wouldn't have hit her if Gabe hadn't brought those flowers over....*

"Mom?" Brent said, pushing the issue.

Faking a good-to-see-you smile for the family's benefit, Hannah nodded. "Sure." She started climbing the bleachers, but something about having to face Patti, Russ and Donny knowing they'd probably spent a great deal of time talking about her and Gabe was too much for Hannah. Bending closer to Brent, she hollered over the noise of the band and the crowd, "You go ahead. I'm going to the snack bar to get some hot chocolate."

"For me, too?"

"Of course."

"Okay!" Always eager for something sweet, Brent smiled broadly and slipped between the crush of bodies ahead of them. She waited long enough to make sure his father had spotted him, then weaved her way to the ground.

The band switched songs, and the cheerleaders once again

joined in. The energy and enthusiasm surrounding her lifted Hannah's spirits—but did little to ease her nervousness. This was Kenny's first big game as starting quarterback for the varsity team. She hoped he'd be happy with his performance. She also wanted him to excel for Gabe's sake. Beating Oakridge would go far toward silencing his critics.

Of course, Gabe didn't have to worry about having any critics in Dundee if he was leaving town, she told herself. He'd be on television, making millions and building a new career. She twisted to look behind her—and she'd be living her old life of constant association with Russ and his family.

She'd still have her boys, she reminded herself. They were the reason she didn't leave herself.

Hannah caught sight of what she wanted to see down on the field and leaned closer. Gabe sat in his wheelchair, as handsome as ever in a dark sweater and khakis. Evidently, he'd decided to leave Lazarus at home. The dog that accompanied him almost everywhere wasn't around.

She watched Gabe confer with a stranger, who had to be the consultant he'd mentioned, and frowned. The man who'd be taking over for him was probably a good coach, but it was tough to accept a replacement.

Finally, the announcer came over the loud speaker. The Spartans won the toss, and the teams lined up for the kickoff. Hannah knew Brent would come searching for her if she didn't find her seat soon, so she bought the hot chocolate and forced her feet to carry her to where her ex-husband and his brother and sister were sitting.

"Hi," she said as brightly as possible and hugged her nieces before sitting down.

"Hey, where's mine?" Russ teased when he saw the cups she carried.

He was obviously on his best behavior, trying hard to compensate for the previous weekend, but it did little to endear him to her.

"Sorry," she said, rather insincerely.

"I'll share with you, Dad," Brent said and took his hot chocolate as Kenny jogged out onto the field.

Hannah held her breath while her oldest son started to play. The first series of downs didn't go well. The Spartans tried to run twice, netting only three yards. Then Kenny nearly threw an interception.

Hannah winced at the poor showing. "We didn't even get a first down," she said when the punting team took over.

She was talking to Patti, who sat between her and Russ with Joseph, her husband, directly behind her and Donny on the far side, but Russ answered. "Don't get your hopes up," he said. "I think the Spartans are going to have a bad game."

"Why?" she said, irritated that he'd make such a prediction so soon, especially when their son was heading up the offense.

"The Wildcats are pretty good this season."

"Kenny's good, too."

"It's not Kenny, it's the *coach*," he said pointedly.

Of course Russ would say that. "Are you're saying we're going to lose?"

"That's what I'm saying." He gave her a hard stare. "And it will all be thanks to *Gabe*."

"I think we're gonna lose, too," Patti said, frowning.

Patti's husband said nothing. He was rubbing Patti's shoulders and didn't appear to be listening.

"I'll bet you we don't," Hannah said coolly.

Russ smiled when the Spartan defense gave up fifteen yards on a simple carry. "*What* are you willing to bet?"

She searched her mind for something she wouldn't mind giving up. "A loaf of my homemade bread against your weekend with the boys."

"Not good enough."

"You love my homemade bread."

"It isn't what I want."

The Wildcat quarterback connected with one of his receivers on a short pass, gaining another eleven yards. But Hannah refused to let what she'd seen so far discourage her. She believed in Kenny; she believed in Gabe, too. "What is it you want?" she asked Russ.

"A date."

Hannah gaped at him. "You're kidding, right?"

"No. Patti's been telling me that I should try to win you back, and that's exactly what I plan to do."

Patti gave her a sheepish smile. "I think it'd be so wonderful, for everyone, if you two could work out your differences."

"Being divorced is no picnic," Donny mumbled, speaking for the first time.

"I want a chance to prove how much I've changed," Russ told her.

The memory of him backhanding her only last week loomed large in Hannah's mind. Not much of an improvement, she thought.

The Spartans made their first great play by stuffing the Wildcats' runningback at the line of scrimmage, and the crowd went wild. Like most everyone else, Hannah jumped up and applauded, but she noticed that Tuck, sitting several rows over and down, didn't move. He looked as though he was concentrating hard, trying to control the game with his mind. Mike and Lucky Hill weren't far away, either. They had their little daughter with them, but their expressions were almost as somber as Tuck's.

"So just how much confidence do you have in this team?" Russ pressed when she didn't respond to what he'd said.

"Enough," she replied, sitting down again.

"Enough to make me that bet?"

"I don't want to bet you."

"Because you know Loverboy can't get the job done," he taunted.

There was a fumble on the field. When the Spartans came up

with the ball, Hannah drew a deep breath and lifted her chin. Kenny and Gabe would pull it off; she knew they would. "Fine," she said. "You're on."

THE SCORE WAS 14-0. With only thirty seconds remaining in the first half, Gabe watched Spartan center Fred Mendoza snap the ball. Kenny backed up and scanned for his receivers, but Moose Blaine missed his block, which allowed Kenny to be sacked. Again. Kenny was good at scrambling, but there wasn't a high school quarterback in America who could have gotten the ball off in that amount of time.

Gabe shook his head. The Spartans hadn't gained more than twenty yards in a single possession. Exactly what he hadn't wanted to see was happening and he had no doubt Coach Blaine was behind it.

"They're not playing like they did in practice," Buzz Smith said, the lines in his weathered face looking as though they'd been etched in granite.

"Maybe it's time for some substitutions," Gabe said.

Buzz dropped the playbook that hung around his neck. "I don't know if we want to do that yet. This is their first game. We need to give 'em a chance to work the bugs out."

Gabe hadn't told Buzz anything about Blaine. He planned to have the problem solved tonight.

He caught Blaine's eye as the team huddled up.

Blaine smiled, seemingly unconcerned. At that point, Gabe decided he couldn't wait any longer. He'd given the front line long enough to prove themselves and they hadn't done the job. Several of them had to be in league with Blaine. Whether or not Kenny had joined the fun remained to be seen. The way the game had gone so far, there wasn't any way to tell. Even if he wasn't involved, Gabe was tempted to pull him. Kenny wasn't getting enough protection, and Gabe didn't want to put any quarterback at risk, least of all Hannah's son.

"Humor me," he said to Buzz, then began calling out names. "Colin, you're in for Moose. Manny, you go in at right tackle."

The smug expression on Blaine's face didn't change. Feeling grim, Gabe turned back to the game. He didn't want to lose to the Wildcats, especially like this. It wouldn't do justice to the boys who were still giving their best—or to the memory of Coach Hill.

The very next play, the Wildcats sacked Kenny again, and Gabe sent out the punting team. Fortunately, the clock ran down before Oakridge could get back into scoring position, but they came dangerously close to being able to kick a field goal.

As the band lined up for the halftime performance, the Spartans jogged off the field with their heads low. They weren't getting beat by their rivals, Gabe thought. They were getting beat by themselves.

Owens and Blaine were already running with the team. "Get things started for me in the locker room, will you?" Gabe said to Buzz and brought up the rear because it was slow going pushing a wheelchair over turf.

As he neared the spectators lining the fence, he heard a woman laugh and say maybe the great Gabriel Holbrook didn't have it in him to be a coach. He could have recognized Deborah by her vitriolic comment, but he didn't have to. She was standing at the gate.

"I tried to warn you that you had a problem with the team," she said as he passed by. "But you were too busy with Hannah to even take my call."

He'd taken it. She was the one who'd hung up. But Gabe ignored her. He didn't need Deborah's help. He needed his boys to come through for him. If Kenny could get off a few passes, it was still possible to recover…unless Blaine had poisoned too many members of the team.

"Gabe."

A strong, familiar hand squeezed his shoulder just before he entered the locker room. Even before he looked up, Gabe knew by the feel of that hand, and the voice, that it was his father. He wanted to pull away and disappear inside the building. He had work to do. But Garth quickly planted himself squarely in the way.

"Yes, sir?"

"You've got to make some adjustments, huh?"

Was his father trying to tell him how to coach? Gabe glanced behind him at the milling crowd, most of which were streaming toward the snack bar. "A few."

"What are you going to do?"

What was his father hoping to accomplish, waylaying him like this? "I don't know yet."

"A lot of folks think you should pull Price out."

"What's happening isn't Kenny's fault. He's getting no protection."

"So you're going to stick with him?"

"Maybe. I know he can do the job."

Garth shoved his hands in his pockets and nodded. "Then I say go with your gut. You know what you're doing. There's plenty of time left."

Suddenly Gabe realized why Garth was standing there. He was offering his support. Gabe could see it in his face. His father wanted him to succeed. His earnest expression reminded Gabe of all the games where his dad had sat in the stands, cheering him on, of all the rides his father had given him to and from practice, of all the trips they'd taken to the sporting goods store for new cleats or pads or other things to help his game. And the endless encouragement. Garth was trying to provide more of the same now....

It was like Reenie had said. Regardless of that incident twenty-four years ago, his father had always been there for them, providing a solid foundation.

A sudden tightness in Gabe's throat made it difficult to speak. God, he missed what they used to have. "I better get inside," he said.

"Right." Garth started to move away.

Gabe watched him for a second, then cleared his throat so he could call out. "Dad?"

Garth turned, looking surprised. It was the first time in months Gabe had addressed him in any way other than "sir." "Yes?"

So many things hovered on Gabe's tongue… Too many. He couldn't sort them out—at least not now. One battle at a time. He needed to get into the locker room and take charge of his team. But something held him back, something that whispered, "Quit being your own worst enemy."

"Thanks," he said simply.

His father smiled and nodded. "Go get 'em, eh?"

HANNAH REMAINED in her seat during halftime while Russ took Brent to the rest room. When he returned, he grinned and had Patti move down so he could sit by her. "Where would you like to go on our little date?" he asked. "We could leave the boys with Patti and take a trip, maybe head to a resort for the weekend."

He'd never offered to take her to a resort when they were married. They'd been too poor, mostly because he rarely had a job. Even if they went now, which was never going to happen, *she'd* probably have to pay for it.

Some new leaf he's turning over… "The Spartans haven't lost yet," she grumbled. "And a date doesn't last the entire weekend. *If* I lose, we're talking a movie with the boys at most."

Russ's face darkened at her response. "It's Gabe, isn't it? It's like everyone's been saying. You really are sleeping with him."

Hannah glanced quickly at Brent, relieved to find him too preoccupied with his cousins to be listening to their conversation. But Patti leaned close, obviously hanging on every word.

Hannah almost denied it. Then she remembered what Gabe had said when he was lying next to her yesterday. *If they say we're sleeping together, we say, damn right, as often as possible. Where can they go after a response like that?* Hannah was fairly certain Russ would go ballistic, but she didn't care. She was tired of restraining her own emotions, tired of caring too much about what everyone else thought and felt. "I am," she said. "And, *man,* is he good."

It was the most blatantly truthful thing she'd ever said to either one of them—and she could tell they knew it when Russ's jaw went slack and Patti's eyes turned into saucers.

"You're telling me the mother of my children, the woman I've known most of my life, is really a cheap slut?" Russ growled.

"Russ…" Patti warned, obviously torn, and nervous about the children overhearing.

Hannah met his eyes and smiled faintly. "No. I'm telling you I'm in love with Gabriel Holbrook, and I don't care who knows it."

"He's using you, getting back at you for what you did to him," Russ said.

"You're making a mistake, Hannah," Patti warned. "You'll never be able to keep him."

Hannah gazed down at the empty football field. "That doesn't change anything."

KENNY SAT SLUMPED against the lockers while Coach Owens chewed out the whole team. "What the hell happened to our front line during the first half of this game?" he yelled. "*Where* were our blocks? Do you want to let Oakridge make fools out of us all?"

Some of the guys shook their heads and mumbled in response, but most sat in depressed silence.

After Owens, it was Blaine's turn to address the team but he had little to say. Kenny couldn't even look at him. He hated Blaine, resented how he'd divided the team— especially because the bad guys seemed to be winning. Kenny couldn't make a difference in the game no matter how hard he tried.

"It's been a difficult few weeks what with losing Coach Hill," Blaine said. "It's not unusual that we'd suffer a setback…" He droned on, keeping up pretenses by saying a lot of nothing.

Finally, Gabe took the floor, but he didn't talk right away. He sat in his wheelchair, waiting until everyone was looking at him. When Kenny could hear a faucet drip in the bathroom, he said, "How many of you think this is just a game?"

Several members of the team glanced at each other, obviously confused. Even Buzz, the new consultant, seemed surprised by the question.

"How many?" Gabe repeated more insistently.

When everyone finally figured out that he actually expected an answer, a few boys raised their hands, then a few more until everyone had a hand up, including Kenny. Somehow Kenny knew it wasn't the answer Gabe was looking for, but it was what his mother always said, and Hannah tended to be right about things in general.

"Well, I'm here to tell you that it isn't just a game." Holbrook drilled the players who made up the Spartan front line with a pointed, steely gaze. "Not tonight. Why? Because life is all about the little things, the decisions we make every day. That's what builds us into who we are." He eyed the twins, who'd done such a halfhearted job keeping Kenny safe in the pocket. "It's about having courage and always holding up your end. It's about making an honest attempt. Nothing else matters. Do you understand?"

No one said anything.

"Do you understand?" Holbrook repeated.

Kenny couldn't help nodding.

"Price, why don't you explain it to the others."

Kenny cleared his throat when he found everyone watching him. He didn't like being put on the spot, especially when he felt guilty for having been tempted to fail his team. But the victorious glint in Blaine's eye told Kenny that Blaine thought he had Holbrook by the throat, and Kenny knew he had to say something.

"This is our defining moment," he said, thinking of Tuck. "This is where we show ourselves and each other who we really are, what we're made of."

"There's no shame in losing once in a while," Blaine said. "Oakridge is a tough op—"

"It isn't about winning or losing," Holbrook interrupted. "It's about character. There are two kinds of men—strong men, who remain true to their internal compass regardless of all else; and weak men who are easily misled and wind up cheating themselves of all they can be."

"That sounds like something I once heard Coach Hill say," Brandon Joseph said, sitting up straighter and taking note.

Gabe's teeth flashed in a smile. "I heard him say it too, Brandon, twenty years ago. And I know if he were here today, he'd deliver the same message. He certainly set the example, didn't he? Coach Hill lived a life he could be proud of. So what do you think? What kind of men do you boys want to be? Will you remain true to your team, to each other, to Coach Hill and to me?"

"I will, Coach!" Dookie Howser yelled.

"Me, too!" someone else called, and the response soon turned into a chorus.

Kenny saw the twins cast each other, and Coach Blaine, an uneasy glance. Finally, Moose stood up. "I'm sorry, Coach," he said, hanging his head. "I don't deserve to play because I haven't been giving you an honest effort. But I hope you'll put me in second half and let me make it up to you."

Blaine went beet red at the defection of his own cousin.

"No one should get past you. You're too good, Moose," Holbrook said and turned back to Kenny. "Kenny, you're the team leader. What can we expect from you this half?"

Kenny met his coach's gaze. Maybe Holbrook would be gone next year, maybe it'd mean that Kenny would never play football again. But for here and now, he was playing for a man he could respect. And he was going to walk away from this game being able to respect himself. "Leave me in, too, Coach," he said. "You'll get nothing but my best."

"I believe that," Holbrook said. "I believe you'll all give me your best. Now get out there and show me what you've got."

CHAPTER NINETEEN

AFTER HALFTIME, the feeling on the field was completely different, but Kenny's job still wasn't easy. Most of the guys on the team seemed to understand what had happened in the locker room. They seemed to be committed. But there were a few, like Sly, who didn't care about internal compasses, respect or team loyalty—which meant those who did care had to work twice as hard.

Midway through the third quarter, the Spartans finally came within scoring range. When Lonny missed his block on third and seven, the defense rushed in. But Kenny managed to roll away from the pressure and head downfield to score the Spartan's first touchdown. A rush of adrenaline shot through him as he saw the referee's arms go up. But then someone flew at him, hitting him when he wasn't expecting it. He landed hard on his left arm, and the resulting pain momentarily paralyzed him.

"Kenny, you okay?" Moose shoved the Wildcat who'd hit him out of the way.

The guy hurried off the moment he saw the size of Moose, and Kenny tried to nod, but he could scarcely breathe.

"You hurt?" Moose pressed.

Kenny had never felt so much pain in his life. But he knew he couldn't show it. He had to stay in the game. The momentum was just beginning to shift—he wasn't done yet.

"I'm fine," he managed to say, but he didn't object when Moose grabbed the front of his jersey and set him on his feet.

"Thanks," he said, trying not to grimace.

Worry showed in Moose's meaty face. "You don't look good," he said. "You're out for the rest of the game. Maybe even next week's game."

Kenny scowled. "No way, man. I'm fine!"

"The hell you are."

It wasn't until Moose glanced at Kenny's left arm that Kenny realized he couldn't move it. "I throw with my other hand," he said. "Don't say anything to the coaches." But he should've saved his breath because the stands were deathly quiet, and Owens and Blaine were already trotting out onto the field, along with the team's trainer.

"Come on," Kenny said from between clenched teeth, and he and Moose started for the sidelines. When they met up with the coaches, Kenny blinked the sweat out of his eyes, which felt mysteriously like tears, and tried to brush past them. "I'm okay. Let's go."

Owens didn't seem convinced. "You took quite a hit out there."

"Did we get the penalty?" Kenny asked, struggling to absorb the pain, to act normal, to think beyond it.

"Fifteen yards."

"Good." Kenny finally reached the bench. He wished he could sink onto it and rock back and forth in misery, but he turned to watch the second-string kicker instead. "That's it," he said when they made the extra point, but Owens wasn't listening. He was frowning over his clipboard.

"You've got to come out," he said. "We'll go with—"

"Is Kenny okay?"

Owens glanced at Coach Holbrook, who was making his way down the sidelines with that Buzz guy. "He's hurt."

"No, I'm not!" Kenny said.

Owens ignored him. "Who do you want to go in for him?"

"Greer," Holbrook answered.

"But I feel fine," Kenny insisted.

Surprise registered on Holbrook's face. "Kenny, if you feel good enough, sit down and watch the game. If you don't, let's get your mother down here and have her take you to the doctor."

"I can play," he insisted.

"What if something's broken?"

Kenny thought that was probably the case. "We'll get it X-rayed after the game. It won't hurt anything to wait."

"Kenny—"

"Come on, Coach. I need this," he said softly and grabbed Holbrook's arm.

Holbook glanced pointedly at the spot where Kenny held him. Kenny let go but couldn't apologize. He could focus only on keeping himself together long enough to finish the game.

"Please, Coach," Kenny said. "I *have* to do this." He had to know that he wasn't going to turn out exactly like his father, always searching for the easy way out and blaming everything and everyone else for what went wrong in his life.

"You could get hit again," Holbrook warned.

Only a few feet away, the defense fought to hold the Wildcats to their own side of the field. Kenny winced at the rough tackles. The thought of simply *jarring* his arm nearly made him faint. But he had to finish what he'd started. This was his Thomas More moment. "If I do, you can take me out."

"Are you feeling much pain?"

"My arm's a little numb, that's all," he lied, even though his whole body felt like it had just been through a meat grinder.

Blaine had come up from behind. Now he suddenly jumped into the conversation. "He's trying to be a hero, letting his ego get in the way. Don't listen to him. Of course he should come out."

Kenny opened his mouth to plead with Holbrook some more. The Spartans weren't going to lose because some fool took a cheap shot and knocked him out of the game. Blaine had already done enough damage to the team. But Kenny didn't need to say any more. Blaine's involvement seemed to be just the thing to get Holbrook to give in.

"You can play," Holbrook said. "But you have to stay in the pocket, do you understand me? If you get sacked or try to run even once—"

Blaine's hands clenched. "You're making a mistake, Holbrook," he said. "This kid has a head as big as yours."

Holbrook ignored him. "*Don't* run," he said to Kenny.

Kenny put his helmet back on with his good hand. "I won't."

"You're going to get fired for this," Kenny heard Blaine warn Holbrook.

"It's a possibility," Holbook said. "But the fact that you won't be here next week is a foregone conclusion."

Kenny couldn't tell which one of them was right. It was too much to think about. All he knew was that Tuck was watching and so were his mother and brother. He was going to show them, and himself, what kind of man he wanted to be.

Determination surged inside him like floodwater tearing through a canyon.

It was the only thing that kept the nausea and blackness at bay.

"HE'S HURT," Hannah said, watching Kenny attempt another pass.

"No, he's not," Russ said.

Hannah considered the way Kenny held his left arm. It didn't look natural. He didn't seem to be moving quite as fast as normal, either. Had that late tackle done more damage than she'd thought?

"He just completed another pass," Patti said. "I think he's fine."

"Can you keep an eye on Brent for a minute?" Hannah asked Russ.

"Take him with you," Russ grumbled. Ever since she'd admitted her feelings for Gabe he'd had very little to say to her. And although Kenny had begun to play brilliantly, Russ didn't seem pleased. Considering how much Russ cared about Kenny's football success, Hannah couldn't work out what his problem was.

"Russ!" Patti said, her tone full of reproach. "He's your son, too. Of course you can keep an eye on him."

"So she can use Kenny as an excuse to get in front of Gabe, hoping he'll invite her over again tonight?"

"Oh, grow up!" Hannah snapped. "I'm worried about my son." Getting up, she hurried down to the fence, so she could see better.

Kenny backed up to throw again, but couldn't get the pass off. A defender broke through the front line. Kenny shifted to the left to avoid the tackle; then, in an amazing feat of strength, Moose Blaine threw off another guy and managed to protect his quarterback well enough for Kenny to toss the ball a few short yards. After the play, Hannah thought she saw Moose check with Kenny to be sure he was okay and watched her son nod.

Was she wrong? Her sixth sense told her no, but…

"Hi, Hannah."

Hannah glanced over to see that Mike Hill had come up next to her and greeted him.

"Kenny's playing quite a game. That kid's something special."

"I'm proud of him," she said absently.

"Is something wrong?" he asked.

"Kenny's hurt. Do you think Gabe knows that?"

"I'm sure he does."

"Then, why isn't he pulling him out?"

"I don't know, but he must have a good reason, don't you think?"

She wasn't sure. Did she trust Gabe that much? She wasn't used to relying on other people to look out for her boys.

"I'm sure Kenny's going to be okay, Hannah," Mike said gently.

She nodded, and he put his arm around her to give her shoulders a gentle squeeze. "Do you need to go down there?" he asked.

She gazed at Kenny, then Gabe, and drew a deep breath. Gabe was different from Russ. He wouldn't let her down. "No."

"Would you like to come sit with me and Lucky?"

Hannah had never had much of a chance to speak to Lucky. Lucky was younger, so they hadn't attended school together, and she'd left town for several years. Now that she was back, they only passed on the street occasionally. But Lucky was Gabe's half sister, and Hannah couldn't help being drawn to anyone even remotely connected to him. Certainly sitting with Mike and Lucky would be better than watching the rest of the game with Russ.

"Okay," she said and let Mike lead her back into the bleachers.

AN HOUR LATER, Gabe sat on the empty football field and stared up at the scoreboard, which, like the lights, would probably be shut off any second. The glowing numerals read twenty-one to twenty.

"Can we go yet?" Brent asked, finally growing bored with playing in the mud over by where the team's water cooler had been.

"In a minute." Gabe had met Hannah at the door to the locker room when she came to check on Kenny and insisted she leave Brent with him. She had to go to Dr. Hatcher's to have Kenny's arm X-rayed and, evidently, Russ wasn't speaking to her, so she would've had to take Brent with her or ask someone else to watch him. Gabe had volunteered for the job because he wanted to help—but he also liked the fact that if he had Brent, he'd definitely get to see Hannah tonight.

Brent followed the line of his gaze to the scoreboard, looking puzzled that Gabe could still be interested in what was posted there when everyone else had gone home. "We won, didn't we, Coach?"

"We won," he said. "Thanks to Kenny." It had come down to the final few seconds, but on third and twenty, Kenny had thrown a long bomb that resulted in a spectacular, game-winning touchdown. The other team got the ball back after the extra kick, of course, but there hadn't been enough time to do anything. It was over. The clock wound down to the cheers of everyone on the Spartan side, with the band playing the fight song, while the dejected Wildcats dragged themselves off the field.

"How'd Kenny win the game?" Brent asked.

Gabe wasn't sure how Hannah's oldest son had even managed to jog out whenever the offense took the field, but Kenny wouldn't let Gabe pull him. Every time Gabe tried, Kenny rounded on him with determination so fierce it bordered on defiance, letting Gabe know he needed to keep playing.

Obviously, this game meant far more to him than just another matchup against Oakridge. Basically, Kenny had been trying to prove something and, right or wrong, Gabe had given him the opportunity.

"He played with heart," Gabe answered, then added more softly to himself, "He remained true to his internal compass."

Before Brent could question him further, Gabe heard someone call his name. Surprised that anyone besides the groundskeeper and he and Brent were still around, he turned to see Mike and Lucky walking toward him.

"Good game," Mike said, only the bottom of his smile visible beneath the shadow of his cowboy hat.

"Thanks." Gabe let his eyes flick toward Lucky. She possessed a delicate face and a curvy body, but he'd already known that his half sister was uncommonly pretty. He also knew how much Mike loved her, how happy his friend was in his marriage.

Maybe it would be possible to accept her for that alone....

I like her. I think you would, too, if only you'd give her a chance, Reenie had said.

"I'll bet you're proud of Kenny," she said.

It was rare that Lucky ever spoke directly to him. Gabe could tell by the hesitant smile on her face and the way her hand tightened on Mike's arm that she wasn't sure she'd get a response, but he couldn't ignore her. As much as he didn't want to have a half sister, his father hadn't given him a choice. And as his mother said, Lucky wasn't to blame.

"I am," he said.

She glanced at Mike, as though getting that much out of him was some sort of victory, and the strain in her face eased slightly.

"You think he's gonna be okay?" Mike asked.

"We'll know soon enough. Hannah took him over to Hatcher's."

"I hope nothing's broken."

"Me, too." Gabe was worried about Kenny, but he was also sure that the kid would never have forgiven him if Gabe had taken him out.

"Blaine was doing exactly what I thought he was doing, wasn't he?" Mike asked.

Gabe nodded.

"What are you going to do about it?"

"Make sure he's permanently removed from coaching." Gabe had no choice. Especially now that he was leaving. He wouldn't turn the team, *his* team, over to anyone as long as Blaine was involved.

"Blaine's demise has been too long in coming," Mike said. "He should have been fired after what he did to you twenty years ago."

"Fortunately, getting rid of him shouldn't be too hard," Gabe said. "Moose is willing to talk."

"Really? Blaine's nephew?"

"He doesn't like what his uncle did, and he wants to tell the truth."

"Good for him! Did Kenny say anything about Blaine?"

"I didn't get a chance to talk to him after the game."

Mike adjusted his hat. "It certainly didn't look as though he was involved."

"He wasn't," Gabe said. He wanted to keep the whole mess as far away from Kenny as possible, but he suspected the situation hadn't been quite as simple as he'd just stated. There was a reason Kenny and Sly had gotten into a fight. And there was a reason Kenny had played like the devil was after him.

"Will you be glad to have Blaine gone?" It was Lucky again. Gabe sensed her eagerness to befriend him and felt his resistance slip a little.

"In a way," he said, but even that wasn't as straightforward as it should have been. Blaine deserved what he was going to get, but Gabe couldn't help feeling sorry for him. He knew what it was like to lose a cherished career. The fact that Blaine had no one to blame but himself made the loss even worse.

"Do you like coaching?" she asked.

"I do," he said, realizing just how much.

"Not enough to stick around and finish the job, though, huh?" Mike cocked an eyebrow at him, and Gabe realized that his friend knew about New York. Gabe had told himself numerous times that he needed to call Mike and explain. But the same kind of reluctance that had made it difficult to tell Hannah had kept him from actually picking up the phone.

"Who told you?"

"Hannah sat with us for the last part of the game."

Gabe pinched the back of his neck. "I'm just checking it out. It's not a sure thing. And the team will be fine. ESPN has sent a guy out to replace me. He's a good coach."

"He won't be any better than you."

Brent tugged on Gabe's sleeve. "Is it time to go home yet?"

"Almost.

"Baby-sitting tonight, huh?" Mike said.

Gabe remembered Mike telling him to invite Hannah out and grinned. "Just trying to be a good coach."

Mike chuckled. "I didn't buy that before, and I'm not buying it now."

"Gabe?" Brent interrupted. It was the first time Brent had used his first name. Obviously, Hannah's boy was getting impatient. "Can we go? Please?"

"Why are you in such a hurry?" Gabe asked.

"I want to play with Lazarus."

So *that* was it. "But we're not going to my house, we're going to yours."

"Can't we pick him up first?"

Gabe opened his mouth to explain about the long drive, then changed his mind. They had a wait ahead of them. They could easily make the trip to the cabin. And Brent's eagerness gave him an idea. He smiled at the little boy. "Hey, Brent. You know, I have to go out of town for a few days. Do you think you can watch Lazarus for me?"

Brent's eyes rounded. "You're going to let him *stay* with me?"

Gabe had planned on taking the dog. But leaving something of himself behind with Hannah seemed…comforting. "If it's okay with your mom."

"She won't care. I'll just beg her if she says no."

"Let me ask her first, okay?"

"Okay."

"Gabe?" Mike said.

Gabe turned back to his friend. "Yeah?"

"Whether you come back or not, I want you to know that I appreciate the fact that you were willing to take over for my father. I know he would have been proud tonight."

More emotions ripped into Gabe. With everything that had been going on lately, he felt as though he'd just been taken out of a freezer, that every nerve in his body was burning as the feeling returned all at once. "Your dad was a good man, Mike."

Mike nodded. "I'll be watching the *Countdown* on Sunday. Knock 'em dead," he said with a grin, then put his arm around his wife and walked away.

"Can I push you?" Brent asked, breaking the silence.

Gabe dragged his eyes away from his half sister and his best friend. He almost said the usual, that he'd rather manage on his own. But when he looked into Brent's hopeful young face, he changed his mind. "Sure."

"Cool! You're the only one I know with one of these," he said.

Brent managed to move Gabe only as far as the pavement before his strength gave out. "I'm tired," he complained. "Can I can ride in front with you?"

Gabe shifted in surprise. "Aren't you getting too big to be sitting in someone's lap?"

"I'm only seven," he said.

It'd been a long time since Gabe had held a child. Suddenly he missed his niece and two nephews, wondered how he could have let so much time pass without visiting them.

"I can fit," Brent added encouragingly.

Seeing a strong resemblance to Hannah, Gabe smiled at the boy again. "Okay, come on."

The scent of good old-fashioned dirt lifted to his nostrils as Brent climbed into his lap and, for the first time since the accident, Gabe wondered what it would be like to have a son.

The stadium lights snapped off as they reached the truck. Normally, Gabe knew he'd still be thinking about the game. It had been amazing, and promised great things for the rest of the season, especially with Blaine gone. But something—maybe the protective feeling he had for the young boy in his lap—seemed to beckon him toward a new challenge.

Maybe football wasn't the only thing in the world, after all....

KENNY DIDN'T THINK he'd ever been so tired in his life. The game had taken everything he had. But they'd won. He still couldn't believe it. Even with a broken arm, he'd thrown two touchdown passes.

"You're quiet tonight," Hannah said as they drove home from Dr. Hatcher's office. "Is the pain getting worse?"

Kenny gazed down at his new cast. Because the bones in his arm hadn't shifted, the doctor didn't need to set them, but the X-ray and casting process had taken nearly two hours. Now that it was close to midnight, there weren't many cars on the road, and all the businesses they passed, except the Honky Tonk and the gas station, looked eerily abandoned. "No, the pills helped."

"You tired?"

"Beat." He wished his brain would shut down along with his body, but he couldn't stop thinking. About the pride on Tuck's face as the team carried him off the field. About Tiffany, who'd rushed over as soon as they let him down to make sure he was all right. He could still feel her hand gripping his good arm as if she didn't care that he was all sweaty, the crazy way his heart had thumped when he gazed down into her blue eyes. "Call me tomorrow," she'd said.

Call her... He was going to call Tiffany Wheeler....

Then there was Blaine, who'd glared at Kenny with so much hatred as they passed on the way to the locker room. If Blaine managed to hang on to his job, Kenny would never play for the Spartans again. He knew that, but somehow it didn't seem to matter so much anymore. Tonight was what had mattered—and he'd passed the test.

"Where do you think Dad went?" he asked above the Avril Lavigne song playing on the radio. After the game ended, Russ had checked to make sure he was okay, then stalked off. They'd called from the doctor's office to tell him Kenny's arm was broken, but he hadn't answered.

His mother glanced over at him. "Who knows? He's mad at me again, and when he gets mad at me, you know he makes himself scarce. I'm sure he'll call you first thing in the morning," she added. "He has to be incredibly proud of the way you played tonight."

Russ wasn't be proud; Russ was disappointed that Kenny had gone against his wishes. But his father had only been hoping to hurt Coach Holbrook, which seemed stupid to Kenny. Why should the Spartans have to lose just because his father didn't like the new coach? "Why's he mad at you?" he asked.

His mother seemed to search for the right words. "Well, because..."

"Could you just tell it to me straight this time, Mom?" he asked softly. "I'm not a little kid anymore."

"No, you're not." She blew out a sigh, then smiled briefly. "He's not happy that I've been seeing Gabe."

"How does he know?"

Her eyebrows went up. "Do you think it's possible to keep a secret in this town?"

Kenny thought of Blaine knowing about Tiffany and decided it wasn't. "Dad had his chance and he blew it," he said. "He doesn't have the right to get mad at you over another guy."

"Emotions don't always make sense, Kenny. Just rest assured he's not mad at you."

Kenny knew the game was at least part of the reason his dad was upset, but he didn't correct his mom. He'd done what he'd done. His dad would have to accept it. Kenny had certainly been forced to accept enough things where his father was concerned. In any case, Kenny was more interested in taking the conversation in a different direction. "So, how do you think Coach Holbrook feels about you?"

Hannah pulled into their drive and cut the engine. "I think he likes me okay," she said. "But we probably won't be seeing much of each other in the future."

Kenny paused with his hand on the door latch. Gabe's truck was parked at the curb. "Why not?"

"Because he's been offered a job in New York." Her voice ended on an up note, but Kenny could tell she wasn't happy. "He's going to host *NFL Countdown*."

"Really?" Kenny couldn't help being impressed. ESPN was ESPN.

"It's a great opportunity," she said, but the smile curving her lips was definitely a fake one. He could tell she didn't want Gabe to go.

"What about the team?" Kenny asked, suddenly realizing the full impact of this news.

"Buzz Smith is going to take over."

Great. Another coach. Holbrook was letting them both down. Kenny got out and walked to the house, pausing on the front porch as his mother came up from behind with the key. When she opened the door, it was dark inside, but the television was still on. In the dim, flickering light, he could see the outline of Gabe Holbrook lying on the couch. It was the first time there'd ever been a man other than his father resting comfortably on his mother's couch.

Gabe appeared to be sleeping. But when they walked inside, he lifted his head.

"How'd it go?" he asked.

"Got a cast," Kenny said, lifting his arm.

"But the break is a clean one," Hannah told him. "He should have the cast off in three to four weeks. The doctor said it would protect his arm well enough that he could probably play soon if he wanted to."

Gabe sat up and moved his feet to the ground with his hands. "That's great."

"My mom says you've had some good news, too," Kenny said.

Gabe hesitated. "What news is that?"

"Aren't you going to New York to be part of NFL Countdown?"

"Oh, yeah," he said as if it wasn't any big thing.

"That's cool," Kenny said, but he couldn't inject any real enthusiasm into his voice. Because what he really wanted to say was, "Don't go. My mom and I need you right here."

CHAPTER TWENTY

HANNAH PERCHED on the arm of the couch and stared down at Gabe. She could hear Kenny's footsteps fading down the hall, knew he'd be asleep within minutes. She was tired herself, too tired to face the fact that Gabe would be flying out in the morning.

Suddenly, she heard movement behind her and turned to see Lazarus. "Hi Lazarus," she said, giving him a pat. "Where'd you come from?"

"Brent wanted to play with him," Gabe explained.

"So you drove out to get him?"

He nodded.

"That was nice of you."

"Actually, I had an ulterior motive."

"Sounds like a man," she teased. "What is it?"

"I was hoping he could stay here with you while I'm gone."

Gabe was going to let her keep his dog? "You don't want to take him to New York?"

"I don't think he'd enjoy the trip. He'd have to be in one of those dog carriers, and it's a long flight. He's not used to being so confined."

Lazarus wasn't used to being without Gabe, either. But she wasn't going to point that out. If Gabe's dog was staying, Gabe had to come back at some point, didn't he? "Of course he can stay here."

"Thanks."

"What time does your flight leave?"

"Seven."

"You're kidding," she said. "With the drive to Boise, you'll have to start out at four-thirty. That's in just a few hours."

"I know. I packed when Brent and I went to pick up Lazarus." He nodded toward a suitcase in the corner of the room, sitting so deep in shadow Hannah hadn't noticed until he pointed it out to her.

So, he was spending the night? She wanted to smile but opted for a scowl. "You shouldn't have volunteered to baby-sit for me. You're not going to get enough sleep."

"I wanted to see you before I left, and to make sure Kenny was okay."

"I think he's going to be fine. At the doctor's office, he kept saying, 'Did you see that pass, Mom? Did you see it?'" She fought back a yawn. "Do you want me to take you to the airport?"

"No. It's too early, and it's too far of a drive. I'll leave my truck in long-term parking."

Long-term parking. She didn't like the sound of long-term anything when it meant Gabe would be gone. But she certainly didn't want to stand in his way. He was moving on after the accident, just as she'd wanted. She should be glad, right?

His eyes drifted over her, and she could tell exactly when his thoughts shifted to other things. "Are you going to sit over there all night?" he asked.

She twisted to look down the hall. "The boys could get up," she said hesitantly.

"So?" he responded. "They won't be surprised to find you lying on the couch with me. They already know you love me."

Hannah's jaw dropped. *"What?"*

"At least Brent does," he amended. "He told me all about it tonight."

"Brent doesn't know a thing," she said.

Gabe recovered something he'd stuffed under his head as a pillow. When he shook it out, Hannah saw that it was the Hawaii

T-shirt she'd brought home with her. "He showed me this," he said, his grin turning slightly devilish. "And he told me you sleep with it at night."

Embarrassment prickled the back of Hannah's neck. "There's no privacy in this town," she grumbled.

He chuckled. "It's okay. I already knew things weren't casual between us."

"How?" she challenged, folding her arms.

"Are you kidding?" he said. "I can feel it."

HANNAH DIDN'T WANT to waste the next few hours with sleep. She knew this might be the last time she'd ever have Gabe's arms around her. Once he left for New York, he could easily get caught up in the success, the money, the fame. There was a lot out there waiting for him. His withdrawal from the public's view for the past three years would only make his reappearance that much more sensational. In the midst of all the attention, it would be easy to forget the woman back home.

But tomorrow would have to take care of itself. She'd deal with the future when it was no longer the future. Tonight she had her cheek pressed to his chest, where she could hear the steady beat of his heart. She felt safely cocooned in the warmth of his body.

They already know you love me. She hadn't argued too loudly when he'd said that. There wasn't any point. He was right. She was so far gone that she melted every time she looked at him. How could she hide an emotion so all-consuming?

Maybe she would've been able to salvage some of her pride if she could've concealed her feelings a little better. But she didn't care too much about pride. Let Patti and anyone else who wanted to say "I told you so," do it. After struggling for so long to fall in love with Russ, Hannah was just glad to know she was capable of loving a man as completely and passionately as she did Gabe. Every woman should experience that once in her lifetime, she decided. Even one who lived in a small town, had a lousy ex and not a lot of hope for a future relationship.

"Why aren't you sleeping?" Gabe muttered, pressing his lips to her temple.

"I'm thinking."

"About what?"

"Everything."

"Are you upset about me going to New York?" he asked.

"No, I'm happy for you."

"Really?" he said, the scratchy quality of his voice indicating he was falling back asleep.

"Really," she repeated. Then she squeezed her eyes closed and prayed with all her heart that her rare bird would indeed take off and soar once again.

"I HEARD GABE'S IN New York," Patti said when she called Hannah the following Wednesday.

Hannah put down the picture she'd been framing and sank into the chair behind her desk. "You heard right."

"Kenny told Russ he's on *NFL Countdown.*"

Hannah and Kenny had watched Gabe on television last Sunday and knew ESPN had to be thrilled with him. He was a perfect commentator: intelligent, articulate, even funny.

"When has Kenny talked to Russ?" Hannah asked. "We couldn't even reach him last Friday after we went to the doctor's."

"He was upset. But he brought Kenny a sandwich for lunch on Monday, and apologized for his behavior."

"Good for him," Hannah said. Kenny hadn't mentioned it. Kenny had been too preoccupied with Tiffany. If he wasn't calling her, she was calling him. They talked on the phone for hours.

"Russ isn't nearly as bad a guy as you like to believe," Patti said.

Hannah swiveled in her chair to check her reflection in the chrome lamp. She wanted to see if the bruise on her cheek was completely gone. The lamp didn't make the best mirror, but she couldn't see anything. "And he's not nearly as good as you like to believe," she replied.

There was a momentary silence. Patti still wasn't accustomed to Hannah's new directness. "So you're going to try and hang on to Gabe?"

"No." Hannah scratched Lazarus, who'd gotten up from where he'd been dozing in the corner and ambled over. "Gabe's gone, and I don't expect him to come back, at least for any length of time."

"Does he call you?"

"Occasionally." He'd called her twice, but they hadn't talked long. She'd assured him that Lazarus was okay, that Kenny liked Coach Smith, that Blaine had resigned the moment he heard that several of the boys had come forward. She told him she was happy and busy, that Russ hadn't been causing her any problems. In fact, she and her ex were back on polite terms. The only thing she didn't say was that she felt hollow inside without Gabe, and that she'd recorded his show and watched it again and again late at night after the boys were asleep.

"And you're still in love with him?" Patti said.

"It's not something I can turn on and off, Patti."

Her ex-sister-in-law sighed. "Well, I hope you'll continue to be willing to attend family events and stuff, for the boys' sake. I don't think it'll help them to have you refuse to go to this or that function just because Russ will be there."

"I've never done that before. I don't plan on starting now," Hannah said.

"Well, Jamie's doing it to Donny. It makes it really hard to plan anything, you know?"

"What are you planning?"

"Dad's birthday is coming up."

Hannah glanced at her calendar. She hadn't written it down. For the first time in twenty years, she would have forgotten Pug's birthday. "When's the party?"

"Sunday. Can you come?"

"Sure. Where is it?"

"My place. One o'clock."

"What would you like me to bring?"

"Dad loves that bowtie pasta you used to always make."

"I'll bring it," Hannah said. "Anything else?"

"That should be enough. We'll have a big barbecue and watch the 49er game. They're playing the Raiders."

Almost everyone in Russ's family was a 49er fan. "Your dad will like that."

"I think so."

"See you soon."

Hannah continued to pet Lazarus after she hung up. Generally the dog spent his time with Brent, but Brent was at school.

"What do you think Gabe's doing right now?" she asked.

The dog whined and shifted his eyebrows, and Hannah laughed.

"He's probably having a great time, being treated like a star by big executives… Meeting women…" The laughter now gone, she took a deep breath and glanced around her office. "But we're having fun here, right? Just look at all this stimulating work. And now we have Pug's birthday to look forward to."

Lazarus obviously didn't give a damn about the birthday party. And, if she was being honest, Hannah would admit that she, too, was less than enthusiastic.

"How exciting," she said flatly and went back to work.

ON FRIDAY NIGHT, Gabe sat in an exclusive black-tie restaurant with Phil Hunt, his wife, Tonya, Phil's boss Harvey Fischer and Harvey's date, Gigi—who looked about half Harvey's age and wore what seemed like twice her weight in diamonds. There was a third woman present, who was supposedly a friend of Gigi's but had to be some kind of porn star or centerfold pinup model. With breasts the size of watermelons, it was easy to tell she'd had more than one appointment with a surgeon. Her revealing, clingy dress and the way she brushed against him at every opportunity, suggested to Gabe that she was there to go home with him, if he wanted.

Ah, the benefits of being rich and famous, Gabe thought sarcastically. He was back, all right. Back where the money and the attention was. Back where it was possible to be unbelievably self-indulgent. If he wanted to, he could go on a sex and drug binge that would last indefinitely—but he wasn't interested in drugs or even in sex, at least with Barbie, if that was her real name. Looking at her, Gabe guessed "Barbie" was part of the package, like the implants, bleached hair and collagen-enhanced lips....

"How do you like New York, Gabe?" Phil's wife asked.

Gabe set his wine on the table. "I've always liked it here," he said. He loved the pulse of the city, the art, the people, the buildings. But only to visit. He couldn't imagine living here indefinitely. There wasn't any room to breathe. No pine trees. No place for Lazarus.

Another voice in his head added, "No Hannah," but he quickly silenced it.

"I've always been a big fan of yours," Phil's wife went on, obviously hoping to engage him in a longer conversation. "I'm glad you could join us tonight."

"I'm happy to be here," he replied, but the happy part was a considerable stretch. He'd only let Phil talk him into dinner this evening because he'd been looking for a distraction. He hadn't wanted to languish in the company penthouse and twiddle his thumbs while the Spartans were playing. He'd already twiddled his thumbs enough this week, thinking about Lucky, Reenie, his father, Kenny, Brent, the team and, most of all, Hannah.

"This has to be the best restaurant in New York," Phil said.

"I know it's one of the most expensive," Harvey added proudly.

Harvey liked to point out all the great things the station was doing for Gabe. ESPN was pushing hard, trying to get Gabe to sign a one-year contract. But Gabe insisted they give him a few weeks. He wanted to see if he could adjust, which was why he hadn't let himself return home yet. If he flew home after every show, his heart would remain in Dundee.

Ignoring the crack about the expense of the restaurant, Gabe glanced down at his watch. The Spartans were playing the Rams this week. It'd be halftime by now. He wondered if—

"Gee, are you in some sort of hurry, Gabe?" Barbie asked, her voice slightly pouty.

Gabe shifted to the left so the waiter could set a bowl of lobster bisque in front of him. "No, why?"

"The way you keep checking your watch, I thought maybe you had another date lined up."

He should've gone home for the game, he decided. He should've gone home to Hannah....

But he hadn't given New York a fair shot. What was wrong with him? Hosting *NFL Sunday Countdown* was a dream come true for a has-been football player who could no longer walk. Now that he knew he'd never play again, what better career could there be?

He remembered holding Brent in his lap, feeling like a father. He remembered sitting on the sidelines long after the Spartan's win last Friday, so proud of Kenny and the rest of the team he could cry. He remembered losing himself in Hannah—

"You feeling okay?" Phil asked, picking up on Barbie's question.

"Fine," he said.

Phil handed around a basket of rolls. "New York's a rat race. You're probably a little tired."

"Bedtime will come soon enough," Barbie said with a suggestive smile.

Harvey leered meaningfully at his jewel-ridden girlfriend, who twirled her bracelet, then turned back to Gabe. "So, how did you like doing the show last week?"

"I enjoyed it," Gabe said. That much, at least, was true. He liked talking about football. It made the sting of being unable to play worse, but he was beginning to grow accustomed to the changes in his life.

"I have to tell you, our ratings last Sunday went through the roof," Phil said. "And you're the reason. You could go far with us, Gabe. Very far."

"You have a way of making it all so interesting," Tonya said.

"I bet you had more female viewers than male," Barbie piped up.

Gabe thought of Hannah again. "Thank you," he said.

"We'd like to sign you up for two years instead of one," Harvey said. "How do you like that?"

Gabe wasn't sure. He'd left Dundee and the accident behind, as he wanted to do. Maybe he should make the commitment and stick it out, force the issue. But something was missing.

"I'll consider it," he said.

Harvey frowned, obviously not pleased with his response, and sent a reproachful glance at Phil that said, "I thought you had this guy." "When can we expect an answer?" he asked.

Gabe set his spoon in his empty bowl. "When do you need one?"

"In a week," Harvey replied. "We've got to have something secure by then or my ass is on the line. There're a lot of guys who'd kill to be in your position, you know."

Gabe raised an eyebrow at the statement, and an awkward silence fell over the table as everyone realized what Harvey had just said. "I'll try to keep that in mind."

"If a week's too soon, you could have a little longer," Harvey said, backing off, probably because of the unyielding tone of Gabe's voice.

Gabe gave him a polite nod. "Thank you, Harvey. In any case, you'll have my answer soon."

HANNAH HEARD the telephone ring and rolled over, fumbling for the handset on her nightstand. "Hello?" she said, still half-asleep.

"Hannah?"

It was Gabe. Sitting up, she blinked quickly and felt her heart start to pound. "Are you home?" she asked hopefully.

"No. I'm still in New York. I just got back from dinner. Sorry to wake you. It's late here, but with the time change, I didn't think you'd be in bed."

Hannah checked the clock. If she had even *half* a social life, she wouldn't be in bed. It was only ten-thirty. "Kenny's spending the night with Tuck, or I'd be waiting up for him."

"Did we win the game tonight?"

"No, but it was close. Twenty-four to twenty-one."

"Kenny still okay with the new coach?"

"He says he likes you better but, fortunately, he's been pretty preoccupied with other things."

"Like a certain cheerleader?"

"You got it."

"They're still calling each other?"

"All the time."

"Do you like her?"

Hannah ran a hand through her disheveled hair. "She seems sweet. I'm just not ready for Kenny to start into this phase of puberty."

"Did you tell him what I said?"

"That you didn't have sex with anyone until college? No, I decided to keep that information to myself, thanks," she said on a laugh.

He laughed with her. "That isn't the part I thought might be helpful. What I wanted to convey is that I'm glad I waited, that there's no rush."

Hannah hugged herself, feeling the soft cotton of Gabe's T-shirt against her body. Since he'd left, she'd given up stuffing it under her pillow and begun to sleep in it. "It's a subject we'll have to cover, but they just started talking this week. I'm going to give it some more time, see what happens."

"Maybe Russ can have a father-to-son talk with him, explain about physical urges and why it's important to be smart about when to give in to those urges, that kind of stuff."

Hannah stifled a yawn. "Are you kidding? Russ would probably ask Kenny if he's gotten down her pants yet."

Another deep laugh made Hannah smile. "How's New York?" she asked.

"It's fine, but…"

"What?"

"I miss you," he said.

Hannah caught her breath. This was the first time he'd ever said anything that indicated she was special to him. "You're probably just homesick," she said, keeping her tone light. She didn't want him to think she misunderstood, believed he meant anything serious by it.

"I miss Lazarus, too."

"At least you mentioned me before your dog."

Another chuckle. "That's not just any dog."

"I know. Brent's taking good care of him. They're inseparable."

"Actually, I miss the cabin, too," he admitted.

"It's a nice place."

"But mostly I miss touching you, tasting you, feeling your naked body pressed against mine as I make love to you."

Heat began to curl through Hannah's blood like smoke. "If this is phone sex, I can see why people like it."

"It gets a lot better," he said.

"Maybe, but I have to admit, when it comes to you, I prefer it up close and personal."

"Is Brent asleep?"

"Out like a light."

"And I'm not there. Damn. Definitely my loss."

"There's a key under the mat. You could always come home," she said, but immediately regretted the suggestion. She'd promised herself she wouldn't cling to him, wouldn't drag him down.

"Just kidding," she quickly corrected. "I know you're right where you need to be. You did an awesome job last week, and you'll do just as good this week."

"They want an answer," he said.

"What kind of answer?"

"Whether or not I'll sign a two-year contract to do the show."

Drawing an unsteady breath, Hannah squeezed her eyes closed. "A contract is probably a good thing, right? It's job stability." And it wouldn't allow Gabe to backslide. He'd be so busy, he'd probably be a whole new person by the time those two years were up.

"Is that what you think?" he asked.

"Of course. You should do it. Definitely."

"Definitely," he repeated.

She didn't add anything, mostly because she couldn't speak past the lump in her throat.

"Will you be watching on Sunday?" he asked after a moment of silence.

"Of course. I've already memorized everything you said from last week. It's time for a new tape."

Another laugh. "There's something about you, Hannah Price."

"I know. I like your furniture, remember? And I'm in love with you. No surprises there."

"You're also good in bed," he added.

"Really?"

"The best."

"I'll have to remember that," she said, smiling.

"Just leave that key under your mat," he said. "I'm coming home sometime."

With that, he hung up, and Hannah went to sleep dreaming that it would be tonight.

CHAPTER TWENTY-ONE

HANNAH DIDN'T WANT TO go to her ex-father-in-law's birthday. Her relationship with Patti was strained by Patti's disapproval of her involvement with Gabe, and Hannah's resentment of that disapproval. And it would be awkward with the rest of the family. For one, Hannah had no idea how Russ might treat her. He'd taken Kenny out to lunch yesterday, ostensibly to apologize for neglecting him the night of the game. In reality, he'd proceeded to bash Hannah for breaking up their family and for just about everything else that had gone wrong in his life. Kenny had repeated a bunch of stuff Russ had said about her and Gabe, mostly things that should never have been said, especially to their sixteen-year-old son. *Did you know your mother is sleeping with Coach Holbrook?*

She hated Russ now more than ever. But she loved her boys, and she wanted them to be able to go to their grandpa's birthday without having to worry about the adults in their lives. Which meant she needed to endure the party.

She'd stay an hour, two at most, then leave, she decided. Patti or Russ could drop the boys off later, if they wanted to stay longer.

"Wow, you look great, Mom."

Hannah smiled as Kenny walked into the kitchen. "Thanks."

"What's the occasion?"

"No occasion." Hannah had been craving something new so badly she'd finally gone shopping. She'd found an attractive teal-colored sweater on sale for forty dollars, and the weather was just cool enough to wear it. Since the truth had come out, Sly's mother had sheepishly backed off the request that Hannah pay for Sly's stitches, so Hannah didn't feel too badly about spending the money on herself.

"Dad's going to be hating life when he sees you in that," Kenny said.

Hannah laughed. She thought, "Russ deserves to be hating life," but said nothing.

The front door slammed shut behind Brent and Lazarus, who finally came running into the kitchen. She'd already called them twice. "Are we going to the party now?" he asked.

Hannah noted the grass stains on her youngest son's knees, considered making him change, then decided not to worry about it. He'd only roll around in the grass at Patti's and get even dirtier.

Retrieving the pasta salad she'd made, she told Kenny to get the gift—a portrait she'd done of the two boys—set her VCR to record *NFL Countdown,* and headed out.

The drive took less than ten minutes. Soon Hannah was jockeying for a parking spot amidst all the vehicles that clogged the drive. She recognized Donny's truck, Pug and Violet's Cadillac, Patti's car. There was even a white sedan parked behind the van. The sight of it almost made Hannah turn around. Patti had invited Deborah Wheeler to the party.

"Mom?" Kenny said when she didn't get out right away. "You coming?"

Hannah took a deep breath and pasted a smile on her face. *I miss you,* Gabe had said. She missed him, too. He'd never know how much…. "Of course."

"Are you sure Patti won't care that we're bringing Lazarus?" Kenny asked as they walked to the door.

"I checked with her," Hannah said. "She told me he could come if we keep him in the backyard."

"I'll stay with him," Brent said. "He won't want to be out there all alone."

Hannah opened her mouth to say that the dog would probably be okay for a little while, but Patti must have been watching for her because the door opened almost immediately.

"Hi, Hannah," she said, but didn't hug her, as usual.

Hannah shifted the bowl in her arms to camouflage the fact that she didn't make any move to embrace Patti, either. "Hi."

"Everyone's watching the pregame show."

"Sounds great," Hannah said, refusing to let Patti or anyone else make her feel any more out of place than she already did.

Patti hugged the boys and took the salad, and Brent ran off to show Lazarus off before the dog had to be relegated to the backyard. Kenny hung back. "You okay, Mom?" he asked.

"Of course."

"Don't let anyone make you feel bad," he said softly. "I know Coach Holbrook really likes you."

Hannah nodded because it was too late to say anything more. Violet had come out of the kitchen.

"Hello, Hannah," she said. "How nice of you to come."

Polite. Distant. They were treating her like a traitor.

"I wouldn't miss it," Hannah said. "Here's Pug's gift. I hope he likes it."

"I'm sure he will."

"I'll tell you what I'd like," Pug called out.

Hannah hadn't realized he was within hearing distance, and braced herself for the worst. Sometimes Pug said the rudest things, all the while acting as though he had the right. At least he was generally undiscriminating with his gruff remarks. "What's that?" she said.

"I'd like my favorite daughter-in-law to get her head out of the clouds and be satisfied with a good man who loves her."

"Gabe *is* a good man," she said stubbornly.

"But that boy's in New York, where he's going to stay. It said in the paper that ESPN is offering him a two-year contract."

"I hope he signs it," she said. "It'll be good for him."

"I don't care what's good for him. I'm worried about what's good for you," Pug said.

"I don't want her anymore, anyway," Russ snapped.

Pug made a noise of disgust. "Then you're an idiot."

Trying not to smile, Hannah sauntered into the living room, where she could hear Gabe's voice on the television.

Deborah Wheeler watched her cross the room and sit down before bothering to say hello. Hannah eyed her for a moment, giving her a taste of her own medicine, then nodded in acknowledgement.

Donny completely ignored her, but not because he felt any animosity. He was just consumed by his own pain. He looked tired and depressed.

"Gabe seems a little nervous today," Deborah said.

Hannah knew she was trying to stir things up. "He'll be fine," she said with a little shrug.

They sat there for a few minutes in silence. Russ kept looking from the television to her, with his lip curled in disgust. And Pug kept shaking his head as if it was a damn shame everyone couldn't just do what he said.

Finally, Hannah got up to see if Patti needed any help. But she only made it halfway to the kitchen before Kenny called her back.

"Mom! Come quick."

"What is it?" When she stuck her head into the living room, no one answered. They were all transfixed by the television.

Hannah shifted her focus to the screen and, for the first time since arriving at Patti's, really listened to what Gabe was saying.

"So you're not going to be a regular part of the show?" Steve Young asked him.

Gabe shook his head. "I'm afraid not, Steve."

"That's too bad. I was hoping we'd see a lot more of you."

"I like it here, but there are a few things at home I'd rather not miss."

"Like..." Steve gave him a you-can-trust-me smile.

Gabe seemed hesitant to answer at first, but when the camera panned to his face, he slowly grinned. "I've met someone I'm hoping to marry."

It was easy to tell that Steve Young was surprised by Gabe's answer. But Steve wasn't an idiot. He knew this would be of great interest to America in general, and football enthusiasts in particular, so he kept at it. "Can you tell us who the lucky lady is?"

Time seemed to stand still. Hannah noticed the open mouths of Donny, Pug, and Violet, could see Russ's eyes nearly bulging out of his head. She could even hear her own heartbeat, thumping loudly in her ears.

Gabe glanced at the camera, his dark eyelashes making the perfect frame for his blue eyes. To Hannah, it felt like he was looking right at her. "Her name is Hannah Price."

"Oh, God," Hannah whispered.

"Where'd you meet her?" Steve asked.

"She's from my hometown."

"Well, I hope you'll be happy."

Gabe's grin turned into a hopeful boyish smile. "I will if she says yes," he said, and the program cut to a commercial.

No one moved for several seconds until, finally, Deborah Wheeler turned to gape at Hannah. "You did it," she murmured. "I can't believe it.... You did it."

Hannah could hardly breathe. Gabe was coming home. He was coming home *to her.* And he wanted to get married. He'd just said so. In front of millions of people including Russ and all of Russ's family. *On national TV!*

It was a lot to take in, especially with everyone staring at her in stunned surprise.

"Mom?" Kenny said, his voice breaking with excitement. "Are you going to do it? Are you going to marry him?"

Could it last? Could he truly forgive her for the accident? "I told him I didn't plan on getting married again," she said, more to herself than anyone.

"So? You can always change your mind," Pug said.

"He hasn't asked me to, yet. At least not officially," she said.

Kenny crossed the room and put his arm around her. "He just told all of America that he wants to marry you. That's pretty official." He leaned down so that they were eye to eye. "You want to marry him, don't you?"

He can't help but resent you eventually. Patti had said that. Was it true?

"I don't know."

"Don't miss your chance, Hannah," Pug said, and Russ shot him a furious glance.

This *was* her chance, Hannah realized. She had the opportunity to live with the man she loved, sleep with him, hopefully share the rest of her life with him. And she was going to take it. Risk it all. "I know," she said.

Brent grabbed her hand. "Does that mean you're going to say yes?"

When she nodded, he let out a whoop. "Lazarus is mine!"

Hannah might have laughed at his response, but she was still reeling. "Hannah Holbrook," she said, practicing. She knew that no one, besides her, Kenny and Brent—and possibly Pug—appreciated the sound of it. But she didn't care. Suddenly she felt as light as air. Maybe she'd even have another baby….

HE WAS ABOUT TO propose marriage. To Hannah Price. He was planning to stay in Dundee, probably for the rest of his life. And he wanted to coach.

Somehow it had all crystallized for him while sitting at dinner in New York, with Barbie cooing over him, Harvey pressing him to sign a multimillion-dollar contract, and Phil constantly stroking his ego. Hosting *NFL Sunday Countdown* was undeniably a great opportunity—but for someone else. He'd offered to be a stand-in when one of the regulars was out, and that would be enough.

The answer had been so simple, he'd almost missed it, Gabe realized as he drove home from the airport, his window down and the cool night air rushing into his truck. He belonged in Dundee, with Hannah, Kenny, Brent, Lazarus, and his own family. He had some ground to make up with his father. Reenie needed him right now, as well.

But he still couldn't believe it. A few months ago, he never would've imagined he'd be getting married so soon. He'd been too busy deluding himself that he'd walk again, that he'd return to football.

He'd hung on to that hope so tightly because he'd feared there'd be nothing to replace it if he let go. But there was. Hannah, even the Spartans, were just as vital to him as anything that had come before.

Holding the steering wheel with his left hand, he reached for the small velvet box sitting in the seat next to him. He'd bought Hannah's ring at Tiffany's before flying home. He'd wanted to get her something special, something beyond anything she'd ever seen before—and he felt certain he'd found it. He just hoped he could convince her that marrying him wouldn't be a bad thing for her boys. She loved him; he knew that. But she'd be worried about them, so much that she'd put their interests before her own wants and needs.

For probably the hundredth time, he ran through what he planned to say to her the moment she offered him any resistance. He'd be good to Kenny and Brent. They needed a better role model than they had. He could teach them a lot, about football, school, woodworking, overcoming adversity. He had the money to buy them things she couldn't. And his best argument of all—how could it hurt a child to have an extra adult around to love him and care for him?

It couldn't. That would have to be her reply. Then he'd tempt her with the ring. He didn't know a whole lot about diamonds, but this one was certainly pretty. The salesgirl at Tiffany's had nearly fainted when he bought it. *That's the most beautiful ring we've got....*

Which is what made it perfect for Hannah. She was the most beautiful woman he'd ever met, especially on the inside, where it really mattered.

The "Welcome to Dundee, Home of the Bad to the Bone Rodeo" sign came up on his right, and he felt a smile tempt his lips. To him, that sign might as well have said, "Welcome home, Gabe."

HANNAH SAT ON HER PORCH in Gabe's chair, staring out over her moonlit yard. The boys were asleep. As she pulled a blanket tighter around her shoulders to ward off the chill, she could hear the cicadas, smell the dew gathering on the grass. She liked this time of night. It was late, calm and peaceful. But she couldn't relax. Gabe had called from the airport in New York an eternity ago to say he was on his way home. He told her he'd stop by, but he'd been in a big rush to catch his plane and hadn't said anything more than that. She'd wanted to ask if he meant what he'd said on TV, if he was really planning to marry her—because she was having a difficult time believing what she'd heard.

From the reaction she'd already witnessed, so was almost everyone else. Russ had immediately gotten up and stormed out of Patti's house. In the ensuing silence, Deborah had burst into tears and slipped away. Although Patti and Violet had glanced worriedly at each other when Russ left, they'd largely refused to acknowledge that anything unusual had taken place. Pug was the only one in Russ's family who seemed pleased. He'd grinned and clapped her on the back. "See if you can get me a couple of 49ers tickets, will ya?" he'd said, and she'd hugged him.

Kenny and Brent didn't seem to care if anyone else was excited. They were ecstatic. Kenny had grinned from ear to ear. Brent had started running through the house with Lazarus, yelling frenziedly that they belonged to a family now.

A family... Hannah smiled as she gave up her grip on the blanket to pull her hair back. Father, mother, two kids and a dog. All living together. Just when she'd given up on the whole concept.

Headlights appeared at the end of the street, making Hannah's pulse speed up. It was Gabe.

As he pulled into her driveway, she walked over to the driver's window. "Hi," she said.

He let the engine idle, looking nervous for the first time since she'd known him. "Hi."

She dragged the blanket up around her shoulders again. "I watched the show today."

"What'd you think?"

"That you're crazy."

He seemed taken aback. "Why?"

"What about the accident?"

"What about it?" he responded.

"It cost you so much, Gabe. *I* cost you so much. Do you really think you'll be able to forgive me for that?"

"Hannah..." His eyes grew intense. "The accident cost me a lot," he admitted. "But I don't see any reason to let it cost me any more than it already has, do you?"

Hope swelled inside Hannah. "So you were serious when you said you wanted to marry me?"

A lazy grin spread across his face. Seeing it, her heart nearly pounded right out of her chest. He *was* serious. She knew right then the dream was real. "What do the boys think of the idea?"

"They like it," she said.

At this, some of the tension seemed to drain from his body. He turned off the truck and opened his door, and she stepped closer to him. "I'm glad to hear that," he said. "Now I don't have to worry about all the things I've been planning to say."

"What kinds of things?"

"Things that I hoped would convince you I'd be a good stepdad."

"You were worried I wouldn't think so?"

His eyebrows shot up. "Knowing how much you love those boys? Yes."

She chuckled softly.

"So?" he said.

She gave him a grin of her own. "So, what?"

"What do you say?"

She opened her mouth to respond, but he held up a hand. "Wait, I think I'll have a better chance if you see the ring. The salesgirl convinced me there wasn't a woman on earth who could say no to this."

What the salesgirl had probably meant was that there wasn't a woman on earth who could say no to *him,* but Hannah didn't clarify. She was too busy staring at the ring he'd thrust in front of her. He'd bought the biggest emerald-cut diamond she'd ever seen, set in white gold.

"Wow," she breathed.

"Is that a yes?" he asked eagerly.

She was having trouble finding words. This ring had to have cost more than her house. It was hard to believe that yesterday she'd hesitated about buying a forty-dollar sweater and today she owned the biggest diamond in Dundee; that yesterday she'd thought she'd never remarry and today she was ready to set the date.

"I know you have money, Gabe, but…can we really afford to spend so much on a ring?"

He laughed and shook his head. "You don't have anything to worry about, Hannah. I can afford whatever I want to buy you. And this isn't just a ring—it's a promise."

"Of what?" she murmured, still staring down at it.

He took the ring out of the box and slid it on her finger. The weight of the diamond felt foreign to her hand, but good. "That I'll never hold the accident against you. That I'll love you forever," he said. Then he tilted up her face and kissed her gently on the mouth.

* * * * *

Come back to Dundee in September! BIG GIRLS DON'T CRY features Gabe's sister, Reenie, who discovers that her husband—and her marriage—may not be everything she thinks....

*Please turn the page to read
an excerpt from Brenda Novak's
exciting new romantic suspense novel.
EVERY WAKING MOMENT
is available from
HQN Books next month.*

CHAPTER ONE

VANESSA BEACON'S HANDS SHOOK as she stared down at the California driver's license she'd had her gardener purchase for her several months ago. The photo was hers, along with the physical characteristics. Hair:Bld; Eyes:Bl; HT:5-06; WT:120. The name, birth date and address, however, were not. The name read *Emma Wright*. Vanessa had chosen "Emma" because it was her mother's middle name. "Wright" she'd selected as a reminder. She was doing the *right* thing. She had to believe that wholeheartedly, or she would never have the courage to take such a risk.

The clock ticked loudly on the wall of her expansive chrome-and-marble kitchen. It seemed even louder than Manuel's new plasma television, which she'd turned on in the living room to occupy their son, Dominick. She'd gone through her and Dominick's suitcases, checked for his new birth certificate, her driver's license and the two prepaid credit cards she'd purchased as additional identification, plus the teaching credential in her new name. She also counted her cash and packed her maps. But she couldn't help worrying that she'd forgotten *something*.

God, she couldn't make a mistake. Dominick's life might depend on what she'd forgotten.

Mumbling a silent prayer that she could think straight despite her racing heart, she once again sorted through the backpack she'd hidden in the attic for the past three weeks. A small, hand-held cooler contained three types of insulin—NPII, Regular and the fast-acting Humalog. Outside the cooler and loose in the backpack, she'd packed two hundred Ultra-Fine needles for Dominick's three or more daily injections, two blood-glucose monitors, arm and finger pokers with plenty of test strips and two boxes of extra lancets. There was also a biohazard sharps collector, which was so large and bulky she'd almost taken it out a number of times but didn't in the end because she had to have somewhere safe to toss the needles. She'd included Keto-Strips to test for protein in Dominick's urine, an emergency glucagon kit—in case he ever passed out, God forbid—and a tube of oral glucose gel for use in smaller emergencies. Besides all that, she'd packed his logbook to record his blood-sugar readings, and plenty of carbohydrates disguised as granola bars, trail mix, fruit and individually packaged chips for her son's mid-morning and mid-afternoon snacks. She'd nearly required a small suitcase just to transport his diabetes supplies. But every item was absolutely essential. One missed insulin injection could quickly result in ketoacidosis, a life-threatening condition.

I have everything. There's nothing to worry about.... Vanessa closed the bag. But a glance at the clock made her feel weak in the knees. It was after ten. Juanita should've been here fifteen minutes ago. Would she come at all? Or had Manuel gotten to her?

Vanessa cautioned herself against the paranoia that threatened. Manuel always watched her closely, but she was sure he had no idea she was about to disappear. She could trust the gardener. Carlos had proved himself with his secrecy on the false ID and the car he'd bought for her. Juanita would come through, too—*if* her loyalties were what Vanessa believed they were, and *if* she clearly understood what Vanessa wanted her to do. Vanessa thought she did. Manuel had insisted on hiring a nanny who could speak only Spanish, so his son would learn his native tongue, he said. But there were plenty of bilingual nannies, especially in San Diego where they lived. No, it wasn't solely for Dominick that Manuel had selected Juanita. Manuel liked the idea that Vanessa wouldn't be able to communicate with her. Isolating Vanessa gave him that much more power and control.

Fortunately, it wasn't quite that simple. He didn't know it, but during the four years they'd been living together, she'd taught herself enough Spanish to speak and understand most of what she heard. At first, she'd done it to help while away the empty hours of her day, since Manuel wouldn't let her return to school or get a job. Later, she'd wanted to understand the strange phone calls he received at night and to decipher what the Rodriguez family discussed during the frequent meetings they held in the conference room off Manuel's home office.

But she didn't want to know about Manuel's business dealings anymore. Or his family's. His family was the main reason Manuel had never married her, even after she'd had Dominick. His mother refused to accept her, ostensibly because of her nationality, but Vanessa knew it went a little deeper than that. Mama Rodriguez couldn't tolerate the thought of another woman in her favorite son's life. Period. It was a fact Vanessa had once lamented, but no more. She'd learned enough about Manuel's mother, his whole family, to be thankful for their rejection.

Dominick came in from the living room, his round face a picture of impatience. He'd just turned five two months ago and would've been starting kindergarten in a few weeks. She hoped she'd be able to get them situated soon, so he could go to school this year. "Mo-om, I thought you said we were going to leave!" he said.

Vanessa attempted a reassuring smile, even though she was sweating profusely and feeling as though she might faint. Juanita *had* to come. She had the car Carlos had bought. And if she didn't appear soon, it meant Manuel had figured out what was happening. He'd take Dominick to Mexico and Vanessa would probably never see her son again. Manuel had certainly threatened that often enough—whenever she tried to establish some independence. He'd made his point when she'd tried to leave the first time. Her father had passed away several years before she met Manuel, and her brother had been killed in a motorcycle accident not long after, but her mother and married sister lived in Phoenix. She'd gone to them, and wished she could do so again.

But she wouldn't make the same mistake twice. Manuel had tracked her down and dragged her back—then let her know, in no uncertain terms, that he wouldn't tolerate her leaving in the future.

Don't think of that. Don't remember…

"We're waiting for Juanita," she said, aching to pull her child into her arms. She didn't know what she'd do if she could never hear Dominick laugh again or tell her how much he loved her. But she knew a clingy, desperate hug wasn't what he needed at the moment. She didn't want to communicate her anxiety to him any more than she already had.

"You said she was coming a long time ago," he complained. "Where *is* she?"

Vanessa had no idea. Juanita had worked for them for nearly a year and was never late. Where could she be today? Without her support—and the car—Vanessa and Dominick would never get away.

"Maybe she had a flat tire." *Please let it be that.* "I'm sure she's coming."

The phone rang. Vanessa quickly gave Dominick some markers so he could write on the dry-erase board attached to the fridge and approached the desk in the corner.

Anxiety stabbed through her when she recognized Manuel's cell-phone number on caller ID. He was supposed to be on a plane to Mexico. He left the country often and stayed, sometimes for several days, sometimes for a couple of weeks. He claimed to import marble from Culiacán, but Vanessa had long suspected that he imported more than marble.

The steady bursts of noise jangled her already frayed nerves. Should she answer it?

She wasn't sure she could keep her voice level. Hoping that his plane had simply been delayed, that he'd be gone soon, she decided to let the answering machine take it. But she should've known she couldn't avoid him so easily. Her cell phone, which was sitting on the counter, started ringing only a few seconds later. Manuel hated it when he couldn't reach her. She knew he'd keep trying, again and again and again, until she finally picked up, even if it meant missing his flight.

She couldn't let him miss his flight.

When she continued to hesitate, Dominick glanced up from his drawing. "Mommy?"

Spurred by the curiosity in her son's voice, Vanessa arranged her expression in a blank mask to hide the fear and loathing Manuel elicited, and retrieved her cell. "Hello?"

"What's going on?" Manuel demanded without a greeting.

"Nothing. Why?"

"You didn't answer the house phone."

"I told you last night that I might run a few errands this morning."

"You haven't left the house."

A prickly unease crept up Vanessa's spine. He'd spoken with such certainty. "How do you know?"

"A good guess."

She didn't believe it was a guess at all, and judging by his flippant tone, he didn't care whether he'd convinced her. Somehow he always knew where she was. She'd scoured every inch of the house and been unable to find any type of listening device or video camera, so he must have hired someone to watch her. Which made Juanita absolutely integral to her plan.

Dominick went back to drawing, and Vanessa moved to the sink to stare out the kitchen window at the perfect summer day, wondering for the millionth time who was out there.

"Why didn't you pick up?" Manuel pressed, unwilling to let the subject go.

"I was—" she swallowed to ease the dryness in her throat "—in the bathroom."

"I had a phone installed there, remember? For your convenience."

Not for her convenience. So she wouldn't have even the bathroom as an escape from him. "I refuse to answer the phone while I'm in the bathroom," she said. "I haven't used that extension since you put it in. You know that."

He chuckled softly. "*Querida,* you can be so stubborn."

Manuel had no idea. But he was about to find out—if only Juanita would arrive as promised.

"What do you need?" she asked.

"I'm calling to check on you."

Check on her? Not in a loving way. Vanessa could hardly tolerate the sound of Manuel's voice or the pretense of his caring. When she'd first met him, at twenty-two, she'd just graduated with a teaching degree. He'd been older, twenty-five, and had seemed energetic and ambitious—but loving and kind, too. He'd changed so fast....

Maybe she'd never really known him. Maybe the man he used to be was simply a persona he adopted when it suited him. In any case, she barely recognized him anymore. His dark eyes, once the color of melted chocolate to her, watched her too carefully, frightening in their obsessive intensity. And the thick black hair she used to love, especially when it fell across his brow, he now slicked back in a dramatic style that added to the impression he gave of being as hyperaware as he was hypercritical.

She brought a hand to her chest, preparing herself for the answer to her next question. "Aren't you going to Mexico today?"

"The trip's been postponed."

Her muscles tightened. *No! Not when I'm so close.* "Until when?" The knocking of her heart against her ribs made it difficult to speak.

"Come on, *mi amor*. You know better than to bother your pretty head with business."

A dodge. Typical of him. As was the condescension in his voice. He didn't like her knowing his schedule. Except for the odd occasion, he typically sprang news of an impending trip only the night before.

But Juanita still wasn't here, and Manuel hadn't said why his trip had been postponed. Did he realize she was planning to leave him?

"Will you be home for dinner, then?" she asked.

"Of course. I always spend my evenings with you, if I'm available."

Bile rose in Vanessa's throat at the thought of postponing her escape until Manuel's next trip to Mexico. Holding out until he was far from home would be the wisest course. She and Dominick needed the lead time. But everything was already arranged. And staying meant she'd have to suffer through more nights in Manuel's company, nights that always ended, at some point, with her lying beneath him. Manuel had an insatiable sexual appetite and demanded she perform some kind of sex act for him daily, often two or more.

"Maybe you could mention to Juanita that I'm in the mood for *meñudo*," he said.

Even the prospect of sharing another interminable dinner with Manuel made Vanessa ill.

She frowned at the cigarette burn her husband had inflicted on the inside of her wrist four days ago. Manuel loved to deal out little reprisals for anything that displeased him—

Dominick rounded the kitchen island. Quickly hiding the injury, she rubbed her son's back as he came over to hug her leg.

"What's wrong, Mommy?" Worry clouded his innocent eyes.

She held a finger to her lips to indicate silence. She didn't want Manuel to overhear.

"I'll tell her to make it for dinner," she said into the phone.

"And I'm going to need those suits I had you take to the cleaners," he added. "Can you pick them up for me while you're out?"

Her life was closing in on her again. "Of course."

"Thank you. You're such a wonderful wife."

"I'm not your wife," she said.

"As far as I'm concerned, you are. Every man should be so lucky."

Vanessa's nails curled into her palm at his assumption and false praise. He threw her a few compliments from time to time—figuring that would keep her happy. But he'd never trusted her or loved her enough to let her be truly happy. Or to stand against his family and marry her, as she'd once wanted. Or to treat her as an equal instead of chattel.

"How do you want me to pay for it?" she asked, because she knew he'd expect this question. Their gated, ten-thousand-square-foot mansion provided proof of his wealth. But he kept such a tight rein on their money that it had taken her nearly two years to save the funds she'd given Carlos for the car. She'd only managed to accumulate that much by returning small items she hoped Manuel wouldn't miss, even groceries, and hiding the money between the insulation and the wall in the attic.

"I'll call the bank and add an extra hundred to your account," he said.

"Fine." She grimaced at his stinginess. He allowed her no standing balance. He waited until she had a specific need, one he could easily verify. Then he called and transferred enough to cover the expense. One hundred bucks would barely pay his dry-cleaning bill; Manuel clothed his lean, sinewy body almost exclusively in the finest hand-tailored suits.

"Thank you, *querida,*" he said. "What else do you have planned for the day? What is my *hijito* doing?"

She glanced at their son. Dominick was so unlike his father, so much more similar to her side of the family—especially the younger brother she'd lost the year she and Dominick had moved in with Manuel. Large for his age, Dominick had sandy-blond hair, eyes that were an unusual shade of green, and golden skin that still retained the softness of a baby's. "He's standing here, waiting to go to the store."

"He should be reading, Vanessa. You know I want him to read."

"We'll read when we get back."

"Let me transfer the money to the credit card I've given Juanita. She can do your shopping and pick up my dry cleaning. I don't know why you like doing such menial tasks."

Maybe it was because she had nothing else to do. Manuel insisted that Dominick needed one hundred percent of her attention, but she believed there should be more to life than following her son around, watching over his every move, correcting all his mistakes, stealing the same privacy and independence from him that Manuel had already taken from her.

"I like to get out once in a while," she said. *If you only knew how badly I'm dying to get out right now.* "It's good for me."

"So you're always telling me."

She *had* to leave. Right away. She couldn't survive the helplessness any longer.

"But today…today you might be right," she said. "I've got a headache. Why don't you go ahead and put the money on Juanita's card. I'll have her take Dominick out to run errands while I lie down."

"Fine."

"I'll see you tonight," she said, eager to get off the phone. Tears burned at the backs of her eyes, tears of disappointment and bitterness toward the man who had systematically cut her off from friends and family.

At least he didn't know what she had in store for today. If he did, he would've said something about the way she'd set him up—wouldn't he?

"Te amo," he said.

She couldn't say it back. She hadn't been able to for years.

"Goodbye." She hung up then slumped over the kitchen sink, afraid she was going to be sick.

The sound of keys jingling and the front door opening, brought her head up. Dominick dashed off and, a moment later, marched into the kitchen ahead of Juanita, who met Vanessa's eyes with a fearful expression.

"Are you ready, my friend?" she asked in Spanish.

"Where have you been?" Vanessa replied in the same language.

"I had a neighbor check the engine of the car. I couldn't let you go without knowing you and Dominick would have a reliable vehicle."

Vanessa feared the car might be stolen property. It should've cost a lot more than it did. But Carlos hadn't admitted anything, and she hadn't asked. What was the point? She had to take what she could get; she didn't have a choice. "Why didn't you tell me? Or call?" she said in English.

Juanita scowled and moved closer, gazing around the kitchen as if looking for the camera Vanessa had searched for repeatedly. "I thought of it too late yesterday, and we agreed never to discuss this over the phone." She lowered her voice so Dominick, who'd started using the Dry-Erase board again, couldn't hear. "He called me last night, you know. He asked how Dominick was doing in his studies, but he also asked many questions about you."

"Like what?" Vanessa whispered.

"What you do while he's gone, where you go, whether you try to communicate with me."

"What did you tell him?"

"Nothing." She removed the long heavy coat, sunglasses and head scarf Vanessa had asked her to wear. "Put these on and go. Right away. It isn't odd for a little old lady like me to dress so warmly, even in the summer. And the engine of the car is good, strong. You should be fine."

Vanessa hesitated as she accepted the clothing. "But he didn't go to Mexico, Juanita. He's still here, in town. He wants you to make *meñudo* for dinner!"

"So...are you going to wait?" Juanita leaned around the island to check on Dominick.

Vanessa could see that he was still happily occupied. But she put Juanita's belongings on the center island and pulled Juanita into the formal dining room. "I don't know what to do."

"You have to go," Juanita said. "He senses something. I know he does."

"But now that he's coming home tonight, you won't be able to tell him I was here when you left at dinner but gone when you returned in the morning. What will you say to him?"

"Don't worry. I'll say I was running late and you were already gone when I arrived."

Vanessa checked Dominick again. He'd given up on the Dry-Erase board and was busy arranging magnetic letters into the small words she'd taught him to spell. "He'll want to know why you didn't call him when I didn't return."

Juanita pulled thoughtfully at her lip with her teeth. "I'll have Carlos take me home early," she decided, "before I would expect you back, the tell Manuel I felt ill and didn't want to infect Dominick."

"And if someone's watching the house? What if they see me like this and tell Manuel you left with Dominick—and never came back? With Manuel coming home, it's all so much more *immediate*."

"Calm down, my friend. We've talked about this before. I'm just the housekeeper. No one pays attention to when I come and go. If someone says I left with Dominick and never came back, I'll say they are *loco*. My son dropped me off in the morning. Carlos took me home when I felt ill. In between, I never went anywhere or saw anything out of the ordinary. How can Manuel argue with that? It is simple, eh? Besides, he doesn't even think we speak the same language, remember?"

"Sí." Vanessa struggled to regulate her rapid breathing. He'd never suspect Juanita. He trusted her. Everyone trusted Juanita.

Nodding decisively, she ducked back into the kitchen, covered her head with the scarf and pulled on the coat. It was now or never. She was leaving; there was no looking back. Somehow she'd provide a life for herself and Dominick that had nothing to do with the man who tried to own her.

Their return distracted Dominick from his magnets. "Why are you dressing up like Juanita?" he asked with a scowl.

"This is the special game we've been practicing for," she told him, adding Juanita's sunglasses and dark lipstick to her disguise. She'd been terrified that Dominick might mention the "game" to Manuel. But it was a risk she'd had to take. Fortunately, they played games of pretense quite a lot, and it had never become an issue. "We're going to see if anyone can tell who I really am."

"Am I going to dress up, too?"

"No, you're going to act like I'm Juanita, remember? When we step outside, you'll hold my hand and walk to the car the same as you do whenever Juanita takes you shopping or to the library."

"That's not how it goes. I'm Max, from *Where the Wild Things Are,* and you're a lady named Emma."

Vanessa had chosen the name Max because it came from Dominick's favorite book. He responded well to it. And, equally important, it was a name Manuel would never connect with him. "We'll do that, too. Just as soon as we drive away."

"Oh, I get it! You're going to be Juanita first, *then* Emma." He seemed excited—until he followed them into her bedroom and noticed, for the first time, the two suitcases she'd packed. He watched Juanita cover one with a big black garbage bag and take it out to the back porch.

"Why are we throwing away our suitcases?"

"We're not," Vanessa said, doing the same with the other one. "Carlos is going to get them for us."

"Is he playing, too?" Dominick asked as they returned to the kitchen.

Vanessa slipped the backpack into a garbage bag and carried it to the back. "Sort of. We'll meet him down the street."

"But why do we need suitcases? Are we going somewhere far away?"

"Yes," Vanessa said, feeling such relief in the word that she reached out to squeeze Juanita's hand.

"Where?" Dominick asked.

Across the country, as far as I can take us. "You'll see. It's a surprise." She stood in the living room to make sure Carlos saw their luggage. Had he noticed Juanita pulling up outside?

The gardener came almost immediately. Good. Glancing inside the house from the patio, he nodded as he picked up the first bag and carried it around to the front, as if he was loading more clippings into the bed of his truck.

Fear turned Vanessa's legs rubbery as she hurried to the front door and gave her nanny a tight hug. "You'll be okay?" she asked in Spanish.

"Of course. We have it all planned out."

"I could never thank you enough."

Juanita took a piece of paper from her pocket and slipped it into Vanessa's hand.

"What's this?"

"My sister Rosa's number. We can communicate through her. Call me if you need anything."

Vanessa stared down at the crumpled piece of paper balled in her hand. "But you never even told me you had a sister—"

"Exactly. Manuel doesn't know about her, either. I keep my business to myself, eh?"

"Where does she live?" Vanessa asked.

"About an hour from here."

In a moment of pure panic, Vanessa squeezed her friend's arm. "Go to her, Juanita. Go and never come back here." She leaned close so she could whisper the rest into Juanita's ear. "Manuel, he...he isn't right."

"You're the only one he hurts," Juanita whispered back. "Just be safe, my beautiful friend. And be happy."

Vanessa waited while Juanita said goodbye to Dominick. Then she took her son's hand. Keeping her face down and stooping a bit like the older woman, she led him out the front door into the mellow sunshine of a clear August day.

The nondescript white sedan she'd asked Carlos to purchase sat in the circular driveway, representing the freedom she'd craved for so long. She wanted to race toward it, buckle Dominick safely inside and put the metal to the floor as she tore away. But she forced herself to walk very slowly, like Juanita. She'd be gone soon. Then she wouldn't be Vanessa Beacon anymore. She'd start over as Emma Wright, and Dominick would be Max.

HARLEQUIN *Super*ROMANCE

BLACKBERRY HILL MEMORIAL

Almost A Family
by Roxanne Rustand
Harlequin Superromance #1284

From Roxanne Rustand,
author of *Operation: Second Chance*
and *Christmas at Shadow Creek*,
a new heartwarming miniseries,
set in a small-town hospital,
where people come first.

As long as the infamous Dr. Connor Reynolds stays
out of her way, Erin has more pressing issues to
worry about. Like how to make her adopted children
feel safe and loved after her husband walked out on
them, and why patients keep dying for no apparent
reason. If only she didn't need Connor's help. And if
only he wasn't so good to her and the kids.

Available July 2005 wherever Harlequin books are sold.

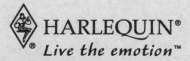

HARLEQUIN®
® *Live the emotion*™

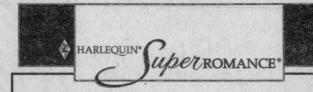

HARLEQUIN *Super*ROMANCE®

Single FATHER

He's a man on his own, trying to raise his children. Sometimes he gets things right. Sometimes he needs a little help....

On-sale July 2005

To Protect His Own
by Brenda Mott
Harlequin Superromance #1286

All he wanted was peace and quiet. Alex moved to the ranch to make a better life for his daughter far away from the city, where one senseless act had changed everything. But compassion has no limits, and he can't turn his back on Caitlin Kramer, a woman struggling to recover from a tragedy of her own.

On-sale August 2005

A Mom for Matthew
by Roz Denny Fox
Harlequin Superromance #1290

Zeke Rossetti has a young son—and he's trying to cope with the child's deafness. Grace Stafford, a teacher, is on a mission for her grandmother. Can these two help each other find what they need?

Available wherever Harlequin books are sold.

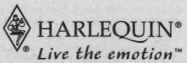

HARLEQUIN®
Live the emotion™

If you enjoyed what you just read,
then we've got an offer you can't resist!

Take 2 bestselling
love stories FREE!
Plus get a FREE surprise gift!

Clip this page and mail it to Harlequin Reader Service®

IN U.S.A.	IN CANADA
3010 Walden Ave.	P.O. Box 609
P.O. Box 1867	Fort Erie, Ontario
Buffalo, N.Y. 14240-1867	L2A 5X3

YES! Please send me 2 free Harlequin Superromance® novels and my free surprise gift. After receiving them, if I don't wish to receive anymore, I can return the shipping statement marked cancel. If I don't cancel, I will receive 6 brand-new novels every month, before they're available in stores. In the U.S.A., bill me at the bargain price of $4.69 plus 25¢ shipping and handling per book and applicable sales tax, if any*. In Canada, bill me at the bargain price of $5.24 plus 25¢ shipping and handling per book and applicable taxes**. That's the complete price, and a savings of at least 10% off the cover prices—what a great deal! I understand that accepting the 2 free books and gift places me under no obligation ever to buy any books. I can always return a shipment and cancel at any time. Even if I never buy another book from Harlequin, the 2 free books and gift are mine to keep forever.

135 HDN DZ7W
336 HDN DZ7X

Name	(PLEASE PRINT)
Address	Apt.#
City	State/Prov.	Zip/Postal Code

Not valid to current Harlequin Superromance® subscribers.

Want to try two free books from another series?
Call 1-800-873-8635 or visit www.morefreebooks.com.

* Terms and prices subject to change without notice. Sales tax applicable in N.Y.
** Canadian residents will be charged applicable provincial taxes and GST.
   All orders subject to approval. Offer limited to one per household.
   ® are registered trademarks owned and used by the trademark owner or its licensee.

SUP04R   ©2004 Harlequin Enterprises Limited

eHARLEQUIN.com

The Ultimate Destination for Women's Fiction

Visit eHarlequin.com's Bookstore today
for today's most popular books at great prices.

- An extensive selection of romance books by top authors!

- Choose our convenient "bill me" option. No credit card required.

- New releases, Themed Collections and hard-to-find backlist.

- A sneak peek at upcoming books.

- Check out book excerpts, book summaries and Reader Recommendations from other members and post your own too.

- Find out what everybody's reading in Bestsellers.

- Save BIG with everyday discounts and exclusive online offers!

- Our Category Legend will help you select reading that's exactly right for you!

- Visit our Bargain Outlet often for huge savings and special offers!

- Sweepstakes offers. Enter for your chance to win special prizes, autographed books and more.

**Your purchases are 100%
guaranteed—so shop online
at www.eHarlequin.com today!**

INTBB104

HARLEQUIN *Super*ROMANCE®

Montana Standoff

by Nadia Nichols

Harlequin Superromance #1287

Steven Young Bear is ready to fight
the good fight against the mining
company whose plans threaten to
destroy a mountain. Molly Ferguson
is fresh out of law school and
representing the other side. Steven
and Molly are in a standoff!
Will love bring them together?

Available July 2005
wherever Harlequin books are sold.

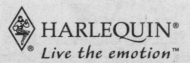

HARLEQUIN®
Live the emotion™

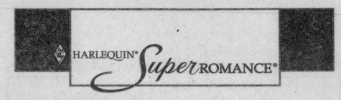

COMING NEXT MONTH

#1284 ALMOST A FAMILY • Roxanne Rustand
Blackberry Hill Memorial

Erin can't believe she's working with Dr. Connor Reynolds—the man her family blames for what happened to her cousin. And that's not the only thing she has to worry about. She's just divorced and living in a tiny town with three adopted children who aren't taking her husband's desertion well. And as hospital administrator, she also has to figure out why the town's residents are refusing to use her hospital. If only she could act as if Connor was simply another colleague....

#1285 THE PREGNANCY TEST • Susan Gable
9 Months Later

Sloan Thompson has good reason to worry about his daughter once she enters her "rebellious" phase. And that's before she tells him she's pregnant. Then he discovers his own actions have consequences. This about-to-be grandfather is also going to be a father once again.

#1286 TO PROTECT HIS OWN • Brenda Mott
Single Father

All Alex wanted was to be left alone on the ranch so he could have a second chance with his daughter—to make a better life for them, far away from the city and the drive-by shooting that had changed everything. But he can't turn his back on new neighbor Caitlin Kramer, a woman struggling to recover from her own shattered past....

#1287 MONTANA STANDOFF • Nadia Nichols

Environmental lawyer Steven Young Bear is in Moose Horn, Montana, to fight the good fight against the mining company whose plans threaten to destroy a mountain. Molly Ferguson is fresh out of law school representing the mining company. Steven and Molly are on opposite sides and it doesn't look as if anything can break this standoff.

#1288 IN HER DEFENSE • Margaret Watson
Count on a Cop

He thinks she's a bleeding heart. She thinks that's better than having *no* heart. But the case of a missing waitress and an abused mother and child have Mac MacDougal and A. J. Ferguson working together to find the man who is responsible—before he finds them.

#1289 THE DAUGHTER HE NEVER KNEW • Linda Barrett
Pilgrim Cove

Guilt and anger made Jason Parker turn his back on his home and his family after his twin was killed in a car crash. Now, after nine years, he's returned to discover that nothing and no one in Pilgrim Cove is the same—and that he left behind more than he had ever guessed.